FIGHTI

Durant's instincts kicked dodging behind a telephone pole, and pulled the Luger from his waistband. The two gunmen fired almost simultaneously, one shot nicking the telephone pole and the other whistling past his ear. He crouched, arm extended at shoulder level, and caught the sights in the reflection from the streetlight. He ripped off three quick shots.

The first shattered the car's windshield. The second plucked at the sleeve of the man by the passenger door. The man by the rear door grunted with surprise, a starburst of blood covering his shirt front from the third slug. He lurched sideways, his legs collapsing, and slumped face-down on the curb. The driver shouted a curse.

The other man jumped on the running board as the Buick roared away. Durant rose from behind the telephone pole, glancing at the dead hoodlum, and decided to make tracks. The cops, given the opportunity, would charge him with murder.

ST. MARTIN'S PAPERBACKS TITLES
BY MATT BRAUN

WYATT EARP
BLACK FOX
OUTLAW KINGDOM
LORDS OF THE LAND
CIMARRON JORDAN
BLOODY HAND
NOBLE OUTLAW
TEXAS EMPIRE
THE SAVAGE LAND
RIO HONDO
THE GAMBLERS
DOC HOLLIDAY
YOU KNOW MY NAME
THE BRANNOCKS
THE LAST STAND
RIO GRANDE
GENTLEMAN ROGUE
THE KINCAIDS
EL PASO
INDIAN TERRITORY
BLOODSPORT
SHADOW KILLERS
BUCK COLTER
KINCH RILEY
DEATHWALK
HICKOK & CODY
THE WILD ONES
HANGMAN'S CREEK
JURY OF SIX
THE SPOILERS

THE OVERLORDS

Matt Braun

St. Martin's Paperbacks

Note to Readers

This is a work of fiction. Names, characters, places, and incidents either are the product of the author's imagination or are used fictitiously, and any resemblance to actual persons, living or dead, business establishments, events or locales is entirely coincidental.

THE OVERLORDS

ISBN: 0-312-98172-4

Printed in the United States of America

St. Martin's Paperbacks edition / January 2003

St. Martin's Paperbacks are published by St. Martin's Press, 175 Fifth Avenue, New York, NY 10010.

10 9 8 7 6 5 4 3 2 1

To
My Classmates
Oklahoma Military Academy
Those Were the Days

Author's Note

Galveston was the Las Vegas of the Roaring Twenties. There were casinos, nightclubs, Broadway entertainers, bookmaking parlors, and a red-light district with over a thousand ladies of the evening. The Roaring Twenties was also the era of the Volstead Act, a federal law prohibiting the sale of alcoholic spirits anywhere in America. The Island, as Galveston was called by locals, was nonetheless home base to the largest rumrunning operation west of the Mississippi.

Overlooking the Gulf of Mexico, and located off the coast of Texas, Galveston was controlled by modern-day mobsters. A triad of gangsters, crooked politicians, and unscrupulous businessmen transformed the Island into a paradise of sun-and-surf resorts, with a nightlife that rivaled New York and Paris. Millions of tourists flocked to the Island, and tens of millions of dollars were siphoned off by an underworld empire that lasted more than fifty years. There is nothing remotely similar to Galveston in all of American history.

The Overlords is historical fiction. Literary license has been taken with names and places, dates and events, and a large part of the story is pure invention. In fact, *The Overlords* bears testament to the hoary adage that truth is stranger than fiction. The historical reality of Galveston Island often beggars belief.

The Roaring Twenties was an era of booze, jazz, and "let the good times roll." Galveston Island was a microcosm of a people and a nation involved in a decade-long party orchestrated by the mob. *The Overlords* is their story.

Chapter One

A horseman in a black hat thundered over the hill. Not an instant later a rider in a white hat topped the rocky crest and spurred his barrel-chested stallion. He closed the gap with a burst of speed.

Off to the side, not twenty yards away, a Ford truck barreled along in a sputtering roar. The back of the truck was rigged with a wooden platform, enclosed by a sturdy metal railing. A cameraman fought to maintain his balance, his camera mounted on a tripod and the legs of the tripod bolted to the platform. He furiously cranked the handle on his camera, tracking the action.

The horseman in the white hat leaped from his stallion. He slammed shoulder-first into the black-hatted desperado and drove him out of the saddle. The men tumbled to the ground in a gritty cloud of dust.

The director yelled, *"Cut!"*

The command was amplified through a megaphone held by the director. He was standing behind the cameraman, gripping the metal railing to steady himself. The truck lurched to a halt as the two horsemen levered themselves off the ground. The director looked pleased.

"Good job," he said. "Someone get Tom and Tony in there while we still have sun. Earl, move your horse out of camera."

Earl Durant was the stuntman who doubled for Tom Mix. His white stallion doubled for Mix's famed movie horse, Tony. He dusted himself off, nodding to the black-hatted stuntman, and led his horse behind the truck. A wrangler led Tony into camera.

The sun dropped steadily toward the Pacific Ocean.

The motion picture, titled *The Drifter*, was being shot in the tree-studded hills north of Hollywood. The crew had been at it since early that morning, and the director was fearful of losing the sun. He waved his megaphone.

"People, *please!*" he said in an agitated voice. "We need Tom *now!*"

Tom Mix stepped out of a Dodge touring car parked in the shade of a tree. He was handsome in the way of matinee idols, with hawklike features, dark flashing eyes, and a muscular build. At forty-six, he was still in good shape, though he seldom did his own stunts these days. He stopped beside Durant.

"How about it, Earl?" he said quietly. "Did our great leader get the shot?"

Mix didn't trust directors. He was particularly at odds with Reave Eason, who had little experience at directing Westerns. Eason strutted around in breeches and riding boots, with all the airs of a Prussian cavalry officer commanding a regiment. He wielded his megaphone like it was a baton of power.

"I reckon he got it," Durant said. "Just be careful with the fight scene. He doesn't know a right cross from an uppercut."

"How would you handle it?"

"Let Dusty knock you down. Then get up and trade punches even-steven. Show the audience it takes grit to win a fight."

"Yeah, that's the ticket," Mix agreed. "Give 'em a real knock-down-drag-out."

For all his success, Mix was never hesitant to seek advice. He had fought in the Spanish-American War, following Teddy Roosevelt in the charge up San Juan Hill. Some years later he'd caught on as a bronc-buster with the Miller 101 Wild West Show, which toured out of Oklahoma. Then, after being discovered by a movie producer, he went directly from the rodeo arena to the silver screen.

There were other popular motion picture stars who

made Westerns. William S. Hart, Ken Maynard, Buck Jones, and Hoot Gibson all had a loyal following. But Tom Mix was billed as the "King of the Cowboys," and by 1926, he earned a staggering $20,000 a week. He was the highest paid actor in films, eclipsing such luminaries as Douglas Fairbanks and Charlie Chaplin. Some thought the better billing would have been the "King of Hollywood."

By contrast Durant made fifty dollars a day for risking his neck in death-defying stunts. Yet stuntmen were the daredevils of Hollywood, relying on nerve and finely tuned reflexes to deliver action scenes that amused and amazed audiences. They were the gladiators of the motion picture amphitheater, and even the stars accorded them their due. None was more respected than Earl Durant.

Mix always insisted that Durant work on his pictures. Durant was slightly taller, lithely built, with chestnut hair and gray eyes. He was in his late twenties, broad through the shoulders, athletic in appearance. But he had a chameleon quality on film, and he easily doubled for such diverse actors as Mix and Fairbanks, and the master of illusion, Lon Chaney. Mix looked at him now.

"Told you before, you ought to be a director. You know more about pictures than Eason and that artsy crowd. When are you gonna take the leap?"

Durant smiled. "One of these days."

"Don't wait too long."

Eason was fussing about losing the sun. Mix rounded the truck and walked to where Dusty Miller, the black-hatted stuntman, was waiting. Durant listened as Eason set the scene, a climactic moment for any Western, the big fight. He thought he would have staged it differently, and wondered if perhaps Mix was right. Maybe it was time to take a shot at directing.

Durant's journey to Hollywood had been one of chance rather than purpose. In 1918, like many young idealists, he had joined the army in the belief that he was off to fight the war that would end all wars. Yet he had

soon discovered there was nothing chivalrous about the
poison gas and machine guns found in the trenches of
France. Instead there was something in the killing which
suggested humanity's end—and oblivion.

On the day Armistice was declared, over ten million
people had lost their lives. As quiet fell across the battle-
fields, there was little rejoicing in the trenches. The stench
of death was still too strong, and the men huddled there
felt the taint of barbarism deep within their souls. The
doughboys who survived were disillusioned, shorn of innocence. They had seen man at his worst.

For Durant, the revulsion of war was compounded
by personal loss. In 1918, while he was fighting in
France, what was called Spanish influenza ravaged continent after continent. Worldwide, in just nine months,
over 21,000,000 people died, and the toll in America
climbed above half a million. Among the dead were Durant's parents, and his only sibling, a younger sister.

In early 1919, after his discharge from the army, Durant came home to an empty house. His father had been
a cattleman, and the family ranch, located in the Texas
Panhandle, encompassed a hundred thousand acres and
almost ten thousand head of cows. Embittered, with no
purpose in life, he sold the ranch, banked the money, and
drifted from job to job, ever heading westward. He came
at last to Hollywood.

Western motion pictures were a staple of the film
industry. Durant, who had been raised on a horse, gravi-
tated to the studios and caught on as an extra. Stuntmen
were better paid, and he soon made the switch, unconcerned that a stuntman's life expectancy was a slim proposition. Defying the odds, he'd suffered only a concussion
and a broken leg during his six years in films. In the
process, he became a student of the men who were rev-
olutionizing motion pictures.

The film industry was born in New York City. Thomas Edison demonstrated a crude projection system in
1889, and a few years later, his newest invention, the Ki-

netograph projector, assured the future of motion pictures. *The Great Train Robbery*, the first film with a running storyline, was a one-reel Western made in 1904. By 1908, there were five thousand Nickelodeons across the country, a nickel being the price of admission. Vaudeville houses in many cities were swiftly transformed into theaters.

Hollywood, eight miles outside Los Angeles, was mostly farmland at the time. Moviemakers began migrating there, attracted by a Chamber of Commerce claim of 350 sunny days a year. By 1914, Hollywood had become the center of the motion picture industry, home to Paramount Pictures, Universal Films, Twentieth Century-Fox, Metro-Goldwyn-Mayer, and Warner Brothers. Neighborhood theaters and plush movie houses sprang up everywhere, with the Strand Theater in New York seating 3,300 patrons. The industry moguls were quick to brag that more people went to the movies than read books.

By the 1920s, motion pictures were big business. D.W. Griffith's masterpiece, *The Birth of a Nation*, cost $100,000 to produce and grossed over $50,000,000. Other directors readily imitated his style, and Earl Durant, in between doing stunts, was their keenest student. One way or another, his future lay in films.

"Earl."

Durant turned at the sound of his name. Neal Cushman, the assistant director, handed him a letter. "Forgot to give you this," he said. "It came addressed to you at the studio."

"Thanks, Neal."

The envelope bore the imprint of a law firm in Galveston, Texas. Durant tore it open and scanned the contents, his features suddenly grim. The letter was dated August 28, five days ago, and informed him that his uncle, Joseph Durant, had died of a heart attack. As the only living relative, he was the sole heir to his uncle's estate. The bulk of the estate was comprised of the People's Bank & Trust.

Durant slowly refolded the letter. He was reminded

that Uncle Joe's only son and his cousin, George Durant, had been killed at the Battle of the Marne in France. His Aunt Sarah, Uncle Joe's wife, had died in the same influenza epidemic that had killed his parents. The family, he reflected bitterly, was now gone. He was the last Durant.

"Cut!"

Eason's shout came as the sun tilted lower toward the Pacific. The fight scene was completed, good having again vanquished evil, and Tom Mix walked around the end of the truck. He saw the expression on Durant's face.

"What's wrong, pardner?" he said soberly. "You look like you've seen a ghost."

"Guess I have," Durant replied. "Just got word my uncle passed away."

"Well, hell, that's a damn shame."

"Yeah, I'll have to head out for Galveston in the morning."

Mix clapped him on the shoulder. "Get things squared away and hurry on back. We start another picture in a couple weeks."

"I'll be here in plenty of time."

Mix nodded sympathetically, then moved off toward the Dodge touring car. Durant looked down at the letter, struck by a hollow irony. He was the last of the line, and he wished he had made an effort to visit his uncle while there was still time. He hadn't been there since before the war.

He wondered what Galveston was like these days.

Galveston Bay was an immense body of water, seventeen miles wide and more than thirty miles long. The causeway, supported by concrete pylons, spanned the narrowest section of the bay. Three miles from the mainland to the Island, the two-lane ribbon arched skyward over marshes and bayous.

The headlights of a massive, four-door Buick slashed through the silty darkness of night. There were three cars in the convoy, the Buick and two Chevrolets, all bearing the emblem of the Texas Rangers. Captain Hardy Purvis, commander of the Houston district, rode in the shotgun seat of the Buick. He stared straight ahead as the causeway dipped back onto land.

Galveston Island paralleled the coastline, some fifty miles south of Houston. The Island itself was a thin sliver of sand, two miles wide and thirty miles long, and flat as a dime. It was part of a chain of barrier islands, running northeast to southwest along the coast, looking south into the Gulf of Mexico. To the east, at the tip of the Island, was a deep-water passage into Galveston Bay.

The causeway spilled out onto Broadway. The street bisected the Island, along an esplanade of palms and oaks, with a huge sign in electric lights touting *GALVESTON, THE TREASURE ISLAND OF AMERICA*. The town proper was located at the eastern end of the Island, and was alternately known as the "Sin City of the South" and the "Island of Illicit Pleasures." Gambling, bootlegging, and prostitution brought Galveston notoriety as well as prosperity.

"Take a right," Captain Purvis ordered the driver. "Head for the Seawall."

The Buick swerved off Broadway onto Twenty-first Street. Purvis glanced back through the rear window, assuring himself that the cars behind were still in line. There were five Rangers in each of the Chevys, and three in the backseat of his Buick. Tonight was the seventh time he'd raided Galveston, and he reflected all too bitterly that he had yet to arrest his first hoodlum. He told himself now that fifteen Rangers were equal to any job . . . even the Hollywood Club.

Twenty-first Street intersected Seawall Boulevard. A hurricane had devastated Galveston in 1900, and afterward the city had built a seawall seventeen feet high, sixteen feet at the base, and five feet across the top. Seawall Boulevard was a six-lane paved road fronting the wall, lined with luxurious hotels and tourist resorts. The wall was over ten miles long, and on the Gulf coastline, a glittering strip of casinos, nightclubs, and pleasure piers hugged the beaches. An access road bordered the strip.

The Hollywood Club was the swankiest nightspot in town. Dining and dancing, along with top entertainment and a plush casino, attracted thousands of people every week. A pair of searchlights out front revolved in a flashing display that lit the sky and distinguished the establishment from others on the beach. The club was laid out along a four-hundred-foot pier that terminated in a T-head looking out onto the Gulf of Mexico. The casino was reportedly at the end of the pier, strategically located at the head of the T, suspended over water. Purvis and his Rangers, despite their previous raids, had yet to find it.

The owners of the club, Oliver "Ollie" Quinn and Edward "Dutch" Voight, were the acknowledged czars of the rackets on the Island. A year ago, when Purvis had been assigned to the Houston district, he'd undertaken an investigation that quickly identified who controlled Galveston's underworld. He operated on the theory that to kill a snake, you cut off its head, and he'd targeted Quinn and Voight as the first step in routing the Island's vice element. Having been stymied in the effort, tonight's raid was being conducted in utter secrecy, with every Ranger he could muster. He meant to have his snake.

A light breeze from the Gulf brought with it the tangy scent of salt water. As the cars skidded to a halt before the Hollywood Club, Purvis jumped from the Buick. He marched toward the entrance at a brisk clip, the Rangers formed behind him in a tight wedge. The doorman, who was tricked out in a top hat and tails, gave them a snappy salute. He rushed to open the door. "Good evening, Cap'n," he said with a pearly grin. "Hope you enjoy the show."

Purvis ignored the gibe. He went through the entrance, entering a hallway lined with exotic potted plants and two doors. From previous raids, he knew the one on the right led to a business office and the one on the left led to dressing rooms for entertainers and band members.

A busty young blonde waved to him as he went past the cloakroom. Directly ahead were heavy swinging doors constructed of glass.

The doors opened immediately onto the nightclub. The decor was vaguely Spanish, with rattan furniture, intimate shaded lamps on the tables, and crystal chandeliers dangling from the ceiling. Off to the right was a dining room that seated five hundred, and to the left was a dance floor only slightly smaller than a football field. A raised stage with a twenty-three-piece orchestra overlooked the dance floor.

Ollie Quinn hurried forward. He was a man of medium height, attired in a tuxedo, with a square jaw and a humorous mouth. There was a certain Gaelic charm about him, and his eyes, blue as carpenter's chalk, seemed forever lighted by some secret joke. He stopped in Purvis's path.

"Well, Captain Purvis," he said genially. "Welcome again to the Hollywood Club."

"None of your nonsense this time, Quinn. I'm here to close you down."

Purvis brushed past him, followed by the phalanx of Rangers. Quinn smiled, turning toward the stage, and idly signaled the bandleader. A moment later, the orchestra, trumpets blaring, segued into *The Eyes of Texas*. The bandleader stepped to the microphone with a broad grin. His voice boomed out over the nightclub.

"And now, ladies and gentlemen, the Hollywood Club takes great pride in presenting, in *all* their glory— the Texas Rangers!"

The crowd, as though on cue, rose to their feet. All of them, from the tables and the dance floor, moved to block the aisle in the center of the room. Their voices swelled in merry abandon to the beat of the music.

> *"The eyes of Texas are upon you*
> *All the livelong day!"*

The Rangers, formed in a knot around Purvis, bulled a path through the revelers. But the crowd gave way by inches, laughing and singing louder, slowing their progress. Several minutes passed in a jolly little struggle before the Rangers emerged onto the opposite side of the nightclub. There, dressed in tuxedos, were two muscular bruisers, arms folded across their chests. They barred the way to another set of glass doors.

"Stand aside!" Purvis shouted. "Stand aside or be arrested!"

The bruisers patted their pockets, their faces a study in bogus consternation. Finally, one of them came up with a key and fumbled around unlocking the doors. One of the Rangers stepped forward, roughly pushing him aside, and held the door open for Purvis. They entered a hallway, which led to a bar and an elegant lounge, again decorated with rattan furniture and exotic plants. The patrons of the lounge greeted them with knowing smiles and polite applause.

Beyond the lounge was still another set of doors, fashioned this time from sturdy oak polished to a luster. The doors led to the T-head part of the club, which was supported by stout pylons over the waters of the Gulf. Dutch Voight, attired in a double-breasted tuxedo, stood before the doors as though waiting to greet the Rangers. He was short, his barrel-shaped torso solid as rock, and his features had an oxlike imperturbability. He nodded impassively.

"Back again, Captain?" he said in a voice like sandpaper on pebbled stone. "Thought you would have seen the light by now."

Purvis glared at him. "Out of my way, Voight. I intend to shut down your casino once and for all."

"You know we're not in the gaming business. We operate a private club, members only."

"I'm ordering you to move aside."

"Captain, you're just bothering our guests, and for no reason. There's nothing illegal going on here."

Purvis exploded. "Goddammit, get out of my way and do it right now! Otherwise I'll break down those doors."

"No need," Voight said with a sly smile. "Our doors are always open to the Texas Rangers."

The doors swung open as if by magic. A man with strikingly handsome features and alert green eyes waved them inside. Purvis and his Rangers charged through the doors, and then, abruptly, hauled up short. The room was massive, two hundred feet wide by a hundred feet deep, and lavishly appointed with teak paneling and lush wall-to-wall carpet. Tall windows offered a panoramic view of the Gulf of Mexico.

There were two hundred or more people scattered about the room. Some of the men wore suits and ties, others were formally dressed in tuxedos, and the women, dripping jewelry, wore fashionable evening gowns. Eight billiard tables dominated the center of the room, and men with cue sticks stood around watching while others pocketed balls. The onlookers were quick to call out "Good shot!" whenever a ball fell.

Along the walls were at least fifty backgammon and bridge tables. The dice cups rattled at the backgammon tables, and cards with the Hollywood Club logo were dealt to bridge players. At every table, people were gathered around, smoking and sipping champagne, watching with rapt interest. Some turned as the Rangers barged into the room, looking at them with the bemused curiosity normally reserved for acrobats and dancing elephants. Others, as though absorbed in a pleasant social pastime, simply ignored them.

"Disappointed, Captain?" Voight asked wryly. "As you can see, things haven't changed since your last visit. Billiards and backgammon, same as usual."

"Horseapples!" Purvis barked. "You're not fooling anybody, Voight. There's gaming rigs here somewhere."

"Be my guest, search the place to your heart's content. We're a legit operation."

"There's icicles in hell, too!"

Purvis ordered a search. From previous raids, he knew it was a waste of time, and he ground his teeth in frustration. However it was managed, the gambling paraphernalia and slot machines had disappeared from the brief interval between the front door and the moment he'd stormed into the room. He wondered how the hell they pulled it off.

The Rangers conducted a thorough search. They tapped walls, kicked at the flooring with their high-heeled boots, even looked under the billiard tables. At the rear of the room were two offices and an employees' lounge, and they combed through these as well. They found nothing; no gaming chips, no roulette wheels, no sign of a slot machine. Their search was swiftly concluded.

"You're slick," Purvis fumed when it was over. "But don't think you've seen the last of me. We'll get you yet—and damn soon!"

Voight appeared unimpressed. "Captain, you and your men are welcome at the Hollywood Club anytime. Have a nice ride back to Houston."

Purvis and his Rangers passed Ollie Quinn as they went out the door. Voight walked forward to his partner, watching as the lawmen marched back through the nightclub. The orchestra accompanied their retreat with another rendition of *The Eyes of Texas*. The audience merrily chimed in with the lyrics.

Quinn wagged his head. "Dutch, I've never seen such a determined man. I just imagine he'll be back."

"Wouldn't surprise me," Voight agreed. "Nothing worse than a Texas Ranger with egg on his face."

"Yes, too bad we can't buy him off. Honest men are a burden, aren't they?"

"You and your fancy talk, Ollie. Why not just say he's a pain in the ass?"

"Oh, that's much too coarse for an impresario like myself. You have to remember I'm a *showman,* Dutch."

"Yeah, and I'm a magician. Now you see it, now you don't."

Voight turned to their lieutenant with eyes the color of emeralds. "We're losing money, Jack. Let's have some action."

"Whatever you say, boss."

Jack Nolan signaled the housemen. He walked off through the crowd, flattering the women and nodding politely to their husbands. All the while he was checking his watch, herding the patrons this way and that as the housemen went about their business. Not quite three minutes later, the whirr of a roulette wheel and the rattle of dice on a craps table sounded throughout the room. Dutch Voight and Ollie Quinn looked on with approval.

The Hollywood Club Casino was back in action.

Chapter Two

Austin was situated along the banks of the Colorado River. Like ancient Rome, the town was built upon seven hills and spread northward from the rugged shoreline. The surrounding countryside was a pastoral setting of rolling prairie and limestone mountains.

Congress Avenue, the main thoroughfare, rose gently from the river to the state capitol grounds. Early on the morning of September 4, Sergeant Clint Stoner of the Texas Rangers parked his car and walked toward the entrance. A ray of sunlight glinted off the dome as he mounted the sweeping steps to the capitol.

Stoner wondered again why he'd been summoned to the statehouse. He was assigned to the Headquarters Detachment, located on the outskirts of Austin, and worked in the investigative division. When he signed in for duty that morning, his commander, Captain Fred Olson, told him that he had been ordered to report to Colonel Homer Garrison, head of the Texas Rangers. Olson seemed put out that he himself hadn't been informed as to the reason.

On the second floor, Stoner turned down a long corridor. A moment later he entered the reception room of the state headquarters. The secretary was an older woman, her hair pinned back in a severe chignon, and she asked him to have a seat. She wrote his name on a slip of paper and moved to a thick oak door leading to an inner office. Shortly she returned, nodding to him without expression. She ushered him through the door.

Colonel Homer Garrison was seated behind a large walnut desk. His chiseled features and brushy mustache gave him an appearance of solidity and iron will. The office, like the man, was utilitarian, with two leather chairs positioned facing the desk. The sole decorations were the Texas state flag and the national flag, draped from standards anchored to the floor. His greeting was brusque.

"Good morning," he said. "Have a chair."

Stoner seated himself. "Captain Olson told me I was to report to you, sir."

"I suspect Olson was burned at being kept in the dark."

"The captain didn't say one way or the other."

"No, he wouldn't." Garrison opened a folder on his desk. "I've been reading your file, Stoner. You have a commendable record."

"Thank you, sir."

Stoner had been in law enforcement for nine years. He began as a deputy sheriff, later joined the highway patrol, and four years ago, he'd been recruited into the Texas Rangers. In that time, he had killed two men in gunfights, a bank robber and a murderer, and steadily advanced in rank to sergeant. He was thirty-one, the most highly decorated officer in his Ranger company.

"I'm looking for a volunteer," Garrison said, closing the folder. "How would you feel about working undercover?"

There was no question in Stoner's mind that he'd already volunteered. When a superior asked, there was only one acceptable response. "I'm your man, Colonel."

"Excellent," Garrison replied. "Are you familiar with the situation in Galveston?"

"Well, sir, I know it's a hotbed of vice."

"Actually, it's somewhat more complicated, Sergeant."

Garrison went on to explain. The town and the county were controlled by two mobsters, Oliver Quinn and Edward Voight. By all accounts, they operated casinos, a fleet of rumrunners, and were so powerful they collected tribute from lesser gangsters. Their limitless source of funds allowed them to bribe the police chief, the sheriff, the county attorney, and any number of judges. The Island was so corrupt that it had become known as the Free State of Galveston.

Humbling as it was to admit, Garrison noted, the Rangers had conducted seven raids, all to no effect. Captain Hardy Purvis, the Houston District commander, had reported the most recent failure only late last night. Yet Purvis was correct in his assessment of how the war should be waged against Quinn and Voight. The way to bring them down was to dismantle the flagship of their empire—the Hollywood Club.

"The raids simply haven't worked," Garrison concluded. "So I want to send you in there undercover. Plainclothes, a fake identity, a cover story that will withstand scrutiny."

Stoner nodded. "Just exactly what is it I'm looking for, Colonel?"

"The assignment is more difficult than it sounds. Quinn and Voight somehow—mystically, it seems—make their casino disappear."

"Pardon me, sir?"

"Quite literally, Sergeant, the casino vanishes before our raiding party can make their way to the rear of the club. I want you to determine how it's done."

Stoner's eyes narrowed. He was just shy of six feet, whipcord lean, with weathered features and sandy hair. He survived as a lawman on sharp instincts and quick reflexes, striking first and fastest. He sensed a pitfall in the assignment.

"Way I hear it," he said in a level voice, "Galveston's a pretty rough place. An undercover man might get himself killed if he was found out."

Garrison steepled his fingers. "Do I detect a condition in there somewhere, Sergeant?"

"I'm requesting that I report directly to you. Loose talk has a way of getting to the wrong ears."

"In other words, keep Captain Olson in the dark as to your assignment. And neglect to tell Captain Purvis he has an undercover agent operating in his district. Is that about it?"

"I'd feel easier, Colonel," Stoner told him. "Quick as I turn up anything, I'll let you know. Time enough then to plan a raid."

"Point well taken." Garrison was silent, thoughtful a moment. "Your file indicates you're a single man. Is that correct?"

"Yes, sir."

"You'll need a woman along, to complete your cover. Someone to act as your wife. Any ideas?"

Stoner smiled. "Colonel, I've got just the girl. She'd jump at the chance to play detective."

"Known her long?" Garrison asked soberly. "Would you trust her with your life?"

"Well, sir, in lots of ways, she'd be trusting me with her life. I guess it'd be a fair trade-off."

"Very well, I'll accept your judgment in the matter. As of today, you are reassigned to my office. Get to work on your cover story and keep me advised."

Stoner got to his feet. "I'll come up with something airtight. Shouldn't take more than a couple of days."

Garrison thought he'd picked his man well. The Rangers was an organization of long tradition, founded before the Civil War and carried on to the present day. Looking at Stoner, he was reminded of the adage that underscored the tradition: One riot, one Ranger. He felt confident one Ranger was adequate for Galveston.

"A final thought," he said forcefully. "You have but one assignment in Galveston. Bring me the secret of the Hollywood Club."

Stoner grinned. "Colonel, I'll deliver it with bells on and a red ribbon. You've as good as got it."

The train slowed at the top of the causeway. Earl Durant, who was seated at a window, stared down at the bay, which was almost twenty feet below the monolithic arch. He saw oceangoing freighters docked at the city wharves.

A car overtook the train as it started down the grade. Durant always marveled at the engineering feat of the causeway. The concrete span was wide enough to accommodate train tracks, a two-lane highway for automobiles, and an electric interurban railway. The interurban whisked back and forth to Houston on the hour.

The train pulled into the Santa Fe station shortly before noon. Durant collected his suitcase from an overhead rack and followed the other passengers off the coach. His trip from Los Angeles had taken two days, with changes of trains in Albuquerque and Dallas. He felt grungy and soiled, ready for a hot shower.

From previous trips, Durant recalled that the Tremont was one of the better hotels in the downtown area. He walked east on the Strand, which was Galveston's main business street, crowded with shops and stores and ornate Victorian office buildings. A block north, on Water Street, he saw sea gulls floating lazily over ships berthed at the docks.

Durant was reminded that Galveston was a place apart. The Islanders lived by their own values, their own measure of morality, and prided themselves on being different from mainlanders. There was a mystique about the town that flaunted *joie de vivre* and a zestful wickedness, tolerance for the risqué. Life was meant to be a celebration, a somewhat naughty party that never ended.

The hotel was on Mechanic Row, a block south of the Strand at Twenty-second Street. Durant engaged a room for an indefinite stay, and once upstairs, quickly shed his soiled clothing. He unpacked, took a scalding shower and shaved, and then changed into a fresh suit, starched white shirt and striped tie. Downstairs again, he ate lunch in the hotel dining room.

Shortly after one o'clock, he entered the Hendley Building, on the corner of the Strand and Twentieth Street. On the second floor, he found the law offices of

Grant, Kline & Shapiro. After announcing himself, a secretary showed him into the office of Walter Kline, a lanky man with gray hair and sad eyes. Kline offered him a chair.

"Please accept my condolences," Kline said. "Your uncle was a fine man, salt of the earth. We were friends for over thirty years."

Durant shook his head. "Doesn't hardly seem real just yet. Wish I could have been here for the funeral."

"Yes, of course. There were two hundred people, perhaps more, at the services. Your uncle was very highly regarded in the community."

"I'll visit the cemetery while I'm in town."

"Hmmm." Kline's sad eyes appeared sadder. "However sudden his death, his will expresses the wish that you take over the bank. Do I infer you have other plans?"

"Mr. Kline, I work in moving pictures," Durant said equably. "Even if I knew how, I've got no interest in running a bank. I figured to put it on the market." He paused. "Maybe you could help me find a buyer."

"May I make a suggestion?"

"Sure thing."

"Ira Aldridge is the vice president. He was your uncle's right hand for many years, a very capable man. Talk to him before making any hasty decisions."

Durant nodded. "Sounds like he'd be the one to buy the bank."

"Nooo," Kline said slowly. "I'm afraid Ira hasn't the resources."

"Then what's to be gained by talking?"

"Perhaps you owe it to your uncle, Mr. Durant. He held Ira Aldridge in great esteem."

"Yeah, I suppose you're right. I need to find out what's what with the bank anyhow."

"By the way," Kline said, "will you be staying at your uncle's home? He owned a very nice house on Twenty-ninth Street—and it's yours now."

"No, I took a room at the Tremont. I'll probably go

by the house tomorrow. See about Uncle Joe's personal effects."

"Do let me know if I can be of assistance."

"Thanks, I will."

Some five minutes later, Durant walked into the People's Bank & Trust. A Victorian stone structure, the bank was on the Strand, between Eighteenth and Nineteenth Streets, in the heart of the business district. Aldridge's secretary, an attractive young woman who introduced herself as Catherine Ludlow, escorted him to an office at the rear of the bank. She smiled as she closed the door.

"Well, well!" Aldridge said, hand extended in greeting. "I certainly see the family resemblance. Joe spoke of you often, and with great pride, I might add."

Ira Aldridge was a portly man, amiable in manner, somewhere in his early fifties, with a shock of salt-and-pepper hair. They chatted a few minutes about the late Joseph Durant, and Aldridge expressed his deepest sympathy. His eyes went moist as he spoke of the loss of his closest friend.

"But no more of that," he said with an open smile. "We've laid Joe to rest and you're here now to take his place. I know he would be pleased, very pleased."

Durant cleared his throat. "Well, the thing is, I plan to sell the bank. I'm a movie stuntman, not a businessman. It'd never work."

"Of course it would," Aldridge protested. "I'll be right by your side, and banking is far less difficult than people think. You'll catch on in no time."

"Sorry, but it's not a matter of catching on. I've got a motion picture waiting on me in Los Angeles."

"You don't understand, Earl. May I call you Earl?"

"Wish you would."

Aldridge appeared agitated, his hands darting like birds. "Your uncle devoted his life to the People's Bank & Trust. He thought of it as a bank for the common man, the little people. Unless you stay on, it will all have been for nothing."

"You lost me there," Durant said, an eyebrow lifted quizzically. "What've I got to do with anything?"

"William Magruder is the only man in Galveston with money enough to buy this bank. And he was your uncle's mortal enemy. The man's an out-and-out scoundrel!"

"Who's William Magruder?"

"One of the two richest men in town," Aldridge said. "He owns the Galveston City Bank and half the Island. He's old money, and lots of it."

Durant shrugged. "Then he's the man I need to talk to. Sounds like a hot prospect."

"Good God, you can't do that! Magruder tried every underhanded tactic imaginable to force us out of business. Your uncle fought him tooth and nail, just to keep the doors open."

"Not my fight," Durant observed. "How much is the bank worth, in round figures?"

Aldridge sighed wearily. "A hundred thousand, perhaps a little more."

"No kidding!"

"Earl, do you understand what I'm saying? Magruder would shut down the bank and foreclose on every poor soul who's struggling to buy a home or keep from going under in a small business. The man has no scruples. None!"

"Look, don't get me wrong," Durant said uneasily. "I've got nothing against the common man, and I respect what Uncle Joe tried to do. But any whichaway, I wasn't cut out to be a banker. That's it in a nutshell."

"I see." Aldridge deflated back into his chair. "So you plan to contact Magruder?"

"Unless you'd like to buy the place yourself."

"I regret to say I haven't the means."

"Then I guess Magruder's the only game in town."

"Joe Durant would be disappointed in you, Earl. Very disappointed."

"I reckon I'll have to learn to live with that."

Durant walked out the door. A moment later Catherine Ludlow stepped into the office. She was a wholesome young woman, in her early twenties, with a shapely figure, auburn hair, and eyes the color of larkspur. Aldridge was slumped in his chair, and she moved closer to his desk. She gave him a look of concern.

"Are you all right, Mr. Aldridge?"

"I'm afraid not," Aldridge muttered. "The heir to our little kingdom took the wind out of my sails."

"Mr. Durant?" she asked uncertainly. "What did he do?"

"I fear it is what he plans to do."

"Pardon me?"

"Catherine, he intends to sell the bank to William Magruder."

"Omigosh!"

"Yes, indeed."

Ira Aldridge thought he heard the faint knell of doomsday.

The Gulf sparkled with silvery starlight. The moon was down, and apart from the luminous iridescence of the stars, the water spread onward into an infinity of darkness. High clouds scudded northward on a gentle breeze.

The *Cherokee,* a twenty-six-foot Chris-Craft with twin Liberty engines, appeared out of the starlit swells. A salty spray laced off the bow as the sleek mahogany hull sliced through the surface chop. The course was south by southwest out of Galveston.

Diamond Jack Nolan stood in the cockpit. His gangland moniker stemmed from the diamond ring he wore on his pinky finger, and tonight his chiseled features were a study in concentration. Whizzer Duncan, his second in command, stood beside him cradling a .45 caliber Thompson submachine gun. A man of slight build, with wispy hair and pale eyes, Duncan was dangerous as a pit viper.

To the rear, in the *Cherokee*'s wake, was a fleet of fifteen wooden lugger boats. The luggers rode low in the water, powered by twin 100 horsepower engines, and in the dark resembled nothing more than large rafts. Aboard the boats were Nolan's rumrunning crew, hard men armed with Winchester 12-gauge pump shotguns and 1918 A1 Browning Automatic Rifles. Their eyes strained southward into the inky waters.

The dim glow of a lantern appeared off the port bow of the *Cherokee*. The pilot, on Nolan's order, quickly throttled down, the hull of the speedboat plowing roughly through the troughs. A three-masted schooner, the *Shark*, loomed ahead, ninety feet at the waterline and painted a dull black. The ship swayed at anchor against rolling swells, armed men stationed at her gunwale. She was all but invisible except for the guttering lantern.

The *Cherokee* swung in under the lee of the schooner. The weathered rigging of the ship creaked in the breeze, audible over the rumbling growl of the speedboat as it throttled down to idle. The fleet of luggers stood off a hundred yards out, bobbing in the swells, armed crewmen at the alert. Nolan clambered up a rope ladder thrown over the side of the ship and nimbly hopped onto the deck. Whizzer Duncan covered him with the tommy gun.

Captain Rob McBride, master of the *Shark*, waited amidships. He was powerfully built, with a red beard, and in the swaying lamplight, he looked every inch the pirate. He greeted Nolan with a crushing handshake and a booming laugh. "Jack, my darlin' boy, it's good to see you again!"

"That goes double for me, Rob. I take it you found fair winds along the way."

"Aye, laddie, we did indeed."

Nolan and McBride were business associates, not friends. Their relationship was one of wary neutrality, mutual respect underscored by guarded watchfulness. Smuggler and rumrunner, brothers in a dangerous trade, neither of them ever chanced being robbed by the other. Their truce was maintained by parity in firepower.

"I'm bearing a load," McBride said with his pirate's

grin. "Fifteen hundred cases, all as you ordered, Jacko. Scotch, gin and bourbon."

Nolan handed over a fat manila envelope. "Sixty thousand, just as we agreed. You can count it."

"Why, of course I will, no offense intended."

McBride riffled through the cash, all in hundreds. On his signal, one of the crewmen waved the lantern back and forth over the side of the ship. The lugger boats motored in one at a time, idling in the lee of the black schooner. The crew hoisted nets out of the hold, loaded with crates wrapped in burlap, and lowered them to the waiting boats. The rumrunners worked with quick efficiency to stack the crates.

Captain Rob McBride was but one of hundreds of skippers smuggling illegal spirits. The Volstead Act, enacted by Congress in late 1919, had ushered in the era of Prohibition. A decade of campaigning by temperance leaders, who decried the evil of strong drink, was the moving force behind the law that took effect in 1920. Evangelist Billy Sunday cursed the influence of demon rum, arguing that "whiskey would make the world a puking, spewing, staggering, bleary-eyed, tottery wreck." He and his fellow temperance leaders turned off the spigot.

Yet little could they have foreseen that banning liquor would plunge America into the wildest, most turbulent time in history—the Roaring Twenties. Mobsters throughout the country were quick to grasp the potential, and tens of thousands of speakeasies sprang up across the land. Smugglers routinely sailed from Cuba, Jamaica, and the Bahamas, anchoring offshore in international waters, and provided a steady source of booze for the rumrunners. Prohibition backfired, to the tune of millions of dollars in illicit trade.

Jack Nolan, for his part, thought it was laughable. Galveston, with Quinn and Voight at the helm, became the conduit for bootleg liquor throughout Texas, Colorado, Oklahoma, and other states across the Southwest. The Federal Prohibition Agency headquartered in Houston was on the pad, and in six years, there had never been a raid on the bars and nightspots in Galveston. The good times rolled, and with it an avalanche of untraceable cash. The shipment being transferred to lugger boats would later be off-loaded to bootleggers at a deserted beach on the mainland. Tonight's haul, at a return of five for one, would net a cool $250,000.

A veteran of the late war, Nolan looked upon Prohibition as kid's stuff. In France, at Chateau-Thierry and Belleau Wood, he'd been brutalized by the sight of death. The generals on both sides pitilessly waged war by pitting massed strength against massed strength, and victory fell to those who demonstrated a superior ability to bleed. After the armistice, he was awarded the Distinguished Service Cross and the French Croix de Guerre. The medals meant nothing; he was merely thankful to be alive.

Upon returning from the Western Front in 1920, his cynicism was matched only by his ruthlessness. Through a friend, he caught on with Quinn and Voight, and slowly moved through the ranks to become the lieutenant of Galveston's underworld. He often thought the work he did for them was mild compared to the war, and he was sometimes amused that the trenches in France had prepared him well for the life of a gangster. He was head of the rumrunning operation, the mob's chief enforcer, and on occasion, a killer. He did good work.

Shortly before midnight, the lugger boats were finished loading. Nolan shook hands with Captain Rob McBride and went down the rope ladder to the *Cherokee*. By now, after years of running illegal booze, the operation was conducted by a standard drill. The men in the luggers had their orders; and they knew which beach had been selected on the mainland for tonight's delivery. The bootleggers would be waiting with trucks, and Nolan would join them in time for the payoff. He first had to attend to the Coast Guard.

The fleet of luggers turned northeast for the mainland. The *Cherokee* came about, motors rumbling, and took a heading due north. The Coast Guard station was located on the northeastern tip of Galveston Island, and they routinely patrolled the southern waters, searching for rum-runners. Nolan's immediate mission was to intercept the patrol and decoy them west, away from the lugger boats. He felt a rush of adrenaline at the prospect of action.

Twenty minutes later he spotted the silhouette of CG-204 from the Galveston station. The cutter was seventy-five feet long, armed with .50 caliber machine guns and a one-pounder cannon mounted on the forward deck. Intended for pursuit, the cutter was capable of speeds up to thirty-five knots. But Nolan was unconcerned about being overtaken, for the *Cherokee,* powered by Liberty aircraft engines, could outrun any vessel on the Gulf. His purpose was to lure them into pursuit.

Whizzer Duncan snapped a 100-round drum magazine into his Thompson chopper. The magazine was loaded with incendiary rounds, and when he opened fire, a stream of white-hot tracers spewed across the water. Nolan's standing orders were to engage the Coast Guard, rather than kill seamen, and the tracers fell short of the cutter. The response was immediate: a blinding flare soared skyward, illuminating the night, and the one-pounder cannon roared. A geyser of water exploded off the bow of the *Cherokee.*

The Liberty engines thundered and the speedboat took off on a westerly course. The *Cherokee* planed across the water, skimming the surface, its wake pocked by slugs from the machine guns on the cutter. CG-204 gave chase just as the flare died out and the sleek little boat zipped away at fifty knots. The cutter throttled up, her massive screws churning astern, but it was no contest. The *Cherokee* disappeared into the inky waters of the Gulf.

Later that night, Diamond Jack Nolan walked into the Hollywood Club. His smile was that of a cat with a mouthful of feathers, and he carried a satchel stuffed with three hundred grand in cash.

He thought Ollie Quinn and Dutch Voight would be pleased.

Chapter Three

The Strand was one of the major finance centers between New Orleans and San Francisco. From the Civil War to present times, the port of Galveston was also one of the busiest shipping points in the world. The wharves along Water Street handled more exports than any harbor in America except New York. The language spoken along the Strand was the language of commodities and exchange, and money.

High in a windless sky, the sun was a white orb as Durant crossed the Strand the next morning. Yesterday, after leaving the bank, he had called and made an appointment with William Magruder for ten o'clock. He regretted the hard feelings with Ira Aldridge, but he had no qualms about dealing with one of the Island's wealthiest men. Business, after all, was business.

The Magruder Building was a ten-story brick structure at Twenty-second and the Strand. The lobby opened onto a vaulting atrium, towering upward to a domed ceiling limned by a massive skylight. Durant took a birdcage elevator to the tenth floor, the marble corridors flooded by the skylight and the warmth of the sun. A suite of offices for William Magruder & Company occupied the entire floor.

A secretary ushered him into Magruder's lavishly appointed office. Overlooking the wharves, it was furnished with wing chairs and a couch crafted of lush morocco leather. The walls were lined with nautical oil paintings, and at the far end of the room, framed between windows with a view of berthed ships, was a broad desk that looked carved from a solid piece of ebony. The room seemed somehow appropriate to the man behind the desk.

William Magruder was a figure of considerable girth. His hair was plastered to his head like black paint on a boiled egg, and wattled jowls hung from his fleshy features. His beady eyes and stern, scowling countenance left the impression of a man who brought sighs of relief whenever he departed a room. He extended a meaty hand.

"Good of you to come by, Mr. Durant. This is my son, Sherman."

A younger man, somewhere in his early thirties, rose from the leather couch. The resemblance was uncanny, though the son was taller and his puffy, ruddy face was that of a hard drinker. After a round of handshakes, Sherman settled back onto the couch and Durant took one of the wing chairs. Magruder lowered himself into a throne-like judge's chair behind his desk.

"Allow me to offer our sympathies for the loss of your uncle. We never saw eye-to-eye, you understand, but he was a good man. Solid as they come."

"Yes, he was," Durant said. "I appreciate the sentiment."

"So you're here to sell his bank, is that it?"

"Are you a mind reader, Mr. Magruder?"

"Why else would you be here? Matter of fact, who else would you sell it to?"

Durant had done his homework. Last night, over drinks in a bar, he'd talked with a garrulous man who turned out to be a native of Galveston. He learned that the Magruders and the Seagraves were the two aristocratic families of the island. For all practical purposes, they controlled the economic lifeblood of the community. They were, in a very real sense, like feudal lords of old.

William Magruder owned the Galveston City Bank, the Galveston Cotton Exchange, several hotels, and the largest insurance company in the Southwest. George Seagrave, the other financial lion, owned the *Galveston Daily Chronicle*, the largest sugar mills in Texas and Louisiana, and the Gulf Railroad, which had merged with the Atchison, Topeka & Santa Fe, and added several million to his empire. Together, they owned the Galveston Wharf Company, which encompassed the entire waterfront. Galveston was the only deep-water harbor in Texas, and that gave them control of all shipping, domestic and foreign. They extorted a ransom in dockage by virtue of their monopoly.

"So, young man," Magruder said without expression. "What's your proposition?"

Durant spread his hands. "A hundred thousand dollars and it's yours. Ira Aldridge says it's worth that and more."

"Aldridge is a nitwit and everybody in town knows it. I'll give you twenty-five."

"I'm not here to horse trade, Mr. Magruder. A hundred's my price."

Magruder laughed a blubbery roar. "I like a man who sticks to his guns. Let's say fifty and call it a deal."

"No, sir," Durant said, poker-faced. "A hundred, take it or leave it."

"You're out of your league here, bub. Nobody in a thousand miles would buy that ten-cent bank and butt heads with me in Galveston. Your uncle learned that the hard way."

"Maybe so, but I won't be blackjacked into a fast sale. You've heard my price."

"Mr. Durant," Sherman interrupted smoothly. "We had you checked out and we know you're a stuntman in moving pictures. Be prudent, take fifty thousand and consider it a windfall." He paused with an oily smile. "You'll never get a better offer."

Durant knew something about Sherman Magruder as well. Last night he'd learned the heir to the throne was a Yale graduate, considerably more urbane and sophisticated than the old man, and some thought he was even shrewder. He was jokingly referred to as "the bootlegger's friend," a man who loved his sauce.

"The answer's the same," Durant said stubbornly. "I won't let it go for less than market value."

"Market value?" Magruder snorted. "Your uncle was a fool and it appears to run in the family. The market value is what I'm willing to pay. Not a nickel more!"

Durant stood. "I reckon I'll just have to put it on the market and find out. Thanks for your time."

"You listen to me, bub. You won't get an offer between here and Chicago! Nobody would dare come into my town."

Durant walked out the door. When it closed, Sherman slowly wagged his head. "Nice going, Pop. You insulted the man and drove him off."

"Goddammit, Sherm, don't you tell me how to run my business. I know what I'm doing."

"You've missed the point, Pop. We can't tell him we're after the deed to the property his bank holds. He might find out the property is worth more than the bank. Then he'd never sell."

"You're wrong," Magruder said sullenly. "He'll be back."

"I don't think so," Sherm insisted. "Mr. Durant has a stubborn streak, and we're the ones who need the deal. We have to buy his bank."

The tourist and convention trade was immensely profitable in Galveston. The Magruders were deep into secretive plans for a large hotel resort overlooking Seawall Boulevard and the Gulf. Too late, they had discovered that property contiguous to their project, property they needed to complete their hotel resort, was owned by the People's Bank & Trust. The bank and the property were now owned by Earl Durant.

Magruder's brow knotted in a frown. "Durant bought into the wrong game. We'll persuade him to sell."

"Oh?" Sherm arched an eyebrow. "And how will we accomplish that?"

Magruder lifted the receiver off the phone and jiggled the hook. "Central. You there, operator?"

"What number, please?"

"Give me 3154."

"Ringing."

The line buzzed and a man answered. "Oliver Quinn's office."

"Put him on. This is William Magruder."

A moment later Quinn came on the line. "Bill, always a pleasure. What can I do for you?"

"Ollie, I need to see you on a matter of business. The sooner, the better, here at my office."

"I'm booked solid today, Bill. How about tomorrow morning."

"All right, ten sharp and don't be late."

Magruder rang off. He sat for a moment, nodding absently to himself, and then looked across at Sherm. His mouth widened in a gloating smile.

"We'll teach young Mr. Durant some new tricks."

Blanco County was situated in the Hill Country. Johnson City, the county seat, was nestled in the hills some forty miles west of Austin. A ranch community, small but prosperous, it was a dogleg turn south of the Pedernales River.

Sergeant Clint Stoner drove into town under a bright forenoon sun. He circled the courthouse square and found a parking place in front of a hardware store. The car was his own, a Chevrolet sedan, and he was dressed in civilian clothes. He walked across to the courthouse.

The office of Sheriff Frank Shelley was on the main floor. Stoner and Shelley were old friends from the days Stoner had served with the highway patrol. He'd called Shelley yesterday afternoon, requesting a meeting as quickly as possible. His manner had been cryptic, sparse on details.

Shelley was heavyset, in his late forties, the sheriff of Blanco County for the past decade. His view on crime and criminals was that a man who stepped out of line deserved hard time, all the law allowed. He looked up from his desk as Stoner came through the door.

"Well, well," he said with a broad grin. "If it ain't the pride of the Rangers himself."

"Frank, good to see you," Stoner said, exchanging a warm handshake. "Putting on a little weight, are you?"

"The missus says I eat regular, too regular. Have a seat and tell me why you're tricked out in civvies. Your phone call was a mite shy on particulars."

"Not too much I can say at this point. I'm working a case undercover and I need a new identity. Thought maybe you could lend a hand."

Shelley chuckled out loud. "Hell, a crime-fighter like yourself, how could I say no? What d'you need, just exactly?"

"A name," Stoner said. "Somebody legitimate, in case the name gets checked out. It'd help if he was well fixed financially."

"Christ, why don't you ask for the moon, too?"

"I'll also need the credentials to go with the name."

Shelley leaned back in his chair, which creaked in protest under his weight. He stared out the window for a time, his features thoughtful. He finally looked around with a crafty smile.

"Bob Eberling," he said. "Bob won't mind if we borrow his name. Known him all my life."

Stoner nodded. "Who's Bob Eberling?"

"Just the biggest rancher in Blanco County."

Shelley went on to explain. Robert Eberling owned the Lazy E ranch, a hundred-thousand-acre spread along the Pedernales River. He ran a herd of ten thousand cows, and was reportedly worth more than a million dollars. Equally important, Eberling and his wife were on an extended trip to England. The ranch was being managed by Eberling's longtime foreman.

"Off buyin' Hereford bulls," Shelley concluded. "Told me he wants to add a new bloodline to his herd. Won't get home till late September."

"Sounds good to me," Stoner said. "I'll have the case wrapped up long before then."

Shelley proceeded to brief him on Eberling's history in Blanco County, Eberling's wife, who was named Olive, and salient details about the Lazy E Ranch. They had lunch at a café on courthouse square, and Stoner continued to draw out more information about his new persona. They parted shortly before one o'clock.

"Frank, I owe you," Stoner said with genuine warmth. "Nobody else I'd trust to set me up with a cover story."

Shelley laughed. "Folks you're after likely don't care no more about the law than a tomcat does a marriage license. You put 'em behind bars and that's payment enough for me."

"I'll surely do my damnedest."

By early afternoon, Stoner was back in Austin. Colonel Garrison had assigned him a new, canary-yellow Packard touring car, confiscated by the Rangers from a San Antonio bank embezzler. Garrison, calling in favors as chief of the Rangers, had also made covert arrangements with the head of the State Motor Vehicle Department. In short order, Stoner had auto license plates matching those of the car owned by Robert Eberling and a driver's license with his photo in the same name. All that remained was to find himself a wife.

Late that afternoon he called on Janice Overton. She was a part-time legal secretary and a full-time party girl. A dazzler at twenty-three, she was tall and sensuous, with long lissome legs, high full breasts, and skin like alabaster. She could be bawdy or ladylike, as the situation demanded, and she turned heads wherever she went. She had been Stoner's steady girl for the past four months.

Janice listened raptly as Stoner described his assignment. Until she accepted the proposition, he skirted any mention of Galveston. But he embellished on the undercover nature of the assignment, and the fact that it involved mobsters who operated an illicit empire built around gambling and rumrunning. He felt obligated to end on a cautionary note.

"I won't kid you," he said solemnly. "These are tough cookies, and they play for keeps. It could get dangerous."

"Oooo!" Her hazel eyes went round with excitement. "I like dangerous."

"Don't jump too quick. One slip and we'll be dead ducks. I want you to know what you're getting into."

"Are you trying to frighten me?"

"Damn right I am," Stoner said. "There's no second chances when you're working undercover. You'll have to be on your toes all the time."

She went up on her toes and kissed him. "I will, honeybunch. I promise."

Janice Overton was a thoroughly modern girl. The climate of the Roaring Twenties was one of ballyhoo and whoopee, a time when all traditional codes of social behavior were under assault. Hemingway and Fitzgerald, and other expatriate writers, were particularly influential in shaping the attitudes of the younger generation. But the greater revolution was stimulated by a radical new science emanating from Vienna.

Sigmund Freud, and to a lesser extent, his disciples Carl Jung and Alfred Adler, were the new messiahs. A generation devoted to "let the good times roll" began exploring introversion, inferiority complexes, and joyously, with open abandon, their libidos. To be happy and well, according to this liberated doctrine of self-expression, one must obey atavism, the pull of deeper instincts. The stairway to emotional bliss was an uninhibited sex life.

Janice found the new creed of intellectualism boorish and somehow pretentious. She was intelligent, with a mind of her own, and perfectly capable of formulating a philosophy of a more practical nature. So she discarded all the pseudo nonsense about the psyche, and adopted what seemed to her the salvation of liberated women, the libido. She loved making love, and never so much as with the Tarzan of lovers, Clint Stoner. A night in bed with him was a dangerous experience; the thought of it gave her goosebumps.

Undercover work sounded like an adventure too delicious to be missed. She put her arms around his neck. "We'll make a good team, sweetie. You wait and see."

Stoner held her closer. "You'll have to take off from your job. Any problem with that?"

"Oh, foo!" she said lightly. "Jobs are a dime a dozen."

"All right, consider yourself officially sworn in and deputized. You are now Mrs. Olive Eberling."

"Olive?"

"You'd better get used to it."

"Ugh!" She pulled a face. "What a dippy name."

"You'll get to like it," Stoner said with a grin. "Especially when I take you shopping."

"We're going shopping?"

"We have to look the part of ritzy swells. They gave me a thousand dollars to outfit ourselves in sporty fashion. We'll blow the whole wad."

"Godfrey!" she yelped gaily. "Just call me Olive."

"Well, Olive—" Stoner consulted his watch. "Too late to shop tonight. Got any ideas?"

"You naughty man. I just love you to death."

She led him into the bedroom. The late afternoon sun was in the west, flooding through the window with golden, shimmering light. She didn't mind in the least.

She knew he liked to watch her undress.

The nightglow of Galveston marbled the sky with shadow and light. A soft breeze floated in off the Gulf as the swirling waters of the bay lapped at the shoreline. Stars blinked like fireflies high above wispy clouds.

Jack Nolan drove across the causeway into deepening nightfall. His car was a black Ford, indistinguishable from others on the road, and unlikely to draw attention. Seldom introspective, his mind was nonetheless on the man he was to meet in La Marque. He thought Arthur Scarett was another lost soul in a topsy-turvy world.

The universe seemed to Nolan in a state of flux. On

the opposite side of the Atlantic, Benito Mussolini and his Fascist party had overthrown the old order in Italy. Joseph Stalin had taken over as dictator in Russia, annihilating his opposition in a series of purges. And in Germany an ex-corporal named Adolf Hitler had presented his manifesto for the future entitled *Mein Kampf.*

Not to be outdone, America had spawned an original all its own, the underworld mobster. A phenomenon uniquely American, these homegrown gangsters, men like Ollie Quinn and Dutch Voight, were brilliant capitalists. The almighty dollar became the only ideology in a remarkable marriage of free enterprise and brass knuckles.

Prohibition had shifted a market worth tens of millions to a trade controlled exclusively by the underworld. The rackets grew and diversified, proliferating amid a climate of tommy-gun violence, cheered on by Americans who simply wanted a drink. Bootlegging and speakeasies operated openly, and for the most part, law enforcement officials turned a blind eye. The accommodation, buttressed by graft, was made easier by the fact that lawmen were merely mirroring public opinion.

As Nolan came off the causeway, he reflected that Galveston was typical of the country as a whole. The casino, along with the rumrunning operation and protection payoffs from gambling dives and whorehouses, generated illicit revenues of more than five million dollars a year. Everybody in town knew that various city and county officials were on the payroll, and while no one spoke of it openly, it was an accepted fact of life. The payoff that hardly anyone knew of was the one that went to Arthur Scarett.

A few miles north of the causeway, Nolan entered the town of La Marque. On the outskirts of the business district, he pulled into the parking lot of Big Jim's Roadhouse. The nightspot was popular along the southern mainland, with dancing, liquor, and poker tables in the back room. He was carrying a .38 Colt in a shoulder holster, and as he stepped out of the car, he adjusted it to a comfortable position under his suit jacket. The gun, like a necktie, was part of his everyday attire.

The front door of the roadhouse opened onto a hallway. Off to one side was a room with a bar, where girls mingled with customers, and for a slightly higher tariff took them upstairs. On the opposite side was a larger room with a dance floor and a three-piece band. There were tables around the dance floor and cozy booths along the walls. The place was crowded, and waiters scurried back and forth serving drinks. The music, with a trumpeter blasting away, was all but deafening.

Arthur Scarett was seated alone in a booth. He was a squat, fat man with a pocked moonlike face and a gift for duplicity. Few people knew him on sight, even though he was the chief prohibition agent for Houston and the southern counties, including Galveston. His squad of agents routinely raided bootlegging operations and speakeasies that refused to share the wealth. All of which looked good for the record and allowed him to extend preferential treatment where it counted the most. Big Jim's Roadhouse was a longtime client.

Nolan scooted into the booth. "Evening, Art," he said. "Enjoying the music?"

"Music's music." Scarett waved a pudgy hand. "But, then, I'm not much of a dancer anyway. My wife says I have two lead feet."

"So how are things otherwise?"

"Never better, Jack."

A waiter took Nolan's order for bourbon and water. Scarett was drinking scotch on the rocks, and they made small talk until the waiter returned. Nolan sipped his drink, then slipped a thick envelope from his inside coat pocket. He placed it on the table.

"Mr. Quinn and Mr. Voight send their regards."

"The usual?"

"The usual."

The payoff was all part of the cost of operating an illicit business. The federal penalty for rumrunning was

$1,000 and six months in prison, and repeat offenders were fined $10,000 and sentenced to five years. The law also mandated forfeiture of all property, including boats, trucks and cash seized at the time of arrest. Bribing a prohibition agent was considered an investment in the future.

Scarett pocketed the envelope. "I got a call from the Coast Guard today. How many cases did you bring in last night?"

"Does it matter?" Nolan said. "You know our deal."

The deal was simple. Galveston Island, from the Hollywood Club to the lowest hooch joint, was immune to raids. The rumrunning operation was immune as well, at least on the beach, where smuggled liquor was transferred from boats to trucks. Once the trucks cleared the Galveston County line, the rules changed and bootleggers became fair game. Everyone understood the rules, including the bootleggers, who scattered like quail when they crossed the county line. Scarett was paid ten thousand a month to abide by the rules.

"I've been thinking," Scarett said in an exploratory tone. "Maybe we ought to up the ante."

"Why spoil a good thing?"

"Jack, you're running God knows how many cases a month. I deserve a bigger piece of the action."

Nolan's gaze was empty of emotion. "You wouldn't want to try that, Art."

"Are you threatening me?"

"Call it a word to the wise."

Their eyes locked and several moments elapsed in silence. Scarett blinked first, some inner voice telling him not to push too hard. "Well, like you said, why spoil a good thing?"

Nolan slid out of the booth. "Enjoyed our little talk, Art. See you next month."

Outside, as he pulled away in the Ford, Nolan thought there was no accounting for greed. But he didn't fault Scarett, or particularly think the worse of him. There was no great harm in throwing out a line and seeing if the fish took the bait. No harm if a man knew when to call it quits.

Nolan arrived back at the Hollywood Club shortly before nine o'clock. He found Quinn and Voight in the office at the rear of the casino. They were involved in a discussion about the astronomical salary needed to import Al Jolson from Broadway. Jolson was opening at the club Friday night, and Voight was still complaining about the price. Nolan thought the ongoing argument typified the differences between the two men.

Quinn was a polished gentleman, a bon vivant and raconteur with an easygoing manner. He was always impeccably dressed, his wardrobe tailored in London, and he frequently traveled to New York booking headliner entertainment for the club. Voight, apart from his tuxedo attire at the casino, wore off-the-rack suits and always appeared a little rumpled. His manner was polite but quietly sinister, no laughter in his eyes. He looked like he might hurt you, given the slightest pretext.

For all their contrasts, the partners ran a smooth operation. Gulf Properties, their holding company, employed over a thousand people, fully five percent of the adult population on the Island. They owned gambling clubs, bars, a restaurant and an amusement pier, and several other legitimate businesses. The Hollywood Club was nonetheless the jewel of their empire.

Yet, for all their gangland activities, they were astute businessmen. They realized that public relations were key to success and they allowed only wealthy Islanders inside the casino. Their patrons were drawn instead from the upper financial strata of Houston, Dallas and other cities throughout the Southwest. To show Galveston in the best light, they also maintained their own brand of law and order with a squad of hooligans known as the Night Raiders. No one feared to walk the streets after dark.

Quinn finally noticed Nolan waiting by the door. He broke off the argument about Al Jolson, and looked around with a quick smile. "Everything status quo with our friend, Mr. Scarett?"

"Went off fine," Nolan replied. "He tried to sandbag us for a raise, but he backed off when I spelled it out. He didn't like the options."

"Damned ingrate," Voight grumped. "We've made him rich as Midas. His only option is to go for a swim."

"I told him as much."

Quinn kept a blue macaw parrot in the office. The bird was named Cuddles and sat perched on a stand behind the desk. A master mimic, Cuddles often joined in the conversation. He cocked his head now and looked at them with a puckish glare.

"Oh, boy! Oh, boy! Take him for a swim. Kiss my ass!"

"See there, Dutch," Quinn said ruefully. "He's picked up all your bad habits."

Voight chuckled. "Smart bird."

Chapter Four

Ollie Quinn occupied the penthouse suite at the Buccaneer Hotel. The hotel was located on Seawall Boulevard, and the balcony of his suite offered a sweeping view of the Gulf. A morning sun, bright as new brass, reflected off waves lapping gently at the beach.

Breakfast, weather permitting, was always served on the balcony. Quinn was in shirtsleeves and tie, seated at a table covered with spotless linen, a napkin tucked into his collar. A waiter from room service fussed over him, setting out a ripe melon, bacon and eggs, and coffee. The breadbasket was filled with piping hot buttermilk biscuits.

Maxine Baxter wandered out of the master bedroom as the waiter left the suite. She was a honey blonde with a ballerina's grace and blue eyes the color of a tropical lagoon. Her hourglass curves amply strained a sheer peach peignoir and high-heeled satin slippers covered her dainty feet. She was small, a pocket Venus.

"Mornin', sugar," she said, moving onto the balcony. "Aren't you up early?"

Quinn spooned a bite of melon. "Today's a big day, Maxie. Al Jolson arrives this afternoon."

"Oh, sure, I guess I forgot. You're excited, aren't you?"

"The king of Broadway! Who wouldn't be?"

Quinn and Maxine were both native Texans. She began as a hatcheck girl at the club, and her lilting Southern drawl, as well as her other charms, quickly caught his attention. A little over a year ago she had moved into the penthouse, happy as a clam to be his only girl. Their lives were filled with luxury and interesting people, and languorous nights dreamily exhausted from love. Neither of them asked for any promises, and there were no strings attached. They lived it one day at a time.

Dutch Voight, by comparison, shunned the limelight. Apart from Quinn, who was occasionally invited to a modest house on Twenty-ninth Street, few people in the sporting world had ever seen Voight's wife. She was a deeply religious woman who lived in denial that her husband was a gangster. A great many people were unaware that Voight had two teenage children, a son and a daughter, who attended Galveston High School. He adroitly kept his personal life separated from his business affairs, and his gangland associates. Quinn often thought his partner needed a girlfriend.

"What a gorgeous day," Maxine said, pouring herself a cup of coffee. "Maybe I'll run downtown and do some shopping. What would you like to buy me, sugar?"

Quinn layered jam onto a biscuit. "Anything your little heart desires. Find a new dress for Jolson's opening."

"Why, I just believe I will! Won't you come help me pick it out?"

"Sorry, buttercup, I have a meeting at ten."

"Business, business, business. You're never any fun."

"That's not what you said last night."

"Oh, you wicked man!"

"I accept the compliment."

For all his cheery banter, Quinn's mind was on the day ahead. At ten, he had a meeting with William Magruder, and he was still wondering what that was all about. Yesterday, on the phone, Magruder had sounded harried, which was unusual. William Magruder was what he'd always thought of as collected, even a bit calculating. A cold fish.

Whatever it was, Quinn was determined that it wouldn't spoil his day. Early that afternoon, Al Jolson was arriving by train, and he meant to celebrate the major coup of his career as a showman. He kissed Maxine on the cheek, and left her to plan a shopping spree that would likely cost him a fortune. In the bedroom, he shrugged into his suit jacket, tilting his Panama hat at a jaunty angle, and hurried out of the suite. The elevator operator gave him an express ride to the lobby.

Turk McGuire, his chauffeur and bodyguard, was waiting outside. There was small chance of anyone trying to rub him out in Galveston, but he believed in playing the odds. McGuire was robust as an ox, his head fixed directly on his shoulders, with the vacant eyes of a man who spent his time contemplating deadly acts. More to the point, he was loyal, quick with his hands and fast with a gun, and seemingly robbed of fear the day he was weaned. No one messed with Turk McGuire.

Quinn's car was a Cadillac Phaeton with a V-16 engine. The body was gold, the teardrop fenders a rich maroon, with a gleaming silver grill and wide whitewall tires. The Phaeton was sleek and rakish, the only one in Galveston, and everyone in town knew it on sight. The day was bright and sunny, and the collapsible top had been folded down, which highlighted the car's lush leather interior. Turk McGuire kept the Caddy washed and polished, every ornament glittering in the sunlight, a rolling tribute to the impresario of the Hollywood Club. He held the rear door open for Quinn.

Some ten minutes later McGuire parked in front of the Magruder Building. The distinctive Cadillac was like a pronouncement of Quinn's presence, but he hardly gave it a thought. Galveston's biggest open secret was that the two reigning families, the Magruders and the Seagraves, occasionally worked with the mob for the civic and economic betterment of the community. Quinn strolled into the building with the brisk air of a man on important business and not a moment to waste. He took the birdcage elevator to the tenth floor.

A secretary escorted him into Magruder's office. The old man was behind his desk and Sherm was seated on the couch. Their relationship with Quinn was one of wary civility, for they preferred to distance themselves from mob activities on the Island. After perfunctory handshakes all around, Quinn was offered one of the leather arm-chairs. Magruder went straight to the point.

"We have a minor business problem. Your assistance would be most appreciated."

"Anything at all, Bill. How can I help?"

"People's Bank & Trust," Magruder explained. "Upon Joseph Durant's death, the bank was inherited by his nephew. The man's name is Earl Durant."

Quinn nodded. "I believe I heard something about the bank changing hands."

"A change for the worse, no question about it. Mr. Durant is a stuntman in moving pictures. Hardly a wel-come addition to Galveston."

"I see."

"In any event," Magruder went on, "we wish to pur-chase People's Bank & Trust. Despite our generous offer, Durant refuses to sell. Therein lies our problem."

"These things happen," Quinn said equably. "What assistance may I offer you?"

"Joseph Durant was respected by a certain segment of our community. I daresay the townspeople would not have condoned violence in his case. On the other hand, his nephew is a stranger. . . ."

Magruder paused, underscoring the thought with weighty silence. Quinn saw now that he'd been asked here not as a fellow businessman, but rather because of his reputation as a gangster. He found it ironic that Galves-ton's guardian of morality and good taste would recruit him to join in a criminal conspiracy. He decided it might work to advantage at some later time.

"Let me understand," he said. "Do you want this Du-rant fellow killed?"

"Good God, no!" Magruder huffed. "We simply want him frightened."

"Roughed up, put on warning."

"Yes, that's it."

"I'm with you now," Quinn said without inflection.

"And is he to be told the reason? The purpose of the beating?"

Magruder exchanged a quick, somewhat startled glance with his son. Their bemused looks indicated they clearly hadn't thought that far ahead. Sherm finally lifted his shoulders in a shrug.

"Why not?" he said. "The purpose is to persuade him to sell us the bank. I think he should be told."

Magruder pursed his mouth. "All very discreetly, of course. Nothing that associates our names with violence."

"Naturally," Quinn agreed. "I'll see that it's handled with the necessary discretion. Durant will get the message."

"Fine, fine," Sherm said hurriedly. "We realize there are expenses involved in this type of thing. Let us know what you think is fair."

"No charge," Quinn said. "Call it a favor among friends."

"That's very decent of you," Magruder said. "I assure you we won't forget your courtesy."

Quinn couldn't have agreed more. On his way out of the building, he wondered why they were so interested in a nickel-and-dime bank. Whatever the reason, he told himself, it wasn't all that important. Today's transaction, with the debit on their side, was what counted most.

Somewhere down the line, he intended to call in the chit.

The train chuffed to a halt with a belch of steam. Several people waited on the cobbled platform outside the Santa Fe depot, there to greet passengers. The stationmaster, pocket watch in hand, noted the train had arrived at 12:59, one minute early.

Quinn was almost dancing with excitement. He wore a smartly tailored linen suit, creamy beige in color, topped off by his Panama hat. As passengers began debarking the train, he moved through the crowd, his expression eager and alert. Then, with a sudden laugh, he hurried forward.

Al Jolson stepped onto the platform. He was a man of medium height, with broad features, snappy electric eyes, and a perpetual moonlike grin. He was attired in a blue tropical worsted suit, an exotic silk handkerchief draped from his breast pocket, the brim of his fedora rolled at a natty angle. The effect was one of casual elegance, faintly continental.

"Mr. Jolson!" Quinn bugled, pumping his hand. "Welcome to Galveston. I'm Oliver Quinn."

"Glad to meet you, pal." Jolson wiped a trickle of sweat off his brow. "Never expected a heat wave in September."

"Well, it's not the heat, it's the humidity. We're right on the Gulf."

"You could've fooled me, sport. Feels like the equator."

"Then you'll like the club, Al—may I call you Al? We had it air-cooled."

"Thank God for small favors."

Quinn signaled a porter. The baggage car door slid open and the porter moved forward with a rolling handcart. Jolson's luggage included three suitcases and two large steamer trunks, which the porter manhandled off the train. He trundled along behind as Quinn led the way around the side of the depot.

"Traveling light," Jolson quipped, waving idly at the luggage. "I might decide I like it in California."

"No question about it," Quinn said. "Motion pictures are all the rage."

"Wait till you see my talky. We're gonna call it *The Jazz Singer*."

Jolson was on his way to Hollywood. Warner Brothers had signed him to star in the first talking movie ever made. Until now, motion pictures were silent, with sporadic dialogue displayed on-screen through subtitles. *The Jazz Singer* would have recorded songs, accompanied by live music.

Quinn felt very fortunate. He had been able to secure

a booking of one week only because Jolson was traveling to California. Jolson was in such demand on Broadway that he seldom made an appearance outside of New York. He was billed as "The World's Greatest Entertainer," and it wasn't mere hoopla. His was the rags-to-riches story of show business.

Al Jolson was the immigrant son of a Jewish cantor. His voice, a brassy blend of warmth with a sob, first made him the preeminent star of the vaudeville stage. From there, seemingly overnight, he catapulted to fame at the fabled Winter Garden Theater in New York. Millions listened to his weekly radio show, and he recorded a new hit record every two weeks. He was the brightest light on Broadway.

A renowned braggart, with a monumental ego, he was widely acknowledged as the musical comedy star of the century. Just within the last year, a New York columnist wrote: "Al Jolson is to show business what Jack Dempsey is to the ring and Babe Ruth to baseball." And now, he was to make the first talky film in motion picture history.

But first, he would play the Hollywood Club. Quinn was beside himself, for it would garner publicity from coast to coast. A phone call earlier had arranged the opening salvo; a reporter and photographer from the *Galveston Daily Chronicle* waylaid them as they crossed the platform. Jolson quickly took center stage, always at his best in front of a camera. He regaled the newsmen with stories of the one he loved the most, himself.

Quinn, meanwhile, had Turk McGuire call for a truck to collect the luggage. A suite was booked for Jolson at the Buccaneer, and he ordered that the luggage be taken ahead to the hotel. When the interview concluded, he steered Jolson to the Cadillac, explaining the band was waiting for them at the club. Jolson gave McGuire a casual once-over as they climbed into the car. He smiled knowingly when they pulled away from the curb.

"I see we're well protected. Dempsey himself wouldn't tangle with your driver."

"Al, we look after our guests on Galveston Island. You're in safe hands."

Quinn, playing the good host, acted as tour guide. He explained that the Strand, which took them east from the depot, was christened to honor London's famed thoroughfare of the same name. Farther uptown, he motioned to the bayside wharves, subtly easing into a point of interest. He knew the story of Jolson's heritage and he related that Germans, Czechs, and Russian Jews had immigrated to the new world by way of the port. Galveston, no less than New York, was a melting pot.

On Twenty-first Street, where they turned south, he pointed out the Grand Opera House. The immense baroque structure was modeled after the great opera houses of Europe during the time of the Renaissance. The elite of the operatic world, as well as Sarah Bernhardt and Anna Pavlova, the Russian ballerina, had all performed there. The auditorium seated 1,600 and was constructed without square corners, a marvel of perfect acoustics. Galveston, he noted, was a city rich in culture.

A few minutes later they crossed Seawall Boulevard. Quinn proudly recounted that the Hollywood Club was the only nightspot in the greater Southwest with top-notch entertainment, gourmet dining, and a plush casino, all under one roof. Dutch Voight met them as they entered the nightclub, and Quinn performed the introductions. Voight took Jolson on a tour of the club and casino, explaining that it was the first air-cooled nightspot in America. He kept the temperature at 69°, confident that gamblers who were cool didn't feel their liquor. Drunk gamblers, he observed, were happy losers.

Jolson, who had known many New York gangsters, recognized Voight as one of the breed. The menacing attitude, however carefully suppressed, was there in mannerism and tone of voice. He thought Quinn, who came off as a dapper devotee of arts and entertainment, was probably no less dangerous. Yet he was impressed by their club and casino, a grand nightspot literally at land's end, suspended over water. He was taken as well by the welcome comfort of air-cooling. He'd finally stopped sweating.

"Are you a gambler?" Voight asked as they left the casino. "We'd be happy to reserve you a table."

"I'm a gambler," Jolson said with an immodest grin, "but only on Al Jolson. I know I can't lose on myself."

Voight covered his disappointment. Entertainers were notoriously poor gamblers, and typically dropped a large part of their salaries at the tables. A few, the worst of the lot, left the Hollywood Club owing the casino money. He'd had similar hopes for Jolson.

Ben Pollack was waiting with his orchestra in the nightclub. Popular all across the country, and a draw in itself, the orchestra featured rising young musicians such as Glenn Miller and Benny Goodman. Jolson had met Pollack once before, in New York, and it was something of a reunion when he hopped onto the stage. They began talking music—particularly Jolson's kind of music—and it soon became apparent that there was a new leader of the band. Jolson, as he did anywhere he went, got it his way.

Quinn and Voight watched from the dance floor. Jolson was a star of the first magnitude, certainly the top entertainer who had ever played the Hollywood Club. Quinn felt as though he had capped his career as a showman, and he could hardly contain his excitement. He looked around at his partner.

"Dutch, do you believe in providence?"

"You talking about divine intervention?"

"Call it what you will," Quinn said. "Somebody was watching over us when he got the role in that moving picture. Otherwise we'd never have been able to book him into the club."

"Tell you what I believe," Voight said crossly. "The bastard's not gonna drop a nickel at the tables. He'll leave town with our ten gees in his pocket."

"Yes, but we'll get that back ten times over in publicity."

"Nobody sings that good. Not even Jolson."

"Wait a week, old friend. You'll change your tune."

"Not likely," Voight said. "I'm tone deaf."

Quinn smiled. "That's exactly why I hired Jolson."

The Turf Club was headquarters for mob activities on Galveston Island. The Hollywood Club was the showpiece, but all serious business was conducted at a three-story building on Twenty-third Street. Quinn and Voight operated their criminal enterprises from an office on the third floor.

A small sign over the main door identified the Turf Club. The building, constructed of white brick, was located between Market and Postoffice Streets, a few blocks from the Strand. The ground floor was a bookmaking parlor, where sporting men could wager on baseball, boxing matches, or horse races at tracks across the country. There were four betting windows at the back of the room.

The atmosphere was congenial and comfortable. A bar along the south wall looked over groupings of tables and leather club chairs, where customers could follow the action at their leisure. On the north wall was a tote board, posted with up-to-the-minute results from racetracks and various sports events. Two men, chalk in hand, constantly worked the tote board.

On the back wall, near the betting windows, was an elevator. The elevator operator took patrons to the second floor, where there were two lounges dispensing alcoholic beverages. The Western Room, done in a nouveau Texas motif, was appointed in leather, rodeo murals, and broad, spear-pointed longhorns affixed to the walls. The Studio Lounge, all modernistic Art Deco, was lights and mirrors and bright geometric designs. One lounge featured Country Western music and the other a jazz quartet.

The third floor was restricted to employees of Gulf Enterprises. On one side of a long hallway was a billiard room, with three pool tables and two snooker tables. On the opposite side was an athletic club, with a boxing ring, weightlifting equipment, and a steam room. Voight, in particular, believed the strong-arm boys and gunsels employed by Gulf Enterprises should be in tip-top shape. Every man on the payroll was required to work out three times a week.

The far end of the hallway was guarded by a gorilla in a pin-striped suit. There, on the street side of the building, was the central headquarters of the mob. Quinn and Voight, from an office paneled in dark wood and furnished in leather, directed the myraid aspects of their underworld empire. The proceeds, upwards of $100,000 a week, flowed from the casino, the rumrunning operation, and payoffs from their cohorts in crime. Entrance into their inner sanctum was by appointment only.

Late that afternoon Fred Crowley stepped off the elevator. He was short and lantern-jawed, attired in a sharkskin suit, spit-shined cordovans, and beige spats. A derby hat was perched atop his head and his eyes flicked left and right, to the billiard room and the athletic club, as he moved along the hallway. He prudently stopped in front of the gorilla.

"I'm Fred Crowley," he said. "Mr. Voight knows I was comin' by."

"Act like a gent in there or I'll break your legs. Take off the lid."

Crowley removed his derby as the gorilla swung open the door. Voight was seated behind a desk, and the man everyone knew as Diamond Jack Nolan occupied a leather armchair. Tall filing cabinets were aligned along one wall and a massive double-door safe was wedged into a corner. Bright sunlight splashed through a window that overlooked the street.

"Come on in," Voight said. "Grab a chair."

Crowley glanced at Nolan, who was paring his nails with a penknife. He seated himself in one of the arm-chairs, his derby balanced on his knees. "I appreciate you takin' the time to see me, Mr. Voight."

"Business is business," Voight said. "So you want to buy the Roseland?"

"Yessir, I've already worked a deal with George Napoli. He said I'd need your okay to buy him out."

The Roseland Supper Club was one of many joints spread around town. Despite its elegant name, the Roseland was a bar with a short-order cook, a dozen slot machines, and a poker room. All of the joints paid tribute on their gaming operations.

"You're new to town," Voight said. "Where are you from?"

"Spring Valley, west of Houston," Crowley replied. "I ran card games there for a couple years. Decided to move where there's more action. Galveston's the place to be."

"You know I'll have you checked out?"

"Yessir."

"You know what will happen if you don't check out."

Crowley fidgeted. "I'm clean, Mr. Voight. You got my word."

"Just so you understand," Voight said. "Did Napoli explain the rules?"

"Yeah, he did. I buy all my liquor from your boys, and I never welch on a bet with a customer. Always pay up."

"You pay up with us, too. We get ten percent off the top on slots and games. You get protection from the cops and the feds."

"Worth every nickel of it, Mr. Voight. Protection's the main reason I decided on Galveston."

"There's one last rule," Voight told him. "Never try to skim and short us on the grease. You skim and you're gone. You follow me?"

"Yeah, sure," Crowley said weakly. "I'm out of business."

"No," Voight corrected him. "You're gone, like forever. Got me?"

Crowley swallowed hard. He darted a glance at Nolan, who was reputed to be a stone-cold killer. He cleared his throat.

"I'll never hold out, Mr. Voight. You got no worries about me."

"Come see me in a week," Voight said. "We find you're on the up and up, you can close your deal with Napoli. You'll make good money with the Roseland."

"Thank you. Mr. Voight. I'll be here same time, next Friday. You can bet on it."

Crowley, hat still in hand, went out. When the door closed, Voight took a cigar from a box on the desk. He deftly clipped the end, struck a match, and lit up in a haze of blue smoke. He looked at Nolan.

"Make a few phone calls, Jack. Somebody we know in Spring Valley will likely know Crowley."

"Larry Hebert," Nolan said. "He's our bootlegger up that way. I'll get on it."

Ollie Quinn came through the door. He dropped into a chair with an exhausted look. "Jolson's a handful," he said. "I finally got him settled into the hotel. I think he would've gone on tonight without any rehearsal."

Voight grunted. "Why didn't you let him? We could've got eight nights for our money instead of seven."

"Dutch, it doesn't work that way. I have the newspapers coming from Houston and Dallas for the opening tomorrow night. We'll make headlines, believe you me."

"I'm surprised you're not playing nursemaid with Mr. Showbusiness. What brings you over here?"

"William Magruder," Quinn said. "You'll recall I met with him this morning."

"Now that you mention it," Voight said, puffing his cigar. "What'd he want, more charity donations?"

"Nothing quite so simple."

Quinn went on to relate the gist of the meeting. He outlined Magruder's designs on the People's Bank &

Trust, and the impediment of the heir, Earl Durant. He ended with a shrug.

"We've been asked for a favor we can't refuse. He wants the fear of God put into Durant."

"Fear of God," Voight amended, "or fear of Bill Magruder?"

"I suppose it's all one and the same. Anyway, we put him in our debt by doing the favor. So I told him we'd handle it."

"Christ, he could've called Western Union if he wants a message delivered. Sounds like small potatoes."

"Not to him," Quinn said. "I gave him my word, Dutch."

"Oh, hell, I'm not arguing with you, Ollie. How do you want it done?"

"We'll leave that to Jack." Quinn turned, nodding to Nolan. "Get a line on this Durant and take care of it. You know the drill."

"Shouldn't be too hard," Nolan said quietly. "I'll have a talk with him in private, put him on notice. He'll see the light."

"Velvet glove on a mail fist?"

"Usually works," Nolan said. "Time enough for the rough stuff if reason fails."

"You're a hot ticket, Jack." Quinn considered a moment. "All right, but make sure you scare the bejesus out of him. Let's fix it so Magruder knows who owes who for what."

Nolan bobbed his head. "I'll look after it."

"And no miscues," Voight added. "Lay it out in spades for him. Get the message across."

Quinn laughed. "What happened to Western Union?"

"Last time I heard, they don't break legs."

Diamond Jack Nolan thought that said it all.

Chapter Five

Saturday was the busiest day of the week in Galveston. Tourists there for the weekend swarmed the town sightseeing and visiting the amusement piers on the beach. Stores were crowded with shoppers and traffic jams were constant on the Strand. The police were hard-pressed to control the circuslike atmosphere.

The People's Bank & Trust, like other businesses, stayed open six days a week. A large segment of the bank's customers were workingmen, struggling to make ends meet, and rushed in on Saturday to cash their paychecks and catch up on mortgage payments. Long lines began forming at the cashier cages soon after the noon hour.

Durant was technically the new president of the bank. Yet he asked few questions and left daily financial operations to Ira Aldridge. After his meeting with Magruder, he had explained the situation to Aldridge, and hardly to his surprise, the older man's reaction was somewhat euphoric. Aldridge was clearly delighted with the turn of events.

"William Magruder is a scoundrel," he'd observed with obvious relish. "He'll try to steal the bank out from under you. He has all the ethics of a jellyfish."

"That won't happen," Durant had avowed. "I'll just have to find another buyer."

"Earl, I'd say your chances are somewhere between slim and none. No one wants to compete with Magruder in his own backyard. He's simply too powerful."

Aldridge had nonetheless put together a list of banks on the mainland. From thirty years in the business, he

knew the executive officers of every financial institution
in southern Texas. He allowed Durant to use his name as
an entrée, and agreed to stay on if the bank was sold to
an outside party. He expressed the opinion that the likelihood was on the order of snowballs in hell.

Today, as he had for the past two days, Durant was
working the phone. So far, he had called bankers in the
towns of Hitchcock, La Marque, Santa Fe, and Texas
City. The response in each instance had been a polite but
very definite lack of interest, and by now, he had spoken
with the presidents of seven banks. Disappointed, though
undeterred, he had exhausted the list of banks along the
coastline. He was calling institutions farther inland this
morning.

The man on the line now was Horace Taylor, president of a bank in Dickinson. "Look, Mr. Taylor," Durant
said. "I'd be happy for you to audit the books and see for
yourself. I know you'll find it fair value for the price."

"Not questioning value," Taylor said on the staticky
line. "I've known Ira Aldridge most of my life, and he's
honest as they come. If he says it's worth it, then it's
worth it."

"Why don't I drive up there Monday and let's talk
about it? I'll even bring Ira along if you like."

"Mr. Durant, it'd be a long drive for nothing. I'm not
the first banker you've approached, am I?"

"No, sir, you're not."

"And I'd venture to say they've all told you the same
thing. Nobody wants any part of Galveston because of
that sorry bastard William Magruder. Am I right?"

"Well, most of them called him a son of a bitch. But
that's been the general thought."

"You've got a tough row to hoe," Taylor said. "I
suspect you'll have a deuce of a time finding a buyer. I
wouldn't tangle with Magruder for all the tea in China."

The conversation ended with Taylor wishing him
well. Durant hung up the phone and slumped back in his
chair. He stared at the list of names on the desk, all too

aware that it was growing shorter by the minute. Dickinson was twenty miles north of Galveston, and apparently that wasn't far enough. No one cared—or dared—to take on William Magruder.

The door opened. Catherine Ludlow stepped into the office carrying a cup of coffee. She was wearing a dark skirt and a white round-collared blouse, with a little blue grosgrain bow at the throat. The outfit showed off her figure without being obvious, and he thought she looked cute as hell. She placed the cup of coffee on the desk.

"Time for some java," she said brightly. "How's it going?"

"More of the same," Durant admitted. "You'd think they're all reading off the same script. Always ends with 'thanks, but no thanks.'"

"You must be getting discouraged."

"No, I'm a regular brute for punishment. I'll find a buyer yet."

She lowered her eyes. "I really shouldn't say this. Mr. Aldridge wouldn't like it. . . ."

"Go ahead," Durant coaxed her. "I'm the original Silent Sam."

"Well—" She looked at him, and he was suddenly aware of the larkspur blue of her eyes. "Mr. Aldridge truly, truly wants you to take over the bank. He says you're your uncle all over again." She smiled shyly. "And I think so, too."

"I appreciate the sentiment. But it wouldn't work out in a million years. I'm not interested in being a banker."

"Mr. Aldridge says you're a stuntman in moving pictures. That must be fascinating."

"Why, do you enjoy the movies?"

"Oh, do I!" she said engagingly. "I see every picture that comes to the Bijou. That's our movie theater."

"I saw it when I was walking around town."

"Do you know any of the—?"

A man appeared in the doorway. Durant's first impression was that he would be perfect for moving pictures.

He was unbearably handsome, with eyes so green they glittered like gems. Aldridge, flushed with anger, was right behind him.

"I tried to tell him he couldn't come in here. He just barged on past me."

Durant got to his feet. "What's the problem?"

"No problem at all, Mr. Durant. I'm Jack Nolan and I'd like to talk with you. In private."

"Jack Nolan, the gangster!" Aldridge shouted. "He's the hatchet man for the mobsters that run Galveston."

Nolan looked wounded. "Give a fella a break, old man. You might hurt my feelings."

"Ira. Catherine." Durant got their attention. "Would you mind stepping outside? I'll talk to Mr. Nolan alone."

Aldridge waited at the door until Catherine went out. He gave Durant a concerned look, clearly reluctant to leave, and then closed the door. Durant motioned to a chair.

"I've never met a gangster," he said as Nolan seated himself. "Or was Mr. Aldridge mistaken?"

Nolan rocked his hand, fingers splayed. "I work at the Hollywood Club. Hottest spot in town."

"I heard Al Jolson's opening tonight."

"Come on by and be my guest. I'll save you a good table."

"I get the feeling you're not here to talk about show business. What can I do for you, Mr. Nolan?"

"Let's talk about your bank," Nolan said casually. "The people I work for, they're friends of William Magruder. They think you ought to sell him the bank—at his price."

"Well, that's a twist," Durant said, openly surprised. "Magruder in bed with the mob. One hand washes the other, is that it?"

"Don't worry yourself about that. What's important here is your health, follow me? You need to put Galveston behind you."

"Are you threatening me, Mr. Nolan?"

"I'm delivering a message, and it's real simple. Take the money and run."

"And if I don't?"

Nolan eased his suit jacket aside. The Colt revolver, nestled in the shoulder holster, spoke for itself. "Save yourself some grief, chum. Nobody wants trouble."

"I'll give you a choice," Durant said with a hard stare. "Pull that gun and I'll take it away from you. Or you can hit the road. Which is it?"

"You ought to get your hearing checked."

"You're the one that's not listening. What'll it be?"

"I'll see you around, tough guy. Real soon."

Nolan rose with a tight smile and walked to the door. As he moved through the bank, Aldridge and Catherine hurried into the office. Durant gave them a funny look, shook his head. A ghost of a grin touched his mouth.

"Try this on for size," he said. "The mob's playing fetch and carry for Magruder. I've been warned to sell him the bank—or else."

"Or else what?" Aldridge demanded. "Are you saying Nolan threatened you?"

"Yeah, I think it qualified as a threat."

"Good Lord!" Catherine said on a sudden intake of breath. "What will you do?"

"Just what I intended to do," Durant said. "Sell the bank to somebody on the mainland."

Aldridge frowned. "I wouldn't take it lightly if I were you. These are dangerous men, very dangerous indeed." He paused, his eyes dark with fear. "They might well do you harm . . . great harm."

"Ira, I guess I'll have to take my chances. I never learned how to cut and run."

Catherine thought he was either incredibly brave or incredibly stupid. Then, looking closer, she saw something in the cast of his face. Something implacable and cold.

Her heart went out to him, and she wished he would

run and keep on running. Yet she somehow knew he wouldn't. Or couldn't.

She wondered if Diamond Jack Nolan knew it as well.

The Turf Club was packed. Saturday was a big day for the sporting crowd, particularly on the opening day of football season. The horse tracks were still open as well, and several important races were scheduled around the country. The betting cages were lined with men waiting to get down a wager.

Nolan paused halfway across the room. He ignored the hubbub of conversation, and stood for a moment studying the tote board. He saw that the Chicago Bears were playing the New York Giants in the Windy City that afternoon. The Bears were favored by five points, and he idly wondered if anyone would bet against Red Grange. But then, on second thought, he knew it was a book-maker's dream. The suckers always took the long odds.

Joe Reed, the elevator operator, greeted him with a loopy grin. "How's tricks, Jack? Sleep late, did you?"

"Don't I wish," Nolan said. "Out and about on a little business."

"Well, business before pleasure, that's our motto. Gotta keep the gelt rollin' in."

The car lurched upward. The interior walls were mir-rored in an Art Deco design, and Nolan's gaze was drawn to the older man's reflected image. Reed was in his late forties, with a lung condition, and he'd been retired to elevator operator. In his heyday, he had been a rough customer, one of many strong-arm boys for the mob. Time and asthma had sapped his strength.

Nolan thought it spoke well of Quinn and Voight. Rather than give Reed the boot, they had pensioned him off as an elevator operator. There were seven men on the payroll in the same situation, men who now ran errands, or answered telephones, or worked the betting cages. Still, while he respected the benevolence of his bosses, he was determined never to end up as an elevator operator. There were better ways to die, and quicker.

On the third floor, Nolan walked along the hallway. Elmer Spadden, the ape who guarded the office door, would never wind up on an elevator either. Of all the men in the organization, Nolan gave Spadden and Turk McGuire a show of respect. He feared no man, but he'd seen them in action, and he knew he couldn't whip either one in a fight. Before it came to that he would resort to a gun, and he liked them too much. They reminded him of overgrown boys with an aptitude for breaking bones.

Quinn and Voight were seated at their desks in the office. Saturday was their most hectic day, busy from morning until late at night with the action at the Turf Club and the crowds jamming the Hollywood Club. Earlier, he'd phoned and told them he planned to drop by the People's Bank & Trust. They were expecting results.

"How'd it go?" Voight asked. "Durant ready to sign over the bank?"

Nolan took a chair. "I'd have to say he surprised me. He's a cool one."

"What happened?"

"Well, for openers, he doesn't scare. I gave him the pitch and he never blinked an eye. Told me to hit the road."

"I'll be damned," Voight said, amazed. "Not losing your touch, are you, Jack?"

"You be the judge," Nolan countered. "You know how you accidentally-on-purpose show a man your gun? Just to put him in the right frame of mind?"

"Yeah, so?"

"I showed him mine and he threatened to take it away from me. How's that for brass balls?"

Voight and Quinn were shocked. Their years on the Island had made them masters of extortion and intimidation, overlords who were never challenged. What they'd just heard mocked their authority, insulted them. Their reaction was predictable.

"Does he know who we are?" Quinn said hotly. "Does he know we *run* this Island?"

"Aldridge told him," Nolan replied. "Followed me through the door and told him I'm the hatchet man for the mob. That got things off to a fast start."

"I'm sure," Quinn said. "You didn't let Aldridge stick around, did you?"

"Didn't have to lift a finger. Durant shooed him out of the office pretty as you please. Everything said was said in private."

"So you told him we represent Magruder and it's in his best interests to sell. Does that cover it?"

"More or less," Nolan said. "I dropped the hint it's not healthy for him on the Island. Told him to take the money and run."

"And?"

"He as much as told me to stuff it."

Quinn and Voight exchanged a look. Nolan knew what they were thinking, for he'd had the same thought himself. But it was not his place to point out the obvious, or step on their authority. He waited for them to speak.

Voight took the lead. "No way we can keep this from getting out. People are gonna hear a wise-ass nobody told us to go screw. We've got to turn that around."

"And quickly," Quinn added. "We gave our word to Bill Magruder. We have to deliver."

"Magruder's second on my list," Voight said. "Durant's made us look bad, and I won't have it. We'll send a message to the whole damn Island. Nobody fucks with the organization."

Nolan was always amused by the euphemism. Everyone on the Island, and the mainland as well, referred to them as the mob. The Texas Rangers, and the occasional reformer, labeled them gangsters and racketeers. Voight and Quinn, who considered themselves businessmen, opted for a more respectable term. Impervious to the irony, they called it the organization.

"Dutch, I think you're right," Quinn said. "What we

need here is an object lesson. One that will impress our associates."

Voight nodded soberly. "Hoods and bootleggers understand only one thing, and that's cracked heads. We'll give them a little reminder not to step out of line."

Nolan shook a cigarette from a pack of Lucky Strikes. He lit up with a gold lighter and exhaled a streamer of smoke. He looked at his bosses.

"Why go halfway?" he said, as though offering a suggestion. "Why not clip Durant and leave him dead on the street? That'll send the message loud and clear."

"No, I think not," Quinn said quickly. "Magruder has a weak stomach when it comes to killing. He was very definite on the point."

"The hell with him," Voight growled. "We're the ones with egg on our faces. Jack's got the right idea."

Quinn shook his head. "Dutch, it just won't do. I agreed to the terms with Magruder, and that's that." His expression was stolid. "We have to stick with the original plan."

Voight was reluctant to concede the point. But he would never compromise his partner's honor, and dismissed it with a wave of his hand. His gaze settled on Nolan.

"We'll do it Ollie's way," he said. "Catch Durant on the street, lots of witnesses, out in the open. Let everybody see what happens when we're crossed."

Nolan took a drag on his cigarette. "How bad do you want him hurt?"

"Stop just short of killing him. Use McGuire and Spadden for the job. They do good work."

"When do you want it done?"

"Tomorrow's Sunday," Quinn said, as though thinking out loud. "No need to get the preachers harping about violence on the Sabbath. Wait till Monday."

"Monday, it is," Nolan said. "Anything else?"

Quinn checked his watch and suddenly jumped to his

feet. "Dutch, will you take it from here? Jolson starts rehearsal with the band at one o'clock. I want to be there."

"Leave it to me and Jack."

A moment of silence slipped past as Quinn hurried out the door. Voight fired up a cigar in a thick wad of smoke. He laughed with satiric humor.

"What a joke. Magruder wants to play dirty, but with rules, for chrissake! By all rights, we ought to ice Durant."

"I'd second the motion, boss. Too bad we've got our hands tied."

"Just make sure you bust his big brass balls. You hear me?"

"I hear you."

A picture of McGuire and Spadden at work flashed through Nolan's mind. He thought Earl Durant would wish he was dead.

The spotlights arced through a sky bright with stars. A warm evening breeze wafted in off the Gulf, the rolling waves of high tide pounding the beach. Far out across the darkened waters a streak of lightning briefly lit the horizon.

The Hollywood Club was chaos in motion. A long line of expensive automobiles dropped off guests from as far away as Colorado and New Mexico. The ladies were clad in evening gowns, dripping with jewels, and the men wore white tie and tails. They were drawn there, in all the glitter and crush, by a once-in-a-lifetime occasion. Tonight was opening night for the man billed as "The World's Greatest Entertainer."

The club was sold out. Tickets were thirty dollars, an outrageous price for the time, and did not include dinner or drinks. Still, the clamor for admission kept the phones jangling and even the lounge by the casino was filled to capacity. The crowd, apart from those few who had been to New York, knew Jolson only by his radio show or his records. They were there to see him in person—to actually see him perform—to say they had attended opening night. The air was electric with excitement.

Quinn was in his element. He was the consummate showman, and never more alive than when he was staging an extravaganza. His vigor was contagious, infecting every employee of the club with pulsing enthusiasm. His charm, cranked up several notches, overwhelmed arriving guests and the raft of newsmen there to cover the event. He dispensed bottles of champagne to the favored few, constantly on the move, hopping from table to table, shaking men's hands and beguiling their ladies. He was everywhere at once, never still.

Dutch Voight, on the other hand, watched it all from the hallway by the lounge. He was still of the very strong opinion that Jolson had picked their pockets; but he begrudged his partner none of the glamour or the accolades from customers and press alike. He and Quinn had fought their way to the top, all too often in the literal sense, and tonight was yet another affirmation that everything on the Island, legitimate or otherwise, revolved around their enterprise. As for Al Jolson, he was pragmatic, perhaps a little philosophical. He knew the casino would have a record night.

The show was to begin at eight o'clock. A few minutes before the hour, Quinn crossed the dance floor and made his way backstage. He found Ben Pollack, the bandleader, talking with some of the musicians off to the side of the bandstand. Pollack, a dandy himself, was quick to admire Quinn's white dinner jacket, lavishly tailored from silk shantung and set off by a scarlet boutonniere. Quinn, who was usually vain to a fault about his appearance, sloughed off the compliment. His interest was fixed on the star of the show.

"Quite a crowd," he said, moving fluidly into a non sequitur. "How'd you think Jolson sounded in rehearsal?"

Pollack laughed. "Ollie, c'mon, stop worrying. You asked me that right after rehearsal."

"I did?" Quinn drew a blank. "What'd you say?"

"What everybody in the band says. He's never been in better voice."

"Yes, that's exactly what I thought. I saw him perform at the Winter Garden in June, when I was in New York. I think he sounded even better in rehearsal."

"I know."

"You do?"

Pollack patted him on the shoulder. "You told me the same thing, almost word for word, this afternoon. Calm down, Ollie. Everything's fine."

"Who's worried? I believe I'll have a word with Al. Wish him luck."

"Careful, Ollie."

"Careful of what?"

"Don't make him as nervous as you are."

"Who's nervous?"

Quinn rushed off backstage. Jolson's dressing room was along a corridor with rooms where band members and entertainers changed, and a lounge where they could relax between acts. A gold star was affixed to one of the doors, and below it, painted in gold script, the words "*Al Jolson.*" Quinn rapped lightly on the door.

"C'mon in, it's open."

The dressing room was appointed with a plush couch and an easy chair, a mirrored makeup table, and a tiled bathroom. Jolson was seated before the mirror, putting the finishing touches on his makeup. He glanced at Quinn in the mirror.

"Hey there, kiddo. How's the crowd?"

"Full house," Quinn said. "You packed them in, Al."

"What the hey, I'm the greatest thing since sliced bread! I always pack 'em in."

Jolson dabbed greasepaint on his nose. He was made up in blackface, with a kinky black wig, his mouth and eyes outlined in clown white. To complete the costume, he wore a baggy black suit, a white shirt with a floppy black bow tie, and white gloves. He'd gotten his start in minstrel shows on the burlesque circuit, and later found it drew raves on Broadway. Blackface was his signature act in the world of show business.

"Everything all right?" Quinn asked anxiously. "How are you feeling?"

"Top of the world!"

"Can I get you anything?"

"Not unless you've got a blonde stashed in your pocket."

"No, sorry, Al. No blondes."

"Whatta way to treat a star!"

Jolson was at the height of his fame. He was forty years old, charismatic and full of vigor, completely taken with himself. The fact that Quinn was a mobster, and probably had people killed on the slightest whim, impressed him not in the least. He treated it all with jocular insouciance.

"Well—" Quinn hesitated, uncertain how to make his exit. "You're sure there's nothing I can do?"

"I've got my pipes tuned and I'm truckin' along to the melody. I'll lay 'em in the aisles."

"Well, then, as they say in the theater, break a leg, Al."

Jolson mugged a blackface grin. "Hang on tight, sport. We're off and runnin'!"

Quinn gave a thumbs-up sign of victory. He went out the door, rushing across the backstage area, and waved to Pollack and the orchestra as they moved onto the bandstand. In the nightclub, he table-hopped his way through the crowd, laughing and pumping hands. His jitters on opening night were linked to a superstition begun with the first act ever to play the Hollywood Club. He always stationed himself at the rear of the room.

Maxine was waiting for him. She wore a silver lamé evening gown, with sapphires at her throat, her flaxen hair piled atop her head in a French twist. She took his arm with a dazzling smile.

"Oh, it's just swell, boopsie. What a crowd!"

"I know," Quinn mumbled. "We could've sold out twice over."

She plumped her hair. "Do you like my dress? You haven't said a word all night."

"Yeah, sure, you look swell."

"A girl likes to be told once in awhile, you know. I bought this dress especially for you."

"Maxie, you look like a million dollars. I'm trying to concentrate on the show."

"Oh, stop worrying, sugar. I mean, after all, you've got Al Jolson!"

"Cross your fingers, anyway."

A murmur swept through the audience as the house-lights dimmed. The stage was faintly lit, and as a hush settled over the room, Pollack raised his baton. The orchestra broke out in a rollicking tune.

Jolson bounded onto the stage. A brilliant spotlight followed him as he opened with *Swanee*. His voice was strong, trained to fill the old vaudeville halls, and he worked without a microphone. He pranced around the stage, white eyes rolling merrily behind blackface, belting out the song. His performance was charged with vitality, energized by raw emotion.

The audience roared as the last note faded. Jolson paused at center stage, framed in the spotlight, and boomed his trademark quip. "Folks, you ain't heard nothin' yet!"

The orchestra segued into *Mammy*. Jolson's voice took on a mournful quality and his features seemed wrought with angst as he warbled the lyrics of a son lamenting for his mother. On the last stanza, he dropped to his knees on a polished ramp attached to the front of the stage. He slid down the ramp, halting in the center of the dance floor, arms spread wide, moist eyes glistening in the spotlight. His anguished voice quavered on the final line.

"My . . . my . . . mammmy!"

The crowd went mad. Women wept, men swallowed

their tears, all of them on their feet, applauding wildly. Quinn whooped and shouted, grabbed Maxine in a tight hug. His face blazed with excitement.

Jolson held them enthralled for the next two hours.

Chapter Six

The day was bright, the sky like blue muslin. A forenoon sun peeped from behind mottled clouds scudding westward on a light breeze. Galveston lay almost somnolent on a lazy Monday morning.

Clint Stoner drove down off the causeway. Janice was seated beside him in the canary-yellow Packard, her hair blowing in the wind from the open window. She pointed with little-girl wonder to the bay and tall freighters lining the portside wharves. Seagulls floated on still wings over the shimmering harbor.

The smell of jasmine and magnolia drifted through the window. Broadway was lined with stately palms, and everywhere there was the pink-and-white profusion of oleander blossoms. Janice breathed deeply, filling her lungs, and scooted closer on the seat. She gaily hugged his arm.

"Oh, Clint!" she said excitedly. "I love it. I just love it!"

"The name's Bob," Stoner corrected her. "And you're Olive and we're the Eberlings. Time to get it straight—Olive, honey."

"I will, I will, I promise. I just slipped."

"No room for slips, now. We're here, and we've got to be on our toes every minute. You remember what I told you."

"I know," she pouted prettily. "One mistake will be our last. I won't forget, sweetheart."

"I sure hope not, Olive."

The date was September 10. They had spent a day shopping, and another day rehearsing their cover story with Colonel Garrison at Ranger Headquarters. The drive from Austin had consumed the weekend, and only now, after crossing the causeway, had it become real. They were on the island where gangsters operated with impunity.

Ten minutes later they sighted the Buccaneer Hotel. To them it was palatial, four hundred rooms overlooking Seawall Boulevard and the Gulf. Intelligence reports from Ranger Headquarters indicated that Oliver Quinn, one of the two gangland kingpins, occupied the penthouse. The plan was to make themselves as obvious as possible, attract attention. They were wealthy tourists on a holiday.

Stoner braked the Packard to a halt at the entrance. A bellman rushed out, greeting them effusively, and began unloading their luggage from the trunk. The four suitcases were expensive, glossy leather tooled with their phony initials, and they were dressed for the part. Janice wore a fashionable day dress of the new artificial silk called rayon, a cloche hat, and a strand of pearls. Stoner was attired in a whipcord Western suit, pointy-toed burgundy boots, and a wide-brimmed white Stetson. They looked like money on the hoof.

The clerk at the registration desk snapped to attention. "Good day, sir. Welcome to the Buccaneer."

"I'm Robert Eberling," Stoner said. "I reserved a suite for three weeks."

"Yessir." The clerk riffled through his file cards. "Mr. and Mrs. Eberling of Johnson City. Is that correct?"

"That's me, pardner."

"You certainly picked the right place for a vacation, Mr. Eberling. The Buccaneer's the finest Galveston has to offer."

"Just make sure we've got a suite facing the Gulf. I won't settle for anything else."

"You have a wonderful view," the clerk trilled. "As a matter of fact, you're on the floor reserved for our special guests. You're just down the hall from Al Jolson."

"Al Jolson!" Janice said, round-eyed. "The New York Broadway star?"

"Yes, ma'am, Mrs. Eberling, the very one. He opened Saturday night at the Hollywood Club. That's the top nightspot on the Island."

"Oh, Bob," Janice simpered, batting her eyelashes at Stoner. "I'd so love to see Al Jolson. Wouldn't you, swee-tie?"

Stoner hadn't planned to move so fast. He'd thought to establish their credentials as wealthy vacationers, and then gain entrance into the Hollywood Club casino. But any plan was governed by circumstances, and he was nothing if not flexible. He seized on opportunity.

"You heard the little lady," he said to the clerk. "Arrange us a couple tickets for tonight."

"I—" the clerk stammered, caught off guard. "I'll talk with our manager, Mr. Anderson. He handles all requests with the Hollywood Club."

"Yeah, you do that. Tell him I expect some good news pdq. Now, we'd like to see our suite."

"Yessir, Mr. Eberling."

The bellman appeared with their luggage on a cart. He led them to the elevator and escorted them to a suite on the fourth floor. The sitting room was appointed with plush furniture and tall doors leading to a balcony that offered a panoramic view of the Gulf. The bedroom was bright and airy, with broad casement windows looking out over the water. Stoner tipped the bellman twenty dollars.

"Thank you, Mr. Eberling!" the bellman said with a horsey grin. "Let me know if there's anything I can do for you. Anything at all!"

"How about you bring a bottle of bourbon and some ice? The missus and I like a nip now and then."

"Yessir, we keep bonded stock for our guests. I'll be back in a jiffy."

"Thank you kindly."

The bellman went out. Janice inspected the bedroom

clapping her hands with delight, then hurried back into the sitting room. She stepped onto the balcony.

"Oh! Oh!" she cried. "Would you look at that. Isn't it marvelous?"

Stoner joined her on the balcony. The noonday sun was at its zenith, the clouds drifting westward on a warm breeze. Light reflected off the water in sparkling colors, rolling whitecaps cresting swells to the horizon. He put his arm around her waist.

"Not bad, huh?"

"Not bad!" she exclaimed. "I think I'm going to like being rich. Can we stay forever?"

"We'll see how things play out."

Stoner inspected the shoreline. The weekend tourists were gone, and the beach was practically empty. Along the seawall, extending five miles east and west, were amusement piers, dance pavilions, restaurants, and bathhouses with indoor salt-water pools. The beachfront was advertised as the "Boardwalk of Treasure Island," and even in the daytime it was impressive. The five-mile strip was known locally as the Gold Coast.

Two blocks east of the hotel Stoner spotted the Hollywood Club. From his briefing in Austin, the pier with a T-head over the water was distinctive, and easily recognizable. He pointed it out to Janice.

"There's our target," he said. "Home base for Quinn and Voight and all their goons."

Janice shuddered. "I wish we really were here on vacation. Just the thought of them spoils the fun."

"We'll have some fun, and you won't have to act, either. People come from all over to see the sights here."

"Don't worry, sweetheart. I am Olive Eberling, housewife and tourist. I won't forget."

The phone rang. Stoner moved into the sitting room and caught it on the third ring. "Bob Eberling here."

"Mr. Eberling, this is Charles Anderson, manager of the Buccaneer. I trust your suite is satisfactory?"

"I think we'll be real comfortable, Mr. Anderson. Have you got those Al Jolson tickets for me?"

"No, sir, I'm afraid not," Anderson said apologetically. "The Jolson show has been sold out for months. I'm really very sorry."

"How long is Jolson appearing here?"

"Only this week. I understand his engagement has been extended through Saturday night."

"Your man at the front desk the same as said you've got pull with this Hollywood Club. Is that so or not?"

"Well, yes and no," Anderson said in a defensive tone. "I usually have a direct line to the club. But to be perfectly honest, I couldn't get my own mother a ticket. Not at this late date."

"I'm disappointed in you," Stoner said in a gruff voice. "We're here for three weeks and I expected better treatment. The little woman's gonna be mighty upset."

"Please extend my most sincere apologies to Mrs. Eberling. I'll make it up in some way during your stay with us."

"In Blanco County, a man's word is his bond. I'll hold you to it, pardner."

"Feel free to call on me at any time, Mr. Eberling."

Stoner hung up and turned to Janice. "Looks like we won't be seeing Al Jolson. The show's sold out."

"Oh, rats!" she said petulantly. "I was counting on it!"

"Well, in a way, it worked out to our advantage. The hotel manager owes me one."

"Owes you one what?"

Stoner grinned. "He's gonna get us into that casino."

The Hollywood Club was all but deserted. Apart from a cleaning crew, working to restore the damages from a weekend of revelry, there was hardly anyone on the premises. Monday mornings were devoted to preparing for the week ahead.

Dutch Voight was seated in his office at the rear of

the casino. Earlier, he'd emptied a safe secreted behind a painting on the wall. The desk was piled high with stacks of cash, the proceeds from the casino and the nightclub for the previous week. He methodically counted the bills.

Cuddles, the parrot, watched sleepily from his perch on the stand. He was Quinn's special bird, grudgingly tolerated by others, and no one knew it better than Cuddles himself. In the way of wild things held captive, he sensed who liked him and who didn't, and when it was best to keep his silence. He never talked when he was alone in the office with Voight.

Today, Voight wasn't in a talking mood anyway. His full concentration was on the task at hand, and he would have brooked no distractions. All of the business at the club, both the casino and the nightclub, was transacted in cash. After counting the week's take, he began skimming fifty percent off the top. Later, an accountant who subscribed to larceny, would dummy a set of books for the government. Voight's own entries were made in a ledger kept in the safe.

The books were cooked to avoid what Voight considered an onerous injustice. In 1913, with passage of the Sixteenth Amendment, Congress had legislated personal income taxes. During the World War, Congress had also enacted an excess profits tax on corporations, which had yet to be repealed. Gulf Enterprises was owned wholly by Voight and Quinn, and the double hit on taxes would have cost them dearly. They were of the opinion that the federal government was run by stick-up artists.

A few minutes after twelve, Voight finished his labors. He made a final entry in his personal ledger and returned it to the safe. From the stacks of cash on the desk, he placed thirty thousand in the safe and thirty thousand in his briefcase. He rarely carried a gun, but Mondays were the exception; he stuck a Colt .38 snub-nose in the waistband of his trousers. He closed and locked the safe, moving the painting back into position, and collected his briefcase. Cuddles, still silent, watched as he went out the door.

Elmer Spadden was waiting in the casino. He wasn't privy to what went on in the office every Monday morning; but he nonetheless knew that the briefcase was stuffed with cash. His sole purpose was to bodyguard the man who paid him liberally and treated him with the respect due someone willing to step into the path of flying bullets. Not that anyone had tried to bump off his boss, or Ollie Quinn, in almost five years. The last time it happened, he and Turk McGuire had killed three gunsels in a shootout in the bookmaking parlor at the Turf Club. The mainland gangs afterward stayed clear of Galveston island.

Outside the club, Spadden took the wheel of Voight's three-year-old Studebaker. Voight was a man of simple tastes, and he never envied Quinn his flashy Cadillac and ostentatious life-style. In many ways, Voight was a prude, and despite the ready availability of women in their business, he'd never considered taking a mistress. He admired his partner's taste in women, but always from afar. He thought one Don Juan in the organization was enough.

Business affairs were another matter entirely. Though he often grumbled about the cost, he deferred to Quinn when it came to contracting acts for the nightclub. To himself, if to no one else, he admitted that Quinn had the flair, and a certain genius, for show business. The nightclub was the engine that generated customers for the casino, and the weekend had convinced him Jolson was the greatest draw ever. He sulked about the price—calling $2,000 extortion—but he accepted Quinn's judgment. Jolson would be held over for another Saturday night.

Quinn was waiting for him at the Turf Club. Their Monday morning routine was by now standard practice, and never varied. Voight tallied the take from the Hollywood Club, and Quinn tabulated the haul from their other activities. The revenue from rumrunning, the bookmaking operation, and payoffs from speakeasies, gaming dives and whorehouses was always substantial. For tax purposes, all of the revenue was accounted as income from the Turf Club. Then fifty percent was skimmed off the top.

"We had a good week," Quinn said, indicating stacks of cash on the desk. "There's twenty-six thousand from the Turf Club. I took off another twelve from the restaurants and the amusement pier."

Voight opened his briefcase. "Some weeks are better than others. I've got thirty here."

"Goes to show you," Quinn said with a wry smile. "Didn't I tell you Jolson was worth every nickel?"

"I still say he's in the wrong business. The bastard's a born heist man."

"You're just burned he won't drop any at the tables. Count your blessings, my friend."

Voight placed the cash from the desk in his briefcase. "I'm running late. I have to get to the bank."

"Give my best to Sherm," Quinn said. "Tell him we'll have his problem solved tonight."

"Ollie, I'd lay eight to five that's the first thing he asks me."

In the hallway, Voight found Jack Nolan talking with McGuire and Spadden. He nodded to them, his expression impassive. "You boys set for tonight?"

Nolan grinned. "Got it all worked out. Nothing to worry about, boss."

"I never worry." Voight looked at Spadden. "Let's walk over to the bank."

Ten minutes later they entered the Galveston City Bank. Spadden waited in the reception area while a secretary buzzed Voight into Sherm Magruder's office. The bank was pivotal to William Magruder's myriad financial affairs, and he had appointed his son to the position of president. Sherm offered Voight a chair.

"Good afternoon, Dutch," he said pleasantly. "You're regular as clockwork. It must be Monday."

"Before you ask," Voight said, "we haven't forgotten about that Durant fellow. He'll get his tonight."

"I'll pass that along to my father. We're most appreciative of your assistance in this matter."

"Glad to lend a hand."

Voight unsnapped the clasps on his briefcase. He neatly arranged the stacks of cash on the desk. "The count's right. Sixty-eight thousand."

"You've enjoyed an excellent week. Would you like the usual?"

"Stick with a winner, that's my motto."

Sherm personally made out certificates for bearer bonds. The bonds were virtually untraceable, and redeemable at any bank. For those in the rackets, it was a foolproof method of hiding money from government tax agents. The certificates were split evenly between Edward S. Voight and Oliver J. Quinn.

There was a certain quid pro quo to the arrangement. Quinn and Voight worked closely with the Magruders and the Seagraves in controlling the political apparatus of Galveston County. Of equal import, the gambling and vice operation attracted tourists, which benefited all the city's businesses and fueled a stable economy. During 1921, when the entire country suffered an economic depression, Galveston enjoyed boom times and full employment. The mob was considered a valuable asset by the old guard of the Island.

The Magruders could have survived and thrived without the mob. The demand for cotton in Europe was such that their Galveston Cotton Exchange represented a veritable money tree. In turn, millions of dollars flowed through the Galveston City Bank from financial institutions in England, France, Germany, and other European countries. But gambling and vice were the lubricants that greased the wheels of the Island's economy, as well as the city and county governments. The Magruders were strong advocates of free enterprise, legal or otherwise.

"Service is our byword," Sherm said amiably. "And

thanks again for arranging that personal matter. We won't forget a favor."

"Consider it our treat, Sherm. What are friends for?"

Voight emerged from the bank with Spadden at his side. He wondered yet again why the Magruders were so intent on buying People's Bank & Trust. Then, just as quickly, he decided it didn't matter.

Any banker he'd ever met was a pirate at heart.

The evening was balmy. A full moon played hide-and-seek high above silvery clouds drifting on a faint breeze. The town was awash in scampering moonglow.

Durant walked along the Strand. Shops and stores were closed for the night, and the street was all but deserted. His hands were in his pockets, his expression thoughtful as he moved along at a measured stride. He occasionally glanced at the displays in store windows, but his mind was elsewhere. He felt himself at a dead end.

All day he'd been on the phone calling bankers. His list had now dwindled to the point that he had exhausted every prospective buyer between Galveston and Houston. The response, as it had been last week, was polite but firm, no interest whatever. William Magruder, even when his name wasn't mentioned, nonetheless pervaded every conversation. He was a specter from hell, all but demonized, in the world of banking.

The next step was to start trying bankers in Houston, perhaps Austin or Dallas. Ira Aldridge gave scant encouragement on that score, noting that Magruder's stranglehold on Galveston was notorious throughout all of Texas. Durant recalled Magruder saying he wouldn't find a buyer between Galveston and Chicago, and after today, he began to think it might be true. He was, for all practical purposes, stymied.

Earlier, he'd had dinner at a café on Mechanic Street. The meat loaf and vegetables, at any other time, would have rated kudos and compliments. But he had picked at his food, his appetite gone, lost in troubled thought. For a moment, he'd even considered going hat in hand to Magruder and striking the best deal possible. Then, angered by the prospect of his own humiliation, he had brushed the idea aside. He wouldn't grovel before any man.

The thing that frustrated him most was being trapped in Galveston. His original plan had been a night or two on the Island, where he would settle his uncle's estate and quickly be on his way. He had a spot waiting in Tom Mix's next moving picture, and he'd planned to return to Hollywood long before now. He wouldn't be surprised but what Mix had hired another stuntman, for Western films were shot on a tight schedule and stuntmen were plentiful. He seriously doubted a phone call to Mix would change things. Not until he was definite on leaving Galveston.

After a forgettable dinner, he decided to go for a walk. He'd been closeted in the office all day, and he thought the exercise might clear his head. He needed a new strategy, some new plan to unload the bank and put him on the road back to Los Angeles. So far no solution had presented itself, and he was surprised to find himself at the end of the Strand, across from the Santa Fe depot. He turned south on Twenty-fifth Street, thinking he would walk over to Broadway and take the long way back to his hotel. The moon was out and he had nowhere else to go, so why not? He had all night.

The intersection of Twenty-fifth and Broadway was the most historic spot in Galveston. As he approached the corner, he saw the Heroes Monument, a towering marble structure with the bronze statue of Lady Victory at the top. He recalled, from a visit before the war, that his uncle had pointed it out, explaining that it had been erected to commemorate the victory over Mexico, and the independence of Texas. He paused at the base of the monument and read the weathered plaque affixed to the marble pillar. He could almost hear the pride in his uncle's voice those many years ago.

Early in 1836, Santa Anna's army overran the Alamo

and swept unchecked across Texas. David Burnet, president of the Republic, retreated with his staff to Galveston and set up a temporary capitol. Two days later, on April 21, General Sam Houston and his volunteer army turned and attacked the Mexican forces on the San Jacinto River. The attack became a rout, lasting only eighteen minutes, with the Mexican troops in full retreat and Santa Anna captured. The battle took place some forty miles north of Galveston, and the Heroes Monument was built to honor the volunteers who brought independence to Texas. The Lady of Victory stood looking at the distant San Jacinto battlegrounds.

Tourists were drawn to the monument. Several couples, out for a stroll under a full moon, paused to stare up at the bronze Lady. The intersection was also a major artery to the Island's residential district, and heavily traveled day or night. Automobiles, as well as passersby on foot, went by in a steady stream. Durant was still thinking of his uncle as he moved through the group of sightseers gathered at the base of the memorial. He paused on the sidewalk to let another couple join the small crowd.

A car swerved to a stop at the curb. Durant turned onto Broadway as the doors slammed and he saw Jack Nolan standing beside a Buick sedan. He would later learn that the two men with Nolan were Turk McGuire and Elmer Spadden. But for now, what his mind registered was two strong-arm thugs, built for rough work. The men started toward him as Nolan lit a cigarette and leaned against the front fender of the Buick. His first instinct was to run, but he knew he'd never get away. They could easily chase him down with the car.

"Hey, tough guy," Nolan called out with a jocular smile. "You should've taken my advice."

McGuire and Spadden spread out. Durant immediately recognized the oldest trick in street fighting. They intended to flank him from either side, and force him to fight two fights at the same time. He backed away, aware that his only chance was to stay on the move and somehow keep them separated. McGuire gave him an evil grin, motioning to Spadden, and they crowded him toward the monument. Some of the men in the crowd of sightseers sensed what was happening, and pulled their women aside. The others quickly caught on, scattering into the street.

Durant saw a police car pull to the curb on Twenty-fifth Street. Two cops stepped out of the car, one of them with the chevrons of sergeant on his sleeves. For an instant, Durant thought the cavalry had arrived just in the nick of time. Then, with a sickening sensation in the pit of his stomach, he saw the sergeant flip Nolan a salute and stand back to watch the fight. He realized there would be no rescue tonight.

McGuire moved swiftly for a man of such enormous bulk. He feinted with a left jab and launched a whistling overhand right. Durant was no rookie to barroom brawls and he was fast on his feet. He slipped beneath the blow and delivered a splintering left-right combination. McGuire's lip spurted blood and a look of surprise came over his face. Before Durant could follow through, Spadden quickly stepped in from the other side and punched him in the kidney. His legs buckled as though whacked by a sledgehammer.

A woman screamed as the men jumped him in a flurry of fists. He tried to fight back, but the blows rained down in a drumming tattoo. McGuire landed a right to the jaw, followed by a crackling left hook. Spadden struck him low in the gut, then straightened him up with a sharp uppercut. The men were professionals, versed in their work, and they beat him to the ground at the base of the monument. McGuire finished it with a thudding kick to the ribs.

Jack Nolan walked forward to inspect their handiwork. He squatted down, exhaling smoke from his cigarette, and examined the wreckage of Durant's face. He smiled a lazy smile.

"Get smart and get out," he said. "You don't want there to be a next time."

Durant was barely conscious. A rivulet of blood leaked down into his eyes and he watched through a reddish mist as they walked back to the Buick. What seemed an eternity later, the car doors slammed and they drove off. The police sergeant ambled across the street. He clucked his tongue with a tsk-tsk sound.

"How you feelin', laddie?"

"Not so . . . good," Durant wheezed.

"Well, all the same, I'm placin' you under arrest."

"Me . . . what for?"

"Disturbing the peace and disorderly conduct. Shame on you."

The cops took him to the hospital to get stitched up. Then they took him to jail.

Chapter Seven

The municipal court was located on the ground floor of City Hall. A jailer brought Durant from the lockup shortly before nine the next morning. Walter Kline, his uncle's attorney, was seated at the defense table.

Durant looked like he'd been run over by a train. His bottom lip was crusted with blood, there were catgut stitches lacing his eyebrow, and his left eye was a splotchy rosette of purple and black. He was unshaven and unkempt, his suit wrinkled and dark stubble covering his jawline. His one good eye burned with anger.

The jailer removed his handcuffs and walked away. Kline rose from his chair, a look of concern on his face, and shook hands with Durant. "I tried to get you released last night," he said. "After you called, I spoke with Judge Hagan by phone. He refused to set bail."

"Doesn't surprise me," Durant said brusquely. "This whole town's as crooked as a barrel of snakes. They intended all along for me to spend the night in jail."

"Who is 'they'?"

"Magruder and his mob buddies."

"I believe you'd better give me all the details."

Until last night, when he was allowed one phone call, Durant hadn't spoken with the lawyer since he arrived in Galveston. He proceeded to brief Kline on everything that had happened, including his meeting with William Magruder and the subsequent threat by the mob. He concluded with an account of last night's beating and Jack Nolan's warning to sell the bank and leave town. He gingerly touched the stitches on his brow.

"Nolan and his hooligans made their point. I feel like I tangled with a wildcat."

"I daresay you do." Kline hesitated, considering a moment. "You've incurred some powerful enemies in a short time. I'm frankly amazed Magruder's so . . . involved . . . with racketeers."

"I'll think about that once I'm out of jail. How do I get these charges dismissed?"

"I seriously doubt you will."

"How's that?"

"Whoever is behind this—Magruder or the mob—has connections here at City Hall. Your arrest was clearly intended to underscore their message."

"To hell with that!" Durant snapped. "I didn't start that fight. It was a setup."

"Let me offer some good advice," Kline said. "Disturbing the peace is a misdemeanor. Usually a fifty-dollar fine . . ."

"I won't pay it. I'm the one that took a beating."

"Consider the alternative. If you insist on a full-blown hearing, there's no question you'll be convicted. Who's to testify you weren't the culprit? Do you have any witnesses?"

Durant's mouth set in a tight line. "You're saying I can't win, right?"

"You will most surely lose," Kline told him. "And the sentence will be thirty days on the county road gang. I strongly urge you to plead guilty."

"What a crock! The whole Goddamn thing's been rigged."

"Unfortunately, that appears to be the case."

Court convened at nine sharp, Judge Wallace Hagan presiding. Sergeant Michael O'Rielly, the beefy Irishman who had arrested Durant, was called to the stand. He told a fanciful tale of how Durant had instigated an altercation with two tourists, who subsequently fled the scene and the Island. He testified he'd witnessed the fracas from start to finish.

Durant entered a tight-lipped plea of guilty. Walter Kline then delivered an eloquent argument for leniency. He explained that his client was a visitor to Galveston, there to settle his uncle's estate, and anxious to be on his way. Judge Hagan peered down from the bench, as though weighing the sentence for an axe murderer. He finally banged his gavel and ordered Durant to pay a fine of fifty dollars. The court clerk accepted the cash with a sly smirk.

Afterward, outside City Hall, Kline assured the younger man that he'd made a wise decision. Durant thanked him for his services, shook hands, and then caught a cab back to his hotel. In his room, he discarded his soiled clothes and took a long, steamy shower. When he shaved, he hardly recognized himself in the mirror, and he swore softly under his breath. Dressed in a fresh suit, he emerged from the hotel a few minutes after ten. He walked toward the Strand.

Everyone in the bank stared at him. Catherine gasped, unable to take her eyes off his face, and Aldridge began peppering him with questions. They followed him into his office where he told the story again, including his experience in municipal court. He appeared unnaturally calm for someone who had suffered a beating and been subjected to a night in jail. The black eye and the ragged line of stitches across his brow made it all the more unusual. Aldridge studied him with a look of weary regret.

"Earl, it's time to quit," he said. "These men are dangerous, and things will only go from bad to worse. It's time for you to get out."

Durant stared at him. "Get out?"

"I never thought I'd hear myself say this. But under the circumstances, I think you should sell the bank to Magruder. You have no choice."

"Mr. Aldridge is right," Catherine said in a small voice. "You can't fight those gangsters by yourself. You're just one man."

"I had a lot of time to stew on things last night.

There's nothing to do but think when you're locked in a jail cell. I've decided to stick around."

"You're angry," Aldridge said, "and that's perfectly understandable. But you mustn't let anger cloud your judgment. These men could kill you."

"Ira, it's not debatable." Durant's gaze was steady. "How long will it take you to teach me the banking business?"

"Listen to this madness! Do you honestly believe Magruder will turn back when he's gone so far? Do you, after last night?"

"I plan to have a talk with Magruder."

"Talk?" Aldridge said incredulously. "Talk about what?"

"How to take your lumps and like it."

Some twenty minutes later Durant entered the Magruder Building. The elevator operator gave him a strange look, darting glances at his battered features as they rode to the tenth floor. In the reception room, he walked past the secretary. She hurried around her desk.

"Just a moment, sir!" she cried, rushing after him. "Do you have an appointment?"

"Mr. Magruder is expecting me."

Durant barged into the office. Magruder was seated at his ebony desk, slowly working through the morning's correspondence. He peered across the room with a startled expression. His secretary hesitated in the doorway.

"I tried to stop him, Mr. Magruder. He just—"

"Quite all right, Ellen," Magruder said with a dismissive wave. "Please close the door, and hold my calls."

Durant halted before the desk. Magruder examined him with clinical detachment. "You appear to have met with an accident, Mr. Durant. How very unfortunate."

"Magruder, I'm staying in Galveston. I'm here to tell you to call off your dogs."

"I'm sure I don't know what you're talking about."

"Don't waste my time with crapola," Durant said

bluntly. "Your gangster pals did their best and it backfired on you. I officially took over the bank this morning."

"How impressive," Magruder said in a mocking tone. "You're quite the determined young man, aren't you?"

"Determined enough to take you over the hurdles. And like it or lump it, you'd better get used to it. I'm not going away."

Magruder, despite his blasé manner, was concerned. Things weren't working the way he'd planned, and he felt a stab of anxiety about the land owned by People's Bank & Trust. Without it, he would never complete his new resort hotel. He lifted a hand in a conciliatory gesture.

"Let's both reconsider," he said in an avuncular voice. "Your life's in Hollywood, not here on Galveston Island. So I'll make it easy to overlook our little misunderstanding. I'll pay the hundred thousand you originally asked."

"Too late," Durant said. "The bank's not for sale."

"Never make rash decisions, Mr. Durant. Haste inevitably leads to regret."

"That sounds like more of your threats."

"Nothing so crass."

"Do yourself a favor," Durant said with a level stare. "Live and let live, or you're the one that'll regret it."

"Are you threatening me now?"

"Definitely."

Durant walked out of the office. Magruder's features flushed to the hairline, and he took a moment to collect himself. He'd been threatened once or twice in his life, but never before by anyone of the lower classes. Particularly a motion picture stuntman. His eyes hooded with outrage.

He put in a call to Ollie Quinn.

The meeting began at two that afternoon. George Seagrave and his son, John, arrived shortly before Quinn and Voight. Magruder, with Sherm in attendance, welcomed them to his office. The men gathered there were the mov-

ers and shakers of Galveston. Theirs was an alliance of
the underworld with civic leaders, and everyone benefited
equally. The businessmen never socialized with the mobsters, and that was mutually acceptable. Their single link
was the future of the Island.

Politics was the glue that tightly bound their alliance.
Ostensibly, the Magruders were the leaders of the Inde-
pendent Party and the Seagraves were the chiefs of the
City Party. In actual fact, they met behind closed doors
with their underworld partners and decided the slate of
candidates for every election. Quinn and Voight, apart
from bribing city and county officials for their own purposes, delivered the swing vote. The sporting crowd was
a major voting bloc on the Island.

Galveston was made for crooked politics. The city
itself represented eighty percent of the population in Galveston County, far outweighing the towns scattered along
the southern mainland. The city was governed by a five-
member commission, which included the mayor, the
police chief, the tax collector, the waterworks superinten-
dent, and the head of public improvements. Like the
county officials in similar posts, they were all elected by
popular vote. They owed their jobs to the small coterie of
men gathered in Magruder's office.

The meeting today had been set a week ago. The men
were there not to discuss politics, but rather civic devel-
opment. A municipal pleasure pier was being planned by
the city, for construction at Twenty-fifth Street and Seawall Boulevard. The pier was to include a dance pavilion,
shops and restaurants, and an outdoor amphitheater for
public events. Investors were needed for the bond issue
to cover construction costs, and each of the men had com-
mitted to raising funds. George Seagrave was the first to
deliver an update.

"I'm pleased to report," he said in an expansive voice,
"we have pledges for over a hundred thousand dollars.
We'll easily double that in the weeks ahead."

Seagrave was a fleshy man, with curly gray hair and

a determined jaw. John, his son, was a Princeton graduate and very much a chip off the old block. The family mansion was at Twenty-ninth and Broadway, not far from the Magruder mansion, in the heart of an enclave for the city's aristocracy. Seagrave's other son, Frank, was a playboy who spent his time drunkenly wandering about Europe. His name was never mentioned in polite company.

"George, my heartiest congratulations," Magruder said. "You and John have made a splendid contribution to this project. Absolutely splendid."

Seagrave preened. "We all have to do our share, Bill. As President Coolidge is fond of saying, the business of America is business." He paused, a quizzical birdlike expression on his face. "May I inquire how your efforts are going?"

"Gentlemen, I couldn't be more pleased. Sherm has spearheaded our campaign, and we expect to bring in a quarter million, perhaps more. High goals inevitably lead to high achievement."

Magruder basked in his own admiration a moment. Then, like a rajah of financiers, he looked at Quinn. "Ollie, what have you and Dutch to report?"

"We've done pretty well, Bill."

"Any specific number as yet?"

Quinn plucked a check from inside his suit jacket. "We're happy to present a cashier's check for two hundred and ten thousand. Courtesy of Gulf Enterprises."

Seagrave cocked his head like he had a flea in his ear. "All of that from you and Dutch? From your company?"

"Well, not all," Quinn said with a wry smile. "We solicited donations from our business associates. They were generous in their support."

Quinn and Voight believed public relations was a necessary business expense for the rackets. They were co-founders of the Galveston Beach Association, sponsors of a yearly Christmas party for underprivileged children, and ready contributors to any charity's fund-raising efforts. Their generosity bought good will throughout the community.

"Ollie, Dutch," Magruder said with approval. "Allow me to commend you for your civic spirit."

Seagrave concurred. "You've set the pace for the rest of us. Very well done, indeed."

"Speaking of pace," Magruder added. "We absolutely must reach our goal by the middle of November. You know how Christmas diverts people onto personal affairs."

Construction on the Pleasure Pier was scheduled to begin in early 1927. Their objective was to have the million-dollar bond issue fully subscribed before the end of the year. They fell to discussing other avenues of raising funds, and agreed to redouble their efforts in the month ahead. The meeting broke up a few minutes before three.

Magruder asked Quinn and Voight to stay behind. He alluded in vague terms to a matter of personal business. Seagrave understood, for he occasionally did business with the mobsters himself. Just last year they had arranged a squad of goons to rout union organizers at one of his sugar mills. A round of handshakes sent the Seagraves on their way.

Magruder's demeanor changed when the door closed. His eyes narrowed and his voice took on a rasping quality. "I want the matter of Earl Durant settled. You gave me your word on this, Ollie."

Quinn nodded. "We tried persuasion and it didn't work. Our men tell us Durant's a tough cookie."

"I won't have him charging into my office and issuing threats. I want it ended."

"Let's be plain," Voight interjected. "The sure way to end it is to put him on ice. You understand what I'm saying?"

"Yes. . . ."

"No mincing words," Voight persisted. "You want him knocked off. Right?"

"I—" Magruder exchanged an uneasy look with Sherm. "I see no other way."

Voight stood. "Don't worry about a thing. We'll handle it."

"How will . . . ?"

"You don't want to know. Read about it in the papers."

"Yes, of course."

Quinn and Voight managed to suppress smiles. The situation now put Magruder even more in their debt, a chip to cash at a later time. Turk McGuire was waiting outside with the Cadillac, and drove them from the Magruder Building to the Turf Club. They called Nolan into the office.

"The ante's been upped," Voight said. "We got the go-ahead to dust off Durant."

"Huh!" Nolan looked surprised. "What happened?"

"Damn fool braced Magruder this morning. Told him to back off or he'd kill him."

"Some guys have got more balls than brains. You want to take him for a swim?"

"No," Voight said sternly. "The bastard keeps making us look bad and we've got a reputation to uphold. Do it so everybody gets the picture."

"But with caution," Quinn amended. "Catch him alone somewhere and make it look like a robbery. We don't need witnesses who could tie you to the job."

"Good idea," Voight agreed. "Wait a few days till he's forgot about the beating. Take him when his guard's down."

"Few days is better anyway," Nolan said. "That'll give me time to set it up and pick the right spot. Want me to use Elmer and Turk again?"

"Might as well," Voight said. "Let 'em finish what they started."

"I'll get rolling on it right away."

Nolan went out to talk with Spadden and McGuire. He thought it was dumb of Durant not to have taken the warning and skipped town. Some men never got the message until they were dead.

Too bad.

Stoner and Janice stepped out of the elevator. They moved through the lobby, and Stoner waved to Charles Anderson, the Buccaneer manager, who was talking with the desk clerk. Their canary-yellow Packard was waiting in front of the hotel.

Today was their day to play tourists. Janice wore a fetching little day dress, casual yet expensive. The patterned fabric clung to her svelte curves, modestly revealing her figure. But she also wore sensible walking shoes, an unadorned hat, and a muted blue scarf fluttering at her throat. She looked very much the wife of a wealthy Blanco County rancher.

"Oh, Bobby, honey!" she said with a wink as she crawled into the car. "What a wonderful day for sightseeing. Where are we going first?"

Stoner hooked the car into gear. "How about Jean Lafitte?"

"The pirate?"

"Ol' Jean flew the Jolly Roger over these very waters."

"I love it!" she squealed. "A real live pirate?"

"Not just exactly, Olive," Stoner said as he pulled away from the hotel. "Lafitte joined all his buddies in pirate heaven."

"Do pirates really go to heaven?"

"I think maybe this one did."

The hotel had provided a packet of tourist information. As they drove along Seawall Boulevard, Janice called out points of interest. The Island's original settlers were cannibals, members of the Karankawa tribe. They ate other Indians because they believed an enemy's courage was absorbed by devouring choice parts. The first white men on the Island were Spanish Conquistadors, led by Cabeza de Vaca. The expedition landed in 1528.

"All the Indians disappeared," Janice said, studying the tour booklet. "I wonder if the Spaniards ate them?"

Stoner smiled. "I think the church frowned on cannibalism."

"Well, where did they go, then?"

"Guess we'll never know."

Their first stop was where Fifteenth Street joined the coastline. Jean Lafitte's headquarters, La Mansion Rouge, was still visible in ruins maintained by the historical society. A privateer, Lafitte was nonetheless an American hero, having aided General Andrew Jackson during the War of 1812 at the Battle of New Orleans. By 1817, Lafitte ruled Galveston Island, occupying it with his band of buccaneers and claiming it as his personal kingdom. He set about building a colony.

The town was called Campeachy. There were houses and taverns, a dockyard at the edge of the bay and a major arsenal. Pirates who sailed into port were forced to abide by Lafitte's court of admiralty, which was a one-man court with no appeal. The town prospered, at its peak reaching a population of nearly two thousand, all within four years. Then, in 1821, the American and Spanish governments threatened war against Lafitte's sanctuary for privateers. The time had come to move on.

Lafitte put the torch to Campeachy. After burning it to the ground, he boarded his flagship, the *Jupiter*, and sailed off into the Gulf. History failed to record his end, though it was rumored he died at sea, off the coast of Yucatán. Jean Lafitte, ever the enigma, was mysterious even in death.

"Isn't that strange?" Janice said, staring at the ruins of the old fort. "He just sailed away and was never heard from again. What a sad ending."

"The man was a pirate," Stoner said. "Did you expect a happy ending?"

"Well, he wasn't all bad! I mean, except for him, there might not even be a Galveston."

"One thing's for sure."

"What?"

"Lafitte was better than the thugs that run this place today. They make him look like Little Orphan Annie."

"Don't remind me."

The tour guide took them north from the beach. A year after Lafitte sailed away, Texas settlers rebuilt what would become the Port of Galveston. During the Texas Revolution, the Island briefly served as the capital, and later, in the Civil War, it was captured by Union troops only to be recaptured by the Confederates. From that time until the present, Galveston was one of the major deepwater harbors in the world. Millions of dollars in tonnage went through the port every day.

Late that afternoon Stoner and Janice stopped for coffee at a café overlooking the harbor. Along Pier 20, the small boats of the Mosquito Fleet were tying up at the docks. The crews, descendants of Portuguese and Italian fishermen, began unloading their harvest of shrimp and oysters. Towering above them at the wharves were steamships, oceangoing tankers, and freighters, many flying the flags of distant nations. Seagulls kept winged sentinel over the tiny shrimp boats.

The scene was one of bustling industry, but somehow tranquil. Stoner sipped his coffee, watching with interest as the Mosquito Fleet unloaded their catch for the day. There was a strangeness to it, for during his years with the Rangers, he'd never been assigned to the coast. Yet he found it oddly peaceful, the ships, big and small, in harmony with the flat, sunlit waters of the bay. He thought it was a world apart from the nightspots on the other side of the Island.

"Penny for your thoughts," Janice said. "You look like you're a thousand miles away."

Stoner pointed to the wharves. "I was wondering what those fishermen think about the mobsters who run this town. Do they approve of the rackets, or do they just not care?"

"Aren't you the big philosopher today? I can tell you the answer."

"Go ahead."

"They don't care," Janice said with a shrug. "They're tickled pink to make a few bucks and spend the evening at their friendly speakeasy. Nobody cares, here or anywhere else."

Stoner looked at her. "You sound a little jaded."

"Listen to who's talking," she said in a teasing lilt. "You sound like a Boy Scout."

"Me?"

"Yes, precious, you. I love you to pieces, but you're treating this like a holy quest of some sort."

Stoner glanced over his shoulder. The café was almost empty, and their waitress was off somewhere in the kitchen. He lowered his voice anyway.

"I've been sent here to do a job nobody else could pull off. Lots of people are depending on me, and I mean to deliver the bacon. I thought you understood all this."

"Of course I do," she said simply. "Why else would I risk life and limb?"

"You just seemed a little lukewarm all of a sudden."

"Are you kidding? I'm so excited I still get goosebumps. I love this undercover stuff."

Stoner laughed. "All you need's a badge."

"Now that you mention it," she said, her eyes bright. "How do we get into that casino? When do we really start work?"

"We start tonight and we're gonna play it foxy. I have to establish myself as a high roller."

"What does that mean, play it foxy?"

"A loser with money to burn."

Early that evening they drove to the Garden Club, three blocks north of Seawall Boulevard. The club was an octagonal structure with flamboyant columns, stained-glass windows, and a whimsical cupola. There was dining and dancing, and at the rear of the building, a poker room with slot machines along the walls. The buy-in at the high-stakes poker table was a thousand dollars.

Janice developed an instant love affair with the nickel slots. Stoner gave her fifty dollars from the five-thousand-dollar bankroll he'd been provided by Colonel Garrison. His instructions were to use the bankroll however he saw fit to gain entry into the Hollywood Club casino. After leaving Janice with her one-armed bandit, he took a seat in the high-stakes poker game. He made a point of casually dropping his name to the house dealer.

Stoner was no novice to poker. Throughout the evening he caught several hands he knew were certain winners. Yet he was there to lose, and however much it galled him, he folded his cards. Other times, holding a poor hand, he attempted a weak bluff and donated to the pot. He looked like an amateur trying to play with the big boys.

By midnight, he'd lost five hundred and quit the game. The manager of the poker room, solicitous and smooth, lamented with him on his streak of bad luck. His here-today-gone-tomorrow attitude was that of a man who believed luck really had something to do with poker.

He was marked as a pigeon.

Chapter Eight

Arthur Scarett drove across the causeway on Friday morning. The prohibition agent was looking forward to a long relaxing weekend with his family. As head of the Houston office, he had the authority to approve leave for all agents. He'd given himself time off.

Ruby Scarett was a plain dumpling of a woman. On the drive down from Houston, she had acted as referee for their two boys, who were in the backseat. The boys were nine and ten, young hellions who enjoyed nothing quite so much as pounding the whey out of each other. She was exhausted even before her holiday began.

For his part, Scarett ignored the commotion. He was content to leave discipline to his wife, who, he was convinced, had been a drill sergeant in a previous incarnation. His mind was focused instead on sandy beaches and crystalline skies, which were a harbinger of fair weather and sunshine. He planned to spend the weekend working on his tan.

Scarett hoped to avoid running into Jack Nolan. He was on the take, turning a blind eye to the rumrunning operation, but nonetheless prudent. He could have called Nolan and been comped to hotel accommodations, top restaurants, and probably tickets to the Al Jolson show. But he saw no reason to risk exposure by openly associating with gangsters. He figured the ten thousand a month payoff was ample reward.

The Beach Hotel was located at Twentieth Street and Seawall Boulevard. A rambling five-story structure, the hotel was distinguished by its baronial rotunda, marble floors, and a grand stairway sweeping upwards from the lobby. Ruby held the boys in an iron grip while Scarett checked in at the front desk. A bellman, wary of the struggle between mother and sons, escorted them to the elevator.

Their suite was on the fifth floor. Scarett felt a man of his means could afford to splurge, and he'd reserved the best the hotel had to offer. The sitting room was bright and airy, with modernistic furnishings and broad windows that afforded a spectacular view of the Gulf. There were two bedrooms, each with its own bathroom, which ensured Ruby privacy if not security. She thought the boys would have the place wrecked before the weekend was out.

The bellman fled the suite as though escaping a war zone. Scarett, who could be a taskmaster when the occasion demanded, rapped out a command. "Let's have some *quiet!*"

The boys, Fred and Hank, snapped to attention. Their mother was tough as nails, but their father, once he got going, was hell on wheels. They waited like good little soldiers for whatever came next.

"Here's the score," Scarett said. "You break anything in this suite and I'll blister your backsides. Got it?"

"Yes, Pa," the boys mumbled in unison.

"All right, now that we have that settled, get changed into your swimsuits. We're going to the beach."

The boys scampered off to their room. In the master bedroom, Scarett avoided watching his wife change. He loved her, but Ruby in a swimsuit was like stuffing ten pounds in a five-pound bag. From the rear, he thought it looked like two porkers wriggling around in a gunnysack. He was thankful Jack Nolan wouldn't see them on the beach.

Across town, Jack Nolan walked into the Turf Club. His crew had spent the last three nights shadowing Durant, and he wasn't pleased with the results. Upstairs, he proceeded along the hallway and found Spadden, ever the faithful watchdog, posted outside the office door. Spadden greeted him with what passed for a smile.

In the office, Voight was seated behind his desk. The phone rang as Nolan came through the door. Voight caught it on the second ring. "Yeah?"

"How ya doing?" a voice said. "This is Jim Torrence, over in Texas City."

"I remember you, Jim. You run the Dixieland Club, right?"

"That's me."

"What can I do for you?"

"Well, Dutch, I think it's the other way 'round. I called to warn you about a problem you're gonna have."

"Uh-huh," Voight said, lighting the stub of a cigar. "What problem is that?"

"Joey Adonis," Torrence replied. "Him and his gunsels are headed your way."

"Adonis knows better than to set foot in Galveston."

"Not today, he don't."

Joey Adonis was an Italian mobster from Texas City. He operated nightclubs, gambling dives, and a large bootlegging network. He was Torrence's long-standing rival on the mainland.

"I'm listening," Voight said. "Why's he headed over here?"

"You've got another visitor," Torrence said. "Art Scarett, your pal, the prohibition agent? He's staying at the Beach Hotel."

"So?"

"Adonis plans to bump him off."

Voight straightened in his chair. "How'd you get wind of this?"

"I've got a pigeon in Joey's outfit. Pays to keep tabs on the competition."

"And your pigeon tells you what?"

"Adonis is one clever fucker. He'll blast Scarett in Galveston and the Feds will think it was your work. All the blame will come down on your head."

Voight munched his cigar. "You know this for a fact?"

"Think about it," Torrence said. "Suppose the Feds get pissed about Scarett and put you out of business. Who d'you think will take over Galveston and the rumrunning—your whole operation?"

"Sounds like Joey Adonis."

"Kee-recto!"

"Thanks for the tip, Jim. I owe you one and I always look after my friends."

"Hell, just take out Adonis and we'll call it even. I'll have the mainland to myself."

"I'll let you know how it works out."

Voight hung up. He stared at the phone a moment, then quickly related the gist of the conversation to Nolan. There was an instant of weighing and deliberation before Nolan spoke.

"You think Torrence is on the level?"

"One way to find out," Voight said. "Call the hotel and see if Scarett is registered. Don't let on who you are."

Nolan placed the call and spoke with the hotel operator. When he hung up, his features were solemn. "Scarett's registered, him and his family. You'd think he would've told me."

Voight grunted. "Probably didn't want to be seen with you. We've got to stop this thing in its tracks. We don't need heat from the Feds."

"How do you want it handled?"

"Take all the boys you need and put a round-the-clock tail on Scarett. We'll find Adonis by keeping a watch on his target."

"What then?" Nolan asked. "You want me to whack Adonis when I find him?"

Voight wedged the cigar into the corner of his mouth. He puffed thoughtfully, considering alternatives. "Try to take the guinea son of a bitch alive. We don't need any shooting wars." He paused, a cold smile behind the cigar. "I'd like a word with the cocksucker, anyway."

"But if I can't take him alive?"

"Why, hell, Jack, give him one with my compliments."

"Got you, boss." Nolan started out, then turned back. "What about our friend, Durant?"

"Yeah, Durant," Voight said, reminded of unfinished business. "Anything new?"

"Same old story. We've trailed him three days now, and he never goes anywhere but the bank and his hotel. You didn't want him hit anywhere too public."

"Let's put him on the back burner till you collar Adonis. Our first job's to make damn sure Art Scarett gets out of town in one piece."

"I wonder why Adonis decided to put the move on us. We haven't had any trouble in five years, maybe more."

"Who knows how a guinea thinks? You'd have to be a mind reader. Just get him before he gets Scarett."

"I'm on it."

Nolan hurried out the door. Voight leaned back in his chair, took a puff on his cigar. He blew a perfect smoke ring, watched it float lazily toward the ceiling. His mouth razored in a hard smile.

He definitely wanted Adonis taken alive.

Durant left the bank early. His head hurt from all he'd tried to absorb about the world of finance. Three days under Aldridge's tutelage only made him feel like a dullard. He thought he wasn't cut out to be a banker.

On the street, he saw the man for the second time. Over the last three days he'd had some visceral sense that he was being watched. The only one he had spotted was the short, wiry man with red hair and a pug nose. But something told him there were others.

The feeling made the hair prickle on his neck. All the more so because Aldridge was hollow-eyed with worry for his safety. Hardly a day passed that the older man didn't comment on the need for caution. He was troubled that Durant hadn't seen the last of the mob.

To himself, Durant admitted he'd been foolhardy to threaten Magruder. He had let anger override reason, and Aldridge's concern halfway had him convinced that he was in danger. Today that belief was reinforced when he again spotted the red-haired man across the street. Twice in three days seemed something more than coincidence.

Durant stepped into a drugstore. His eye was still ringed a purplish-black and the stitches on his brow had begun to itch. He bought a tube of Vaseline ointment, and while the clerk was making change, he glanced out the window. His shadow was still across the street, three stores down, pretending interest in a window display. There was no question he was being followed.

The drugstore was on a corner, with a side exit on Eighteenth Street. He wandered through the store, as if browsing, and slipped out the side door. At the corner, he peeked around the side of the building and saw the man still feigning interest in the window display. A group of pedestrians waited for a car to pass by, and he fell in beside them as they crossed the intersection. He left his shadow watching the front of the drugstore.

Two blocks down, he entered Brandt's Gun Store. On his walks around town, he had seen the shop and never given it much thought. But now, with a man tailing him and fresh memories of the beating he'd taken, he felt prudence was in order. Perhaps it was all imagined, or Aldridge's constant harping on the mob, and perhaps it wasn't. Better safe than sorry.

Durant found himself in a small ordnance depot. The walls were lined with rows of rifles and shotguns, and a double-shelved showcase was filled with pistols. At the rear of the store, he saw a portly man at a gunsmith's bench, tinkering with the extractor on a hunting rifle. The man rose from the bench, wiping his hands on a rag, and pushed his spectacles up on top of his head. He walked forward as Durant stopped in front of the showcase.

"Good day," he said. "May I help you?"

"I see you're a gunsmith."

"Yes, I'm Willie Brandt, the owner. I do all my own repairs and guarantee every gun in the shop. Are you interested in a pistol?"

Durant nodded. "Something for personal protection."

"Of course." Brandt studied his battered features, but made no comment. "Any particular pistol?"

On the showcase shelves were a wide array of revolvers and semiautomatic pistols. Durant wanted something more serious than a .38 but nothing as cumbersome as a .45. He pointed to a German Luger.

"Is the Luger in good condition?"

"Yes, quite good," Brandt said, taking it from the top shelf. "Some of these came back from France, trophies of war. Good German engineering."

Durant hefted the Luger. A semiautomatic, it was chambered for 9mm, somewhat hotter than the American .38 caliber. He pulled the toggle-bar action to the rear and locked it open. With his thumbnail in the breech, catching light reflection, he looked down the bore and checked the barrel. There was slight pitting in the lands and grooves, but nothing that would affect accuracy. He worked the action several times, then tested the trigger. He nodded to Brandt.

"I'll take it," he said. "How much?"

"Twenty dollars with a box of cartridges."

"Sold."

Durant loaded the magazine with seven rounds. He chambered a round, flipped on the safety, and stuck the Luger inside his waistband, hidden by his suit jacket. He stuffed the box of cartridges in his hip pocket, and placed a twenty-dollar bill on the counter. Willie Brandt looked at him with a curious expression.

"You seem to be a man who knows weapons."

"I was in France," Durant said evenly. "I took one of these off a German and used it most of the war. It does the job."

Brandt squinted. "I hope you don't have to use that one."

"That makes two of us."

Outside the shop, Durant turned west on the Strand. As he walked back toward the drugstore, his eyes searched both sides of the street. He saw nothing of the red-haired man, or anyone else who appeared to be watching him. But he didn't relax, for he knew he was easy to find. There was no place to hide in Galveston.

Up ahead, he saw Catherine come out of the bank. She started toward the streetcar stop at the corner, and he suddenly increased his pace. On the spur of the moment, he decided to ignore the fact that no self-respecting banker would socialize with an employee. He'd eaten too many meals alone in the last ten days, and he needed someone to talk to. Someone so attractive made it all the better.

"Hi there," he said when he stopped her at the corner. "I don't want you to think I'm forward—and I know this is awful sudden—but would you have dinner with me tonight?"

"Dinner?" She looked startled. "Oh, I don't think I could."

"Say yes to a lonely man." Durant raised his hand, palm outward. "No passes, I promise. Scout's honor."

"Oh, it's not that, really it isn't. It's just my mother's waiting dinner for me at home."

"I'll bet she'd understand if you gave her a call. Try it and see."

"Well—" Catherine hesitated with a winsome smile. "All right, I will call her. Let's find a phone."

Durant took her to Guido's Restaurant on Water Street. The place was cozy, with candlelit tables that overlooked the bay. A waiter took their orders and there was a moment of awkward silence. The Luger in his waistband reminded him there were problems he wanted to forget. At least for the night.

"Tell me about yourself," he said, trying to put her at ease. "Have you always lived in Galveston?"

"Always." She laughed softly. "I've only been off the Island twice in my life—both times to Houston."

"So your family's old-line Galveston?"

"No, not in the way you mean. My parents moved here when they were married."

"What does your father do?"

"Why . . . he was in the Coast Guard."

"Was?"

Her smile slipped. "Yes, he was killed in the Hurricane."

Durant knew all about the Hurricane. Early in September of 1900, a storm developed off the western coast of Africa. In the days that followed, it swept north of Cuba, passed by the tip of Florida, and then roared into the Gulf of Mexico. On September 7, by now a full-blown hurricane, it struck Galveston with winds in excess of 120 miles an hour. The Island's highest point was not quite nine feet above sea level, and by nightfall, the Gulf and the bay had converged. Galveston was under water.

The center of the hurricane passed over the Island late that evening. The tide off the Gulf was at least fifteen feet and breakers twenty-five feet and higher battered the shoreline. By midnight the storm had petered out, but the following morning brought a scene straight out of hell. A third of Galveston was leveled to the ground, with 4,000 houses and hundreds of buildings simply washed away. The most devastating hurricane in American history had killed 6,000 Islanders.

Everyone in Texas remembered the Hurricane of 1900. Durant was a boy at the time, but his recollection of it was still vivid. He looked at Catherine now.

"Those were hard times," he said quietly. "Losing your father like that must have been rough."

She smiled wanly. "Actually, I never knew him. I wasn't quite a year old when it happened."

"So it's been you and your mother since then?"

"Yes, she worked in a laundry to put me through high school. She's quite a lady."

"Sure sounds like it."

"Now it's your turn," Catherine said, her eyes bright with interest. "I've always been fascinated by motion pictures. How did you ever become a stuntman?"

"I was working as an extra," Durant said with an offhanded gesture. "In this one scene, the stuntman was on top of a train that was about to crash. He had to leap up and grab a rope stretched between a tree and a telegraph pole. He missed."

"Was he killed?"

"No, but he was banged up pretty good."

"And you took his place," she said excitedly. "You did, didn't you?"

"Yeah, I did," Durant admitted. "I went to the director and told him I could do the stunt. So he gave me a shot and I pulled it off. That's where it started."

"Which stars have you done stunt work for?"

"Well, I do all of Tom Mix's pictures. I doubled for Lon Chaney in *The Hunchback of Notre Dame* and *The Phantom of the Opera*. And some for Doug Fairbanks, like *The Thief of Bagdad*."

"Omigosh!" she yelped. "Do you know Mary Pickford?"

Mary Pickford was a spirited young actress known as "America's Sweetheart." Douglas Fairbanks, her husband, was a dashing hero of the silver screen. They were idolized by fans and courted by every filmmaker in the industry. Their lavish estate, Pickfair, was the focal point of Hollywood society.

Over dinner, Durant held Catherine spellbound with stories of Hollywood royalty and their escapades. He went on to tell her that his ambition was to become a movie director, and his greatest supporter was Tom Mix. But even as he talked, he was reminded that Mix's next picture started in two days. He would have to make a call tonight.

Hollywood, for now, took a back seat to Galveston.

His only other choice was to cave in and sell out. Which was no choice at all.

He refused to run.

The Funland Pier was ablaze with lights. There was a roller coaster, a Ferris wheel, a merry-go-round with painted ponies, and barkers hawking games of chance. Friday night was carnival time in Galveston.

Arthur Scarett and his wife stood in a crowd beside the merry-go-round. Their boys, astride painted wooden ponies, whooped and laughed as they rode round and round. Scarett was pink from an afternoon on the beach, stuffed with hot dogs and orange soda pop. He debated whether his stomach would tolerate the roller coaster.

Joey Adonis waited near the Ferris wheel. He was short and stout, attired in a pin-striped suit and a gray fedora. With him were two shooters, impassive cold-eyed men whose one talent was efficient, indolent murder. Their eyes flicked back and forth between the merry-go-round and Arthur Scarett. They'd had him under surveillance since he checked into the Beach Hotel.

The problem, as Adonis saw it, was how to separate the prohibition agent from his family. Everywhere Scarett went, the wife and kids went, and Adonis, being a religious man, wasn't about to pop mom and her bambinos. He had all weekend to catch Scarett alone, but he wanted to get back to Texas City and business. He was mulling the problem when he felt the snout of a pistol pressed to his backbone.

"No cute moves, Joey, or you're a dead man."

Nolan was directly behind him. Four of Nolan's boys were crowded close around the two shooters, snub-nosed revolvers tented in their suit pockets. Adonis realized he had been so intent on Scarett that he'd gotten sloppy, and now Diamond Jack himself was breathing down his neck. Nolan nudged him with the gun. "Here's the drill," he said with amiable menace. "We'll walk out of here like old pals, no fuss, no bother. Try anything sporty and you're cold meat."

Adonis snorted. "You're gonna give it to me anyway. Why should I play along?"

"No, Joey, you've got it all wrong. Mr. Voight and Mr. Quinn just want to have a talk with you, that's all. Use your beaner and you'll live to a ripe old age."

"Are you on the square with me, Jack?"

"Joey, c'mon, would I lie to you?"

Adonis thought it was highly likely. But the odds dictated that he play for time and hope the Virgin Mary was watching over him. Two cars, motors running and drivers at the wheel, were waiting outside the Funland Pier. Nolan and one of his men got into the lead car with Adonis, and the other men, after disarming the shooters, got into the second car. No one spoke as they pulled away from the curb.

Five minutes later the caravan approached the front of the Hollywood Club. The cars turned right and slowed to a stop outside the rear entrance to the kitchen. The cooks and dishwashers pretended temporary blindness as the men filed through the rear door. Nolan followed a service hallway which led to the employees' lounge at the end of the T-head pier. The croupiers and stickmen in the lounge, like the kitchen help, went momentarily blind.

The casino didn't open until eight o'clock, and it was now seven thirty-one. Nolan, with his men trailing behind, led Adonis and the shooters from the lounge to the office. Voight was seated at the desk and Quinn stood at the picture window overlooking the dark waters of the Gulf. The door closed, and Adonis, with Nolan at his side, halted before the desk. Cuddles, the parrot, cocked his head and croaked "Oh, boy! Oh, boy!"

Adonis straightened his tie. "What the hell's the idea, Dutch? Why'd you have us rousted?"

"I'll get to you," Voight said, then glanced at Nolan. "Where'd you find them?"

"Funland Pier," Nolan replied. "What with the crowd

and the noise, I figured it was time to make our move. They were on Scarett and his family like mustard plaster."

"That's bullshit!" Adonis flared. "Me and the boys was just down here seein' the sights."

"Save your breath," Voight said. "Jack and his boys were on you all day while you tailed Scarett. We're not saps, Joey."

"You don't know what the fuck you're talkin' about. I got no business with Scarett."

"No, you just planned to snuff him and put the Feds on us. After the dust settled, then you'd make your move on the Island. We know all about it."

"Like hell," Adonis snapped. "Whoever told you that's a Goddamn liar."

"Liar! Liar!" Cuddles squawked. *"Pants on fire?"*

Adonis scowled. "What's with the bird?"

"He's a psychic," Voight said with a mirthless laugh. "You're lying, Joey. Caught out by a parrot."

"Dutch, I'm tellin' you the truth. I swear it on the Holy Mother's head."

"Careful lightning doesn't strike you."

"I'm on the square here! I wasn't out to ace Scarett."

Voight snorted. "Ollie, what do you think? Is he a snarf or not?"

Quinn turned from the window. "I believe you're right, Dutch."

"Wait a minute," Adonis said, looking from one to the other. "What the hell's a snarf?"

"That's you, Joey," Voight said with open mockery. "A guy who bites the bubbles when he farts in the bathtub. Fits you to a T."

Nolan and his men chuckled out loud. Adonis glared at Voight. "You got a lotta nerve callin' me names. Come down to it, you're no better'n me, maybe worse. You've whacked a few guys in your day."

"Yeah, but my day's not over, Joey. Yours is."

"What's that supposed to mean?"

Voight nodded to Nolan. "Jack, we're through talking here. Take him for a swim."

"Bye-bye!" Cuddles piped in. "Byebyebye!"

Adonis paled. His expression was that of a man who has just heard death whisper a terrible revelation in his ear. He appealed to Quinn.

"Ollie, for Chrissake, you and me go back a long ways. You gotta stop this! I'm askin' you."

"Too late," Quinn said in a flat voice. "You should've stayed clear of the Island. Let's get it done, Jack."

Nolan and his men pulled their pistols. Whizzer Duncan, his wiry lieutenant, moved to the far corner of the room. He rolled back the carpet, then opened a trapdoor built into the floor, revealing a narrow flight of wooden steps. The sound of water slapping against timbers echoed from below.

Duncan went down first. Nolan and the others then herded Adonis and his two shooters down the steps. A wide landing was bolted between stout pylons that supported the T-head of the casino. Nolan's powerful speedboat, the *Cherokee* was lashed to the landing, bobbing gently in the surf. The prisoners were forced into the boat at gunpoint.

Twenty minutes later Nolan cut the throttles. They were ten miles or so off the coast, the *Cherokee* wallowing in swells from the southern Gulf. On the ride out, Adonis and his cohorts had been bound hand and foot, and then wrapped in heavy logging chains. At Nolan's order, the men got them on their feet, near the stern of the boat. Duncan held Adonis upright.

The two shooters were wild-eyed with terror. For all the men they'd killed, one broke into sobs, mewling pitifully for his life, and the other seemed paralyzed. One at a time, they were hoisted into the air and thrown overboard, sinking beneath the choppy surf the moment they hit the water. Adonis watched them vanish with a look of stricken dread.

"Mother of Christ," he muttered, craning his neck to

look at Nolan. "Jack, I'm begging you, shoot me first. Don't drown me like that. I'm begging you . . . have a heart."

"No can do, Joey," Nolan said with a steady gaze. "Nothing personal, I'm just following orders. Business is business."

Duncan and the other men lifted Adonis off his feet. As they tossed him overboard, his mouth opened in a shrieking curse: "You bastards, I'll see you in hell!" He hit with a splash, taken deep by the roiling waters.

Nolan engaged the throttles. He brought the *Cherokee* around and headed back to shore. Duncan stared at their wake a moment, then turned forward. He chortled sourly.

"Think Joey found his hell at the bottom?"

"No," Nolan allowed. "I'd say long before then."

"Yeah, long before then when?"

"On his way down."

Duncan thought that was rich. He got a mental picture of Adonis trying to swim in chains. Holding his breath. All the way down.

Chapter Nine

The Magruders seldom frequented the Hollywood Club. William Magruder believed entertainment was a foursome at bridge, and nightclubs seemed to him a frivolous pursuit. Gambling, in his opinion, was a pastime for the mentally deficient.

For all that, Saturday night was the exception. Magruder had asked his only daughter how she would like to celebrate her twenty-first birthday. She told him, knowing it would tilt his equilibrium, that she wanted to see Al Jolson's closing night in Galveston. He had no choice but to call Ollie Quinn.

Elizabeth, who insisted on being called Libbie, was a striking young woman. Her tawny hair and sumptuous figure was set off by bee-stung lips and an impudent nose. She was warmly attractive, by turns charming and spoiled, and she generally left men somewhat bewitched. An evening in her company, whatever her mood, was always memorable.

Libbie prided herself on being the ideal of a liberated woman, a flapper. She wore short skirts, rolled her stockings below the knee, and kept her hair bobbed in a shingle cut. She smoked cigarettes, flattened her breasts to affect a slender look, and painted her face with an exotic blend of cosmetics. Her outfit tonight was a sheer champagne slip of a dress, glistening with glass beads, and a matching silk headband. She carried a white plume fan with an air of regal disdain.

Her mother, by contrast, looked the wealthy matron. Opal Magruder, her hair piled atop her head, was pleasingly plump, her face lightly blushed by rouge. She wore an elegant black satin sheath with lace across the top and down her arms, the hem of her skirt touching the floor. Francis Magruder, Sherm's wife, was presentable, if somewhat dowdy, dressed in an evening gown of tulle silk with a scooped neckline. The men were formally attired in tuxedos.

Quinn, with Nolan at this side, greeted them at the entrance of the nightclub. He shook the men's hands, kissed the ladies' fingertips, and turned his high-wattage smile on Libbie. "Allow me to wish you a very happy birthday," he said with glib dignity. "We're honored to have you at the Hollywood Club on such a special occasion."

"Thank you so much." Libbie fluttered her fan with a delicate motion. "I'm so looking forward to seeing Al Jolson perform. Everyone says he's fabulous."

"The world's greatest," Quinn said, ever the showman. "I'm sure you won't be disappointed."

Libbie glanced past him at Nolan. He was impeccably groomed in a white dinner jacket, his piercing green eyes magnetic behind tanned features. His sleek assurance and lithe good looks reminded her of the movie idol Rudolph Valentino. She was suddenly glad she hadn't brought a date tonight.

The orchestra was playing *Japanese Sandman*. The club was packed, and on the dance floor, couples dipped and swayed to the beat of the music. Quinn led the Magruders to a large oval table centered on the stage, seating them on one side with empty chairs awaiting the rest of their party. A flurry of waiters descended on the table.

Quinn rejoined Nolan at the door as the Seagraves arrived. They were the guests of the Magruders, and like them, infrequent visitors to the Hollywood Club. With George Seagrave was his wife, Clara, locally renowned for her obsession with planting oleanders all over the Island. They were accompanied by their son, John and his wife, Mary, a woman more interested in raising children than flowers. Quinn, still playing the courtly host, escorted them to the Magruders' table.

After everyone was seated, he made his way back-stage. He knocked on Jolson's dressing room door, waiting to enter until he heard a voice from inside. Jolson was in the midst of his transformation to blackface, tarlike goo smeared on his hands. He looked up in the mirror.

"Ollie, my boy," he said with a broad grin. "How's the crowd tonight?"

"Full house," Quinn said, crossing the room. "They're hanging from the rafters for your closing night."

"And Dutch was worried about an extra two grand to hold me over. I shoulda asked for five!"

"Dutch would've had a stroke. But I hope you're feeling generous tonight. I'd like to ask a favor."

"Ask away."

"I have a business associate in the audience. The whole family's here, celebrating his daughter's birthday. I was hoping you'd sing her a song—at their table."

Jolson stared at him in the mirror. "You want me to sing *Happy Birthday*?"

"No, no," Quinn said quickly. "One of your regular songs. Just sing it to her."

"Is she a looker?"

"Al, she's a knockout."

"I always was a sucker for a pretty face. What's her name?"

"Libbie," Quinn said. "There are nine of them seated at a table down front. She's the only flapper in the bunch."

"Good for her," Jolson said agreeably. "I'll give her something to remember."

"You're a sport, Al. I appreciate it."

"What the hey, why not? What's your business with her father?"

Quinn smiled. "We have mutual interests in a bank."

Their table was tiny, crammed against a wall at the rear of the room. Stoner was dressed in a double-breasted tux and Janice wore a lavender gown with a deep V in the back to her waist. They were so far away they could barely see the stage.

"I hope Jolson sings loud," she said playfully. "We'll need opera glasses from back here."

"Count your lucky stars," Stoner said. "I got the only table in the place. The *one* and only."

"Well, like they say, money talks."

"Highway robbery would be more like it."

On a hunch, Stoner had dropped by the club early that afternoon. He'd gone to the front office and talked with the business manager, asking if there had been any cancellations for tonight's show. The business manager was a slick operator, an extortionist at heart, who held back tickets for every show, for the right price. A hundred dollars a seat got Stoner a table.

Stoner thought it was worth a shot. For four nights in a row he had gambled at the Garden Club and a couple similar poker rooms. He was nursing his funds, for he needed a sizeable bankroll to pull off the last step in the plan. But he'd lost a few hundred here and a few hundred there, and his name was now known at the gaming dives. Tonight, he intended to talk his way into the only casino that mattered.

Over dinner Stoner observed how the club operated. From his briefing in Austin, he knew something of the routine as well as the personnel. He identified Oliver Quinn from the description he'd been given at Ranger Headquarters. He assumed Dutch Voight, who ran the gaming end of the business, was busy with the casino. He would verify that only if his plan worked.

Quinn held his attention throughout dinner. He watched as Quinn seated two groups of people at the same table on the edge of the dance floor. There were nine people in the party, and Quinn's manner toward the two older men was ingratiating, curiously deferential. Stoner wondered who they were, and why they rated special treatment. He made a mental note of their faces.

The other man who caught his attention was Diamond Jack Nolan. Intelligence files at Ranger Headquarters indicated that Nolan was the enforcer for the Galveston mob. His reputation, though he'd never been arrested, was that of a cold-blooded killer. Stoner saw the easy smile that never touched Nolan's eyes, and he could believe the reports were accurate. He marked Nolan as the most dangerous of the lot.

Stoner finished his steak while Janice was still savoring her shrimp Touraine. The service was faultless, and he had to admit that the Hollywood Club warranted its reputation for gourmet dining. After a glance around the room, he decided it was time to make his move. Quinn had gone backstage, and Nolan had escorted a few people to the glass doors that led to the casino. He looked across at Janice.

"I'll be right back," he said. "I want to test the waters before the show starts."

She paused, a delicate shrimp speared on the tines of her fork. "You'll be careful, won't you?"

"Careful's my middle name."

Stoner walked to the nightclub entrance. The maitre d' was slim as a greyhound, with a pencil-thin mustache, and an expression of haughty reserve. He inspected Stoner with a patronizing smile.

"Yes, sir, how may I help you?"

"I'm here with my wife," Stoner said amiably. "She's all excited to try the casino after the show. Thought you could arrange it for us."

"I'm afraid our clubroom is open only to members, Mr—?"

"Eberling. Bob Eberling. I'd be glad to pay any membership fee."

"No, I'm sorry, quite impossible, Mr. Eberling. One must be sponsored by another member."

"Well, I'm a regular at the Garden Club. Call over there and ask about Bob Eberling. They'll vouch for me."

"Our clientele doesn't frequent the Garden Club. And vice versa, if you see what I mean."

"Look here—" Stoner pulled a wad of cash from his pocket. "Suppose you get me in the casino and I'll make it worth your while. How's a hundred sound?"

The maitre d' looked down his nose. "We at the Hollywood Club do not accept bribes, Mr. Eberling. Will there be anything else?"

"The little woman's gonna be awful disappointed."

The maitre d' just stared at him. Stoner started away, and then, as if struck by an afterthought, turned back. "Say, tell me something, will you? Who're the people down by the dance floor? The ones with the good-looking girl?"

"The young lady is Miss Elizabeth Magruder. Tonight is her birthday."

"Looks like the whole family's here. Her father must have some pull to get a front-row table. Who is he?"

"William Magruder," the maitre d' said in an imperious tone. "One of Galveston's most prominent businessmen."

"Pays to have influence, huh? I'll bet you roll out the red carpet when he heads to the casino."

"You'll have to excuse me, Mr. Eberling. I have other duties."

"Yeah, sure, I understand."

Stoner filed the information away, curious that a businessman was so chummy with a gangster. He walked back to the table, seating himself, and told Janice he'd struck out on the casino. She played her role and looked properly crestfallen. He shook his head. "Guess we'll have to go back to Plan A."

"The manager at the hotel?"

"Yeah, that and more time in the poker clubs."

"Well, anyway—" She consoled him with a squeeze of his hand. "The evening's not a complete loss, sweetie. We get to see Jolson."

The houselights dimmed. A spotlight hit the stage as

the orchestra swung into a bouncy tune. Jolson exploded out of the wings.

The choo-choo train that takes me
Away from you
No words can tell how sad it makes me.

Jolson was on bended knee. The spotlight framed him and Libbie as he knelt before her at the table. The lyrics were particularly meaningful because everyone knew he was leaving for Los Angeles in the morning. He finished the last refrain of *Toot Toot Tootsie* with outstretched arms.

The audience roared their approval. Jolson took Libbie's hand and kissed it, then skipped back up the ramp to the stage. He concluded the show with a foot-stomping rendition of *California, Here I Come*, which seemed inspired, since he was off to make the world's first talky movie. The crowd gave him a standing ovation that brought him back for four curtain calls.

When the houselights came on, Libbie was the center of attention. Quinn stopped by the table and she kissed him on the cheek for arranging a birthday song by Jolson. The conversation turned to *The Jazz Singer*, the talking motion picture Jolson would start shooting next week. Magruder and Seagrave agreed that talking pictures would prove to be a short-lived fad. Quinn reminded them that people had said motion pictures would never replace vaudeville. And now vaudeville was all but dead!

Libbie excused herself to go to the powder room. She wasn't interested in listening to her father debate the future of motion pictures. All the more pressing, she felt a buzz from too many gin rickeys and an urgent need to pee. Afterward, she paused before a vanity mirror to freshen her makeup, amused by the stares that her flapper look drew from some of the older women. When she came out of the ladies' room, she saw Quinn's green-eyed assistant standing by the doors to the casino. She thought he was devilishly handsome, temptation in a tux. And after all, it was her birthday!

She took a cigarette from her evening bag. Then, stopping directly in front of him, she looked up into his eyes. "May I have a light?"

Nolan clicked his lighter. "Having a good time, Miss Magruder?"

"Just marvelous," Libbie said, exhaling a thin streamer of smoke. "I don't believe we've met."

"I'm Jack Nolan."

"What do you do for Mr. Quinn?"

If only you knew, Nolan thought to himself. He smiled disarmingly. "I'm the club's Mr. Fixit. Whatever needs doing, I fix it."

"How very interesting," she said, vamping him with a look. "What are you fixing tonight?"

"Pardon me?"

"You could fix it quite nicely by dancing with me."

Libbie exuded sensuality. She considered herself a liberated woman, one who rejected the starchy, outdated customs of an older generation. Like many young women of the Twenties, she drank, experimented with sex, and explored everything forbidden by a moral code that seemed unbearably ancient. She had discovered the joys of burning the candle at both ends.

Nolan was tempted. He had a weakness for cute young things with no inhibitions. But rules were rules. "I'm sorry, Miss Magruder," he said with genuine regret. "Mr. Quinn doesn't allow me to dance with guests."

"Why don't you call me Libbie and I'll call you Jack?"

"All right, but that doesn't change anything."

Her voice was warm and husky, softly intimate. "We could change things."

"I don't follow you."

"Oh, I think you do. Why not give me a call at home sometime?"

"Never work," Nolan said ruefully. "Your father

wouldn't like it and Mr. Quinn definitely wouldn't like it.
I'd be in hot water."

"Ummm," she murmured throatily. "I think you like
hot water . . . don't you, Jack?"

Nolan watched her walk back into the club. Her short
skirt revealed shapely legs and her hips wigwagged in a
swishing motion that held his attention. He felt a warmth
in his groin and a knot in his belly, and warned himself
to forget it. Quinn would have his balls if he messed with
Magruder's daughter.

The irony wasn't lost on Nolan. A little bombshell of
a girl coming on to him while her father pulled the strings
to have a man killed. He was amused all over again that
she'd asked him what sort of work he did for Quinn. In
a roundabout way, he was working for her father, and
there was the real irony. She would never know.

The orchestra wailed away in an earsplitting number.
He saw the girl drag her father out of his chair and pull
him onto the dance floor. The crowd went wild with the
music, hopping about like well-dressed acrobats in a frenzied Charleston. Magruder was hopelessly lost, merely
plodding along to his daughter's flailing arms and thrash-
ing legs. Her fluted laughter melded with the tempo of
the beat.

Nolan turned into the casino. Voight gave him a quizzical look, and he nodded in the affirmative, proceeding
on to the employees' lounge. He hung his tux in a wall
locker and changed into a dark charcoal suit. By the time
he stepped into the hallway to the kitchen, he'd forgotten
the girl.

He had work to do.

The organ swelled to a crescendo. Everyone in the theater
sat mesmerized by the action on the screen. The organist
kept his eyes glued to a speeding motorcycle.

Manslaughter was the title of the movie. A motorcycle cop was chasing the unjustly accused heroine in her
car. Catherine clutched Durant's arm as the heroine lost

control and her car skidded around broadside in the road. The motorcycle struck the fender and the cop vaulted into the air, thrown over the hood. The heroine, distraught and shaken, staggered from her car.

Theaters across the country were equipped with organs. A skilled organist could provide a wide array of sound effects—thunder, gunfire, the rumble of an earthquake—and accompany the shifting moods of a film. Tonight, the organist dropped the tenor to a haunting refrain as the heroine stumbled around the car and looked down at the cop's body. A gasp went through the audience.

After the movie, Durant and Catherine walked south on Tenth Street. Last night, when he'd run into her on the corner and invited her to dinner, it had been a spur-of-the moment thing. But he had enjoyed her company, and sensed it was mutual, and tonight he'd asked her out for an early dinner and a movie. As he walked her home, she eagerly questioned him about the stunts. She was particularly intrigued by the motorcycle crash.

"I can't imagine it," she said. "A motorcycle going that fast and him flying through the air! How on earth did he live through it?"

"Well, good judgment helps," Durant said. "You have to think a stunt through, and then plan it step by step. It's all in the timing."

"Timing?"

"Let's take the split second of the crash. He had to time it perfectly to let go of the motorcycle. To let the momentum throw him over the car. Everything's timing."

Her hand was nestled in the crook of his arm. She hesitated, but curiosity got the better of her. "Have you ever misjudged the timing?"

"Oh, boy, did I," Durant said with a laugh. "I had to jump from the top of a double-decker bus to an elevated girder. I missed and hit the street like a lead brick. Broke my leg."

She winced. "How awful."

"Yeah, that's when I started thinking seriously about directing. Directors don't wind up in the hospital."

"But it's really more than that, isn't it? I think you want to create films of your own."

"Doing stunts is like a classroom. I've learned a lot from watching the way directors work. King Vidor and Tom Ince are two of the best."

Durant went on to explain that Ince had formulated a blueprint for making pictures which included a detailed shooting script and a scene-by-scene shooting schedule. King Vidor had pioneered dramatic camera techniques, where the camera moves as if it were the actor, revealing the shot from the actor's point of view. Imagination, looking at things from the camera's perspective, was the key to visual narrative.

Catherine could have listened to him all night. Everything about moving pictures captivated her, and she was engrossed by his behind-the-scenes description of Hollywood. Before she knew it, they crossed the corner of Tenth and Avenue K and turned into the walkway of her house. She didn't want the evening to end, but her mother would have gone to bed, and it was too late to invite him inside. She turned to him at the door.

"I had a wonderful time," she said, smiling happily. "I don't know when I've enjoyed myself so much."

"Same here," Durant said. "Hate to call it a night."

"Me, too."

"Maybe we could do it again."

"I'd love to."

Durant kissed her softly on the lips. Her hand went to his cheek, caressing him, and then she stepped back. She laughed nervously.

"Well . . . good night for now."

"Good night."

Durant went down the walkway as she opened the door. He looked back, waving to her, and crossed the street. His spirits were so high he felt a little drunk, and he wondered at himself. Then, thinking about it, he realized it wasn't just having a good time, or even loneliness. He was really attracted to her.

Halfway down the block he got his bearings. He decided to follow Avenue K west and cut over to his hotel. His mind was still on Catherine and he thought he would call her tomorrow. Maybe she would enjoy an outing to one of the amusement piers, or a walk along the beach. A solitary Sunday suddenly took on brighter prospects.

There was no traffic at Fifteenth Street. As he crossed to the opposite corner, he heard the muffled idle of an automobile engine. He glanced around and saw a four-door Buick sedan coasting silently toward him with the lights out. His every sense alerted as the passenger door and the right-side rear door opened, and two men stepped out with pistols. He recognized them from the beating he'd taken at the Heroes Monument.

Durant's instincts kicked in from the war. He sought cover, dodging behind a telephone pole, and pulled the Luger from his waistband. The two gunmen fired almost simultaneously, one shot nicking the telephone pole and the other whistling past his ear. He crouched, arm extended at shoulder level, and caught the sights in the reflection from the streetlight. He ripped off three quick shots.

The first shattered the car's windshield. The second plucked at the sleeve of the man by the passenger door. The man by the rear door grunted with surprise, a starburst of blood covering his shirtfront from the third slug. He lurched sideways, his legs collapsing, and slumped face down on the curb. The driver shouted a curse.

"Get the *hell* in the car!"

The other man jumped on the running board as the Buick roared away. Durant fired a departing shot, trying for the gunman and blowing out the rear window instead. He rose from behind the telephone pole, glancing at the dead hoodlum, and decided to make tracks. Houselights were coming on in the neighborhood, and he couldn't afford to be identified. The cops, given the opportunity, would charge him with murder. He hurried north on Fifteenth Street.

Four blocks away, Nolan skidded around the corner of Nineteenth. He switched on the lights, letting off the accelerator, and the Buick slowed to a moderate speed. Beside him, Turk McGuire blew out a gusty breath, still clutching his revolver. His eyes were wild with fury.

"That cocksucker killed Elmer! Where the fuck'd he get a gun?"

"I don't know," Nolan said. "But he sure as Christ knows how to shoot. Look at the windshield."

"Hell, look at the back window," McGuire snarled. "Bastard was still shootin' at us when we took off. Who the fuck is this guy?"

"Turk, that's a damn good question."

Nolan headed for the Turf Club. The car was riddled, and he wanted to get it out of sight in the garage behind the building. But as he drove, his mind returned to the shootout, and the man who took cover behind a telephone pole. The man calmly blasting away with an automatic.

He thought he wanted to know more about Earl Durant.

Chapter Ten

Late Monday morning, Dutch Voight walked into City Hall. Nolan was acting as his bodyguard, until the right replacement was found for Elmer Spadden. The funeral was set for the next day.

The morning paper had carried a story about the shooting. According to the police, who had interviewed everyone in the neighborhood, between six and ten shots were fired. But there were no witnesses, no leads, and little to investigate. There was also no mention of who Elmer Spadden worked for.

Voight was enraged. Earlier, with Nolan at his side, he had made the weekly trip to the Galveston City Bank. Sherm Magruder, who suspected the truth, acted as though he'd never heard of Spadden. Instead, ever the friendly banker, he exchanged bearer bonds for a briefcase full of cash. The transaction was conducted in terse silence.

But now, entering City Hall, Voight put on a cheerful face. Dealing with politicians was a dirty game, and the first rule was to never let them know what you were thinking. Every Monday Voight made the rounds, and there was nothing secretive about the meetings. Vice fueled the economy of Galveston, and the public, for the most part, approved. Voters already knew their political leaders were on the pad.

The first stop was the office of the mayor. Margie Clark, the mayor's longtime secretary and occasional lover, was expecting Voight. She showed him and Nolan into the office, and gently closed the door. Edward Pryor rose from behind his desk with the smile of a man who knew how his bread got buttered. His hair was snow-white and his manner was gracious, a politician to the core. He never thought of himself as a crook.

"Good morning, Dutch," he said, waving them to chairs. "I was most distressed to hear about Elmer. Terrible thing, just terrible."

"Elmer was a good man." Voight placed his briefcase on the desk and unsnapped the latches. "Send some flowers to his funeral. He'd like that."

"I most certainly will, Dutch. Depend on it."

There was no question of Pryor or any other politician attending the funeral services. That would have been too open an association, even for the voters of Galveston. Flowers were more discreet.

Voight removed two thousand in cash from his briefcase. The mayor was his conduit to the police force and other departments of the city government. A hundred thousand a year ensured protection for all the mob's activities.

Pryor placed the cash in his desk drawer. "I'll make the usual distributions," he said. "And once again, my most sincere condolences. I know Elmer was unstintingly loyal."

"Fact is, Eddie, he wrote the book on loyal. I'll see you next week."

Nolan held the door for Voight as they went out. Their next stop was the county courthouse, where they called on Sheriff Leonard Beebe. A lanky man with a salt-and-pepper mustache, Beebe had been the sheriff of Galveston County for three terms. He was their pipeline to various judges and the county prosecutor. He greeted them with a somber look.

"Helluva note," he said. "I know Elmer was one of your top boys. Any idea who did it?"

Voight scowled. "We know exactly who did it."

"Whatever way it happened, I'd be glad to arrange murder charges. Wouldn't be any trouble at all."

"Let's just say it's a private matter. We'll take care of it ourselves."

Beebe expected nothing less. The mob operated by its own code, and transgressors were dealt with in brutal fashion. Someone would disappear, and the likelihood of his office ever learning the name was practically nil. He accepted the weekly payoff with no further reference to Elmer Spadden.

On the street again, Voight and Nolan turned toward the Turf Club. All the talk that morning about Spadden left Nolan even more puzzled than before. Saturday night, after the shooting, he'd reported back to Voight and Quinn at the Hollywood Club. They were dumbfounded that Durant had armed himself with a gun.

Voight, who was closer to Spadden, was particularly enraged. Quinn, though angry, was calmer, and assured Nolan they didn't hold him responsible. Yet, all day Sunday, he'd expected an order to snuff Durant, the faster, the better. Instead, his bosses had kept their own counsel, and kept him in the dark. He felt like it was time to ask the question.

"Tell me if I'm out of line," he said as they walked along. "Back there, you told Beebe we'd take care of business ourselves. When are we going after Durant?"

Voight frowned. "Ollie got a call from Magruder Sunday afternoon. He's meeting with him now."

"What about?"

"Magruder didn't want to talk on the phone. Just said to hold off on that 'personal matter' till him and Ollie could get together."

"I'll be damned," Nolan said in a bemused tone. "What do you think he wants?"

"We'll find out soon enough."

They walked on toward the Turf Club.

Monday mornings were always slow. The few merchants who traded with People's Bank & Trust brought their weekend receipts in for deposit. But the bank was otherwise at a standstill.

On his way in that morning, Durant had spoken

briefly with Aldridge. He'd waved to Catherine, greeting her with a smile, and thought she looked hurt that he hadn't stopped to talk. Then he retreated to his office, and stayed there all morning, with the door closed. He was still trying to piece things together.

Sunday he'd gone out of his hotel only for a late breakfast and an early supper. He hadn't called Catherine about a date, for fear of putting her in danger as well. The short time he was out of the hotel, he fully expected a car loaded with gunmen to run him down. He wondered why they were waiting.

Today, over breakfast, he'd read the newspaper story. He learned the man he had killed was named Elmer Spadden, and felt no surprise that his own name wasn't mentioned. Nor was he surprised that the police hadn't busted into his hotel room and arrested him. The mob wouldn't lower themselves to call on the cops, even crooked cops. They would settle the score on their own.

Saturday night continued to scroll through his mind like a scary movie. He was convinced Jack Nolan was the driver of the car, for Nolan had been involved from the beginning. The other man, the one built like a mastodon, he remembered from the fight at the Heroes Monument. He wasn't sure he wanted to know the man's name.

The odds dictated that he run. He had survived Saturday night only because he'd had the foresight to buy the Luger. That and the kill-or-be-killed lessons he had learned in the trenches of France. The next time, they might catch him off guard, or send thugs armed with tommy guns rather than pistols. And he had no doubt there would be a next time, for it was now a matter of payback. He had killed one of their men.

Despite the odds, he'd decided not to run. All day Sunday he had weighed the risk of staying on against the more prudent measure of fleeing Galveston. By nature he was not a quitter, and it went against the grain to be driven out by Magruder and a bunch of gangsters. No less telling, the war had taught him that a man with the guts to stand

and fight was, more often then not, a match for the bullies of the world. He was resolved to see it through.

A knock at the door interrupted his woolgathering. Aldridge stepped into the office, his features at once quizzical and concerned. He closed the door, moving across the room, and took a chair. He tried a tentative smile.

"Everything all right?" he asked. "You've hardly spoken to anyone all morning."

"Just one of those days," Durant said dismissively. "Nothing to worry about."

Aldridge studied his face. "Why don't I believe you?"

"What's not to believe?"

"You act like a man with a load too heavy to carry. Sure you don't want to talk about it?"

Durant hesitated a moment. He trusted the older man and perhaps it wouldn't hurt to confide in someone. He told himself Aldridge need to know anyway. Just in case. . . .

"You heard about the shooting Saturday night?"

"I read about it in the paper," Aldridge said carefully. "One of the hoodlums who work for Quinn and Voight was killed. Why do you ask?"

"I killed him."

"No!"

"Afraid so."

Durant quickly related the events of Saturday night. He explained his decision to buy a gun, and how he'd used it to kill Elmer Spadden. He concluded with an empty laugh.

"I didn't stick around to wait for the police. Unless I miss my guess, they'd jump at the chance to charge me with murder."

"Wise decision," Aldridge said. "But I can't say the same about staying in Galveston. You should have left town yesterday."

"Where would I go?" Durant said hollowly. "I killed one of their men and there's nowhere to run. They'd just track me down in Los Angeles."

"Yes, now that you mention it, you're right. Even selling the bank to Magruder wouldn't solve anything. Quinn and Voight are vengeful men, and you've made them look bad. You're not safe anywhere."

"Ira, I hate to say it, but it's not just me. I've been sitting here thinking about it, and these bastards make their own rules. They might try to get at me through you."

"Oh, I don't think so," Aldridge said. "What would that possibly gain them? You're the one they want."

Durant rubbed the bridge of his nose. "Do me a favor and watch your step, anyhow. Why take chances?"

"Yes, of course." Aldridge held his gaze. "I wasn't aware you were seeing Catherine. Do you think she's in any danger?"

"I doubt they'd harm a woman. Gangsters think of themselves as tough guys, and that would spoil their image. She's probably safe."

"On the other hand, you very definitely are not. How will you protect yourself?"

"Guess I'll have to grow eyes in the back of my head."

"Do you really believe that will stop them?"

Durant shrugged, let the question hang. He already knew the answer.

Quinn was waiting in the office at the Turf Club. The moment Voight and Nolan came through the door, they knew something was wrong. His features were clouded with anger.

"I've got a feeling it's bad news," Voight said. "What happened with Magruder?"

"Our friend lost his nerve." Quinn wagged his head with distaste. "He wants us to back off on Durant."

"What the hell do you mean, back off? He's the one that asked us to ice the bastard!"

"Dutch, I made that very point. I made it several times and it was a waste of breath. He wouldn't listen."

"Screw him!" Voight's dark eyes shone like nuggets

of coal. "We're burying Elmer tomorrow, and Durant killed him. Are you telling me we let the sonofabitch skate?"

"No, I'm not," Quinn said in a controlled voice. "I'm telling you Magruder's one of the big reasons we *own* the rackets in Galveston. We can't afford to offend him."

Voight stalked to the window. He stood looking out at the street, his jaws clenched. There was a moment of oppressive silence, the air thick with tension. He finally turned around.

"How about this?" he said. "We take Durant for a swim and nobody'll know the difference. He just disappears."

"Easier said than done," Quinn noted. "You'll remember he's got a gun and he's willing to fight. How do we take him without another shooting?"

"I don't know and I don't give a rat's ass. I just want him dead."

"Listen to me, Dutch. Magruder's as nervous as a whore in church. Durant knows he's behind everything that's happened, the shooting, the whole works. He's scared Durant will start broadcasting it around town."

Voight laughed bitterly. "All the more reason to clip the bastard."

"You'll get no argument from me," Quinn said. "But Magruder thinks we have to hold off, let things settle down. Let Durant think it's over. Let him think he's won."

"How about it, Jack?" Voight said, turning to Nolan. "You think Durant will think he's won?"

"Not a chance," Nolan replied with conviction. "We learned the hard way he's a sharp cookie. He knows it's not finished."

"See!" Voight said, looking at Quinn. "Magruder's talking through his hat. Nothing's solved till we nail Durant."

"And we will," Quinn told him. "Just try to be a little patient for once. Give Magruder time to get his nerve back."

"Goddamn amateurs," Voight grumped. "Never yet seen one that wasn't a pain in the ass."

A rap sounded on the door. Turk McGuire stuck his head inside, nodding to Nolan. "Jack, there's a broad on the phone for you. She won't take no for an answer."

"Always the ladies' man," Quinn said, relieved by the interruption. "How do you work them into your schedule, Jack?"

"Talking about schedules," Voight said. "You've got a ship loaded with booze coming in tonight. Don't let your love life interfere with business."

"I'll have the fleet there with time to spare. Everything's all set."

Nolan slipped out the door. He crossed the hall to a cubbyhole office, where the phone for Gulf Enterprises rang through. He picked up the receiver. "Hello."

"Hello yourself, handsome."

"Who's this?"

"Libbie Magruder. You haven't forgotten our tête-à-tête Saturday night . . . have you?"

"You'd be hard to forget."

"How very gallant. I love it!"

"What can I do for you?"

"Ummm." She laughed, a throaty growl. "I can think of several things."

Nolan wondered if she was as wild as she sounded. "I thought we settled this Saturday night."

"No, I asked you to call me and you didn't. So I've called you. Aren't you flattered?"

"Even if I am, it's not a good idea."

"Oh, I think it's a marvelous idea. And if you were truthful, so do you . . . don't you?"

"I think you're trouble."

"Yes, but you like to play with fire. I know you do."

"You don't know anything about me."

"I know enough," she purred. "Why fight kismet when it's all in the stars? Meet me for a drink this afternoon."

Nolan told himself he was nuts. But she was right about one thing. He liked to play with fire.

"There's a place in La Marque where nobody's likely to see us. The Rendezvous Roadhouse."

"Ooo, a rendezvous . . . what time?"

"How's two sound?"

"See you there, handsome."

The line went dead. Nolan replaced the receiver on the hook, certain he'd made a mistake. But then, on second thought, he shrugged it off.

Like she said, why fight kismet?

The sun stood like a blinding fireball against an azure sky. There was little traffic on the causeway, for the weekend tourists had fled the Island like lemmings. The interurban cars to Houston were running practically empty.

Nolan drove with the window down. The sparse traffic somehow reminded him of Arthur Scarett, the prohibition agent. Scarett and his family had departed yesterday, never aware that their lives had been in danger. Joey Adonis, now feeding the fishes, would become part of the lore of what happened to those who trespassed on the Island.

Today, Nolan drove his own car, a sporty Stutz Bearcat with a collapsible top. At no small cost, he'd had the latest innovation installed, a customized compact radio. The automobile, with its range and mobility, had shattered the isolation of rural America forever. Yet it was the magic of radio that had shrunk the size of the planet.

A flick of a switch brought instant access to the outside world. People clustered around their sets, already addicted to favorite programs, and sat mesmerized before the talking box. Today's news was reported today, and in a way, it was as if they were eavesdropping on the curious, and sometimes bizarre, secrets of distant places. There was a verve and excitement of immediacy about the broadcasts.

A stock market report came on as Nolan approached

La Marque. The Dow Jones was up to 102, a new benchmark, and apparently headed to dizzying heights. Listening to the report, he remembered the crash of 1921, and how get-rich-quick investors had become overnight paupers. His view was that the stock market was run by shady New York financiers who periodically bilked the public. His own road to wealth was simpler, and far more certain. He invested only in himself.

The Rendezvous Roadhouse was on the highway south of La Marque. A two-story structure, it was part speakeasy, part dance hall, and a trysting place for lovers, married or otherwise. There was a bar and gaming room on the ground floor, and cozy bedrooms for rent by the hour on the second floor. On a Monday afternoon there were few customers, and Nolan virtually had the place to himself. He took a booth on the far side of the dance floor.

Libbie arrived a fashionable ten minutes late. A cloche hat set off her bobbed hair, and she wore a slinky crepe de chine dress with pleated flounces, her stockings rolled below her knees. Nolan watched as she crossed the dance floor, and felt more amused than flattered that the performance was solely for his benefit. She was decked out as Little Miss Sexpot.

"Forgive me for being late," she said, scooting into the booth. "I had the most dreadful time deciding what to wear."

Nolan chuckled. "I'll bet you ransacked your closet."

"Well, honestly, what's a girl to wear to a *roadhouse*? I've never been to one before."

"I guess there's a first time for everything."

A waiter drifted over. Libbie ordered a gin rickey and Nolan asked for bourbon with a water chaser. They made small talk, skirting anything of a meaningful nature, until their drinks were served. She lifted her glass in a suggestive toast.

"Cheers to our very first date."

Nolan clinked glasses. "I thought we were just getting together for a drink."

"You big fibber." She fluttered her eyelashes. "You thought nothing of the kind. You know very well I have my sights set on you."

"Never try to kid an old kidder. You don't even know me."

"Oh, don't I? Diamond Jack Nolan, rumrunner, gangster, and all-around bad boy. I know *everything* about you."

Nolan thought that wasn't quite true. Only that morning her father had called off the hit on Durant, a job put on hold but not canceled. His amusement was tempered by the irony of the situation. He looked at her over the rim of his glass.

"How'd you learn all my better traits?"

"A girl's entitled to her secrets. I'll never tell."

"What makes you think I'm the guy for you?"

"Kismet, the stars," she said with a sultry laugh. "We were fated to be lovers."

Nolan stared at her. "What is it, little rich girl has a fling with a gangster? Something you can shock all your society pals with?"

She looked wounded. "Now you're being mean. I fell for you the minute I saw you. I haven't thought of anything but you since Saturday night."

"You don't pull any punches, do you? Are you always this pushy with men?"

"No, I usually let them chase me. But you would never have called me, and that would have been the end of it. So I called you."

Her honesty was strangely appealing to Nolan. He understood that liberated women of the Jazz Age were uninhibited, scornful of the old moral taboos. His own view of things was similar to hers, for he followed no rules, and few laws. Even more, she was young and vivacious, stunningly attractive. His kind of woman.

"We'd have big problems," he said seriously. "You know I can't be seen with you in Galveston. I'd get my butt kicked if anybody found out."

"No one will ever know," she said airily. "We'll meet in out-of-the-way places . . . just our secret."

"You're used to parties, and dancing, and good restaurants. Might not be much fun."

"Oh, yes, it will!" She scooted closer, shoulder to shoulder. "You must think I'm a wicked woman."

Nolan grinned. "What the hell, I'm a wicked man."

"Jeepers, I'm all tingly just thinking about it. Did you book us a room in this den of infamy?"

"Are you trying to seduce me?"

"Silly man, I already have."

They spent the afternoon entwined in fierce love.

Chapter Eleven

The red-light district was on Postoffice Street. For four blocks, between Twenty-fifth and Twenty-ninth, sin was for sale. The locals jokingly referred to it as Fat Alley.

The bordellos were conveniently wedged side by side, two-story houses with narrow porches and wooden shutters painted in garish colors. Whores tricked out in skimpy dresses posed in lighted doorways, or leaned out open windows. They offered their wares to a randy stream of seamen, dockworkers, vacationers, and college boys. The going rate for quick lust was three dollars.

There were almost sixty houses of prostitution along Fat Alley. Galveston's business leaders believed that a segregated red-light district was the only practical way to control the oldest profession. They agreed as well that ladies of the evening, like gambling dives and speakeasies, were essential to the Island's well-oiled economy. Over a thousand whores plied their trade on Postoffice Street.

The brothels operated on a time-for-hire policy. Turnover was the key to a profitable venture, and the madams kept the traffic moving. Customers were shown into a parlor where they were encouraged to buy popskull whiskey while they inspected the merchandise. Those who refused to be rushed might feed quarters into a slot machine, but they soon found themselves upstairs with one of the girls. The love-for-sale transactions rarely lasted more than a few minutes.

Fat Alley, oddly enough, was one of the safest neighborhoods on the Island. The combustible mix of whiskey, men, and whores in any other town often led to muggings, brawls, and assorted forms of mayhem. But in Galveston there was a higher law than the one enforced by the police, and it had nothing to do with courts or time in jail. Anyone who caused a disturbance would be accosted by the Night Riders, the hard-fisted thugs who worked for Quinn and Voight. The penalty was a swift and brutal beating.

On Tuesday nights business began to pick up along Postoffice Street. Mondays were a day of rest for the girls, the trade slack from the departure of weekend tourists. But by sundown on Tuesday, Fat Alley came alive with men intent on getting their wicks dipped. The girls, after lazing about for a day, thought of Tuesday as the beginning of their workweek. They greeted the johns with restored vigor.

Harry Johnson and his buddy, Fred Doolin, were out for a night on the town. They were young and single, with good jobs at the Galveston Ice Company, and regular customers on Fat Alley. Their work, loading blocks of ice from the plant onto ice wagons, kept them in top shape and ever in need of a woman. Tonight, their first stop was a speakeasy, where a few drinks would get them primed for bedroom gymnastics. They loved to hear the girls squeal.

The speakeasy was jammed with workingmen. Mae Hager, who owned the establishment, circulated through the crowd. She was the only woman in the place, for men never brought girlfriends with them to Fat Alley. Her manner was brassy, with a loud, horsey laugh, and her customers enjoyed her ribald sense of humor. Johnson and Doolin, who dropped in two or three times a week, were among her favorite customers. She was in her forties, henna-haired and overly plump, but still a flirt. She liked young men.

Mae squeezed in between Johnson and Doolin at the bar. She ordered a drink on the house, and told them a dirty joke about a virgin and a duck. As their laughter faded, the door opened and her features suddenly turned sober. She rolled her eyes and said, "Shit!"

"What's the matter?" Doolin asked.

"Trouble, that's what," she grouched. "Lera and his Goddamn one-armed bandits. He's after me to put in his slots."

Johnson, who was feeling his liquor, pushed off the bar. "Mae, you say the word and I'll clean his clock. Nobody dumps on a friend of mine."

"Yeah," Doolin chimed in. "We'll toss his ass out."

"Boys, you don't want nothin' to do with Lera. Keep out of it."

Lou Lera was a thickset man, who fancied himself a gangster. He wore a dark suit and a black shirt with a white tie, and carried himself with a cocky attitude. Quinn and Voight, who believed competition stimulated business, had split the slots concession on the Island between Lera and another distributor. Lera had been pressuring Mae Hager to switch to his machines.

Mae walked forward to meet him. "Evenin', Lou," she said with a phony smile. "Stand you a drink?"

"Let's talk business," Lera said roughly. "I gave you a deadline and tonight's the night. What's it gonna be?"

"I've told you a dozen times and the answer's still the same. I'll stick with what I've got."

"You always was a stupid old cow. What say I send my boys in here and bust this joint to splinters? Think that'd change your mind?"

"Just you try it," Mae snapped. "You don't scare me."

"I'll do more'n scare you, you dumb cunt."

"Fuck you and the horse you rode in on!"

Lera backhanded her in the mouth. Her lip split, smeared with blood, and she fell against the bar. Harry Johnson took two long strides forward and slugged Lera with a looping haymaker. Lera went down hard, sliding on his butt across the floor. His flattened nose sprayed blood over his face.

Johnson started toward him to finish the job. Lera

jerked a revolver from his shoulder holster and fired two shots as fast as he could pull the trigger. The first slug nipped Johnson's arm and the second struck him squarely in the chest. His shirt colored as though a rosebud had been painted on the cloth by an invisible brush. His eyes went blank and his legs buckled at the knees. He dropped dead on the floor.

"Don't nobody move!"

Lera waved the gun at the crowd. He scrambled to his feet, backing away, and disappeared through the door. Mae Hager stared down at the body, huge teardrops puddling her eyes, her mouth dripping blood. She tottered, almost fell, then recovered herself. She shook her fist at the bartender.

"Goddammit, don't just stand there! Call the *cops!*"

The murder made the front page of the *Galveston Daily Chronicle.* The newspaper account was graphic, with all the gory details related by several eyewitnesses. The police were searching for Louis R. Lera.

Early the next morning, representatives of the Galveston Ministers Association stormed into City Hall. Reverend Josiah Baldwin, speaking for the Baptists, and Reverend Tyler Adair, the Methodist pastor, demanded an audience with the mayor. They were accompanied by Herbert Cornwall, perennial reform candidate in the mayoral elections.

Mayor Edward Pryor greeted them with a conciliatory smile. Elections on the Island were decided, in large part, by the political machine and the sporting crowd's swing vote. But an astute politician nonetheless courted the clergy. No one wanted to be crosswise of God.

"Unconscionable!" thundered Reverend Baldwin. "An innocent man shot down in cold blood. We will *not* tolerate it."

Reverend Adair railed on in condemnation. "Mr. Mayor, the Christian community decries this foul and dastardly act. We demand justice!"

"Gentlemen, please," Pryor pleaded. "The police are combing the Island as we speak. I assure you an arrest will be made."

Herbert Cornwall brayed laughter. "You and your administration are corrupt. *Corrupt!*" He pointed an accusatory finger. "The good people of Galveston will unite behind a coalition to put you out of office."

"Come off it, Herbie," Pryor countered. "You'd kill somebody yourself to be mayor. Don't deny it, either."

"This isn't about politics," Reverend Baldwin pronounced. "This is about gangsters running amuck in our streets. *We—will—have—action!*"

The shouting went on for a half hour. Mayor Pryor, promising results, was finally able to usher them out the door. He immediately called Chief of Police Axel Norton to his office.

"We're in deep shit," he said, explaining the situation. "Just the excuse they needed for a reform movement. And if it goes too far, we'll be thrown out on the street."

Norton squirmed. "We're doing our damnedest, Eddie. I'm turning the Island upside down."

"Not good enough," Pryor said sternly. "I'm going to call Magruder and Seagrave, and alert them. You deliver the word to Quinn and Voight—personally."

"What do I tell them?"

"Tell them killing civilians crosses the line. Lera's their man and we're holding them responsible. We want him in custody today—*now!*"

Ten minutes later Chief Norton walked into the Turf Club. Upstairs, there was a new guard on the door, Barney Ward, who had replaced the dead-and-buried Elmer Spadden. Ward stuck his head in the door, announcing a visitor, and got the okay. He admitted Norton into the office.

Quinn and Voight were seated behind their desks. Voight was in shirtsleeves, puffing a long, black cigar. He waved Norton to a chair.

"We don't often see you around here, Chief. What's up?"

"The shit's hit the fan," Norton said, seating himself. "Your boy Lera started the reformers yapping. They jumped all over the mayor this morning."

"Who, exactly?" Quinn asked. "Which reformers?"

"Same old crowd," Norton said. "The Ministers Association, Adair and Baldwin. Herbie Cornwall was with them, too."

Quinn nodded. "And the mayor sent you to deliver a message, is that it?"

"Yeah, he did." Norton swallowed, his Adam's apple bobbing. "He says Lera's your responsibility, what with a civilian being killed. He wants you to hand him over to the police . . . today."

"Hand him over!" Voight said, puffing furiously on his cigar. "We don't even know where the son of a bitch is."

Quinn and Voight were both in a state of rage. Yesterday they had buried Elmer Spadden, and last night, Lera had violated their rule about no violence against civilians. They had a crew out searching for him, even though he'd seemingly vanished without a trace. Their orders were to shoot him on sight.

"I'm just doing what I'm told," Norton said nervously. "The mayor puts it on your head because Lera's your man."

"Screw that!" Voight exploded. "We give the orders around here, not Eddie Pryor. Tell him I said to shove it—"

The phone rang. Quinn lifted the receiver, listening and nodding, and hung up with a perplexed expression. He exchanged a quick glance with Voight, then looked at Norton. He managed a tight smile.

"Thanks for coming by," he said. "Assure the mayor we're on top of things."

Norton understood he'd been dismissed. He rose, relieved to be on his way, and moved to the door. When it closed, Voight turned to Quinn with a questioning look. He raised an eyebrow.

"Who was that on the phone?"

"Magruder," Quinn said. "We're invited to a meeting in his office at one. Seagrave will be there."

"Let me guess," Voight said. "We're gonna talk about Lera, right?"

"Dutch, I'd say it's the safest bet in town."

The bank was crowded for a Wednesday morning. Durant sat at his desk, trying to decipher balance sheets for the previous week. His mind was elsewhere.

Four days had passed since he'd killed the hoodlum named Spadden. He was still looking over his shoulder, no less convinced the mob would try to settle accounts. But he was preoccupied at the moment with an article he had read in the morning paper. There had been another killing in Galveston.

According to the newspaper, the police were scouring the Island for a thug named Lera. There was speculation that Lera had fled to the mainland, and police agencies there were on the alert. Durant toyed with the notion that the mob, with one of its own branded a murderer, would be reluctant to try another killing anytime soon. Then, on second thought, he doubted he'd gained a reprieve.

Catherine knocked, stepping inside the door. "Someone to see you. Reverend Adair and Reverend Baldwin."

"Preachers?"

"And Herbert Cornwall, who's *always* running for mayor. They say it's very important."

"Wonder what they want?"

"They didn't say."

"All right, show them in."

The men trooped into the office. They introduced themselves and Durant got them seated. There was a moment of awkward silence, as though no one had been appointed spokesman for the group. Reverend Adair finally took the lead.

"Mr. Durant, we represent the decent people of Galveston. Perhaps you've heard of the murder last night?"

"I read about it in the paper."

"Not to mention," Adair went on, "the shooting of a gangster Saturday night. Two killings in four days!"

Durant's expression was sphinxlike. "I'm not sure I follow you, Reverend. Why come to me?"

"We very much want to enlist your support in our cause."

Adair offered a quick explanation. The Galveston Ministers Association was opposed to gambling, vice, bootleg liquor, and mobsters in general. Herbert Cornwall, the Association's foremost ally, was their candidate for mayor in every election. Yet their reform movement met resistance from both the mob and many of the Island's legitimate businessmen. Money being the root of all evil, greed too often prevailed. Filthy lucre was the driving force in any election.

"We desperately need your support," Adair concluded. "You are new to town and yours will be viewed by all as an objective voice."

"I wouldn't say it's much of a voice," Durant observed. "I only got into town a couple weeks ago. Hardly anybody knows me."

"On the contrary," Reverend Baldwin announced. "Your uncle was widely respected in our community, and you have taken his place here at the bank. Your views will carry considerable weight, Mr. Durant."

"And there's William Magruder," Adair hastily added. "He actively works to defeat all reform, and he and your uncle were archenemies. You would be marching to the cause in your uncle's footsteps."

"I don't know," Durant said uncertainly. "I've never been much for politics."

Cornwall cleared his throat. "There's talk around town that the mob subjected you to a terrible beating. Diamond Jack Nolan was reported to be the ringleader." He paused, head cocked in scrutiny. "May I ask what you did to incur their anger?"

"Hard to say," Durant lied, his features deadpan. "I'd like to know myself."

"But you don't deny it's so?"

"No, I don't deny it."

Cornwall spread his hands. "Then all the more reason for you to join our cause, Mr. Durant. You will be standing foursquare against the mob *and* William Magruder."

Durant was all too aware that they were attempting to use him for their own purposes. But by joining the reform movement, there was the possibility it would deter the mob from coming after him. As he thought it through, there semed every likelihood the mob would hesitate to kill a man aligned with the clergy. There was the added bonus of hitting back at Magruder. He liked it.

"All right," he said after a prolonged silence. "I'm on the bandwagon. Count me in."

"Excellent!" Reverend Adair crowed. "We are delighted to have you with us. Absolutely delighted!"

"How do we go about it?" Durant asked. "What do you want from me?"

"Nothing just yet," Adair said. "We first have to formulate a plan to win public support. Perhaps we'll be able to get something in the newspaper."

"Our congregations are the starting point," Reverend Baldwin said, nodding sagely. "On Sunday, we'll deliver sermons condemning gangsters and murderers. We must rally the Christian brotherhood to our cause."

"Amen," Reverend Adair added. "God loves a righteous scrap."

The meeting ended on that note. Durant showed them to the door with a round of handshakes, and returned to his desk. A moment later, Aldridge stepped into the office, clearly overcome by curiosity. His expression was one of bemusement.

"Aren't you the popular fellow," he said. "What was that all about?"

Durant wagged his head. "Believe it or not, they recruited me into the reform movement."

"Yes, they've been trying to reform Galveston for years. I assume the Johnson boy's murder last night has them steaming?"

"Yeah, they're steamed, all right. They're talking about taking the fight to the mob. God against the gangsters."

"You already have a bull's-eye on your back. Doesn't joining them put you at even more risk?"

Durant smiled. "Ira, it might just save my life."

Chapter Twelve

Quinn and Voight arrived at Magruder's office shortly before one o'clock. The moment they came through the door, they knew there was trouble in the works. The air was all but frosty.

Magruder was enthroned behind his desk. George Seagrave was seated in a wingback chair, and Sherm was in his usual spot on the couch. They looked like barnyard owls, their features solemn.

"Have a chair," Magruder said without preamble. "I've called you here on a matter of the utmost urgency."

Quinn and Voight seated themselves. Seagrave gave them a perfunctory nod, then averted his gaze. There was a moment of terse silence while Magruder seemed to collect himself. His color was high.

"We have an untenable situation," he said in an orotund voice. "Last night one of your homicidal maniacs killed a man in cold blood. What do you have to say for yourselves?"

Voight glowered at him. "Who the hell are you to call us on the carpet? I don't like your Goddamn attitude."

"Nor I yours," Magruder said sullenly. "The reformers are out bleating their usual denouncements of George and myself, and the political structure of Galveston County. They threatened the mayor with everything short of crucifixion."

"Pryor scares too easy," Voight retorted. "So do you and George, if you want my opinion. These reformers are all hot air. Always have been."

"No, you're wrong," Seagrave said sharply. "The

murder of an innocent man gives them the underpinnings of a moral crusade. They could bring us all down."

Quinn shifted in his chair. "We've beaten back the reformers any number of times over the years. All this will blow over in a few days."

"You miss the point entirely," Magruder informed him. "George and I provide immunity for your activities on the Island. If they bring us down, they bring you down." He paused, staring across the desk. "We must find a solution—quickly."

"Quickly, as in today," Seagrave added. "We have to defuse these reformers before they get started. By tomorrow, they'll be pounding their drum all over town."

Voight laughed sourly. "You want 'em defused? Hell, we'll just kill Lera and dump his body outside City Hall. How's that for a solution?"

Magruder and Seagrave appeared startled. They exchanged a wary glance, weighing the repercussions of so final a solution. Magruder finally shook his head.

"However fitting, it simply won't do," he said. "We can't afford another dead man, even a murderer. More violence would add fuel to the fire."

"So what's the answer?" Quinn asked. "You don't like our solution—what's yours?"

Magruder steepled his fingers. "George and I have talked it over, and we feel there's only one prudent measure. Your man Lera must stand trial for murder."

"You're nuts!" Voight woofed. "You expect Lera to strap himself into the electric chair? That'll be the day!"

"What we expect," Seagrave said firmly, "is for you and Ollie to convince him to surrender. Only a jury trial will take the wind out of the reformers' sails. We need a public display of justice."

Quinn and Voight looked at each other. They suddenly realized that the matter had been discussed, and settled, long before they arrived. Magruder and Seagrave were playing them like violins. Cleverly, a step at a time, they were being manipulated.

"You boys are dreaming," Voight said. "You want us to convince Lera to commit suicide. Why not ask pigs to fly?"

"There is no other way," Magruder said with conviction. "The community must have its spectacle—a catharsis—see him tried and convicted in a court of law. Only then will we squelch the reformers."

Voight snorted. "How the Christ are we supposed to pull that off? Lera's on the lam and we don't have a clue where he's at. He could be in China by now."

"Yes, but you're looking for him," Seagrave said with a studious gaze. "He broke your rule—*your* law against violence—and you intend to kill him. Isn't that true?"

"So what?" Voight said gruffly. "We take care of our own in our own way. Nobody's complained so far."

"But we must have him *alive!*" Magruder trumpeted. "How can I make you understand the salient point in all this? We cannot allow the reformers to mount a crusade in the name of God and church."

"Dutch—" Quinn waited until he had Voight's attention. "I've been sitting here thinking about it, and they're right. A murder gives the reformers all they need to preach hellfire and damnation. They could bust our balloon."

"And?" Voight stared at him. "What's the rest of it? What are you saying?"

"I think we should listen to what they're saying about Lera."

"Even if we found him, so what? You think he's gonna roll over and agree to stand trial?"

"I think we could *make* him agree."

Something unspoken passed between them, and Voight finally nodded. "All right," he said, looking from Seagrave to Magruder. "No promises, but we'll give it a try. Our boys are already looking for him, anyway."

"I couldn't be more pleased," Seagrave said with a sigh of relief. "We knew we could count on you and Ollie."

The meeting concluded with a sense of harmony restored. Magruder mentioned that he would like to have a word with Quinn and Voight, on a matter of personal business. Seagrave, as usual, preferred not to know what such business entailed. He left after an exchange of handshakes.

When the door closed, Magruder sank back in his chair. "I am reminded of the line from *Macbeth*. 'Double, double, toil and trouble.' "

Voight gave him a blank look. Quinn, who had some passing knowledge of Shakespeare, suddenly became alert. "Don't tell me there are more problems?"

"I'm afraid so," Magruder said, his eyes glum. "I've learned that Earl Durant has joined forces with the reformers."

Voight frowned. "How'd you find that out?"

"Like you, Dutch, I have my sources. I received a call just before lunch."

"Talk about odd company," Quinn said speculatively. "I wouldn't think Durant has much in common with preachers. Not after the way he shot it out with our boys."

"Be that as it may," Magruder said. "So long as he is involved with the reformers, you cannot harm him. That would merely galvanize Adair and Baldwin to greater action."

"How long do we wait?" Voight said, his eyes cold. "Maybe it slipped your mind, he killed one of our men."

"You wait until I say otherwise. I must insist you follow my wishes in this matter."

"You're hurting yourself, you know," Quinn smoothly intervened. "You'll never get that bank till we get Durant."

Magruder waved him off. "We have more pressing problems at the moment. Specifically, this fellow Lera."

"And after we deliver him?" Voight persisted. "How about we tend to Durant?"

"All in good time, Dutch. All in good time."

Magruder was struck by a wayward thought. He told

himself he had much in common with Daniel Webster. So much so the irony was difficult to escape.

He too had sold his soul to the Devil.

A brilliant orange sunset shimmered off the waters of the bay. Guido's was slowly filling with the early evening dinner trade. Waiters scurried back and forth through the restaurant.

Durant and Catherine were seated at a window table. Tonight was the first time he'd asked her out since the shooting incident. He had waited, concerned for her safety, certain the mob would try to exact revenge. But his alliance with the reformers, by now public knowledge, had altered the scheme of things. He thought he'd bought himself some insurance.

Catherine was confused. She was immensely attracted to him, and after their date Saturday night, she believed it was mutual. Then four days had passed with hardly a word or a smile, his manner somehow distant, strangely impersonal. She had accepted his invitation tonight, hoping she'd imagined his odd behavior. She tried to put a bright face on things.

"You're the talk of the office," she said, after the waiter had taken their orders. "Two pastors and Herbert Cornwall calling on you! Everyone's dying of curiosity."

Durant chuckled. "Believe it or not, I've been enlisted into the reform movement. Just about the last thing I ever expected."

"What are they reforming against?"

"You heard about the shooting last night?"

"Yes, it was dreadful," she said with a little shudder. "No one's safe from these gangsters."

"That's the whole idea," Durant said. "The preachers and Cornwall intend to use the murder as a political springboard. They want to run the mob out of town."

"Oh, they've been trying to do that for years. I'm not surprised a murder has set them off again. But why would they come to you?"

"Couple reasons, the first being Magruder. They know I'm at odds with him because of the bank, and they say he's involved in dirty politics. They figured I'd be a natural to hop on the bandwagon."

"Magruder's certainly dirty," she agreed. "You said there was another reason?"

"The mob," Durant replied. "They knew I'd gotten beat up by Nolan and his thugs. Cornwall was especially interested about why I'm on the outs with the mob."

"What did you tell him?"

"Nothing even close to the truth. Fact is, I pretty much lied."

Durant thought he was lying to her as well. A lie of omission, however justified, was nonetheless a lie. Yet he couldn't bring himself to tell her he'd killed one of Nolan's men in the shootout Saturday night. He didn't want her to see him in that light, to think of him in that way. A killer.

"Listening to you—" she hesitated, her features set in a musing expression. "Well, I was wondering if this wouldn't anger those gangsters even more. You joining with the reformers, I mean."

"Ira asked me the same thing. I'm betting they'll think twice now. Wouldn't look good to jump a man associated with preachers."

"I hope you're right."

"That makes two of us."

The waiter brought their plates. He served Catherine veal cutlets with carrots and peas, and Durant a T-bone steak with a baked potato. As Durant cut into his steak, he told himself he'd let the conversation drift off course. A pretty girl deserved to be entertained, not frightened. He tried for a lighter note.

"You remember you told me how crazy you are about motion pictures?"

"Yes, I did, didn't I? What made you think of that?"

"I got to wondering—" Durant paused, a hunk of

beefsteak speared on his fork. "What's your favorite movie of all time?"

"Oh, there's no question!" her eyes shone with excitement. "It would definitely have to be *Don't Change Your Husband*."

"What was it you liked about it?"

"The laughs and humor—you'll think I'm terrible . . . and the marvelous naughtiness."

Cecil B. DeMille, the director, was ever aware of the box office. Cynicism was an outgrowth of the World War, and he sensed that audiences were bored with traditional heroes and histrionic villains. The Victorian Age was falling before the Jazz Age, rapidly being replaced by a new morality. Sex and sex appeal were in.

DeMille introduced avarice and lust, human frailty and fallibility in *Don't Change Your Husband*. In the end, virtue triumphed over infidelity, but not until the audience had a full serving of vice. DeMille's star in the movie, and a sequel, *Why Change Your Wife?*, was Gloria Swanson. She projected the glamour of a Roaring Twenties emancipated woman.

"I just adore Gloria Swanson," Catherine said gaily. "She's so beautiful, and all those furs and jewels. Have you ever met her?"

"Only in passing," Durant said with a crooked smile. "She's a real card, though. Regular prima donna."

"Oh, I love Hollywood gossip. Tell me!"

"Well, they play music on some of the sets. Directors like to put their actors in the mood."

Catherine forgot her veal cutlets as he went on to explain. The cranking grind of cameras often intruded on the concentration of actors. The noise of nearby sets being constructed or dismantled unsettled the mood as well. The sets were built next to one another, and sometimes, three or four films might be shooting at once. Every studio kept several small orchestras on hand to work different sets.

"So this one day," Durant elaborated, "Pola Negri was shooting on one set and Gloria Swanson was on the set beside her. Keep in mind, they hate each other. Couple of real cutthroats."

"I can't stand it!" Her eyes sparkled with merriment. "Don't stop, go on!"

"You have to remember movie actors take themselves pretty seriously. Especially when they're into emoting hearts and flowers."

Pola Negri, he went on, was faced with a particularly difficult emotional scene. She insisted on the soft, woeful strains of a single violin to establish the mood. She insisted as well that musicians on other sets stand down until her scene was completed. Gloria Swanson, who was piqued by the demands, quickly recruited a brass band and played a rousing military march at the critical moment. Pola Negri threw a fit, and a Hollywood feud was born.

"I love it!" Catherine said with a mischievous laugh. "I can just see it now. Gloria Swanson at the head of a brass band!"

Durant grinned. "Yeah, it blew the lid off things. Turned into a real catfight."

Her expression was still animated with laughter. "You're better than a movie magazine," she said, picking at her veal. "Do you know Greta Garbo, too?"

"I've seen her around the studios."

"Is it true what they say about her and John Gilbert?"

John Gilbert was a handsome matinee idol of the day. Greta Garbo was an exotic Swedish actress, recently imported to Hollywood. Their torrid love affair was the talk of fans everywhere.

"You haven't heard the half of it," Durant said. "Movie magazines leave out all the good stuff."

"Nooo," she breathed. "You mean there's more?"

"Lots more."

"Oh, I can't wait. Tell me!"

Durant told her all the racy details.

Bubba's Roadhouse was located on the outskirts of Texas City. The ramshackle structure was a dive that catered to the rougher crowd. Gambling, prostitution, and bootleg hooch were housed under one roof.

The dimly lighted parking lot was full. A black four-door Buick was positioned with a view of the main entrance to the roadhouse. Nolan was in the passenger seat, with Whizzer Duncan at the steering wheel, and Turk McGuire in the backseat. They waited in stony silence.

Two days had passed in their search for Lou Lera. Since Tuesday night, when he'd killed the man in Galveston, they had put out feelers to all their contacts on the mainland. Tonight, not an hour before, Nolan had received a call from a bootlegger in Texas City. Lera was bedded down with a whore at Bubba's.

Not long after ten o'clock, Lera emerged from the roadhouse. He was still dressed in the dark suit, black shirt, and white tie he'd worn the night of the shooting. As though he hadn't a care in the world, he walked toward his car, shoulders squared in a cocky manner. Nolan and his men stepped out of the Buick.

"Hello there, Lou," Nolan said in a breezy voice. "Don't try to run or I'll have Turk break your legs."

Lera's face went chalky. McGuire boxed him in from one side and Duncan the other. His mouth ticced in a weak smile, his teeth as yellow as old dice. "How'd you find me?"

Nolan shrugged. "Got a tip you were here."

"Not a smart move," Duncan said, relieving him of his pistol. "Pussy's put more'n one man in his grave. You shoulda stayed hid out."

Lera flinched. "You boys gonna kill me?"

"Depends," Nolan said cryptically. "Let's go for a ride."

"Where you takin' me?"

"Lou, the pleasure of your company has been requested. Leave it at that."

The ride back to Galveston passed in terse silence. A half hour later the Buick rolled to a stop at the side of the Hollywood Club. Nolan led the way through the kitchen entrance, with Lera sandwiched between Duncan and McGuire. The foursome followed the hall to the employees' lounge, where Duncan and McGuire stayed behind. Nolan escorted Lera next door into the office.

Quinn was seated at the desk. Voight stood by the window, a cigar jutting from his mouth. There was a cold stagnancy in his eyes as he turned, waiting for Nolan to close the door. He crossed the room, puffing his cigar, and slugged Lera with a straight shot to the jaw. Cuddles, the parrot, screeched, hiding his eyes behind a wing. Lera hit the floor on the seat of his pants.

"You stupid sonovbitch," Voight raged. "Why'd you kill that guy?"

Lera got to his knees. "Dutch, he coldcocked me, just like you done. What was I supposed to do?"

"You weren't supposed to kill him. Why didn't you stand up and fight him like a man?"

"Honest to Christ, you should've seen the fucker. He was built like a barn."

Voight walked away in a cloud of smoke. Lera slowly levered himself off the floor and got to his feet. Quinn stared at him across the desk.

"You know the rule, Lou. We never harm civilians and we never *ever* kill them. Where was your brain?"

"Ollie, it happened too fast." Lera massaged his jaw, blood leaking from the corner of his mouth. "The cocksucker popped me, all because of that bitch Mae Hager. I just reacted, that's all."

"You just *reacted*," Voight mocked him. "That's the lamest excuse I ever heard. You went dumb in the clutch, admit it."

"Look, I'm sorry," Lera said. "I know I didn't handle it right. I got hot and lost my head."

"Too late for hindsight," Quinn said sternly. "You've put the organization in a bad light, and brought the reformers out of their holes. There's hell to pay."

"I'll do anything you say, Ollie. I swear to God I will. How do I make it right?"

"I'm glad you asked," Quinn said. "We want you to stand trial for murder."

Lera blanched. "How's that again?"

Voight's laugh was thick with anger. "Get the wax out of your ears and pay attention. You're going to stand trial and no two ways about it. Understand?"

"Gimme a break, Dutch." Lera's mouth tightened in a ghastly grimace. "They'll jam my ass in the electric chair. I'm not gonna ride Old Sparky."

"Well, you've got a choice," Voight said. "Go to trial and take your chances with a jury. Or we'll let Jack take you for a swim—right Goddamn now."

"Ohboyohboy!" Cuddles squawked. "Take him for a swim!"

Everyone looked at the parrot. Cuddles held their gazes a moment, then cocked his head and pretended interest in the ceiling. Quinn shifted in his chair.

"Lou, it's not as bad as it sounds," he said. "We'll hire the top defense attorney in Texas, whatever it costs. You'll probably walk out of court a free man."

Lera broke out in a frosty sweat. "Ollie, there's witnesses. Mae Hager'll put me in the hot seat! They'll fry my ass."

"Not to worry," Quinn assured him. "We'll send Jack around to have a talk with Mae. Depend on it, she'll have a loss of memory. Won't she, Jack?"

Nolan nodded. "She won't remember her own name. Guaranteed."

"I dunno," Lera said hesitantly. "There must've been ten or twelve people in the joint that night. How you gonna shut 'em all up?"

"Leave it to me," Nolan said confidently. "The whole bunch will turn dummy. Nothing to it."

"Yeah, but they already identified me to the cops. How you gonna get around that?"

"Quit weaseling!" Voight roared. "You've only got one choice here. Stand trial or go for a swim. Take your pick."

Lera ducked his head. "I'll stand trial."

"Good thinking," Quinn counseled. "Just make sure you keep your mouth shut about the organization. Anybody asks, you just stopped off in Mae's for a drink."

"I got it, Ollie."

"Damn sure better," Voight warned him. "You rat us out and you're a dead man. We'll get to you in jail or anywhere else."

"Hey, I'm no squealer," Lera protested. "I never met you guys in my life. Don't even know your names. How's that?"

"Keep it that way," Voight said. "You walk over to the police station and turn yourself in. Tell 'em you're surrendering voluntarily."

"I won't let you down."

"Jack will be right behind you. Change your mind between here and there, and guess what?"

Lera swallowed hard. "I'm dead."

"You finally got smart," Voight said with a mirthless laugh. "Trot on over to the cops and keep your lip buttoned. We'll have a lawyer there first thing in the morning."

Lera obediently bobbed his head. Nolan ushered him out of the office, and Quinn waited until the door closed. He looked at Voight.

"Think he'll stay mum?"

"Sure he will," Voight said with cold conviction. "Dumb as he is, he knows we mean business."

Quinn took the receiver off the phone. He jiggled the hook. "Operator, get me 8414."

There was a tinny ring on the line and William Magruder answered. "Hello."

"Bill, Ollie Quinn here."

"Why are you calling me at home? Don't you know what time it is?"

"I thought you'd want to hear the latest. Louis Lera is on his way to the police station. He's turning himself in."

"Well now, that is good news. Excellent work, Ollie. Excellent."

"All's well that ends well, Bill. We'll talk tomorrow."

Quinn replaced the receiver on the hook. He smiled humorously at Voight. "Dutch, we've saved Galveston again. We deserve a medal."

"Forget the medal," Voight said gruffly. "I want Durant."

"And you'll have him. Once the reformers lose steam, he's all yours."

"We'll see if the bastard can walk on water."

"Waterwater!" Cuddles echoed. "Take him for a swim!"

Voight grunted. "Goddamn bird's too smart for his own good."

Cuddles wisely said no more.

Chapter Thirteen

The sun burnished the Gulf waters with coppery flame. The sky was opalescent and there was the smell of salt spray on the wind. Wispy clouds sped westward like ghosts fleeing an exorcism.

Clint Stoner was seated on the balcony overlooking the Gulf. The remnants of breakfast, delivered by room service, lay scattered across the table beside his chair. His attention was focused on the Friday morning edition of the *Galveston Daily Chronicle*.

The article dealt with events of late last night. He got the impression that the paper had held the presses in order to make the morning edition. The gist of the story was that Louis Lera, accused of murder, had surrendered himself to the authorities. County Prosecutor Sherwood Butler was quoted as saying he would press for a speedy trial and the death penalty. A preliminary hearing was scheduled that morning in Superior Court.

Stoner was intrigued by the case. He'd followed developments in the *Chronicle* which reported the killing as taking place Tuesday evening. Several identified Lera, and there was little question he was guilty of cold-blooded murder. There seemed no question as well that Lera was in the rackets, operating the slot machine concession. A henchman of Oliver Quinn and Dutch Voight.

The manhunt that followed was heavily reported in the paper. Every lawman from Houston to the Gulf was on the lookout, and Lera had clearly gone into hiding to avoid arrest. Yet, out of the blue and with no explanation, he had surfaced last night and voluntarily surrendered to the police. All of which raised the question of why a man facing the electric chair would suddenly turn himself in. Why indeed?

Janice came out of the suite onto the balcony. She was dressed for the day, wearing a navy skirt and a pastel blue blouse, with a scarf at the throat. Stoner gave her an appreciative look remembering last night in bed, when she wore nothing at all. Their eleven days on the Island seemed to have passed in a blur, except for the nights. She made the nights memorable.

"Look at you," she said, kissing him on the cheek. "A man of leisure sunning himself with his newspaper."

"I need my rest," Stoner said with a sly smile. "You keep me all wore out."

"I recall I had a little help, pumpkin. I think I'll rename you Randy Andy."

"Things come over me when the lights go out."

"You're telling me!"

She poured coffee and nibbled on toast, ever conscious of her figure. Stoner laid the paper on the table, tapping the article, and gave her a nutshell version of Lera's surrender. She glanced at him over the rim of her cup.

"That's one for the funny farm," she said, puzzling on it a moment. "Why would someone who's sure to get electrified just up and surrender? It doesn't make sense."

"Maybe it does," Stoner said. "What if there was something worse than the electric chair?"

"Cripes, what could be worse than that?"

"I've been sitting here thinking about it. Only one thing comes to me."

"Aha! Sherlock at work again. Go ahead, enlighten me, Mr. Holmes."

"Glad to, Dr. Watson." Stoner leaned forward, elbows on the table. "Suppose Quinn and Voight somehow got their hands on this guy Lera. Suppose they put it to him in a way he couldn't refuse."

"Ummm," she said, munching toast. "Why couldn't he refuse?"

"Suppose there were only two options. One, you turn yourself into the cops. Or two, you get killed right now, something tough and dirty. Which would you choose?"

"You think they would really do something horrendous?"

"Jan, they're gangsters," Stoner said grimly. "Forget the Hollywood Club and all the glitz. They've got ways to kill people that would spoil your breakfast."

"Now you tell me!" she yelped. "What happens if they catch us?"

"I warned you before we came here. Don't get nervous on me now."

"Who, me? For your information, I have nerves of steel. Nothing fazes me."

"I'll hold you to it," Stoner said with a smile. "You're my number-one undercover operative."

"I'm your *only* undercover operative," she informed him. "Something bothers me about this Lera, though."

"What's that?"

"Why would Quinn and Voight want him to stand trial? What do they gain?"

Stoner thought it was a key question. Over the last week or so he'd eavesdropped on conversations in bars and gaming dives, and studiously read everything printed in the paper. Slowly, like an intricate mosaic, he had pieced together who was who in the Galveston power structure. Quinn and Voight, with their army of hoodlums, controlled the rackets. Yet the real power brokers, from all he could determine, were William Magruder and George Seagrave.

Magruder and Seagrave, by all accounts, controlled the political apparatus of Galveston County. Quinn and Voight, by virtue of bribes and payoffs, operated under immunity from law enforcement and the courts. So it followed, as he fitted the pieces together, that some link existed between the mob and the two most prominent men on the Island. Corrupt politicians wedded to racketeers required the blessing of those who ruled the ballot box.

Magruder and Seagrave were the names that came to mind.

Stoner recalled as well the evening he'd tried to bluff his way into the Hollywood Club casino. He remembered that Oliver Quinn had shown special treatment to a large party celebrating a girl's birthday. The maitre d' had told him the girl's father was William Magruder, and, in retrospect, it made sense that the other older man at the table was George Seagrave. Thinking about it now, Stoner wasn't surprised that Quinn was playing footsy with the Island's royal families. Even racketeers sometimes went on bended knee.

How all that played on his investigation was, for the moment, a matter of conjecture. His assignment was to bring down Quinn and Voight, and he warned himself not to muddy the waters with dirty politics. He suddenly realized he'd drifted off into woolgathering about things beyond the scope of his investigation. Janice was watching him with a pixilated expression.

"Knock, knock, anybody there? Aren't you going to answer my question?"

"I don't know the answer," Stoner said with a shrug. "Why Quinn and Voight put Lera in jail is anybody's guess. We've got other things on our plate anyhow."

"Let me consult my crystal ball." She wrinkled her brow in mock concentration. "Yes, I believe I see it now—the Hollywood Club."

"Give the little lady a cigar. I think it's time we made our move."

"Dare I ask why, Mr. Holmes?"

"Elementary, Dr. Watson." Stoner wagged a hand back and forth. "We've built our cover story with me the rich sucker and money to burn. Today's our day."

"So how do we work this magic act?"

"I'd say it's more of a tap dance. Let's go see our buddy Charlie Anderson."

Downstairs, they walked through the lobby to the office of the manager. By now, with their lavish suite and generous tips, they were familiar to every employee in the hotel. Charles Anderson, the manager, welcomed them into his office with the courtesy reserved for wealthy guests. He offered them chairs before his desk.

"Mr. Eberling. Mrs. Eberling," he said unctuously. "Hope you're enjoying your stay with us. How may I help you today?"

"Need you to use your influence," Stoner said, adopting his rancher persona. "You'll recollect you told me to call on you for a favor? Anything at all?"

"Why, yes, of course, I certainly do. How may I be of assistance?"

"The missus and me would like to have a whirl at the casino over in the Hollywood Club. I figured you're just the man to open the door."

"Easier said than done," Anderson remarked. "The Hollywood Club requires membership for the casino. They're very selective about their patrons."

"Hell's bells and little fishes!" Stoner grumped. "I've been losin' money hand over fist at the Garden Club and all these other crooked joints. I hear the Hollywood Club's got square games. I want you to fix it for me, Charlie."

"Well—" Anderson appeared uncomfortable. "As I said, they are very, *very* selective."

Stoner slapped a hundred-dollar bill on the desk. "Lookit here now, Charlie, I'm plumb serious. Olive'll tell you so herself."

"Oh my, yes," Janice said, jumping into her role of the good little wife. "Bob just has his heart set on this, Mr. Anderson. Couldn't you help us . . . *pleeeze?*"

"Perhaps I could." Anderson deftly palmed the hundred-dollar bill. "I'll make a call and see what might be arranged. No promises, you understand. I can only try."

"Good enough for me," Stoner said with a broad grin. "I knew you'd pull it off, Charlie. Let me know, you hear?"

"I'll definitely be in touch, Mr. Eberling."

Outside the office, Janice laughed gaily. "What a ham

you are, *Mr. Eberling*. I think you tap-danced us into the
Hollywood Club."

"Olive, darlin', I think you're right. Damned if I
don't!"

They went off for a day of sight-seeing.

"Your friends are here again."

"What friends?"

"Reverend Adair and Reverend Baldwin. And of
course, our mayor in waiting, Herbie Cornwall."

Durant's brow furrowed. "Wonder what they want?"

"I don't know," Catherine said with an ingenuous
smile. "Should I ask them?"

"No, send them in."

Durant was immediately on guard. In the morning
paper, he'd read that Louis Lera had surrendered to the
police last night. His first reaction was one of surprise,
for men who faced the death penalty rarely surrendered
themselves voluntarily. His second was that Lera's surrender would largely defuse the reform movement. The
preachers would have little to preach about on Sunday,
for the accused was now in jail. Justice was taking its
course.

The clergymen, followed by Cornwall, filed into the
office. Their manner was that of Crusaders who had been
thwarted in their quest for the Holy Grail. Durant got them
seated as Catherine gave him a waggish look and closed
the door. Reverend Baldwin went straight to the point.

"I assume you've read the paper?"

Durant nodded. "Most men wouldn't turn themselves
in, not with the evidence that's been reported. Curious
thing."

"Curious indeed," Baldwin said. "We've talked it
over, and we're of the opinion there was nothing volun-
tary about his surrender. He was forced into it."

"That's even curiouser," Durant commented. "How
do you force a man to risk the electric chair?"

Adair grunted. "Oliver Quinn and Dutch Voight are in league with the Devil. I'm sure they found a way."

"All part of a greater conspiracy," Baldwin added. "The objective being to derail the impetus of our reform movement. Which they have accomplished with infuriating ease."

Cornwall arched an eyebrow. "Does the idea of a conspiracy surprise you, Mr. Durant?"

"I'm not sure I follow you," Durant said. "Are you talking about Quinn and Voight?"

"Think back to our last visit," Cornwall said. "Do you recall I asked about the beating you took at the hands of Nolan and his thugs?"

Durant held his gaze. "What's that got to do with anything?"

"Your answer was quite evasive," Cornwall said. "Something to the effect you weren't sure of the reason yourself."

"So?"

"So we think you were less than candid."

"Are you calling me a liar?"

"Nothing of the kind!" Baldwin interrupted. "Let us raise a hypothetical. Is that agreeable?"

Durant shrugged. "Fire away."

"Everyone accepts without question that William Magruder and George Seagrave are the political kingpins of Galveston County."

"And it's hardly a secret," Adair chimed in, "that Magruder and Seagrave tacitly condone the mob's illegal enterprises. All for the sake of a booming economy."

"Which leads to the conclusion," Baldwin carried on, "that Magruder and Seagrave have a working relationship—perhaps mutual interests—with the underworld element. From that, we might naturally assume there is a reciprocal arrangement of some nature."

"So we could hypothesize," Adair said, "that if—*if!*—Magruder had designs on your bank, and you refused to sell. . . ."

"Presto!" Baldwin took his cue. "Magruder might well request assistance from his underworld cronies. . . ."

"And have you beat to a pulp," Cornwall concluded. "All to intimidate you into selling your bank. How does that sound for a hypothetical?"

Durant stared at them. "How long did you boys rehearse this act?"

"We beg your candor," Adair said. "Is it true or not?"

"Sticking to the hypothetical," Durant replied, "what if it was? What's your point?"

"We have a common foe," Adair said earnestly. "Our community is under siege by a criminal conspiracy. Your bank is in jeopardy."

"Not to mention you, personally," Baldwin observed. "The next time these hooligans attack you they may not stop with a simple beating. And I believe you'll agree, Magruder will ensure there is a next time."

Durant's expression betrayed nothing. He wasn't about to tell them that there had already been a next time, men with guns intent on killing him. Nor was he willing to entrust them with the knowledge that he'd killed one of the mob's men. His gut warned him that no secret was safe with holier-than-thou reformers.

"Why the big sales pitch?" he said at length. "What is it you want from me?"

"We want proof," Baldwin said simply. "Proof that links William Magruder to these mobsters."

"And everyone benefits," Adair hurried on. "We obtain substantial grounds for reform, and you save your bank as well as eliminating the risk of further violence. Nothing could be more perfect."

"You just lost me," Durant said. "How am I supposed to get proof on Magruder?"

"Trick him," Cornwall said slyly. "By outwitting Magruder this long, you've shown yourself to be a clever man. Trick him into an admission of his dealings with Quinn and Voight."

"What if I did?" Durant said skeptically. "It's his

word against mine, and he's top dog in Galveston. Who'd believe me?"

Baldwin laughed softly. "We're not talking a court of law, Mr. Durant. We're talking a court of public opinion, as preached from our pulpits. That is where the next election will be won."

"And your private fight as well," Cornwall rushed to add. "Your bank will be saved, and your personal safety will be assured. Neither Magruder nor the mob will defy public opinion."

Durant looked from one to the other. Their argument was persuasive, for public opinion was not a force to be ignored. Yet he saw even greater risk if he tried to trick Magruder into something incriminating and failed. He warned himself not to jump too fast.

"I'll think about it," he said finally. "No promises, but I'll think it over."

"Time is of the essence," Baldwin persisted. "How long will you need?"

"I'll give you an answer tomorrow."

"Splendid!" Adair grinned like a horse eating briars. "We know you won't let us down. Nor yourself, for that matter. All in a good cause!"

The three men left after wringing his hand in fellowship. Durant leaned back in his chair, his eyes fixed on the middle distance. Nothing was ever as simple as it seemed to the schemers of the world.

He wondered how the hell he could trap Magruder.

The men began trooping into the Turf Club shortly before eleven o'clock. They took the elevator to the third floor, where they were frisked by Jack Nolan and Turk McGuire. Firearms, knives and brass knuckles were consigned to a box in the athletic club.

The meeting was held across the hall in the billiards room. The men gathered there were the vice chiefs of the Island, operating under the largesse of their overlords. Quinn and Voight had summoned them, though the purpose of the meeting was not announced. None of the men felt bold enough to ask.

Dan Lampis ran part of the slot machine concession. His counterpart, Lou Lera, was in jail for murder, and he hoped to take over the entire business. Sam Amelio owned seven whorehouses, and Gus Allen operated two of the larger gaming joints, the Garden Club and the Grotto Club. The other men, five in all, had various concessions for juke-boxes, pinball machines, and bootlegging. They were the underbosses of Galveston's underworld.

The men seated themselves in chairs arranged along the back wall of the billiards room. Nolan and McGuire took positions on either side of the door, there to ensure that the meeting was conducted in a businesslike manner. Quinn and Voight walked through the door at the stroke of eleven, and halted behind the snooker table, facing their underbosses. The room fell quiet as the men ranged along the wall waited to hear the purpose of the meeting.

Voight nodded around the room. "You boys are here because of what's happened over the past week. Anybody that's not deaf, dumb and blind knows we damn near handed the reformers our operation on a silver platter."

The men murmured their assent. Quinn silenced them with an upraised palm. "We got off the hook with some fast moves and a little luck. Lou Lera's surrender to the cops was the only thing that saved us. Otherwise the reformers would have started a crusade to clean us out."

"Holy roller cocksuckers," Sam Amelio grated. "Why don't we bump off a couple and teach 'em a lesson? They'd learn to keep their traps shut."

"You always were a stupe," Voight said, fixing him with a hard glare. "Lera killin' that civilian was what got us into hot water. Wise up, for chrissake."

Amelio looked stung. "I didn't mean no harm, Dutch."

"That's the trouble with you lunkheads," Voight said hotly. "Your mouth gets ahead of your brain, and before you know it, you've done something stupid. All that's gonna end today."

"Lera's a case in point," Quinn said. "He pulled a gun when he should've walked away, or at worst, fought the guy even-steven. Everybody has to put the good of the organization first. Forget the rough stuff."

The men swapped glances. They thought it was an odd statement, considering the fate of Joey Adonis. A week ago today Adonis and a couple of his goons were spotted at the Funland Amusement Pier. They seemingly vanished that evening, and while no one had the moxie to ask what happened, everyone in the room knew. Adonis and his boys were at the bottom of the Gulf.

"Talkin' about Lera," Dan Lampis said, his expression one of guileless curiosity. "How'd you and Dutch get him to face charges . . . if you don't mind my askin'?"

"Lou's a stand-up guy," Quinn said with genuine duplicity. "He understood what was best for the organization and he did it. Our hats are off to him."

No one believed a word of it. There was talk that Quinn and Voight had brought in a top defense attorney from Houston, and Lera intended to enter a plea of not guilty. The consensus was that he would nonetheless ride Old Sparky into the next life.

"The reason I asked about Lou," Lampis said, pressing his case. "Somebody's got to take over his end of the slots, and it ought to be somebody that knows the territory. I was thinkin' it might be me."

"Hold that for another time," Quinn said. "We're here to talk about other things."

"Get the wax out of your ears and pay attention!"

Voight's tone was like the rasp of sandpaper. He leaned forward, his hands gripping the edge of the snooker table, and his cold stare ranged over the men along the wall. His attitude was one of open menace.

"The *Rule*," he said coarsely. "The Rule says you don't touch a civilian, don't rough him up, and you Goddamn sure don't kill him. That's the way we've operated from day one."

"And for good reason," Quinn added. "We need good public relations to keep things perking along. Harm a civilian and you put the organization at risk."

"Lou Lera's the exception," Voight told them. "We needed him to stand trial to get the reformers off our back. But starting today, there's not gonna be any more exceptions. No way, no how."

The men returned his gaze as though under the spell of a hypnotist. A leaden stillness settled over the room as he glowered at them, his icy stare touching one, then another. His eyes were hooded.

"Here's the story," he said. "From now on, you break the Rule and there's no excuses, no second chances. Jack will take it from there."

Every eye in the room shifted to Diamond Jack Nolan. He looked back at them with an ironic smile, and they understood exactly what the smile meant. He would kill any man who broke the Rule.

"Everybody got it?" Voight demanded. "You screw up, we're not gonna go through this again. Now's the time to speak up if you've got any questions."

There were no questions. Quinn, never one for loose ends, decided to tie it off. "One last thing," he said. "Spread the word to everybody who works for you, anybody you're associated with, anybody who could get you in hot water. No matter what, no matter why—" he paused for emphasis—"live by the Rule."

The alternative, they all understood, would be unpleasant, and final. The men filed out of the room, bobbing their heads with nervous smiles as they turned toward the elevator. Quinn and Voight walked down the hall to their office. The phone rang as they came through the door. Voight lifted the receiver.

"Yeah."

"Mr. Voight?"

"How'd you get my private number?"

"You gave it to me, Mr. Voight. This is Charles Anderson, manager at the Buccaneer."

"How're things, Chuck? What can I do for you?"

"I have a guest in the hotel," Anderson said. "A wealthy rancher with more money than sense. He's set on trying his luck at your casino."

"Where's he from?" Voight said. "You know anything about him?"

"His ranch is in Blanco County. I know he's lost considerable money at the Garden Club and other spots. He's heard you have the only honest games in town."

"How long's he been at the hotel?"

"Almost two weeks."

"Would you vouch for him?"

"Well, yes, I suppose," Anderson said hesitantly. "He and his wife are big spenders. Very generous."

Voight laughed. "Gave you a tip to call me, did he?"

"Only a hundred, Mr. Voight. I didn't see any harm."

"What's his name?"

"Robert Eberling."

"I'll get back to you."

Voight disconnected. He waited a moment, then jiggled the hook. "Operator? Get me 3684 in Austin."

"Yessir, connecting your call."

There was a metallic buzz on the line, three rings, and a man answered. "Burnett Detective Agency."

"John, this is Dutch Voight. I want you to check somebody out for me."

"Glad to, Mr. Voight," Burnett said. "Who's the party?"

"Robert Eberling," Voight told him. "Supposed to have a big ranch in Blanco County. Find out if he's legit."

"I'll call you with the rundown, Mr. Voight. Probably later today."

Voight replaced the receiver on the hook. One gambler more or less was of no great concern, and he dismissed the matter from mind. He looked around at Quinn.

"So how'd we do, Ollie? Think the boys will toe the line?"

Quinn smiled. "Dutch, I just suspect our troubles are over. No more grist for the reformers."

Voight thought brute force and sudden death were the most persuasive of arguments. He told himself the message would spread through town by noon. Live by the Rule. . . .

Or say hello and good-bye to Diamond Jack Nolan.

Chapter Fourteen

The Rice Hotel was located in downtown Houston. One of the city's older hotels, it was home away from home for visiting salesmen and businessmen. The lobby was appointed with heroic murals of the Texas Revolution.

Nolan, right on time, arrived at two o'clock. He went into the coffee shop and took a table with a view of the door. Earlier, after the meeting with the underbosses, he'd told Quinn he needed the afternoon off. The hours he worked entitled him to free time whenever he could fit it into the schedule. He wasn't expected at the Hollywood Club until that evening.

Libbie entered the coffee shop a few minutes after two. She had taken the interurban railway from Galveston, rather than be seen driving her sporty Chevrolet coupe. Her simple day dress was conservative compared to her flapper outfits, worn so she wouldn't attract undue attention. She crossed to the table and took a seat, her cheeks flushed with excitement. She breathed a nervous little laugh.

"God, I feel like Mata Hari. Do I look like I'm spying for the Germans?"

"You look beautiful," Nolan said, trying to calm her nerves. "Sorry for all the sneaking around, but it couldn't be helped. I'd be up the creek if my bosses found out."

Four days had passed since their afternoon of lovemaking at the Rendezvous Roadhouse. They had talked on the phone in the interim and decided the roadhouse was too close to Galveston. Nolan had suggested Houston, and the Rice Hotel, for their liaison today. Neither of them questioned that their affair was worth any risk.

A waitress drifted by and took their orders for coffee. Libbie waited until she was out of earshot. "I hate to sound naïve, but I've never done this before. How do we arrange a room?"

"Already done," Nolan said in a low voice. "I registered before you got here. We're in Room three-o-four."

"Do we just take the elevator up there—in broad daylight?"

"No, I'll leave and you finish your coffee. Give it five minutes and then come on up."

"Now I do feel like Mata Hari."

"Just act natural and nobody's the wiser. See you upstairs."

Nolan dropped a dollar on the table and left the coffee shop. A few minutes later he opened the door of Room 304 and Libbie quickly stepped inside from the hallway. Her cheeks were even rosier.

"The elevator operator ogled me all the way up. I don't think we fooled him."

"Elevator operators don't bother me."

Nolan enfolded her in his arms. She pressed herself against him, her arms around his neck, and their mouths met in a feverish kiss. They'd both spent four days thinking about the last time, and there was an urgency in their need. He lifted her in his arms and carried her to the bed.

Their haste left clothes strewn across the floor. Her passion was wild and atavistic, and he marveled again at her total lack of inhibition. Their lovemaking was filled with the zest of discovery, playful yet lustily fierce, unbounded by convention. When at last they parted, exquisitely sated, he was still amazed by the depth of her hunger. A welter of claw marks on his back bore testament to her fiery nature.

She snuggled close, her head against his shoulder. A warm breath, soft and velvety, eddied through the hair on his chest. He glanced around and found her watching him with an impish smile. She hugged him in a tight embrace.

"Do you believe in love at first sight?"

Nolan looked away. "I'm not the kind of guy you want to love."

"Because you're a gangster?" She plucked a hair from his chest, laughing when he winced. "I'll choose my own man, thank you very much."

"We're from worlds about as far apart as you can get. I don't think you'd much like mine."

"Oh, so it's just a quick roll in the hay. Wham, bam and thank you, ma'am?"

"You know better than that."

"'Fess up, tough guy." She wrapped a knot of his hair around her finger and threatened to pull. "Did you fall for me or not? Am I your girl?"

Nolan was forced to grin. "You're my girl if that's what you want. You're asking for trouble, though."

"I'm perfectly content to worry about that when it happens."

Libbie was less certain than she sounded. She was a spoiled rich girl, her father's favorite, even though Sherm was the heir to the throne. She had attended Bryn Mawr, a college for rich girls in Pennsylvania, where she became a convert in the struggle for women's emancipation. Her heroine was Susan B. Anthony, who had founded the suffrage movement almost seventy-five years ago. She often thought Susan B. would have approved of flappers.

Women got the vote when the Nineteenth Amendment cleared Congress in 1920. Four years ago, Libbie had cast her ballot for Warren G. Harding, who disappointed her by being branded the most corrupt president in history. But she had studied Lenin and the Bolshevist movement in school, and later waded through the uneasy marriage of democracy, free enterprise, and capitalism. Whatever the form of government, corruption seemed an integral part of the system, and if America could survive a crooked president, she saw nothing wrong with a gangster for a boyfriend. She wasn't so sure about her father.

Nolan, for his part, was crystal clear about their situation. Before the war, like his father and his father's father, he had worked on fishing boats operating out of Texas City. He had known poverty and hardship, scrimping to pay the rent and put food on the table, and it shaded his outlook on life. During the war, his father had died aboard a boat caught in a Gulf storm, and a few months later, his mother passed away of a broken heart. His background, a workingman who won some medals in France and then turned gangster, was not the stuff of high society. He thought Libbie was fooling herself if she believed it didn't matter.

Then, as she snuggled closer in his arms, he realized he was just as foolish. Quinn and Voight, if they ever learned he was sleeping with Magruder's daughter, would probably take *him* for a swim. Their political ties to Magruder, and the continued prosperity of their criminal enterprises, would cast him as the sacrificial goat. Yet, even as he considered the possibility, he knew he wouldn't stop seeing her. He'd survived the Krauts and the trenches of France, and working for the mob, he lived with danger every day of his life. A little more danger, in the form of the girl cuddled next to him, added spice to the game.

She darted his ear with her tongue. She laughed, her mouth moist and inviting, and he kissed her. His hand covered one of her high, jutting breasts, and the nipple swelled instantly. For several moments they caressed and fondled, until finally, aroused and aching, she drew him on top of her. A shudder racked her, and her legs spidered around him, pulling faster and faster with the rhythm of his stroke. Her nails pierced his back like talons as they joined in an explosive spasm.

Afterward, breathing heavily, time lost all meaning. She clung to his hard-muscled frame, carried far beyond her most vivid fantasies. A while later, drifting on a quenched flame, they kissed again, their bodies warm and their legs intertwined. She pressed her mouth to his ear in a throaty whisper.

"Any doubts now?"

"About what?"

"Love at first sight."

Nolan chuckled softly. "You want the truth?"

"Nothing but."

"I think we're stuck with one another."

"Oh, God, isn't it great!"

She kissed him so hard his ears rang.

Durant sat staring at the wall. All morning, and during a solitary lunch at a nearby café, he'd mulled over his meeting with the reform committee. He still hadn't made a decision.

The problem was twofold. First, he kept asking himself if an attempt to trap Magruder would provoke further action by the mob. And second, he stewed on how he might gull Magruder into what amounted to a confession. Hard questions with no ready answers.

Around three o'clock he came to the conclusion he was getting nowhere. He generally kept his own counsel, but today he realized the road walked by an individualist was a lonely one. If nothing else, he needed a sounding board, or maybe a devil's advocate, to put things in perspective. He buzzed Aldridge and Catherine, and asked them to come in.

They already knew something was up. He'd hardly spoken to anyone since the meeting that morning with the reformers. Even more telling, he had put Aldridge off on pending bank affairs, and done it in a rather abrupt manner. Neither of them doubted that it somehow involved the clergymen and Herbert Cornwall. But they couldn't have imagined what he was about to tell them.

Durant waited until they'd taken chairs before his desk. He then explained that he faced a difficult decision, and asked for their opinion. As they listened, he summarized the salient points, stressing the fact that the surrender of Louis Lera, the accused murderer, had undercut the chances of a reform movement. He went on to relate the plan that had been proposed, and how the reformers believed it would ignite their crusade. He admitted he was stumped.

"I'm damned if I do and damned if I don't," he concluded. "Whichever way I turn it, I don't see a smart choice."

"Good Lord," Aldridge said with a troubled frown. "Confronting Magruder would most certainly trigger another assault by his mobster friends. How can you even consider it?"

"Question is, would it?" Durant said. "It's been almost a week since they jumped me. Maybe siding with the reformers bought me a pass."

"A week?" Catherine sounded confused. "It was almost two weeks ago they beat you up. Has something happened I don't know about?"

Durant realized he'd made a slip of the lip. He involuntarily glanced at Aldridge, who kept a straight face. His lie of omission—not telling Catherine he had shot and killed a gangster—seemed in retrospect a mistake. Yet he saw nothing for it but to carry on with the deception. He gestured in an idle motion.

"You're right," he said dismissively. "Too many things on my mind. It's closer to two weeks."

Catherine searched his eyes. "Well, anyway," she said after a moment, "I'm not sure I agree with Mr. Aldridge. I hope you won't be offended. . . ."

"No, no," Aldridge said hurriedly. "Say whatever's on your mind."

"I think Earl—Mr. Durant—was right. Working with the reformers might protect him rather than harm him. Even gangsters have to be concerned with public opinion."

"Yes, that's true," Aldridge conceded. "Earl and I talked it over and came to the same conclusion. The thing that bothers me most is the idea of confronting Magruder."

"What's the option?" Durant said, probing for a reaction. "Without a strong reform movement, we're back to status quo. Magruder could sic his pals on me and nothing to stop him. He still wants to get his hands on this bank."

"No question of it," Aldridge agreed. "Nothing has changed with respect to his designs on the bank."

"So the only solution is to bring him down. Him *and* his mob buddies."

"Yes, that's what I meant a moment ago," Catherine said. "To protect yourself and the bank, you have to put them on the defensive. You really have no choice."

"You know—" Durant rubbed the bridge of his nose, thoughtful. "I think you just helped me to make up my mind. It's time to take the fight to them."

"And then what?" Aldridge asked. "Even if Magruder admits his complicity, it's your word against his. What would you have accomplished?"

"Ira, I raised the same point with Adair and Baldwin. They plan to expose Magruder in their sermons, take the whole thing public. They all but guaranteed me it'll work."

"Nonsense!" Aldridge grumped. "William Magruder owns half this town and the people in it. Whose word do you think they'll accept?"

"I know the problem," Durant countered. "What's the solution?"

"You need corroboration. A witness to whatever Magruder says."

"And where would I find a witness?"

"I volunteer," Aldridge said dryly. "However reluctantly, I enlist in the cause."

"I don't know." Durant hesitated, scratching his jaw. "Magruder might not open up with just me. Why would he talk with two of us there?"

"We'll think of something," Aldridge said. "Perhaps something to do with the bank that involves me. The point is, you have nothing unless you have corroboration."

Durant looked at him. "You'd be putting yourself at risk, Ira. You ought to think about it."

"I already have," Aldridge told him. "More than the bank—or for that matter, you or me—we're talking about the community, what's best for Galveston. I believe it's time to take a stand."

"Don't turn noble on me. That's no reason to go in harm's way."

"Noble has nothing to do with it. I'm just tired of being kicked around by Magruder and his crowd. I realized it here today."

"You're sure?"

"Yes, I am."

Durant called Magruder's office. He spoke to a secretary, who connected him with Magruder. He kept the conversation vague, piquing Magruder's interest with the thought that a discussion about People's Bank & Trust might be beneficial to all concerned. He hung up with a tight smile.

"We're on," he said. "Tomorrow morning at nine."

Catherine was silent, her eyes suddenly filled with concern. Aldridge steepled his fingers, nodding wisely. "So there we are," he said. "I believe we need to talk strategy."

They began discussing ways to snare William Magruder.

The Santa Fe depot was like an overturned beehive. On Friday the railroad put on extra trains to handle the weekend tourists bound for Galveston. A thousand people or more were looking for a taxi.

Quinn waited outside the station house. The four-thirty train, having disgorged its load, finally pulled away toward the switching yard. He checked his watch, wondering if the five o'clock train would be on time. He had to be at the club by six.

Today, a figure of sartorial splendor, he wore a dove-gray tropical worsted suit, with a striped shirt and a blue tie, and a light-gray fedora. Rags Martin, the comedian, was closing tonight, and Quinn was there to meet the Hollywood Club's latest attraction. Sophie Tucker, direct from Broadway, would open tomorrow night.

All in all, Quinn thought things were going his way. The surrender of Lou Lera, engineered with perfect timing, had put the quietus on the reformers. The meeting that morning with the underbosses had put everyone on notice about further violence. He liked an orderliness to things, and he felt the situation on the Island had returned to normal. His mind was now free to concentrate on his newest sensation, a stage spectacular. Yet another coup for Galveston's Mr. Showbiz!

The five o'clock train chuffed to a halt, belching steam, at five-o-one. The weekenders swarmed off the coaches like revelers late for a party. There was a mad dash for taxis and the jitney buses that trundled back and forth between hotels. The weather was balmy for late September, and the tourists had visions of sandy beaches and warm surf. The amusement piers and nightspots would be packed over the weekend.

Sophie Tucker stepped off the private compartment car. She was a small, plumpish woman with a saucy disposition and a kind of bustling vitality. She wore a floral dress with a fur stole and a hat bedecked with bright feathers. Her oval features were framed by hair red as a sunset, and something puckish lurked behind eyes as wide and dark as buttons. Quinn hurried forward to meet her.

"Miss Tucker!" he called affably. "Welcome to Galveston. I'm Oliver Quinn."

"A pleasure," she said with a dimpled smile. "I began to wonder if the train ride would ever end. Is this still the United States?"

"Only for a couple miles, Miss Tucker. The next stop from here is Mexico."

"I can't sing a note in Spanish. And enough already with that Miss Tucker stuff. All my friends call me Sophie. What do I call you?"

"Ollie," Quinn said, doffing his fedora in a gallant gesture. "Your most ardent admirer."

"Well, now," she said, a pudgy fist on her hip. "I do like my men ardent, Ollie. Galveston's looking better all the time."

Sophie Tucker was a show-business icon. A star of burlesque, vaudeville and nightclubs, her career had spanned twenty years. On Broadway, she had captured national fame in the *Ziegfeld Follies* and Earl Carroll's *Vanities*. At forty-two, with a zoftig figure, her brassy, flamboyant style was perfectly suited to risqué ballads. Her show was so bawdy, sometimes raw and ribald, that she'd been arrested three times in New York for indecent performances. She was billed as "The Last of the Red Hot Mamas."

"Tell me, Ollie," she said with amused eyes. "I'm an inquisitive broad and no apologies for it. You mind a couple questions?"

"No, not at all . . . Sophie."

The depot platform was pandemonium in motion, tourists rushing off in every direction. She flung out an arm. "Who the hell are all these people?"

"Your fans," Quinn said with sly eloquence. "Come all this way for your opening night."

"Sold out, are you?"

"Full house, every night."

"I knew I shoulda charged you more."

Quinn was paying her six thousand for a week's appearance. She was not a star on the order of Al Jolson, but he'd casually dismissed Voight's objections about her pricey fee. A Red Hot Mama, he'd argued, would be a sellout. And she was.

"A deal's a deal," he said to her now. "Besides, you'll like it so much here, you'll never want to leave. We had to shanghai Jolson onto the train out of town."

"You're a card, Ollie." She swatted him with the tip of her fur stole. "Anyway, I started to ask you something else. Where's a gal get a drink around here? My pipes are parched."

"We have a suite for you at the Buccaneer. Overlooks

the Gulf with the best view on the Island. And the bar's fully stocked."

Sophie wasn't surprised. Some of her oldest friends in New York were gangsters, and she'd heard all about Oliver Quinn and Dutch Voight. Their control of the Island, the Hollywood Club and the rumrunning operation, made them the envy of every hood east of the Mississippi. She thought she was going to enjoy her stay in Galveston.

Quinn got a porter busy collecting her luggage. He offered her his arm and led her around the depot to the parking lot. Turk McGuire was waiting with the Cadillac Phaeton, the teardrop fenders and gold body polished to a gloss. He knuckled the brim of his hat, nodding with his gravedigger's smile, and held open the rear door. Sophie gave him a slow, appreciative once-over.

"Ummm," she murmured, glancing sideways at Quinn. "You grow them big in Texas. Just my style."

"Hear that, Turk?" Quinn said with a chuckle. "What do you say when a lady pays you a compliment?"

McGuire blushed like a schoolboy. "Guess I'd tell her it's mutual."

Sophie batted her lashes. "Your boss says I'm in a suite stocked with booze. Why don't you come up and see me sometime?"

On the way to the hotel, though she was talking to Quinn, she kept dropping suggestive remarks directed at McGuire. Quinn realized she wasn't merely flirting, that she was indeed a Red Hot Mama. McGuire, staring straight ahead over the steering wheel, was beet red from his neckline to his ears. He seemed relieved when they pulled into the circular drive outside the Buccaneer.

Quinn escorted her to her suite. She marveled at the view, the westerly sun splashing the waters of the Gulf with splotches of orange and vermilion. Then she checked out the bar, clucking approvingly, while a bellboy carried her bags into the bedroom. Quinn waited until she'd inspected the accommodations before mentioning he had scheduled a rehearsal with the band the next morning. She laughed.

"Honey, I could sing if you tap your foot. I've been known to drown out the band."

"We'll let you rehearse the band," Quinn said jokingly. "I'll have Turk pick you up in the morning."

"Um-hmm." She stared him boldly in the eye. "I have a free night and nobody but little ol' me in this great big suite. How about you give Turk the night off?"

Quinn, for one of the few times in his life, was nonplussed. "Sophie, I'll be happy to let him have the night off. Whether he drops by to see you—well . . . that's up to him."

"Tell him he'll never know what he missed if he doesn't. I'm a lotta woman, Ollie."

"I'll relay the message."

Quinn escaped before the conversation went any further. On the short drive to the club, he gave McGuire the gist of her invitation. McGuire was silent a moment, his ears as red as oxblood. He finally found his voice.

"What d'ya think, boss?" he said. "Was she jokin' or what?"

"Turk, I think it might be the experience of your life."

McGuire lapsed into a prolonged silence. "Well—" he said as they pulled into the club. "Okay with you if I take the night off?"

"I'd be disappointed if you didn't. See you in the morning."

Quinn walked from the car to the office at the rear of the casino. He found Voight seated behind the desk, in the midst of lighting a cigar. Before he could speak, the phone rang. Voight lifted the receiver.

"Yeah?"

"Mr. Voight," a voice said at the other end of the line. "This is John Burnett, in Austin. You asked me to run a check for you on Robert Eberling."

"Yeah, sure, the rancher. What's the story?"

"Well, it turns out he's on the square. Owns a big

cattle spread in Blanco County and folks say he's worth a million, maybe more. Solid citizen."

"Anything else?"

"I called a friend at the Motor Vehicles Department and got the plate numbers on Eberling's car. Maybe you want to check 'em out against what he's driving."

"No, from what you say, he's legit. Thanks for hopping on it, John. Send me a bill."

Voight disconnected and called the manager's office at the Buccaneer. A moment later Charles Anderson came on the line.

"Yessir, Mr. Voight."

"Chuck, you know that fellow you asked about, the rancher? Tell him he's been approved for the casino. Have him ask for me when he comes in."

"Yessir, I certainly will. I know Mr. Eberling will be pleased."

"Always happy to take a man's money. See you around, Chuck."

Voight rang off. Quinn gave him a curious look and he shrugged. "Another sucker with money to burn. I had him checked out."

"We can always use another high roller. I just came back from picking up Sophie Tucker."

"Yeah, what's new with 'The Last of the Red Hot Mamas'?"

Quinn laughed. "Dutch, you're not gonna believe it."

Chapter Fifteen

The Strand got busy early on Saturday morning. Stores and businesses opened at eight, and soon thereafter the sidewalks were crowded with weekend shoppers. Intersections were clogged as more tourists in cars spilled over the causeway.

A warm sun rose higher against banks of cottony clouds. Durant and Aldridge left the bank a few minutes before nine and turned west along the Strand. Earlier, in Durant's office, they had reviewed their strategy one last time. Aldridge, though nervous, felt it would work.

"Just remember," Durant said as they walked along. "Let me do the talking and try to stay out of it. I want his attention on me."

"You needn't worry," Aldridge said, a light sheen of perspiration covering his face. "I have no intention of speaking unless spoken to. I'm along strictly as an observer."

"Whatever happens, don't cross swords with him. Getting him mad won't turn the trick. We have to finesse him."

"Earl, we've gone over it a dozen times. You needn't concern yourself with me. I'm fine."

"All right, Ira, let's do it."

They crossed Twenty-second Street and entered the Magruder Building. Dappled streamers of sunshine filtered through the skylight as the birdcage elevator took them to the tenth floor. In the anteroom of Magruder & Company, the secretary greeted Durant by name, darting a curious glance at Aldridge. She ushered them into the inner office.

Magruder was seated behind his ebony desk. His eyes touched on Aldridge, then shifted back to Durant. He motioned them to chairs.

"You asked to meet alone," he said. "Not that it isn't a pleasure to see Mr. Aldridge. But curiosity forces me to ask why?"

"Saves time," Durant replied. "If we make a deal, Ira's included in the package. I wanted him involved in our discussion."

Magruder pursed his mouth. "You said on the phone you might consider selling the bank. How does that involve Mr. Aldridge?"

"Ira comes with the bank," Durant said flatly. "It's not a negotiable point. Without him, there's no deal."

"In what capacity would he remain with the bank?"

"You'd agree to keep him on as vice president. And you'd guarantee it with an airtight, ironclad contract for five years."

"Indeed?" Magruder said slowly. "You drive a hard bargain on behalf of Mr. Aldridge."

Durant shrugged. "Like I said, it's not negotiable."

The strategy was to provide a credible reason for Aldridge's presence at the meeting. Until that was established, there was nothing to be gained in probing more sensitive matters. Durant waited for a response.

"Very well," Magruder said at length. "I assume all of that is acceptable to you, Mr. Aldridge?"

Aldrige held his gaze. "Yes, it is."

"You don't like me much, do you?"

"Business is business, Mr. Magruder. Personal likes or dislikes have no place in the scheme of things."

Magruder's jowls shook with silent laughter. "So long as everyone benefits, who cares about a son of a bitch? Is that the idea?"

"Your words, not mine."

"You always were the tactful one."

Magruder looked back at Durant. "Your uncle and Mr. Aldridge here never approved of my business tactics.

Of course, your uncle was always outspoken about it. No diplomacy."

"No hypocrite either," Durant said. "Was that what you held against him?"

"On the contrary," Magruder said magnanimously. "I respect a man who speaks his mind."

"So where are we with Ira? Do you agree or not?"

"I will provide him with—what was your term?—an airtight, ironclad contract. Which brings us to the matter at hand. How much to buy you out?"

"A hundred thousand," Durant said evenly. "And that's not negotiable, either."

"You surprise me," Magruder said, his eyes narrowed. "You once refused my offer in the same amount. Why accept it now?"

"I've had a bellyful of Galveston. On top of that, I'm bored stiff trying to act the part of a banker. Time to head back to California."

"And your motion pictures."

"That's about the size of it."

"A wise decision," Magruder announced. "Of course, I will require an agreement in writing that you sever all connections with these so-called reformers. Adair and Baldwin, and that jackass, Cornwall. No statements from you, public or otherwise . . . even from California."

"Now that you mention it—" Durant hesitated, set the trap. "I have a condition of my own."

"Condition of what sort?"

"I want an apology."

"Do you indeed?" Magruder appeared amused. "Apology for what?"

"For putting the mob on me."

"I haven't the faintest idea what you're talking about."

"Sure you do," Durant said equably. "You sicced those hoods on me, and had me beat up and almost shot. I want to hear you say you're sorry."

"You've been misinformed," Magruder said, shaking

his head. "Whatever happened to you was not of my doing. You have my word on it."

"Do you want the bank or not?"

"One has nothing to do with the other."

"Don't play me for a fool," Durant said shortly. "You
made a call to Quinn or Voight, and they sent their boys
looking for me. You know it and I know it."

"You are mistaken," Magruder said. "I resent the im-
plication."

"No apology, no deal," Durant told him. "Phrase it
any way you choose, but that's the only way you get the
bank. I want your apology."

Magruder leaned back in his chair. He stared across
the desk, and then, abruptly, some inner revelation lighted
his features. His eyes went cold.

"You're a clever one, bub. Damn me if you're not."

"Nothing clever about it," Durant said. "All I'm asking is to hear you say you're sorry."

"Yes, indeed, very clever." Magruder's gaze flicked
to Aldridge. "You brought along a witness and threw out
the hook. I almost fell for it."

"Fell for what?" Durant tried for a note of confusion.
"I offered you a pretty sweet deal. Do you want it or not?"

"No, I do not," Magruder said in a dismissive tone.
"I believe that concludes our meeting. Good morning,
gentlemen."

"You went from hot to cold mighty fast. What's the
problem?"

"I have nothing further to say to you, Mr. Durant.
Get out of my office."

Magruder began shuffling papers on his desk. Durant
nodded to Aldridge and they walked to the door. On the
elevator ride to the lobby they were silent, wondering
where it had gone wrong. Outside the building, they
turned back toward the bank.

"Don't feel too bad," Aldridge said. "In a way, I'm
not surprised he caught on. He always was a shrewd one."

Durant grunted unpleasantly. "Ira, I'm sorry I got you involved in this. There'll be hell to pay."

"How do you mean?"

"Guess who Magruder's calling right now."

"Quinn and Voight?"

"Nobody else."

There were always large crowds for the opening night of a new act. Everyone wanted to say they were the first to see an entertainer imported from the Great White Way in New York. Tonight was no different at the Hollywood Club.

Clint Stoner looked dapper in his tuxedo. Janice, who had gone to the beauty shop at the hotel, was a vision of loveliness. Her hair was upswept, coifed in the latest Parisian style, and she wore an elegant satin sheath trimmed with lace to accentuate her décolletage. She turned heads.

The maitre d', who had snubbed them on their last visit, practically fawned over them tonight. Charles Anderson, the manager of the Buccaneer, had assured them of special treatment, and guest membership to the casino. Their table in the nightclub was beside the dance floor, near the stage. The maitre d', with only slight exaggeration, called them the best seats in the house.

"How about this!" Janice said as a waiter appeared with menus. "Last time we were at the back of the room."

"Well, Olive, honey," Stoner said, opening his menu, "it pays to know people in high places. All this and the casino, too."

"I can't wait to see Sophie Tucker. Everything I've read says she's absolutely shocking!"

"Hope she doesn't offend your sensitive nature."

"Every little housewife lives to be shocked. Didn't you know that, sweetheart?"

Stoner ordered a bottle of champagne. They dined on foie gras, terrapin soup, and braised pheasant. Between the main course and dessert, the orchestra swung into a medley of lively tunes, and they joined other couples on the dance floor. Janice, her spirits soaring on champagne, dragged him into a fast-stepping fox-trot. He clumped around in his cowboy boots like a rancher stomping crickets.

A while later the houselights dimmed. Sophie Tucker shimmied onstage, centered in a rosy spotlight, as the orchestra segued into show numbers. Her scarlet gown hugged her ample figure and she carried a glittery fan of peacock feathers. Her first song, playing off her trademark billing, was *There'll Be a Hot Time in the Old Town Tonight*. Her voice, a booming alto trained for vaudeville halls, rang throughout the club.

The show became steadily more risqué. Sophie strutted around the stage, belting out songs laced with sexual innuendo and naughty words. She paused for a bawdy wink here and a roll of her eyes there, and punctuated suggestive bedroom lyrics with a flip of her peacock fan. On her last number, she blink-blinked her hips like a hootchy-cootchy dancer and ended on a warbling high note. The audience roared their approval.

By the time she did an encore, and pranced offstage with a bump and grind, it was approaching ten o'clock. Janice applauded until the houselights came up, her eyes merry with excitement. "Did you ever!" she said, giddy with laughter. "No wonder they call her the Red Hot Mama!"

"Time to go to work," Stoner said, lowering his voice. "Let's drift on back to the casino."

"Spoilsport, just when I was enjoying myself."

"No more champagne for you, Olive. Keep your mind on who we are and why we're here."

"Do you think Sophie Tucker will come to the casino? I'd love to get her autograph!"

"Maybe tonight's your lucky night."

They walked to the far side of the room. Stoner gave his alias to the bruisers guarding the glass doors, and they were admitted with courteous smiles. As they moved through the lounge, the oak doors to the casino opened, and a stocky man in a double-breasted tux waited at the entrance. Stoner pegged him immediately as Dutch Voight.

"Mr. and Mrs. Eberling," he said with an amiable nod. "Welcome to our casino."

"Thank you kindly." Stoner made a mental note that there was a hidden intercom between the doors to the lounge and the casino. Otherwise Voight would not have known their names, or appeared so quickly. "Are you the manager, Mr.—"

"Voight," Voight supplied. "You might say I look after things. What is your game, Mr. Eberling?"

"Dice, roulette," Stoner said with a touch of bravado. "Anything that's got numbers on it. I play 'em all."

"We'll do our best to accommodate you. I've arranged an opening line of credit for five thousand. Will that be satisfactory?"

"Well now, that's mighty neighborly of you, Mr. Voight. You make a fella feel right at home."

"We do our best, Mr. Eberling. Enjoy yourselves— and good luck."

"Take all the luck I can get. I'm obliged, Mr. Voight."

"Not at all."

The casino was rapidly filling with patrons. Stoner collected a thousand dollars in chips from the cashier's cage, signing a chit with his alias. Janice, who smiled shyly, playing the part of the little woman, turned with him to survey the action. There were roulette tables, craps tables, and blackjack layouts aligned in orderly precision around the room. Banks of slot machines lined the walls.

"Olive, honey," Stoner said, "how'd you like to try them one-armed bandits? Think I'll have a crack at the roulette wheel."

"Anything you say, sweetie. I believe I might just break the bank!"

"That's the spirit."

Stoner signed another chit with the cashier for a hundred dollars. The cashier gave him a silver bucket, adorned with mother-of-pearl handle, filled with a hundred silver dollars. Janice, cradling the bucket in her arms, made a beeline for the nearest bank of slots. Stoner wandered over to a roulette table.

The game of roulette was one in which true aficionados played complicated betting systems. Stoner preferred to appear the wealthy high roller who relied on luck rather than skill. He randomly scattered chips around the numbered layout, alternately placing a larger wager on red or black, which was the safest bet. The wheel spun and the ivory ball clattered while Stoner and the other players waited in hushed expectation. He regularly lost more than he won.

The game was played at dizzying speed. The croupiers and pit bosses were cordial yet alert, raking in losing bets and paying winners with quick professionalism. All the while Stoner was casually inspecting the tables, the room, and the office at the rear of the casino. At one point, he clumsily dropped a few chips and knelt down, examining the understructure of the table and the floor. He saw nothing suspicious or unusual.

The mystery of it left him baffled. On previous raids by the Rangers, he'd been told the gaming tables and slot machines vanished in a matter of minutes. The Rangers found instead a well-appointed game room, filled with billiards tables, backgammon boards, and bridge tables. What mystified him was not just how the switch was made, but where all the heavy gambling paraphernalia disappeared to, and so rapidly. He was thoroughly stumped.

Across the room, he saw Voight approach Janice. She stopped playing the slot machine, and Voight, acting the convivial host, engaged her in conversation. Stoner pretended he'd lost interest in roulette and moved to one of the craps tables, where he whooped loudly, coaxing Lady Luck every time he tossed the dice. By the time he dropped a couple hundred, Voight had walked away from

Janice with an encouraging smile. He meandered over to the slot machines.

"Act happy," he said to Janice, motioning back at the tables, "while I act like the big-time gambler. What did Voight want?"

"Sweetie, I just got interrogated." Janice fed a dollar into the machine and jiggled with excitement as cherries and lemons and numbers spun. "He was smooth as silk, just making friendly conversation."

"About what?"

"Oh, he asked about the ranch, and the house, and how long we've lived in Blanco County. Things like that."

"And?"

"And I gave him all the right answers." She pouted prettily when the wheels stopped spinning without a winner. "No wonder they call these things one-armed bandits. Would you look at that!"

"Honey, you'll beat it yet. Just keep pumpin' in them dollars. Think I'll try my hand at blackjack."

Stoner took a seat at one of the blackjack tables. He wasn't particularly surprised by Voight's questions, and he was pleased by Janice's artful talent for guile. But he was at a loss as to how the casino was converted into a social club, and irritated with himself that he hadn't readily solved the problem. He mulled it over as the dealer dealt him a blackjack on his first hand.

For the night, Stoner lost seven hundred and Janice dropped two hundred more at the slots. As they were departing, Voight walked them to the door, properly conciliatory over their losses. He wished them better luck next time.

Stoner laughingly assured him they would be back.

Saturday night was the busiest night of the week on Post-office Street. The bordellos and speakeasies were mobbed with weekend tourists as well as Islanders. The four-block stretch that encompassed the red-light district was like a seedy carnival that separated workingmen from their wages.

Late that night, Sam Amelio emerged from a brothel near the intersection of Postoffice and Twenty-sixth Streets. He owned seven whorehouses, and on Saturday nights, he made it a practice to visit them at regular intervals. His madams were terrified of him, but he trusted no one, and he periodically dropped by to collect the proceeds. He was carrying almost two thousand in cash.

Amelio turned toward the corner. He never worried about carrying so much cash, and he saw no need for a bodyguard. Everyone in the district knew him on sight, and they knew as well his reputation for violence. He owned seven houses by virtue of having intimidated his rivals, and, in two instances, beating pimps so badly they left town. He prided himself on being known as the "Prince of Pussy."

One of Amelio's houses was located between Twenty-sixth and Twenty-seventh. As he approached the corner, mentally calculating the take for the night, he heard someone call his name. He stopped, looking south on Twenty-sixth, and saw Jack Nolan leaning against the fender of a Buick. Amelio considered himself a tough nut, but Nolan was one of the few men he genuinely feared. He turned down the block with a sense of something not quite right.

"Hey, Jack," he said, trying to sound jocular. "What brings you to nookieville?"

Nolan flicked an ash off his cigarette. His diamond pinky ring caught the light from the corner lamppost, glinting fire. He smiled a lazy smile.

"Just call me an errand boy, Sam. The boss wants to see you."

"Which boss is that?"

"Mr. Voight."

Amelio felt a tingle along his backbone. He wasn't fooled by Nolan's relaxed manner, the easy smile. He was even more concerned that Voight had sent the mob's chief enforcer out on a Saturday night. Something was definitely wrong.

"C'mon, Jack," Amelio said, suddenly wary. "You know Saturday's my big night. What's Mr. Voight want?"

"Search me," Nolan said, exhaling a thin streamer of smoke. "Probably won't take long, whatever it is. Your girls won't even miss you."

"Look, tell him I'll come by later tonight. Quick as things slow down, I'll be right there."

"No, he wants to see you now."

Turk McGuire stepped out the rear door of the Buick. The driver's door opened and Whizzer Duncan leaned out, his ferret eyes bright with malice. Nolan took a final drag, then crushed his cigarette underfoot. He pushed off the fender.

"Don't make it hard on yourself, Sam. Get in the car."

Amelio looked on the verge of running. His features went taut, the skin tight over his cheekbones, and he took a step back. McGuire, moving quickly for a man of his bulk, strode forward and gripped Amelio's arm in a vise-lock. Duncan, almost as quick, grabbed the other arm. They shoved him into the backseat.

Nolan moved around the car. Duncan slipped behind the steering wheel, and McGuire got in beside Amelio. No one spoke as Duncan started the engine and drove off in the direction of Seawall Boulevard. Five minutes later, the Buick slowed to a stop outside the Hollywood Club, near the kitchen door. The club, even on Saturday nights, closed at two, and the lights out front were already extinguished. The kitchen workers were busy scrubbing down for the night.

"Listen to me, Sam," Nolan said, twisting around in the passenger seat. "You make any trouble and I'll turn you over to Turk. You understand?"

"Who, me?" Amelio's mouth jerked in a rictus of a smile. "Why would I cause you any trouble? I haven't done nothin' wrong."

"Well, it's late and the kitchen help's got enough to

do without you raising a stink. Just mind your manners. Got it?"

"Yeah, sure, I got it."

Nolan led the way through the kitchen. They followed the hallway to the employees' lounge, and then into the casino, which was closed. The croupiers and dealers were sorting chips, waiting for the pit bosses to make a count, and paid them no attention. Nolan rapped lightly on the office door and stepped inside, McGuire and Duncan on either side of Amelio. Duncan shut the door.

Voight was seated behind the desk. Quinn was slumped in an easy chair, his bow tie undone, a drink in his hand. Amelio looked from one to the other, still uncertain as to why he was there, but nonetheless petrified. Voight wagged his head with disgust.

"You dumb guinea bastard. What the hell was that meeting we had yesterday? Tell me, what?"

"Up at the Turf Club?" Amelio said, rattled. "Me and Gus and Dan?"

"What the hell else would I be talking about? What'd I tell you? Ollie and me both?"

"You told us no more rough stuff. Lay off the civilians."

"So you were listening?" Voight said sarcastically. "You got the message?"

Amelio seemed confused. "I'm not following you here, boss. I haven't done nothin' out of line."

"Then how come I got a call from the police chief tonight?"

"I don't know what you're talkin' about. On my mother's head, honest."

"Forget your mother," Voight said. "Sally Urschel runs one of your houses, right? The one off Twenty-fifth and Postoffice?"

"Yeah," Amelio said blankly. "What about her?"

"One of her girls rolled a john tonight. You with me now?"

"No—"

"And when the john started yelling, Sally's bouncer whipped his ass and tossed him out the door. Get the picture?"

Amelio paled. "Boss, you gotta—"

"And the john went to the cops, bleeding like a Goddamn stuck pig. And that's why the police chief called me. What do you think of that?"

"Oh, boy!" Cuddles nervously flapped his feathers. "Deeep shit!"

Everyone looked at the parrot. Cuddles hopped to the end of his perch and pretended to ignore them. Quinn stirred from his easy chair, finishing off his drink. His gaze fixed on Amelio.

"Did you tell your people? Spread the word about laying off civilians?"

"You betcha, I did," Amelio said in a shaky voice. "Yesterday, right after the meeting, told 'em all. No more rough stuff."

Quinn stared at him. "The john pressed charges. Sally and the bouncer and the girl that fingered the wallet are being arrested right about now. You've made a big problem for us, Sam."

"*I told 'em!*" Amelio protested. "Honest to Christ, I told 'em!"

"You're lying," Voight said. "It's written all over your face."

"Think you're right, Dutch," Quinn agreed. "Sam's the one who broke the Rule. Not his people."

Voight slapped the desk with the flat of his hand. The sound was like a gunshot in the office, and his eyes went hard. "We told you in plain English. Nobody—*nobody*—breaks the Rule."

"Take him for a swim!" Cuddles squawked. "Swim-swimswim!"

"You heard the bird," Voight said, nodding to Nolan. "Take him out and don't bring him back."

"*No!*" Amelio lunged toward the desk, his features wild. "You cocksuckers can't—"

McGuire slugged him in the back of the head. He went down as though struck by lightning, and lay still. Nolan moved the carpet aside in the far corner and opened the trapdoor. Duncan took Amelio's feet and McGuire his shoulders, and they carried him down the steps. Nolan followed them to the landing below, then closed the door.

A few moments later the engines of the *Cherokee* rumbled to life. The speedboat pulled away from the landing, gaining headway, throttles opened to full pitch. The sound of the engines faded as the *Cherokee* headed south into the Gulf. A stillness settled over the office.

"Too bad," Quinn said, slouching in his easy chair. "Sam ran a good operation. He'll be hard to replace."

Voight snorted derisively. "One thing's for damn sure, Ollie. Nobody'll break the Rule now."

Cuddles, ever the shrewd mimic, merely nodded. There was nothing more to say.

Chapter Sixteen

Galveston's aristocracy lived on Broadway. The street was lined with palatial homes on a wide esplanade bordered by oleanders and palms. Streetcars festooned with electric lights clanged along the esplanade.

Broadway was one of the first streets platted by the original settlers. The name was chosen because it was a broad thoroughfare, and the Island's oldest and wealthiest families built their mansions overlooking the esplanade. One block, between Twenty-eighth and Twenty-ninth, was preeminent among the town's elite. There, on opposite sides of the street, were the homes of William Magruder and George Seagrave.

The Magruder mansion was an imposing structure, with large windows surrounded by heavy stone and Corinthian columns, and covered with a patterned slate mansard roof. In front, the entrance pavilion formed a tower with a series of grotesque superposed orders, ending at the top in a crown of garlands and cornices and iron spikes. Tourists came on weekends just to stand and stare at it.

Late Monday morning Libbie turned off Broadway in her sporty Chevrolet coupe. She pulled into the pavilion, braked to a stop, and hopped out with an armload of parcels. Her morning had been spent in some of Galveston's tonier shops, where she had purchased a cerulean silk dress, high-heeled pumps, and a pert little hat. She hurried up the steps, delighted with her new outfit, certain it would please Nolan. She planned to meet him in Houston that afternoon.

The mansion was on three floors, with twenty-two

rooms, and a lush floral garden in the rear. She came through the foyer, moving quickly toward a sweeping stairway off the main hall. Her bedroom was on the second floor, and she was in a rush to bathe, slip into her new outfit, and catch the one o'clock interurban to Houston. Last Friday, upon leaving the hotel, she and Nolan had made a date for this afternoon. Two days apart seemed an eternity, and she felt like a schoolgirl with a frantic crush. She couldn't wait to see him.

Opal Magruder came in from the back hallway. Her dress was baggy, her hands soiled, and she was carrying a long-stemmed red rose. She had a household staff of eight, including maids and cooks, a chauffeur and a gardener. Yet, while she let the house run itself, she was forever grubbing around in the garden. Her roses were her passion.

"Look, dear," she said, holding the rose out to Libbie. "Have you ever seen anything so beautiful?"

Libbie halted at the bottom of the stairway. "Oh, that is gorgeous, Mother. What a lovely shade of magenta."

"Yes, it's one of the best of the year. I do so dread the season nearly over. How will I survive without my roses?"

"You'll have to start planning early for Christmas."

Her mother prided herself on having not just the largest, but the most elaborately decorated Christmas tree on the Island. Libbie often thought her father was wedded to his business empire, and her mother was the bride of horticulture and holidays. She wondered that they had ever gotten together to produce children.

"Been shopping, dear?" her mother said, eyeing her packages. "I do hope you bought yourself something nice."

"Nothing really special," Libbie said evasively. "I'm meeting some of the girls this afternoon."

"Well, enjoy yourself, dear. A girl can't have too many friends."

The front door opened. William Magruder moved

into the foyer and hooked his homburg on a hat rack. He saw them standing by the stairway and walked forward into the hall. His features appeared flushed.

"Goodness gracious," Opal said, genuinely surprised. "Why aren't you at the office?"

"Because I'm here," Magruder said brusquely. "I have to talk with Elizabeth."

Libbie sensed there was something terribly wrong. Her father never addressed her in a formal manner unless he meant to find fault, or show displeasure. Nor had she ever known him to leave the office in the morning except on business. She was no less amazed than her mother.

"I don't understand," Opal said. "What on earth do you want with Libbie?"

"Nothing that concerns you, my dear. I prefer to speak with her alone."

"Honestly, how can you say that? Anything that brings you home in the middle—"

"Opal." Magruder silenced her with a frown. "I intend to speak with our daughter in private. Go tend to your roses, or whatever it is you do."

Opal was shocked by his tone of voice. She gave him a wounded look, and then, glancing at Libbie in bewilderment, she marched off toward the kitchen. Magruder turned off the hall into his study.

"I'll have a word with you, young lady."

Libbie followed him through the door. The study was a male sanctuary, all dark hardwood and furnished in leather. Magruder seated himself behind his desk and motioned her to a chair. She placed her packages on the floor.

"I had a call not an hour ago," he said. "A call about a man named Jack Nolan."

Libbie was stunned. Her nerves almost betrayed her, but she managed to hold her composure. "Who is Jack Nolan?"

"Don't act the innocent with me," Magruder growled. "You were seen with him at the Rice Hotel in Houston last Friday. I have it from a reliable source."

"Your *source* must be mistaken, Daddy."

"The call was from a business associate. Someone who knows you and someone who knows Nolan from the Hollywood Club. He was not mistaken."

"Oh, really?" Libbie said, trying for a flippant attitude. "Today is Monday and your business associate is talking about Friday. Why did he wait so long to call you?"

"Charity," Magruder said shortly. "He spent the weekend deliberating whether or not to tell me. He finally decided a father should know his daughter is—involved . . . with a gangster."

"Well, what if I am? I don't need your permission anymore, Daddy. I'll choose my own friends."

"Do you realize what you're saying? The man is a criminal, part of the underworld mob. Haven't you any decency?"

"Haven't you?" Libbie fired back. "You're very palsy-walsy with his boss, that Oliver Quinn. Don't you dare lecture me on disgracing the family name."

Magruder inwardly winced. She was too close to the truth, for his involvement with the mob went far beyond what anyone suspected. He decided the situation called for a harder line.

"I forbid it," he said with authority. "You will not see this man again, and there's an end to it. Do you understand?"

Libbie laughed at him. "Please spare me your ultimatums. I'm of age and I'll see whomever I choose." Her chin tilted defiantly. "That includes Jack Nolan."

"I daresay Mr. Nolan can be persuaded otherwise. You leave me no choice."

"What does that mean?"

"One way or another, young lady, it's ended. Mark my word."

Magruder stormed out of the study. A moment later the front door slammed, and she suddenly knew what he intended. She moved to the phone at her father's desk and

placed a hurried call to the Turf Club. She waited impatiently until Nolan came on the line and then quickly explained what had happened. His reaction was much as
she'd expected.

"Forget meeting me today," he said. "Once your dad
tells Quinn, I'm in big trouble. I'll have to do some fast
talking."

Her mouth went dry. "He won't do anything to you,
will he? You'll be all right, won't you?"

"Don't worry, I'll think of something. I've been in
tighter fixes before."

"When will I see you? You won't let them come between us . . . will you?"

"Never happen," Nolan said with certainty. "I'll find
a way, trust me on that. You're my girl."

"No matter what?"

"No matter what."

Nolan promised he would call her later that afternoon.
When they rang off, Libbie sat for a moment wondering
if he meant it. Then, his voice still fresh in her memory,
she heard him say it again. She was his girl . . . no matter
what.

She desperately wanted it to be true.

Durant found it hard to believe. He read the article again,
shaking his head, still dumbfounded. It just didn't seem
possible.

On Saturday, only two days ago, Jack Dempsey had
lost the heavyweight championship. The fight was held in
a pouring rain at the Sesquicentennial Stadium in Phila-
delphia. Over 120,000 spectators saw the underdog, Gene
Tunney, outbox the Manassa Mauler and take the heavyweight crown. Bookmakers across America had lost their
shirts.

Durant could hardly credit it. Dempsey had held the
championship for seven years, defending his title against
such great fighters as Tommy Gibbons, Luis Firpo, and
Georges Carpenter. A savage puncher, inevitably winning

by a knockout, no one in the fight game thought he could ever be beat. The one consolation, as Durant saw it, was that the new champion was a former serviceman. Gene Tunney had served in the Marines.

A light rap sounded at the door. Durant hastily folded the newspaper and dropped it beneath his desk. All morning he'd been absorbed in his own problems, and then, after glancing at the sports page, the astounding defeat of the Manassa Mauler. He hadn't yet so much as looked at the bank's financial summary for last week. Catherine stuck her head into the office.

"Your friends are back again."

"Friends?"

"You know," she said, rolling her eyes. "Your partners in reform."

Durant wondered what they wanted now. Late Saturday morning, following his and Aldridge's meeting with Magruder, they had come by the office. He had related the details of the fiasco with Magruder, and went on to explain that there was no hope of establishing a mob connection. None of them seemed willing to accept the facts.

A heated exchange ensued. Herbert Cornwall took the lead, urging him to issue a public statement regarding Magruder's ties to the underworld. Durant argued that it was speculation on his part, his word against Magruder's; nothing to substantiate the connection. Cornwall pushed, backed by Adair and Baldwin, and he flatly refused. They left the office in a doleful mood.

Saturday night, he and Catherine had attended a movie. On Sunday afternoon, they had toured the amusement piers and finished the day with dinner at one of the seafood places on the beach. While he was with her, he was able to set his troubles aside and simply enjoy her quick laughter and vivacious spirit. But the thought that Magruder had once again unleashed the mob was never far from mind. The reformers seemed to him yet another fly in the ointment.

"Go ahead, send them in," he said in a gruff voice. "I'm ripe for an argument, anyway."

Catherine frowned prettily. "Don't let them get under your skin."

"I'll try."

The clergymen, followed by Cornwall, stepped into the office. Durant gave them a neutral look and waved them to chairs. After they were seated, there was a moment of strained silence. Reverend Baldwin finally cleared his throat.

"We wish to apologize," he said with an offhand gesture. "We've talked it over and come to the conclusion we pressed you too hard on Saturday. Magruder would indeed prevail in a war of words."

The tone was too tactful by half, almost obsequious. Durant was immediately on guard. "Glad to hear we agree," he said. "So what brings you around today?"

Baldwin smiled slyly. "We spent the weekend exploring new avenues, new strategies. We believe we've found one that is—dare I say . . . Machiavellian."

Durant shrugged. "A three-dollar word for deceit and chicanery. I'm surprised at you, Parson."

"All in a good cause," Adair chimed in. "God wages His battle against evil with every weapon at hand. We are but His servants."

"Which is to say," Baldwin went on, "we have evolved a plan with considerable merit. One we believe will bear fruit."

"Why come to me?" Durant asked. "I've burned my bridges in Galveston."

"Hardly, hardly," Adair assured him. "In fact, you are the very man for our crafty little plan. The only man!"

"How so?"

"Shall we say you are on personal acquaintance with one Diamond Jack Nolan."

"Nolan?"

"Permit me to explain," Baldwin said unctuously. "Jack Nolan is foremost among the mob's henchmen.

Every dirty secret there is to know, he knows intimately. Wouldn't you agree?"

"Yeah, I suppose," Durant allowed. "What's your point?"

"Imagine—" Baldwin thrust a finger in the air for emphasis. "Imagine that Mr. Nolan could be persuaded to betray his associates. And in particular, give evidence against William Magruder."

"Nolan?" Durant said incredulously. "A turncoat?"

"Precisely!"

"You're nuts."

"Perhaps not," Baldwin countered. "Particularly if Mr. Nolan was permitted to walk away a free man. A clean slate, let us say."

"That'd be a nifty trick," Durant conceded. "How do you propose to pull it off?"

"Praise the Lord, Herbert has shown us the way."

Cornwall took his cue. "Mr. Durant, I am a longtime friend and supporter of Attorney General Robert Richardson. I spoke with him by phone this morning."

"And?" Durant said skeptically. "What's the good news?"

"The attorney general has agreed to offer Jack Nolan complete immunity. Not only that, he will receive a ten-thousand-dollar reward, courtesy of the state of Texas. He will, in a word, be redeemed."

"Congratulations," Durant said. "Sounds like a sweet deal. He might even accept."

"Indeed so," Cornwall said with conviction. "And we believe you are the man to offer him such a deal. As Reverend Adair so astutely observed, the only man."

"Why me?" Durant said. "You could just as easily offer him the deal yourself. You're the one with the pipeline to the attorney general."

"Nolan has no reason to trust me," Cornwall replied. "On the other hand, he knows you have a vested interest in your own health. He would believe you are sincere . . . trustworthy."

"Would he?" Durant said. "You assume a lot."

"How else will you save your bank, Mr. Durant? Isn't it worth it to bring down William Magruder?"

Durant thought it was a fanciful scheme. Yet, even if it was one in a million, it was better than nothing at all. He hadn't come up with any bright ideas himself, and he was tired of waiting for the mob to make another attempt on his life. The mere notion of Jack Nolan as a turncoat made for intriguing speculation. It might not only save his bank; it might save his neck.

"You're in the wrong business," he said, looking from one to the other. "You fellows ought to be selling used cars."

"I knew it!" Adair crowed. "I knew you wouldn't let us down!"

"Question is, how do I get in touch with Nolan? Any meeting would have to be held in secret."

"Call the Turf Club," Cornwall suggested. "That's the mob headquarters, their hangout. Just be very careful what you say."

Durant got the operator on the line. She rang the Turf Club and a man with a gravelly voice answered. The man asked who was calling and he said to tell Nolan it was an old friend. A moment later Nolan came on the line.

"Yeah, this is Nolan."

"Earl Durant here."

"Old friend, huh?" Nolan laughed. "You've got a sense of humor, slick. What can I do for you?"

"I'd like to meet with you—in private."

"What about?"

"Let's just say it would be to your advantage."

There was a long pause. Durant could almost hear him calculating, suspicious but nonetheless intrigued. "All right," Nolan finally said. "The Rendezvous Roadhouse in La Marque. Tomorrow morning, ten o'clock."

"I'll be there," Durant said. "Do us both a favor and keep it to yourself."

"Don't worry about it, slick."

The line went dead. Durant looked at the three reformers and nodded. "It's on," he said. "Tomorrow at ten."

"Hallelujah!" Adair exclaimed.

"Indeed so," Baldwin intoned. "God helps those who help themselves."

Durant considered it a long shot, even for God.

The Beach Hotel was vaguely reminiscent of Byzantine architecture. The two-hundred-room hostelry was painted mauve and an octagonal dome centered on the roof was adorned with flashy orange-and-white stripes. A fountain bubbled tall jets of water in the middle of a circular driveway.

Frank Nitti emerged from the hotel late that morning. He was accompanied by Sal "Knuckles" Drago, his personal attendant and bodyguard. Drago was built like a block of granite, and his nickname stemmed from his ability with his fists. Nitti, by contrast, was a dapper man with an air of authority. He was accustomed to being obeyed.

A valet waited with their car. "Good morning, Mr. Murphy, Mr. Reilly. You have a fine day for sightseeing."

"Always this bright?" Nitti asked, squinting into the sun. "You'd think we were in the tropics."

"Blue skies and sunshine!" the valet boasted pleasantly. "Galveston Island's own brand of paradise, Mr. Murphy."

Nitti was amused by the alias. He was registered at the hotel as Thomas Murphy, and Drago was listed as George Reilly. He thought a couple of wops posing as Irishmen was a fine joke on everyone. None more so than Ollie Quinn and Dutch Voight.

The car was a loan from Johnny Renzullo, a gangster who controlled many of the rackets in Houston. Nitti and Drago had arrived by train last night, and after meeting with Renzullo, they had driven on to Galveston. Renzullo, a friend of the late Joey Adonis, was an associate and their chief source of intelligence. He was interested in avenging Adonis, now assumed to be at the bottom of the Gulf. He meant to share in the spoils of the Island as well.

Drago climbed behind the wheel of the car. "Where to, boss?"

"Where else?" Nitti said. "Let's have a look at the Hollywood Club. We'll go on from there."

"Whatcha think, boss, wouldn't Mr. Capone like this place? He's big on all this sunny stuff."

"Knuckles, that's one reason he sent us. All that snow up north gets to him in the winter."

"Yeah, I wouldn't mind havin' a place to go myself. When it snows, I mean."

"I've got a feeling Galveston's our spot."

Frank Nitti was the right-hand man of Al Capone. The most notorious gangster in America, Capone was ruthless and wily, the overlord of nearly all criminal enterprises in Chicago. Nitti was known as "The Enforcer," and he savagely defended Capone's empire from rival mobs. Almost four hundred men had been gunned down in Chicago within the last year.

Today, Nitti was on a reconnaissance mission. Capone was a man whose reach exceeded his grasp, and he was forever searching for ways to expand his empire. Galveston Island was all but fabled in the underworld, a sunny paradise where tourists were fleeced of millions of dollars a year. To Capone, it seemed a peach worth plucking.

Nitti's assignment was to scout out the possibility of a takeover. As the car rolled past the Hollywood Club, he wasn't particularly impressed with the look of the place from the outside. But he knew the interior was lavishly appointed, and he felt a grudging admiration for the crafty move of positioning the casino over the Gulf. He thought a club that could afford Al Jolson was a joint worth stealing.

In fact, all of Seawall Boulevard was a revelation.

The amusement piers and nightspots reminded Nitti of Coney Island in New York. His intelligence sources told him that Quinn and Voight extorted a king's ransom in protection payoffs from gaming dives and speakeasies throughout town. The rumrunning operation, which represented a monopoly on illegal booze, was even sweeter. He figured a couple million a year, easy.

"So what d'ya think, boss?" Drago asked as they neared the eastern tip of the Island. "Like what you seen so far?"

"Not bad," Nitti admitted. "Quinn and Voight have done a good job. Built themselves a regular money tree."

"Johnny Renzullo says they got a big organization, too. Lots of heavy artillery."

"I'm not planning a war, Knuckles. Way I see it, what works in Chicago won't work in Galveston. Too many dead men in the streets might turn the law against us."

"Yeah, right." Drago muddled on it a moment, suddenly grinned with comprehension. "You're gonna knock 'em off, aren't you, boss? Just Quinn and Voight."

"Simplest plan is the best plan," Nitti said, as though thinking out loud. "We'll import some shooters from Renzullo's outfit and let them do the job. Renzullo wants payback for Adonis, anyway."

"You know, boss, that's a funny thing. Johnny don't seem the kinda guy to go all hearts and flowers. Why's he so pissed about Adonis?"

"Adonis was his brother-in-law. Married his little sister and left her with three or four kids."

"No shit!" Drago's jaw hung open. "How come you never told me that?"

"Just drive the car," Nitti ordered. "I never told you because I don't want you cryin' in your beer for Renzullo and his sister. We might have to ice him before it's over."

"Why's that?"

"Once we take over Galveston, we don't want any partners. Renzullo will likely figure he deserves a piece of the action."

"Oh." Drago's bulldog features appeared melancholy. "Too bad it's gotta be that way. Johnny's a stand-up guy."

Nitti sighed. "Take a right at the corner. I want to have a look at the red-light district."

On the way across town they saw the Garden Club and several other nightspots. Nitti was impressed by the fact that every time he turned his head he saw yet another dive dangling off the money tree. A few minutes later Drago parked the car on Postoffice Street, between Twenty-sixth and Twenty-seventh. They got out for a walking tour of the district.

A strong mix of avarice and admiration came over Nitti. Within a block he stopped counting speakeasies, and after a couple blocks he gave up counting whorehouses. He was impressed all over again by the orderly arrangement of things in Galveston, something they had never been able to accomplish in the far-flung environs of Chicago. Everything seemed engineered for the sole purpose of taking down the loot.

Quinn and Voight, of course, would have to go. Yet Nitti was hopeful it wouldn't be necessary to kill Jack Nolan. His sources told him Nolan was a master rumrunner, tough but brainy, and an inside player with the Feds. Keeping Nolan on was the smart move, for there were always unforeseen twists and turns in any takeover. A smooth transition of power required someone familiar with the local ground rules.

Nitti could visualize it in his head, see it all coming together. Sun and surf, a place to escape the wintry winds of Chicago. A pleasant little island all but floating on money.

He thought Capone was going to like Galveston.

Chapter Seventeen

Sherm Magruder knew something was definitely wrong. Every Monday morning at ten o'clock he and his father got together for their weekly planning session. Today, just before ten, the old man had canceled the meeting.

What bothered Sherm the most was that his father was a man of habit. The meeting was part of their weekly ritual, immutable as stone, and it had never before been called off. William Magruder always devoted Monday morning to their diverse business affairs.

Even more, Sherm was troubled by the way it had happened. Ellen Morse, his father's secretary, had called and canceled the meeting without offering an explanation. When he'd asked to speak with his father, she had told him Mr. Magruder was not taking any calls. She seemed perplexed herself by the situation.

Later, around eleven o'clock, he had called her back. She informed him that his father had rushed out of the office, with no word as to where he could be reached. Sherm started to call the house, then thought better of worrying his mother until he knew something more. Never in memory could he recall the old man leaving the office on a Monday morning.

Then, shortly before noon, he'd been summoned to the office. Ellen Morse still had no explanation, but she said his father wanted him to come right away. All the way over from the bank, he tried to fathom the events of the morning, but none of it made any sense. Ellen merely gave him a shrug and a look of concern when he hurried through the waiting room. He found his father staring out the window at the harbor.

Sherm knew it was bad. Magruder turned from the window with cloudy features and something strange in his bearing. He walked to his desk, seating himself, and motioned Sherm to a chair. His eyes were leaden.

"We have some serious problems," he said. "One with Earl Durant and the other with your sister."

"Libbie?"

"Yes, I just came from the house and a very unpleasant conversation with your sister. I sometimes wonder she's a Magruder."

Sherm suddenly knew why the morning meeting had been canceled. He was curious as to the reason. "What's she done now?"

"I'll get to that," Magruder said. "Oddly enough, both of our problems involve Quinn and Voight." He paused, slowly shook his head. "I never thought I'd hear myself mention your sister's name in context with those two."

"I'm a little lost here, Pop. How's Libbie involved with Quinn and Voight?"

"For the life of me, I'm not sure I can discuss it in a rational manner. Let's deal with Durant first."

"All right," Sherm replied, now thoroughly confused. "What's he done?"

"Young Mr. Durant came to see me Saturday morning, on the pretext of selling People's Bank & Trust. He brought Ira Aldridge with him."

"Why didn't you tell me?"

"I wanted the weekend to think it over. Time to decide."

"Decide what?"

Magruder briefly recounted the meeting with Durant and Aldridge. He explained that it was all a trap, an attempt to trick him into admitting illicit dealings with the mob. With Aldridge as a witness.

"I don't get it," Sherm said dubiously. "Even if you admitted it, what good would it do Durant?"

"The very question I asked myself," Magruder acknowledged. "We know Durant is involved with those damnable reformers. What does that tell you?"

"I'm not sure it tells me anything."

"Suppose they meant to start a smear campaign? Tie me to the mob—with Aldridge the unimpeachable witness—and blacken my name. Think about it."

Sherm considered a moment. "For one thing, public opinion would swing to Durant and we wouldn't be able to touch him. Not to mention the damage it would do you politically."

"Exactly my thought," Magruder agreed. "Durant clearly believes the way to save himself *and* his bank is to vilify me in public. So what should we do?"

"Pop, I think you've already made up your mind. Why ask me?"

"I value your judgment, my boy. After all, you will one day assume the helm of Magruder & Company. What would you do in my position?"

"Call Quinn and Voight," Sherm said without hesitation. "Have them remove Durant before it goes any further. He's turned it into a vendetta."

"What about the reformers?"

"I'm sure they'll make the most of it. But when you come down to it, Durant's the problem. He has to be stopped before he can do *real* harm."

Magruder nodded. "Today seems to be our day for Quinn and Voight. I have to call them about Libbie as well."

"I'm still in the dark," Sherm said. "What's all this about Libbie?"

"Your sister. . . ."

"Yes, go on, Pop."

"How can I say this?" Magruder's voice was dull with anger. "Libbie has become romantically involved with a gangster. One of Quinn and Voight's men. His name is Jack Nolan."

Sherm was appalled. "Are you saying she's . . . you know?"

"Yes, I regret to say I am. She was seen with Nolan last Friday in Houston—at the Rice Hotel."

"Who saw her?"

"Oscar Whitney. We both know Oscar wouldn't lie about such a thing. He wrestled with it over the weekend and finally called me this morning. He felt friendship demanded it, one father to another."

Sherm went from shock to anger. He loved his sister, but he thought she was a spoiled brat. All her flapper nonsense, and the women's liberation, and now she was bedding a gangster. He looked at his father.

"Do you think Oscar will keep it quiet?"

"Yes, I do," Magruder said firmly. "Oscar does a good bit of business with us. He knows better than to gossip."

"Let's hope so," Sherm said. "Jack Nolan isn't just any gangster. He does the dirty work for Quinn and Voight."

"I'm all too aware of his reputation. We have to put a stop to it before it becomes public knowledge. I won't have the family name disgraced."

"What did Libbie say? Surely she'll stop seeing him."

"No, I'm afraid not," Magruder said harshly. "Your sister is headstrong and stubborn as a post. She told me to mind my own business."

"Sounds like her," Sherm admitted. "So what's the solution?"

"I plan to have a talk with Quinn. In no uncertain terms, he can lay down the law to this Jack Nolan. We will not tolerate it one day longer."

"I'm not sure that's a good idea, Pop."

"Why not?"

"Quinn might be insulted. By association, you're implying he's no better than Nolan. He has a high opinion of himself."

"I see your point," Magruder said with a thoughtful frown. "We're asking him to take care of Durant, and it wouldn't do to offend him. What do you suggest?"

"An intermediary."

"Isn't that somewhat risky? Who could we trust with . . . this?"

"Monsignor O'Donnell," Sherm said without hesitation. "Quinn donates quite heavily to the Catholic Church. And the monsignor would understand the need for discretion."

Magruder thought there was something to be said for an education at Yale. His son understood the nuances of diplomacy, circuitous rather than direct, exactly what the situation demanded. Still, in the scheme of things, the more immediate threat came first. He placed a call to Quinn at the Turf Club.

"Good morning, Bill," Quinn said when he came on the line. "What can I do for you today?"

"Old business, Ollie," Magruder replied. "That worrisome fellow we've ignored for too long? Find a way to resolve the matter . . . quickly."

"A wise decision, Bill. I know just who you mean. Consider it done."

Magruder hung up, nodding to Sherm. Then he jiggled the hook and asked the operator for another number. A courteous young man answered.

"St. Mary's Rectory."

"Monsignor O'Donnell, please."

"May I tell the Monsignor who's calling?"

"William Magruder."

"And the purpose of your call, Mr. Magruder?"

"A personal matter."

"High time!"

"Dutch, I told you he'd come around."

"Yeah, you did," Voight said. "Wonder what took him so long?"

Quinn smiled. "Magruder works at his own speed. You wanted Durant and you've got him. Don't ask questions."

"Who's asking?"

The phone rang. Voight lifted the receiver, still grinning. "Yeah."

"Dutch, this is Dan Lampis."

"What's up?"

"I was out checking the slots this morning. Guess who I saw on Postoffice Street?"

"Who?"

"Frank Nitti."

Voight's grin slipped. "You're sure?"

"Dead certain," Lampis said. "How could I forget his ugly mug?"

Voight was formerly from Chicago. Four years ago, he had imported Lampis from the Windy City to handle part of the slots concession. They both knew Frank Nitti on sight.

"Keep it to yourself for now, Dan. I'll get back to you."

Voight replaced the receiver on the hook. "Frank Nitti's in town," he said to Quinn in a cold voice. "Dan Lampis saw him on Postoffice Street."

"Nitti?" Quinn repeated hollowly. "You're talking about Nitti from Chicago?"

"One and the same. He's Al Capone's right-hand boy. And I don't need a crystal ball to tell me why he's here."

"You think Capone means to put a move on us?"

"Nothing but," Voight said tightly. "Capone knows there's only one way to get his hands on Galveston. He sent Nitti here to plan our funeral."

Quinn's jaws clenched. "We'll scotch that in a hurry. Capone doesn't know who he's dealing with."

They called Nolan into the office. He listened without expression as Voight told him about Nitti. His eyes narrowed.

"I'll get on it right away. You want him aced?"

"Not just yet," Voight said. "Find him and bring him here. I've got some questions I want answered."

"Whatever you say." Nolan started toward the door,

then stopped. "What with Nitti in town, I almost forgot to tell you. Earl Durant called me a little while ago."

"Durant?" Quinn echoed. "Why would he call you?"

"I haven't got a clue. He said he wanted to meet, something about it would be to my advantage. Sounded pretty mysterious."

"What did you say?"

"I agreed to meet him tomorrow morning. Figured I'd see what's what."

Quinn and Voight exchanged a puzzled glance. After a moment, Quinn looked back at Nolan. "Something screwy's going on here. Magruder just called and gave us the green light on Durant. Said to take him out."

"Why so sudden?" Nolan asked quizzically. "I mean, him and Durant calling at the same time? Doesn't make sense."

"No, it doesn't," Quinn remarked uneasily. "You're sure that's all Durant said?"

"Yeah, he kept it short and sweet."

"I don't like it," Voight interjected. "Somebody knows something we don't. Too much coincidence for my money."

"Dutch, I couldn't agree more." Quinn walked to the window, gazed down at the street. "I think we'd better go slow here. See how it plays out."

"Damn right," Voight said sternly. "Could be somebody's playing us for a patsy. Question is, who?"

"How about Durant?" Nolan said, looking from one to the other. "Do I meet him or not?"

Quinn turned from the window. "String him along and see what he wants. We might learn what we're missing in all this."

"Good idea," Voight said. "We can settle his hash anytime. Nitti's our first order of business."

Nolan nodded. "I'll take some of the boys and hit the streets. He shouldn't be hard to find."

Voight grunted. "Look for a wop with a hooked nose. Fancy dresser, about my size. Always wears spats."

"I'm on it."

Nolan went out. When the door closed, Voight bit off the end of a cigar and lit up in a dinge of smoke. Quinn again turned his gaze out the window.

"What do you make of it, Dutch?"

"I think something's fishy. Stinks to high heaven."

"Yes," Quinn said quietly. "I can smell it from here."

Catherine invited Durant to dinner that evening. She expressed the opinion that he was in desperate need of a home-cooked meal, and she also wanted him to meet her mother. Durant readily accepted.

The Ludlow home was pleasantly comfortable. The living room was filled with overstuffed furniture, bric-a-brac scattered here and there in playful groupings. A sideboard with hand-carved garlands dominated the dining room, and the table was piled high with steaming dishes. Durant's invitation was clearly an occasion.

Alma Ludlow was a slim woman in her early fifties. She was animated and cheery, with bright blue eyes and wisps of gray in her hair. Durant thought it was apparent where Catherine got her good looks and spirited disposition. Her mother would have been a beauty in her day.

Alma stifled her curiosity until they were seated at the dinner table. Then, much like her daughter, she proved to be a devotee of motion pictures, and more particularly, movie stars. She began peppering Durant with questions once his plate was loaded with food.

"Catherine tells me you're a stuntman in motion pictures?"

"Yes ma'am," Durant said, ladling gravy onto his mashed potatoes. "I've been working at it pretty regular the last few years."

"Well, then, you must know everyone's juicy secrets. Is it true, what the papers say? Did Fatty Arbuckle really kill that girl?"

Scandals gave Hollywood the unsavory image of a modern Babylon. Fatty Arbuckle, a popular comedian, allegedly raped an actress, adding a sadistic twist by using a Coke bottle. The actress died and he was charged with murder, facing trial three times. Twice he got a hung jury, and in the third trial he was acquitted. The scandal nonetheless resulted in him being blackballed from movies forever.

Durant wasn't surprised by Mrs. Ludlow's interest. The story had been covered extensively in the press, and movie fans everywhere were fascinated by the sordid headlines. He tried to answer the question without getting drawn into details.

"Everyone in Hollywood thought Arbuckle was guilty. The general feeling was that he got away with murder."

"How terrible," Alma said with a little shudder. "And is it true what they say about John Barrymore? Is he a drunk?"

"Yes, ma'am, it's a fact." Durant paused, a chunk of pot roast speared on his fork. "Barrymore's half stiff all the time and sloshed most of the time. He's still a good actor, though."

"Oh, I think so, too. You must think it's silly of me, but I just love all these handsome leading men. Did you know Rudolph Valentino?"

"Well, I wouldn't say we were buddies. I doubled for him in stunts on *The Four Horsemen of the Apocalypse*. He seemed like a pretty nice guy."

Rudolph Valentino was the matinee idol of the day. He had died little more than a month before from a peritonitis infection following an appendicitis operation. Thousands attended the funeral of the man who would forever be known for his role in *The Sheik*. Women across America were still in a state of mourning.

"How tragic," Alma said weepily. "To die so young, at the height of his fame. I read he was only thirty-one."

"Mother!" Catherine scolded. "Let Earl eat his dinner. You haven't stopped to catch a breath."

"Well, honestly, dear, how often do you meet someone from Hollywood? I'm just making conversation."

"I don't mind," Durant said with a smile. "For a meal like this, I'd talk all night. You're a mighty fine cook, Mrs. Ludlow."

"Aren't you the flatterer," Alma simpered. "All right, I'll ask only one more question and then I'm through. Does Mary Pickford really earn a million dollars a year?"

Durant verified it was true. He went on to explain that Mary Pickford's husband, Douglas Fairbanks, as well as Charlie Chaplin, made a million a year. Not long ago, he noted, the threesome had pooled their resources to form United Artists Studio and produce their own pictures. They were now millionaires many times over.

Alma clapped her hands with delight, and then true to her promise, let him finish his dinner. Later, while she was clearing the table, Catherine led Durant into the living room and took a seat beside him on the sofa. She shook her head with a rueful smile.

"I apologize for Mama," she said, clearly embarrassed. "She's even more star-struck than I am. Do you forgive me?"

"Nothing to forgive," Durant assured her. "Tell you the truth, it was good to talk about something else. Took my mind off my problems."

"Things were so hectic today I didn't have a chance to ask. Are the reformers still pestering you to make a public statement about Magruder?"

"No, we're into a whole new game. I'm meeting with Jack Nolan tomorrow."

"My God!" she blurted. "What on earth for?"

Durant shrugged it off. "Let's just say he might be able to help out. I'll know more after I've talked with him."

"You've said any number of times how dangerous he is. Aren't you taking an awful chance?"

"Sometimes you've got no choice but to take a chance. Don't worry, I'll keep both eyes open."

She felt clotted with emotion, and fear. She took his hand in hers, squeezed tightly. "Promise you'll be careful."

Durant smiled. "Cross my heart."

Alma bustled in from the kitchen. "Now!" she said eagerly, seating herself in an overstuffed chair. Her eyes sparkled with excitement.

"Tell me everything unprintable about Greta Garbo."

The car pulled into the Beach Hotel early that evening. Knuckles Drago was at the wheel, and Nitti, stuffed with seafood, was in the passenger seat. He was pleased with himself, satisfied he'd learned all he needed to know about Galveston. He planned to call Capone when he got to his room.

There was no valet attendant out front. Drago honked the horn, peering past Nitti through the doors into the lobby. The back doors of the car suddenly popped open, and Drago automatically reached for his gun. Turk McGuire jammed the snout of a pistol into his neck with a rumbled warning. Nolan scooted in behind Nitti.

"Easy does it, Nitti," he said in an amiable voice. "Mr. Voight just wants to talk. Let's keep it simple."

Nitti craned around. "I'd lay odds you're Jack Nolan."

"You win your bet."

"How'd you get on to me?"

"Wasn't all that hard, Mr. *Murphy*. We have friends here at the hotel."

"I'll make it worth your while to forget you found me."

"Save your breath and enjoy the ride."

Ten minutes later the car pulled into the garage behind the Turf Club. McGuire relieved Drago of his gun, and after Nolan unlocked the back door, they were marched inside. A narrow stairway, closed to the public, led them to the third floor. Barney Ward waited at the end of the hall, posted outside the office. He knocked three light raps, then opened the door.

Voight was seated behind his desk. His eyes were coldly impersonal, touching an instant on Drago, then shifting to Nitti. Nolan shoved them forward as Barney Ward closed the door. A moment of strained silence slipped past.

"Well, Frank," Voight said without a trace of warmth. "Long time, no see."

"Too long, Dutch," Nitti replied evenly. "What's the idea of rousting us?"

"I've got a better one for you. What's the idea of sneaking into Galveston on the q.t.?"

"We're here for a couple days' vacation. Little surf and sand."

"You're a fucking liar."

Nitti was a man of carefully calibrated composure, mandarin inscrutability. He stared back across the desk with a level gaze. "It's a free country, Dutch. I don't owe you any explanation."

"Let me guess," Voight said, as though contemplating some arcane riddle. "Capone sent you here to scout out the territory. Arrange a nice funeral for Ollie Quinn and me. How's that sound?"

"Sounds like something out of left field. I told you why we're here."

"Don't try to play dumb on me. How many shooters was Johnny Renzullo gonna supply? What'd he promise you?"

Nitti smiled a frosty little grin. "Who's Renzullo?"

"What do you take me for?" Voight said coarsely. "You think I don't know Joey Adonis was married to Renzullo's sister? I had it figured the minute I heard you were in town."

"Nobody ever gave you much credit for smarts. Good thing you left Chicago when you did."

"You guinea son of a bitch! I ought to send you back to Capone in a box."

"Dutch, you don't have the guts for it. You never did."

Voight opened the desk drawer. He took out a .38 snub-nose and moved around the desk. He pressed the muzzle between Nitti's eyes.

"Say that again, hotshot. Let's see who's got the guts!"

Everyone in the room went stock-still. Nitti stared into the bore of the pistol, and his eyes blinked once, then twice. He drew a deep breath.

"You don't want to kill me, Dutch. All that would get you is a war with Capone."

"Looks like I've already got a war. What's the difference?"

"Let me go and that'll be the end of it. You know I never break my word."

Voight cocked the hammer on his pistol. "Say 'please.' "

A doomsday silence settled over the room. Nitti swallowed against a rush of bile in his throat. His voice, when he spoke, was almost inaudible.

"Please."

"You just bought your life." Voight eased the hammer down, lowered the pistol. "Get out of Galveston tonight. Don't go back to the hotel. Don't even stop to take a piss. Got it?"

Nitti slowly nodded. "Got it."

"Tell Capone to stick to Chicago. The climate down here's not good for his health—or yours."

"I'll give him the message."

Voight dismissed him with a curt gesture. McGuire opened the door, where Barney Ward waited in the hall, and motioned Nitti and Drago out of the office. Nolan started after them.

"Jack," Voight said. "Wait up a minute."

"Yeah, boss?"

"Follow them over the causeway. Let Nitti know he's being tailed."

"Good as done."

"One other thing," Voight said with quiet malice. "I want the score settled with Johnny Renzullo. Figure out a way to pop him in Houston. The sooner, the better."

"I'll take care of it."

Nolan went out. Voight returned to his desk and lit a cigar. He chuckled to himself, puffing smoke. Sometimes things worked out just right.

Al Capone would never set foot on Galveston Island.

Chapter Eighteen

On Tuesday morning, Stoner and Janice came down in the elevator a little before ten. As they moved through the lobby, Charles Anderson stepped out of his office. He greeted them with an effusive smile.

"Good morning," he said, nodding politely to Janice. "Off for more sight-seeing?"

"You bet," Stoner said with a chipper manner. "The missus never gets enough of the Island. Do you, Olive, honey?"

"Oh, dear me, no!" Janice trilled. "You are so very fortunate to live here, Mr. Anderson. I envy you greatly."

"Yes, ma'am, I sometimes envy myself." Anderson laughed at his own wit, glancing at Stoner. "I trust they're treating you well at the Hollywood Club, Mr. Eberling?"

"Well, I'll tell you, pardner, it's the old case of win some and lose some. I've got a ways to go to get even."

"I am sorry to hear that. Of course, I've heard gambling men say that luck does require patience."

"Yessir, the worm always turns. I'll get mine back and then some."

"I'm sure you will," Anderson said, stepping aside with a little bow. "You folks enjoy your day."

"We plan to, Charlie. We surely do."

Stoner led Janice toward the entrance. He thought the likelihood of getting even was practically nil. They were now welcome guests at the casino, having played there Saturday night, Sunday night, and last night. So far, even though he believed the games were honest, he was down almost two thousand dollars. He felt he was playing against time with a dwindling bankroll.

Their canary-yellow Packard waited outside the hotel. The valet attendant kept the car washed and polished, and it gleamed beneath golden sunlight and a cloudless sky. Stoner marked the date as September 26, slightly more than two weeks since they had arrived in Galveston. Yet, despite his slimmer bankroll, he was still obliged to play the part of the wealthy rancher. He tipped the attendant ten dollars.

A short while later they drove onto the causeway. Seagulls wheeled and circled above the harbor as a freighter slowly maneuvered into the docks. Janice watched the tranquil scene while Stoner concentrated on the road and the rearview mirror. Over the past two weeks, he had called Colonel Garrison twice, always from phone booths in La Marque. He was wary of calling from the hotel, for fear a curious operator might eavesdrop. He was wary as well of being followed.

The Packard was so distinctive that it attracted attention. By now, tooling around Galveston for two weeks, practically everyone in town recognized the car. All the more troublesome, three nights at the Hollywood Club made it known to parking attendants and others who worked at the casino. Stoner was not apprehensive by nature, but he thought it better to err on the side of caution. Someone with a sharp eye might wonder why they drove over to La Marque so frequently. Or even worse, why a wealthy rancher used phone booths.

Stoner was focused as well on what he planned to say to Garrison. In their last talk, almost a week ago, he hadn't yet gained entrance into the casino. Garrison had expressed displeasure with his lack of progress, and urged him to redouble his efforts. Still, after three nights at the gaming tables, he'd learned nothing about how the casino was mysteriously made to disappear. Yet he had formulated a plan—subterfuge mixed with deception—that he was confident would work. He hoped Garrison would agree.

Stoner never used the same phone booth twice. Today, not long after ten o'clock, he turned off the highway onto the main street of La Marque. On previous trips, playing the tourist with Janice, he had scouted about and found that there were three enclosed phone booths. One was in the town's only hotel, which he had used the first week, and another, where he had placed a call last week, was in the pharmacy. The third was in a tobacco shop and newsstand, a couple of blocks off the highway. He parked the Packard at the curb.

Janice came in with him. The phone booth was at the back of the store, with racks of magazines and newspapers on one side, and an array of cigars and packaged cigarettes behind the front counter. He nodded pleasantly to the shop owner, exchanging three dollars for a handful of quarters, while Janice wandered over to the racks and began browsing through magazines. The phone booth had a low seat, and after he'd closed the door, he gave the operator the number in Austin. He began feeding quarters into the coin slot.

A receptionist answered after a couple of tinny rings. "Colonel Garrison's office."

Stoner kept his voice low. "Tell the Colonel it's Clint Stoner. He'll take my call."

Garrison came on the line within moments. "Well, Sergeant, I'd about given you up for lost. I trust you have good news to report."

"Yes and no, Colonel," Stoner said. "I finally managed to con my way into the casino. Matter of fact, I gambled there the last three nights."

"I'd say you've made excellent progress. Why do I detect a note of reservation in your voice?"

"Well, sir, you might say I'm only half there. I haven't found out how they make the casino disappear. I'm just plain stumped."

"Nothing?" Garrison demanded. "Surely you've seen something that raised your suspicion."

"Colonel, there's nothing suspicious," Stoner said. "I've done everything but crawl under the tables, and I still don't have the least notion of how they pull it off. I'll blow my cover if I try anything more."

"Then you'll just have to keep at it. I have confidence you'll get to the bottom of it, Sergeant. Something will turn up."

"No, sir, I don't think so. They're a tricky bunch, and I doubt we'll get anywhere unless we force their hand. We have to smoke 'em out in the open."

"How would we accomplish that?"

Stoner outlined the details of his plan. Garrison listened without interruption, and then considered it a moment in silence. He finally chuckled with approval.

"I like it," he said. "Hoodwink them into revealing their most prized secret. You're a clever tactician, Sergeant."

"The timing's the thing," Stoner said. "I'll have to work it out with Captain Purvis, and that ought to be done in person. How do we handle that, Colonel?"

"Purvis still doesn't know you're working undercover. I'll have to call him and arrange a meeting. Could you drive to Houston today?"

"Yes, sir, I could be there by early afternoon."

"Excellent." Garrison hesitated, as though thinking something through, then went on. "I received a call from the attorney general yesterday afternoon. You're familiar with a man named Jack Nolan?"

"Yes, sir," Stoner said. "He's the enforcer for the Galveston mob. You briefed me on him before I left Austin."

"Now that you mention it, I believe I did. In any event, the attorney general may offer him immunity if he turns state's evidence against Quinn and Voight. I thought you should know."

"Colonel, I'd be floored if it happened. Nolan's not the sort to turn stool pigeon. Who's behind it?"

"A reform committee," Garrison told him. "Apparently they're talking to Nolan through a man named Earl Durant. I gather he's a banker there in Galveston. Have you heard of him?"

"No, sir, that's a new one on me."

"Well, as you say, it may come to nothing. Even if it did, these things take time. No reason to let it delay our plans."

"I'm with you there, Colonel. So far as I'm concerned, a bird in the hand's the way to go. We could wrap this up by Saturday night."

"Nothing would please me more," Garrison said. "I'll call Captain Purvis now and call you back. Give me your number."

Stoner read off the number on the pay phone. When they hung up, he opened the door of the booth and joined Janice at the magazine racks. She glanced up from a copy of *Vogue* and gave him a questioning look. He nodded at the phone booth with a wry smile.

"Mom has to call me back."

Durant pulled off the highway. The only cars in the parking lot were a Stutz Bearcat and a shiny new Ford. He braked to a halt, hooking the gearshift into reverse, and cut the engine. He sat for a moment surveying the Rendezvous Roadhouse.

Ira Aldridge had loaned him the car, a four-door Chevrolet. As part of the loan, Aldridge had again attempted to dissuade him from meeting with Nolan. Aldridge had argued that Nolan was a killer, untrustworthy, and might very well be setting a trap. The Rendezvous Roadhouse was a known hangout for gangsters.

Durant wondered now if he should have taken the advice. Apart from the cars in the parking lot, the roadhouse look deserted, the perfect place for a quiet murder. Still, he was armed, the Luger stuffed in his waistband, and some visceral instinct told him that Nolan's curiosity was a safety net of sorts. He decided there was one way to find out.

The front hall of the roadhouse was empty. Durant heard distant voices from the rear, what was probably the kitchen. Off to the right, he saw a room filled with card tables, all vacant and no one in sight. To his left was a dim bar with tables and booths, and a small dance floor. He thought it was empty as well until he spotted a tendril of smoke drifting toward the ceiling. He saw Jack Nolan seated in one of the booths.

Durant crossed the dance floor. Nolan watched him with the look of a fox eyeing a lone partridge. "Hey, slick," he said with a breezy smile. "I see you found the place."

"Easy enough to find," Durant said, settling into the booth. "First person I asked gave me directions."

"Well, I like a man that's on time. Just so we get off on the right foot—you packin' heat?"

"Yeah, I'm carrying a gun."

"Thought so," Nolan said. "Automatic, is it?"

Durant nodded. "A Luger."

"I prefer a revolver myself. Automatics tend to jam when you need 'em most."

"Depends on how you treat them. I clean mine every night."

"Do you?" Nolan seemed amused. "I guess Elmer Spadden's a testament to that. You stopped his ticker p.d.q."

"I didn't have much choice."

"Elmer was always better with his dukes than a gun. Where'd you learn to shoot so good?"

Durant shrugged. "Mostly in France."

"No kiddin'!" Nolan said, exhaling smoke. "You were in the war?"

"Wasn't everybody?"

"What part of France?"

"Chateau-Thierry. Belleau Wood. Other places I've forgot."

"I'll be damned." Nolan took a drag on his cigarette, oddly pleased. "I was a Leatherneck, Fifth Marines. How about you?"

"Infantry," Durant said. "Just another doughboy."

"No, slick, not the way you shoot. I'll bet you came home with a chestful of medals."

"I'd bet the same about you."

"Something, isn't it?" Nolan's voice was almost nostalgic, tinged with camaraderie. "Funny the way wars turn out. You a movie stuntman and me a . . . what can I say— a jack-of-all-trades."

"Anything's better than war," Durant said, surprised by the tone of the conversation. "How'd you make it back home in one piece?"

"I'd have to put it down to pure luck. And you?"

"Well, like they say, there weren't any atheists in the trenches. God or luck, take your choice."

"A good eye helped, too."

"How do you mean?"

"Knocking off Krauts." Nolan studied him with a crooked smile. "The way you took down Spadden—in the dark."

Durant returned the smile. "You'll recall there was a streetlight. Luck was on my side, too."

"Not God?"

"Who had time to pray?"

Nolan grinned. "Too bad we're on opposite sides of the fence. I might've liked you."

"Not too late," Durant said, spreading his hands. "You might like me more than you thought."

"Time to get down to business, huh? You said on the phone something could work to my advantage. What was that all about?"

"How'd you like to walk away from Galveston with a fresh start? Wipe the slate clean?"

"That'd be some wipe," Nolan said with an ironic smile. "Go ahead, I'm all ears."

Durant leaned forward. "I've got a direct line to the attorney general of Texas. I can arrange immunity for any crime you've ever done." He paused for emphasis. "And ten thousand in cash to seal the bargain."

"Judas only got thirty pieces of silver. Who do I have to betray?"

"Tie William Magruder to Quinn and Voight. That gets the mob off my back and it saves my bank. And you're off scot-free."

Nolan held his gaze. "I suppose you'd expect me to testify in court?"

"It won't come to that," Durant said earnestly. "Magruder will be ruined in politics and your bosses won't be able to help him. A sworn affidavit with all the details should turn the trick."

"Which you and your reformer buddies would publish in the newspaper. Do I hear this right?"

"That's the general idea."

Nolan laughed. "I always said you had brass balls. You really thought I'd rat out Quinn and Voight?"

"They're not important," Durant said. "I'm after Magruder."

"They're important to me, slick. Forget loyalty and talk about staying alive. I couldn't run far enough fast enough. You'd be reading my obituary."

"Something tells me that wouldn't happen. Who'd have the guts to go up against Diamond Jack Nolan?"

"Save the sales pitch," Nolan said firmly. "Tell the attorney general I decline the offer. No deal."

"Why not sleep on it?" Durant said. "A deal like this comes along once in a lifetime. You might feel different tomorrow."

"Yessir, I do admire a man with balls. Too bad we didn't meet someplace besides Galveston."

"That's your final word on it?"

"Yeah, that's final."

"Sorry to hear it, Jack."

"Life's a bitch, ain't it?"

They parted with a handshake in the parking lot. Durant drove off in his Chevy wondering where the deal had gone sour. Nolan followed a short distance behind in his Stutz Bearcat, stewing on just how much he'd tell Quinn and Voight. He hadn't been kidding when he said he admired a man with balls. He hoped he wouldn't have to kill Durant.

Nolan reached for his cigarettes. He discovered the pack had only one left just as he approached the intersection for La Marque. He turned onto Main Street, remembering there was a tobacco shop a couple blocks down. His attention was drawn to a snazzy canary-yellow Packard that looked vaguely familiar. He pulled into the curb.

A bell jingled over the door as he entered the tobacco shop. Off to the side, at the magazine racks, a man and a woman were standing with their backs to him. The phone in the phone booth blasted a strident ring, and the man hurried toward the rear of the store. As he turned into the phone booth, his features were visible for the first time, his profile caught in a moment of hard intensity. He closed the door.

Nolan recognized him immediately. For the last three nights he'd watched Robert Eberling at the tables in the casino. He recalled Voight mentioning that Eberling was a well-to-do rancher and a high roller, and by his play at the tables, a born loser. The woman still had her face buried in a magazine, but Nolan recognized her as well. She was Eberling's wife.

"Morning," the shop owner said. "What can I do for you?"

"Lucky Strikes," Nolan said, turning away from the woman. "Make it a couple packs."

After paying for the cigarettes, Nolan stepped outside and climbed into his car. He pulled away with one eye on the road and the other on the tobacco shop. Some snatch of conversation he'd overheard reminded him that Eberling had a suite at the Buccaneer. He asked himself why a high roller would be waiting for calls at a phone booth. A phone booth in La Marque.

He thought Dutch Voight would definitely be interested. Something about it didn't rhyme.

• • •

"Thirty-one thousand apiece."

"Another good week."

"Yeah, not bad," Voight said, removing the bearer bonds from his briefcase. "Sophie Tucker damn sure doesn't draw as good as Jolson."

Quinn chortled. "Nobody draws as good as Jolson."

They were in the office at the Turf Club. Yesterday, under pressure to deal with Frank Nitti, Voight had completely forgotten about the bonds. Their split was thirty-one thousand each from money skimmed off last week's operations. He placed the bonds in the massive safe which occupied one corner of the office.

"That's that," he said, closing the safe door. "Wonder what's keeping Jack?"

Quinn checked his watch. "You're right, going on eleven-thirty. I expected him back by now."

"Tell you one thing, Ollie. Nothing good will come of him meeting with Durant. We should've stopped it."

"We had our hands full with your old pal Nitti. Besides, I don't see any harm in their getting together. We'll find out what clever new scheme Durant has up his sleeve."

"To hell with his scheme!" Voight grunted, "High time the bastard was dead and gone."

"We'll get to it, Dutch. Let's wait to hear what Jack has to say."

The phone rang. Quinn answered and a quick smile came over his features. "Good morning, Father Rourke. Always a pleasure to hear your voice." He listened, nodding, his expression suddenly quizzical. "Yes, of course, Father. I'll be right over."

"That's odd," he said when he hung up. "Monsignor O'Donnell wants to see me and it sounded a little urgent. Wonder what's up?"

"Probably another contribution," Voight said. "You're the softest touch in town."

"All in a good cause, Dutch. You know how I feel about public relations."

Quinn and Voight donated to every church on the Island. Their purpose was to garner the goodwill of the people, and thus undermine the periodic outcries by reformist clergymen. But the population of Galveston was predominately Catholic, and their largest contributions were to the Catholic church. Quinn, who was Catholic himself, also considered it an investment in the Hereafter. He hoped to be forgiven, if not redeemed, of his sins.

"I'll be back shortly," he said, moving toward the door. "Keep Jack around till I hear what he has to say."

Voight pulled a frown. "Just remember half of these donations come out of my pocket. Don't let the monsignor soft-soap you."

"Think of your immortal soul, Dutch. You might still have a chance at the Pearly Gates."

"That'll be the day!"

Quinn found Turk McGuire waiting in the hall. Downstairs, the Cadillac Phaeton was parked at the curb in front of the club. McGuire held the door while Quinn climbed into the backseat, then got behind the wheel and started the engine. He swung the car around in a U-turn and headed south.

Quinn's thoughts jumped from the monsignor to things that needed doing at the Hollywood Club. Voight's remark about Sophie Tucker popped into his mind, and from there it was but a short hop to the ox behind the wheel. Everyone at the club knew McGuire was spending his nights in Sophie Tucker's hotel suite. Only Quinn dared mention it.

"Tell me, Turk," he said with a straight face. "How are things with you and Miss Tucker? Keeping her happy, are you?"

McGuire glanced at him in the rearview mirror. "Well, tell you the truth, it's the other way round. She's a lotta woman, boss."

"I suppose that accounts for the dark circles under your eyes. Not getting much sleep these nights?"

"Not a whole lot."

"Business before pleasure," Quinn said, forcing himself not to smile. "Don't overdo things in the romance department. We need her fresh for the show."

McGuire flushed with embarrassment. He managed a dopey grin. "Nothing to worry about there, boss. She's a regular firecracker."

"Turk, I'd say you're a lucky dog. Keep up the good work."

"I'll do my best, boss."

A few minutes later, they turned into the seashell driveway beside St. Mary's Cathedral. Tall towers framed the front of the basilica, with a central tower from which a statue of the Virgin Mary gazed out over the Island. The compound, which included the monsignor's quarters, was located on Twenty-first Street near Broadway. A few blocks to the west was the Ursuline Convent for nuns.

Father Rourke met Quinn at the door of the rectory. He escorted him down a long hallway to the monsignor's study. The room was appointed with furniture of dark teak and polished leather, the waxed hardwood floor glistening from a spill of sunlight through broad windows. A marble statue of the Blessed Virgin stood beneath a large, ornate crucifix.

Monsignor O'Donnell rose from behind his desk. He was a bear of a man, with a square, determined jaw, a broad forehead, and dark, bushy brows sprinkled with gray. His robes were plain, though finely tailored, and a silver crucifix hung suspended over the expanse of his chest. He gave the impression of rocklike strength, and authority.

"Oliver," he said, extending a meaty handshake. "How nice of you to come on such short notice."

"A pleasure, Monsignor." Quinn let himself be directed to a leather armchair. "We see each other too seldom."

"Yes, indeed, particularly for old friends."

Their relationship was one of cordial distance. They never appeared in public together, for a prince of the church could not be seen to socialize with the Island's most visible gangster. Yet Quinn, with steamship tickets delivered anonymously every summer, enabled the monsignor to visit his mother in Ireland. They were comfortable with discreet arrangements.

"Yesterday I received a call," O'Donnell said without further ceremony. "I've been asked to intercede in a delicate matter, and I prayed on it overnight. The caller was William Magruder."

"Magruder?" Quinn looked astonished. "Why would he call you about me?"

"There's the rub, isn't it? Mr. Magruder is concerned about his daughter, Elizabeth. A fine girl, I'm told."

"Yes, I know her personally. We hosted her birthday party at the club a week or so ago."

"Twenty-one, I believe she is," O'Donnell said, the trace of a brogue in his voice. "A young lass, so impressionable, and like many, so naïve. I'm sad to say she's become involved with one of your men, Oliver." He arched an eyebrow. "Romantically involved."

Quinn's jaw dropped. "Who?"

"A lad by the name of Jack Nolan."

"Why didn't Magruder come to me? Why drag you into it?"

"Think on it a moment," O'Donnell said with a sage nod. "A direct approach, or so Mr. Magruder believed, might offend you. As you can imagine, he's an outraged father, and properly so. He asked me to speak on his behalf."

"I understand," Quinn said, sitting stiff in his chair. "Monsignor, you have my word that Miss Magruder has seen the last of Jack Nolan. I'll put an end to it today."

"Nothing too drastic, Oliver. A word to the wise should be sufficient. Don't you agree?"

"A word or three, or four or more. You won't be bothered again, Monsignor."

"I knew we'd find a way between us. God bless you, Oliver."

Quinn departed with unusual haste. When he was gone, Monsignor O'Donnell leaned back in his chair and idly fingered the crucifix suspended from his neck. In many ways, he admired Quinn, and privately, he thought of him as a friend. A relationship not all that unusual within the church.

The idea, as he toyed with it, somehow brought to mind the Borgias. A noble Italian family, central figures in the Renaissance, with two popes and a saint to their credit. Then there was Cesare Borgia, son of a pope, ruthless and murderous, once a cardinal of the church. A man who strangled his enemies to death.

O'Donnell told himself there was ample precedent, established centuries ago by those who ruled the Vatican. A prince of the church and a gangster were entitled to be friends.

He thought Jack Nolan might soon appreciate the irony.

Chapter Nineteen

Nolan parked in front of the Turf Club. He knew he was running late, and strangely enough, he didn't care. He'd stopped at a hamburger joint for lunch, and tried to get his mind straight before reporting to Quinn and Voight. He still wasn't sure how it would play out.

The bookmaking parlor was slow for a Tuesday afternoon. There were a couple of horse races later on the West Coast, and die-hard bettors were already gathering to pore over the scratch sheets. Football games, both pro and college, weren't scheduled until the weekend, and there was little action. He glanced at the tote board as he walked through the club room.

Joe Reed, the elevator operator, greeted him with a sly grin. "Late night, was it, Jack? You rumrunners have all the fun."

"No, wasn't that, Joe." Nolan stepped onto the elevator. "We're bringing in a load tonight. I'll save you a bottle."

"Never turn down bonded whiskey. Nosiree, not me."

Reed was closer to the truth than he suspected. Tonight, rather than last night, would be the late night. Early that morning he'd called the Magruder home and spoken with Libbie. She was frantic to see him, and he'd agreed to meet her on a beach west of the amusement piers before tonight's rumrunning operation. He wasn't yet sure how they would get around the problem of her father. Or for that matter, the bigger problem of Quinn and Voight. He wondered that Magruder hadn't already contacted them.

Upstairs, Barney Ward was stationed at his usual post outside the office. Nolan didn't see McGuire in the billiards room or the athletic club and that gave him pause. He had somehow assumed Quinn would be there, waiting with Voight, for his report on the meeting with Durant. There was sure to be fireworks, and he silently wished they were both present. Quinn always had a tempering effect on Voight.

Ward nodded. "How's things, Jack?"

"Good as gold, Barney. Where's Mr. Quinn?"

"Dunno and didn't ask. Him and Turk went out a while back."

Ward held the door and Nolan stepped into the office. Voight was seated at his desk, a cigar clamped in his mouth, scanning entries in a ledger. He looked up with a sour expression.

"Where you been?" he said. "I expected you back an hour ago."

"Stopped off for lunch," Nolan said, dropping into a chair. "Figured it might be a long afternoon."

"Next time don't keep me coolin' my heels. What happened with Durant?"

"I'd have to say he surprised me. Him and his reformer pals cooked up a deal with the attorney general. They offered me immunity."

"Immunity from what?"

"Anything crooked I've ever done."

Voight stared at him. "I think you'd better spell that out."

Nolan recounted the gist of the meeting. He explained that Durant's chief goal was to establish a link between Magruder and the mob. In exchange for turning stool pigeon, Nolan would receive a grant of immunity from the attorney general, plus ten thousand dollars. A neat little package to entice him to turn Judas.

"Dirty bastards!" Voight fumed when he finished. "They really thought you'd go for that?"

"Well, it was worth a try," Nolan said. "Durant's dead set on nailing Magruder's hide to the wall. He doesn't care one way or the other about you and Ollie."

"I don't give a rat's ass whether he does or doesn't. Time to wash our hands of this whole mess. I want you—"

The door opened. Quinn walked into the office like a dragon breathing fire. His teeth were clenched, a knot pulsing at his jawline, and his eyes burned with anger. Voight looked at him with a dumbfounded expression.

"What the hell happened to you?"

"I just had a talk with Monsignor O'Donnell. Bill Magruder asked him to call me in and oh-so-politely slap my wrists. Care to guess why?"

"Why don't you just tell me?"

Quinn paced across to the window, then turned back and stopped. His eyes drilled into Nolan. "So I'm informed, one of our men has been screwing Magruder's daughter. Anything to it, Jack?"

"Not the way you mean," Nolan said, taken aback by the suddenness of the assault. "Sometimes you meet a girl and things just click. I'm stuck on her and it's mutual."

"Who gives a damn!" Quinn exploded. "You put us at risk with Magruder. Get your head on straight!"

"I'll take you off the hook," Nolan said in a reasonable tone. "I'll have a talk with Magruder and explain it to him. He'll see I'm serious."

"Jesus Christ! Do you think he wants a gangster in the family? Where's your brain?"

"What's the harm in trying? Who knows, I might win him over."

"Listen to me, Jack." Quinn's voice was glacial, his eyes suddenly cold. "Dutch and I won't let you jeopardize our business, everything we've taken years to build. Do you understand what I'm saying?"

Nolan understood exactly what he was saying. All it required was for them to open the door and call in McGuire and Ward. There was no loyalty, no friendship, certainly no brotherhood in the rackets. By nightfall, he would be swimming with the fishes at the bottom of the

Gulf. He decided the only way out was to lie. Convincingly.

"I hear you," he said with a lame shrug. "I just wasn't thinking straight."

"Then we're agreed," Quinn persisted. "You'll ditch the girl?"

"Yeah, sure, it's over and done with. I won't see her anymore."

"No pulling my chain here, Jack. You're on the level?"

"Yeah, boss, on the level."

Quinn studied him. "I've got your word?"

Nolan lied with the aplomb of a Chinese bandit. "I give you my word."

"Now you're talking sense."

"Are we through with the hearts and flowers?" Voight said, clearly disgusted with the whole conversation. "We've got business here that needs tending."

"Oh?" Quinn looked around. "What business is that?"

"Tell him, Jack."

Nolan again related the details of his meeting with Durant. Voight, puffing furiously on his cigar, was quick to add his own opinion. Quinn heard them out, then slowly nodded his head.

"Dutch is right," he said. "Time to get rid of Durant."

"Won't be all that easy," Nolan amended. "You mind a suggestion?"

"Let's hear it," Voight prompted with a wave of his cigar. "You're our boy when it comes to rough stuff."

Nolan steeled himself to lie earnestly. After all that had happened, he'd decided he didn't want to kill Durant. Maybe it was the way Durant had stood and fought that night, the night he'd killed Elmer Spadden. Maybe it was the fact that Durant had survived the trenches of France, and understood there were worse things than dying. Or maybe it had to do with Libbie, and Nolan's abrupt realization that he might get himself killed. He wasn't sure in his own mind as to the real reason. He only knew he had to play for time.

"Durant's dangerous," he said, wording it to get their attention. "After this morning, he knows we'll come at him again. He killed Elmer, and if we try him head-on, he could kill me, or Turk, or anybody else. We have to outsmart him to take him out."

"So?" Quinn said impatiently. "How do we outsmart him?"

"We move on him from a different direction. Maybe through the old guy at his bank, Aldridge. Or maybe the Ludlow girl, the one he's been dating. I'll figure out a way, don't worry about it. Something that'll force him to play into our hands."

"Like what?" Voight said. "Kidnap the girl, force him to come to you? Play him for a slip-up?"

Nolan smiled. "Something tricky, boss. Real tricky."

Voight and Quinn exchanged a glance. Something unspoken passed between them, and Voight finally nodded, "All right, Jack," he said. "Do it your way, but get it done by this weekend. I want him dead."

"I'll take care of it, neat and quick."

Nolan got out before they could ask more questions. Only later, after he'd left the Turf Club, did he remember he'd forgotten to mention the rancher, Robert Eberling. The one who hung around pay phones waiting for a call. He decided to keep it to himself.

One problem more might be one problem too many.

Durant drove around the Island for almost an hour. He needed time to think, to weigh what he would do next. All his options seemed foreclosed.

Shortly after one o'clock, he parked on the Strand. He knew he should eat something, but his stomach resisted the idea of food. Instead, he walked into the bank, offering Catherine a forced smile, and returned the car keys to Aldridge. He asked the older man into his office.

Aldridge closed the door, then took a seat. His eyes narrowed in assessment. "I take it things didn't go well?"

Durant laughed without humor. "Am I that obvious?"

"You look a little green around the gills. What happened?"

"Nolan turned me down cold. I think he was amused by the whole thing."

"Amused?"

"You know, like I was a numbskull to even think he'd go for it. He all but laughed."

Durant gave him a nutshell version of the meeting. He left out a good deal, but he covered what seemed to him the relevant points. He finished with a lame shrug.

"For the most part, it was a waste of breath. Nolan said if he took the deal, there'd be no place to hide. Quinn and Voight would have him killed."

"No question of it," Aldridge said. "I told you as much this morning. He would have been signing his own death warrant."

Durant nodded, his expression abstract. "The really strange thing was that I liked him. Once you get past that tough guy attitude, he's a regular joe."

"A regular joe who just happens to murder people for a living. Have you forgotten he tried to kill you?"

"No, I haven't forgotten, Ira. I'm just saying. . . ."

"Yes?" Aldridge prodded. "Saying what?"

"Nothing important," Durant said. "The only thing that counts is that he turned me down. I'm right back where I started."

"Earl, if anything, you're worse off. I tried to warn you of that before you met with him. You've gone from the skillet to the fire."

"How could it be worse than it was?"

Aldridge shifted in his chair. "Nolan will report everything you said to Quinn and Voight. Their view—and, unfortunately, it's correct—will be that you tried to bribe him to betray them. How do you suppose they will react?"

"Don't have to be a mind reader," Durant replied. "They'll order Nolan to plant me six feet under. What's new?"

"What's new is that you've attacked them personally. Before, they were doing Magruder a favor, or perhaps looking for revenge because you killed one of their men. Now you've made it personal, very personal. You've threatened *them*."

"Yeah, you're probably right."

"I know I'm right," Aldridge said soberly. "And to compound matters, Magruder's applying pressure of his own. Do you remember what you said when we left his office Saturday?"

"What?" Durant searched his memory. "That he was already on the horn to Quinn and Voight?"

"Exactly. So now, in addition to Magruder, Quinn and Voight have a personal stake. They want you dead as much as Magruder—perhaps more."

"Got myself in a helluva fix, didn't I, Ira?"

"I'm afraid so." Aldridge sat forward, his concern genuine. "You really need to leave town, the quicker, the better. You're in great danger, Earl."

Durant waved him off. "I told you once before, that's not an option. There's no place to hide, anyway. They could find me."

"You're more resourceful than that. If you really wanted to, I'm sure you could disappear and not be found. And you needn't worry yourself about the bank. I'll protect your interests."

"Hell, Ira, you're the banker around here anyhow. I guess I'm just too stubborn to run. Or maybe too dumb. Take your pick."

Aldridge sighed heavily. "You know you don't have a chance. They'll kill you."

"Maybe, maybe not," Durant said, his features stoic. "But that doesn't change anything. I won't run."

Catherine stuck her head in the door. "The Holy Trinity is here to see you. Should I tell them to wait?"

"No need to wait," Durant said. "Might as well get it over with."

Aldridge rose. "I'll step outside."

"No, stick around, Ira. I could use the moral support."

Baldwin and Adair, followed by Herbert Cornwall, filed into the office. Aldridge leaned against the wall, arms folded across his chest, while they arranged themselves in chairs before the desk. Their faces were expectant, eager for good news.

"We couldn't stand it any longer," Baldwin said. "How did things go with Jack Nolan?"

"Not good," Durant told them. "He refused the offer. Wouldn't even discuss it."

Their features registered first surprise, then shock. Adair fidgeted nervously. "How could he not discuss it? What did he say?"

"What he said was 'Thanks, but no thanks.' A flat turndown."

"I'm sure there was more to it than that, Mr. Durant. Could you be a little more specific?"

Durant once again related the tone of the meeting. He left out anything about the war, and the discovery that he and Nolan had served in France at the same time. When he finished, the men sat for a moment in bewildered silence. Cornwall finally found his voice.

"I don't understand," he said. "Why would anyone refuse immunity? It doesn't make sense."

"Look at it from his standpoint," Durant said. "He figured he wouldn't live long enough to enjoy his new freedom. Why get yourself killed for nothing?"

Baldwin stiffened. "Do I detect a note of sympathy, Mr. Durant? Why would you care what happens to Jack Nolan?"

"Don't put words in my mouth," Durant said bluntly. "I told you why he refused, and what I think doesn't matter. His reasons were good enough for him."

"All's not lost," Cornwall broke in. "You could still issue a public statement."

"A statement about what?"

"Something to the effect that you met with Nolan and offered him immunity. But while he refused the offer, he nonetheless confirmed the link between Magruder and the mob. How does that sound?"

"Sounds like a lie," Durant informed him. "Nolan didn't say that."

"Who's to know?" Cornwall said with a conspiratorial smile. "It's your word against that of a notorious gangster. I think public opinion would be on our side."

Aldridge, silent until now, could no longer contain himself. "Herbie, how bad do you want to be mayor? Enough to make a liar of Earl, not to mention yourself? I don't think I'd vote for you."

"This isn't your affair," Cornwall said testily. "We're discussing what's best for the community. The people!"

Durant stood. "Gentlemen, I think that concludes our business. Today or any other day."

"Wait now!" Baldwin sputtered. "We can still—"

"No, we can't," Durant cut him short. "Ira, would you show these gentlemen the door?"

Aldridge moved across the room and opened the door. Baldwin looked as though he was on the verge of saying something, but he was silenced by Durant's dark scowl. The men trooped out of the office and Aldridge closed the door behind them. He turned back to Durant.

"To paraphrase Lord Bolingbroke—the art of a politician is to disguise vice in a way that serves virtue."

"Who's Lord Bolingbroke?"

"An English nobleman," Aldridge said. "He made that remark about two hundred years ago."

"You a student of history, Ira?"

"Only where it concerns rascals and liars—like Herbie Cornwall."

Durant thought it went further. The Englishman's remark, though he'd never heard it before, seemed to hit the mark for all of Galveston. Politicians, unscrupulous businessmen, and the mob.

Vice disguised as virtue.

• • •

Stoner kept one eye on the rearview mirror. He and Janice were approaching Houston, and he was still wary of being followed. His appointment with Captain Purvis was set for two o'clock.

Earlier, on the telephone, Colonel Garrison had given him directions. The headquarters for the Ranger Company was located on the outskirts of the city, not far from Rice University. The single-story frame building was set back off the road, identified by a sign hung between stout posts. They pulled into the parking lot with time to spare.

The reception room inside was manned by a sergeant and two orderlies. Stoner identified himself by name only, reluctant to say anything more until he'd spoken with Captain Purvis. The sergeant inspected Janice with a quick, appreciative glance, then disappeared into the back of the building. He returned shortly and led them down a hallway to a door without markings. He motioned them into an office.

Captain Hardy Purvis rose from behind his desk. A tall man, he was in his early forties, with angular features and sparse ginger hair. He had served with distinction in the Ranger Batallion posted along the Rio Grande during the war in Europe. His promotion to captain was the result of breaking a German spy ring operating out of Mexico and infiltrating agents across the border. He was known in the Rangers as an officer who went by the book.

"Come in, Stoner," he said, waiting for the sergeant to close the door. "I've been expecting you."

"Captain," Stoner said by way of acknowledgment. "I'd like you to meet Janice Overton. She's working with me on the Galveston case."

"Miss Overton." Purvis gestured them to chairs before his desk. "Colonel Garrison gave you quite a recommendation. He said you volunteered for the job."

"Actually, I got drafted," Janice said with a coy

smile. "I think I was the only girl Clint knew who was crazy enough to go undercover."

"I see." Purvis seemed uncertain how to take her flippant manner. He turned to Stoner. "The colonel tells me you insisted that I not be informed of this operation. Why was that?"

"Mostly for security, Cap'n," Stoner said frankly. "I was told the mobsters in Galveston don't take prisoners. Seemed like the fewer who knew, the better."

"In other words, you were concerned there might be leaks out of my office. Do I hear you right?"

"No, sir, not just exactly. I figured it was safer—for Janice and me—if everything was kept on the q.t."

"You're giving me the runaround, Sergeant. I'd like a straight answer."

Stoner cocked his head. "How long have you been trying to shut down Galveston?"

"Over a year," Purvis snapped. "What's that got to do with anything?"

"Well, Cap'n, we've been there a little over two weeks. So far, one gangster's been killed, and another one killed a civilian in a speakeasy. Galveston's a dangerous place."

"Get to the point."

"I guess the point's pretty simple. Janice and me are at risk every day we're working undercover. I like the odds better if nobody knows we're there."

Purvis knotted his brow in irritation. "Sergeant, I don't like anyone working my district without my knowledge. Just to be frank about it, I don't give a damn what your reason is."

"I understand, sir," Stoner said in a level voice. "Maybe you ought to talk with Colonel Garrison."

A dark look came over Purvis. He had spoken with Garrison at length on the telephone that morning. Garrison told him in no uncertain terms that he endorsed Stoner's plan for the raid on the Hollywood Club. Purvis was to be in nominal command, Garrison said, but Stoner would call the shots on the raid. The order, though tactfully phrased, was nonetheless an order.

Janice watched the byplay with a secret smile. She knew the score, and she knew that Sergeant Stoner was politely reminding Captain Purvis of who was in charge. On the phone that morning, Stoner had presented his case in the strongest possible terms, pointedly noting that it was his and Janice's lives at stake. His arguments were short of insubordination, but he'd insisted that he control the operation. Garrison, impressed by his plan, had finally agreed.

"Let's move on," Purvis said in an attempt to save face. "Colonel Garrison said you've worked out a plan for a raid. Tell me about it."

"Yessir," Stoner said with just the proper note of respect. "You've seen the inside of the club, right?"

"Several times."

"Then you know how they control those doors. The one into the lounge and the one beyond that into the casino."

"Of course," Purvis said impatiently. "They slow us down until, by the time we get there, the gaming devices have disappeared. I'm waiting for you to tell me how they do it."

"I don't have any idea," Stoner said. "That's the whole point of setting up the raid."

"Wait a minute, I'm missing something here. Are you telling me you haven't figured out how they get rid of the gaming equipment?"

"Yessir, that's exactly what I'm saying."

"Judas Priest!" Purvis barked. "You don't know any more about the casino than I do. Garrison led me to believe you have a plan. A foolproof plan."

Stoner wagged his head. "Captain, I don't know that anything's foolproof. But I'd have to say this comes pretty close."

A moment elapsed in turgid silence. Purvis abruptly realized that Garrison had purposely withheld critical information. He'd been painted into a corner and subtly placed at the command of a sergeant. He took a slow, deep breath.

"All right, Sergeant," he said in a resigned tone. "Let's hear your plan."

"Works like this, Cap'n," Stoner said, watching him closely. "Janice and I will be in the casino Friday night. You and your men pull a raid at nine sharp. Any problem with the timing?"

"No problem at all. Go ahead."

"Your raid's the key to the whole thing. They'll slow you down and do whatever they do to make the casino disappear. But this time, Janice and I will be there to see how it happens."

"Won't work," Purvis said. "We have to catch the gaming devices in actual operation. Otherwise we can't make an arrest."

"That's the second step," Stoner informed him. "You and your men will pull another raid Saturday night."

"Saturday night?"

"Yessir, at ten o'clock on the button. Voight and Quinn will never expect you to hit the place two nights in a row. We'll catch them with their pants down."

"No, I'm sure they won't," Purvis said. "But what does that accomplish? We still have to catch them in the act of operating gaming tables."

"You will, Cap'n."

"What makes you so certain?"

"I'm going to hold the casino till you and your men get there."

"Are you?" Purvis scoffed. "How do you propose to do that?"

Stoner grinned like a jack-o'-lantern, and told him.

Chapter Twenty

A crescent moon hung like a crooked lantern in a velvet sky. The Gulf was calm under a light breeze, the tide lapping gently against the shoreline. Silvery beams of starlight skipped and skittered across the dark waters.

Libbie waited in her Chevy coupe. The car was parked at a sheltered cove five miles west of the amusement piers. The spot was a short distance off the road and overlooked the white sand of a moonlit beach. Hers was the only car at the cove.

The call that morning from Nolan had been a godsend. She was still infuriated with her father, and hadn't spoken to him since their argument yesterday morning. Yet her concern was for Jack, and the deeper fear that her father had reported him to Quinn and Voight. She was worried for his safety.

A car pulled in behind her, quickly cut the headlights. She looked around and saw Nolan step out of his Stutz Bearcat, his features visible in the faint cast of the moon. He glanced back at the road, as though assuring himself they wouldn't be seen, and then walked around the side of her car. He slipped into the passenger seat.

"Hi there, gorgeous," he said lightly, cupping a hand behind her neck. "Been waiting long?"

"All my life."

His touch was like fire against her skin. She scooted across the seat, into his open arms, and he enfolded her in an embrace. She kissed him fiercely, wriggling to get closer, her breasts pressed against the holstered gun beneath his suit jacket. She didn't care about the gun, or who he was, or what he might have done. She never wanted to let go.

They finally parted, slightly breathless, his mouth smeared with lipstick. "Damn," he said with a jester's smile. "I think maybe you missed me."

"Don't you dare kid," she said, nuzzling into his shoulder. "I've been worried sick about you."

"Tell you the truth, I felt the same way. How's things with you and your dad?"

"After yesterday, we aren't speaking. Has he said anything to your bosses?"

"No, not directly." Nolan hesitated, suddenly somber. "He sent the message through Monsignor O'Donnell. Quinn got called on the carpet this morning."

"What!" She sat up, rigid with shock. "He told Monsignor O'Donnell about us? About our—?"

"The whole kit and caboodle. Quinn even heard about the hotel in Houston."

"The son of a bitch! I can't believe he's my father. Why didn't he just take an ad in the newspaper?"

"Didn't need to," Nolan allowed. "Monsignor O'Donnell evidently read the riot act to Quinn. I got the story first hand, loud and clear."

"What happened?" she said, a little hitch in her voice. "Are you in trouble?"

A wayward thought flashed through Nolan's mind. Her father was yet another reason why he wouldn't kill Durant, perhaps the best reason. There was revenge of sorts in letting Durant continue to frustrate the old bastard. He liked the idea, a lot.

"Jack, didn't you hear me? Are you in trouble?"

"I was," Nolan said, wishing he could tell her the truth about her father. "Quinn and Voight raked me over the coals pretty good. We finally came to an agreement."

"I don't understand," she said, looking at him. "What kind of agreement?"

"I took a blood oath I'd never see you again. Told them we were finished."

"You're not serious!"

"On my honor."

"But you're here."

Nolan smiled. "I lied like a dog."

"Tell me it's true," she said, staring into his eyes. "Tell me you'll never leave me."

"I'll never leave you, and that is the honest-to-God's truth. What was it you said once, kismet? We're stuck with one another."

"Oh, Jack!" She hugged him desperately. "I love you so much. You just don't know."

"Yeah, I do," Nolan said softly. "It's the same for me."

"Is it, you mean it? You'll never take it back?"

"Never in a month of Sundays. You've got me hooked."

"Good Lord!" Her features went taut. "I just happened to think. What will Quinn and Voight do if they find out?"

"That's not an option," Nolan said seriously. "We have to be damn careful from now on. Double damn careful."

"But we can't sneak around like this all the time. The Island's too small, and there are too many busybodies. We're bound to be seen."

"I'm already working on it. I'll think of something."

"Jack."

"Yeah?"

"Make love to me."

"In a car?"

"Yes, dammit!" she said in a husky voice. "I need you."

Nolan hadn't done it in a car since he was in high school. Though the seat made it awkward, they managed to stretch out just enough by opening the door. She loosened her garter belt and slipped off her panties, and he fumbled his pants down. She took him in a rush of emotion, pulling him deep inside, and they both peaked within moments. When they finished, spent and breathing hard, she clung to him, unwilling to let go. She whispered in his ear.

"Jack."

"Yeah?"

"Next time bring a blanket."

"What for?"

"Silly," she said, kissing him tenderly. "We'll do it on the beach."

"The beach?" he said doubtfully. "Won't that be a little sandy?"

"Well, good-lookin', we're definitely going to make love. So it's the beach or the car. Which would you prefer?"

"I'll bring the blanket."

They decided to leave ten minutes apart. After they were dressed, she walked him to his car. He took her in his arms, holding her a moment in a snug embrace, then stepped back. He looked down at her in the moonlight.

"One last thing, and it's important."

"Okay."

"You've got to convince your dad we're finished. You can't let on we're playing for time."

She laughed wickedly. "Oh, don't worry, I'll convince him."

"You're sure?"

"Yes, sweetheart mine, I'm very sure."

"Good, give me a kiss for luck."

She kissed him soundly on the mouth. "When will I see you again?"

"I'll call you tomorrow."

Delmonte's was one of the finer restaurants in Galveston. A family-owned establishment, it was off the beaten path, and seldom frequented by tourists. The clientele was composed primarily of Islanders who appreciated fine food.

Durant had a reservation. Earlier, at the bank, he'd asked Aldridge to recommend a restaurant for a special occasion. He declined to elaborate even when the older man gave him a questioning look, but Aldridge nonetheless told him of Delmonte's. All that afternoon he had avoided talking with Catherine, and just before closing time, he'd invited her to dinner. She readily accepted.

The special occasion Durant had in mind was an ending. Alone, sequestered in his office, he'd spent the afternoon deliberating his future. He knew the mob would attempt to kill him, and for every attempt that failed, there would be others. His refusal to run was a mixture of pride and anger, and the knowledge that he couldn't live with himself if he turned tail. All that said, he now viewed his prospects with a degree of fatalism. Yet he would not allow fear to make him a coward.

Which left the matter of Catherine. He felt he had at last found a woman who interested him and kindled a depth of affection he'd never known with other women. Those feelings led inevitably to the realization that every time they were together, he placed her life in jeopardy. There was no absolute that the mob wouldn't try to kill him when he was with her, and however inadvertently, catch her in the crossfire. That was a risk he was unwilling to take, one he would never ask her to share. He planned to end their relationship tonight.

The service at Delmonte's was impeccable. They were shown to a cozy booth, where the table was appointed with linen and fine crystal. A waiter materialized to fill their water glasses and present a basket of freshly baked bread. He nodded approvingly when Catherine selected the braised squab, and all but shrugged when Durant ordered a rib-eye steak. Dinner began with a delicate squash soup, followed by salad.

Durant played on Catherine's fascination with motion pictures. He subtly led her into a conversation about some of the more bizarre stunts he'd been involved with, dwelling on humorous mishaps that went with the job. From there, he easily prompted her questions about movie stars, particularly glamorous women, and their madcap eccentricities. He kept it light and entertaining, a last dinner she would remember with fondness. He intended to end it when he took her home.

A story about Gloria Swanson, just as Catherine finished her squab, brought tears of laughter to her eyes. She dabbed away the tears with her napkin, her cheeks flushed with happiness, and calmed herself with a sip of water. She looked at him across the table, still smiling, and shook her head with amusement. He thought he'd never seen her more radiant.

"All right, now," she said, composing herself. "You've kept me in stitches long enough for one night. I want to hear what happened with Jack Nolan."

Durant tried to shrug it off. "Another harebrained idea that went nowhere. There's nothing much to tell."

"No?" Her gaiety of a moment ago suddenly vanished. "Then why is Mr. Aldridge so desperate for you to leave town?"

"How'd you know that?"

"Earl, he's worried to death about you. He said he argued himself hoarse and you wouldn't listen. He asked me to talk with you."

"Nothing to talk about," Durant said, sloughing it off. "Ira's jumping at shadows."

She studied him intently. "You're not telling me the truth, are you? There's something more."

"Why would you say that?"

"Because of the way Mr. Aldridge is acting. I think Nolan threatened you this morning. Threatened you with more than another beating. Didn't he?"

"Yes and no," Durant said slowly. "There's more to it than you know."

"Things you haven't told me."

"Yes."

"Earl—" She touched his hand. "Do you know what I feel for you? Do you?"

"We're probably feeling the same thing."

"Then don't you think I deserve to know?"

Durant saw his good intentions slipping away. Despite himself, he ended up telling her everything, including how he'd killed Elmer Spadden. She was shocked, but at the same time, she felt an incredible sense of relief. She finally understood what he'd been facing alone for so long.

"I'm glad you told me," she said when he finished. "You never again have to hide anything from me."

"Catherine, there's even more to it. These men don't give a damn who they hurt. They're the sort—"

"You believe I'm in danger, don't you?"

"Yeah, I do." Durant was startled by her intuition. "Look, I think it'd be better—"

"You want to stop seeing me, don't you? So I won't get hurt?"

"Only till things shake out. Another week or so and we'll know what's what."

"No."

"No what?"

"I won't stop seeing you," she said in a no-nonsense voice. "And let's not discuss it any further. I've made up my mind."

"Well, I think I've got something to say about that. I'm the one who has to be the judge of what's best."

"Earl."

"What?"

"My mind's made up. Okay?"

Durant knew better than to argue it further. When they left the restaurant, he walked her home, alert and watchful, expecting Nolan and his goons to appear at any moment. He fully intended to end it once they reached the house. A quick kiss and a firm good-bye. Discussion closed.

She surprised him again. The house was dark, even though it was only a few minutes past nine. At the door, when he started to kiss her, she took his hand and pulled him inside. She shushed him with a finger to her lips.

"Mother's already asleep," she whispered. "Just follow me and don't bump into anything."

"Don't you think—"

"Will you please *hush*!"

She led him to her bedroom. A faint blush of moonlight filtered through the window, and she tugged him inside, then gently closed the door. She put her arms around his neck and gave him a smoldering kiss, darting his mouth with her tongue. She pressed herself to his groin, felt him grow hard, and laughed a minxish little laugh.

He knew then they would never argue about it again.

Libbie arrived home shortly before ten o'clock. She sat in the car a moment, composing herself for the charade she was about to play. Her one imperative was that her father be convinced she was the jilted woman.

On the drive back to town, she had come to grips with the reality of the situation. The most vivid part of the evening was Jack's entreaty that she persuade her father their affair was over. She realized what he was saying between the lines, trying not to frighten her too much. Quinn and Voight would have him killed unless they believed it was finished.

The key was her father. She somehow had to dupe him to the point that he believed she'd seen the last of Jack Nolan. Only then would he express a genuine thanks to Quinn and Voight for having ended the affair. Only then would Quinn and Voight feel confident their intervention had brought the affair to an abrupt, and final, halt. Her father was the key to Jack's survival.

She would have to trust Jack to find a way from there. She knew in her heart of hearts that he loved her, and she believed him when he said he would never leave her. Though he hadn't said as much, she knew he would never be content with furtive meetings on the beach, so shabby it was almost gauche. She was certain he had some scheme in mind he hadn't told her about, something he was working on. Something clever and secure, something lasting.

Which meant she had to be equally clever. Her father was quick and perceptive, nobody's fool. On the way into town, she had stopped at a bootlegger's and bought a pint of Old Crow. She'd taken a slug to fortify her nerves, and then dabbed drops here and there on her dress. The whiskey overpowered not only the scent of her perfume, but also the musk of love. She reeked when she walked into the house.

A light was on in her father's study. She was thankful the scene wouldn't be played out in front of her mother. Opal Magruder, unfailingly, retired to the master bedroom suite around nine o'clock. Her father was generally not far behind, for he arose at sunup and was in the office precisely at seven every morning. The light in the study indicated he was waiting for her to come home. She braced herself for a convincing performance.

Magruder was seated in a leather wingback chair. He was reading the *Southwest Cotton Journal*, and he lowered it to his lap when she stepped through the door. He wrinkled his nose in distaste. "You smell like a brewery."

"Wrong again, Daddy." She crossed the room and flopped into a chair, legs spraddled. "Your little angel wouldn't drink beer on a bet. I'm oh-too-much the sophisticate."

"Where have you been?"

"At Mary Lou Henley's."

"I could check on that, you know?"

"Why, please do. Give her a call."

Libbie wasn't worried. Mary Lou Henley was her best friend, and they had a pact to cover for each other in case their parents inquired. She took a cigarette from her purse and lit it with a gold lighter. Magruder folded his trade journal.

"What were you doing at Mary Lou's?"

"Drowning my sorrows." She exhaled a streamer of

smoke. "Girls love to exchange sob stories. Didn't you know that, Daddy?"

"Not particularly," Magruder said. "What sorrow are you drowning?"

"Oh, I have so many to choose from. How about my father's a cheesy, unfeeling bastard?"

"How dare you!"

"How *dare* you!" she fired back. "How dare you involve other people in my personal life. How *dare* you go to Monsignor O'Donnell!"

Magruder blinked with surprise. "I intended that to be a private matter. How did you find out?"

"Jack told me."

"Jack who?"

"Innocence doesn't become you. What other Jack are we talking about? Jack Nolan, my lover."

"You've seen him?" Magruder demanded.

"No, I regret to say." Libbie deliberately tapped ash from her cigarette on the Persian carpet. "He called me this afternoon and told me about Monsignor O'Donnell. How could you reveal my innermost secrets to a stranger? We're not even Catholic!"

"Monsignor O'Donnell is a man of discretion. He and Oliver Quinn are friends, and I needed a suitable intermediary. I could hardly go to Quinn myself."

"Why go to him at all?"

"You left me no choice," Magruder said churlishly. "I will not have this family dragged into a scandal and held up to public ridicule. Your *lover,* as you shamelessly portray him, is a gangster. A common hoodlum."

"Ex-lover," she said softly, concentrating on forcing a tear to her eye. "He broke it off on the phone this afternoon. I've lost him."

"Good riddance," Magruder pronounced. "You're far better off for it, my dear. The man would have ruined your life."

"You are so callous it scares me. Do you have any idea why he called it off? Do you, Daddy?"

"I presume Quinn spoke to him."

"Spoke to him!" she said sharply. "Oh, yes, Quinn and the other one, Voight, spoke to him all right. They threatened his life unless he jilted me. They all but put a gun to his head!"

"You make my point," Magruder admonished. "These men are thugs, very lower-class indeed. And Jack Nolan is one of them."

"You don't know anything about him! Nothing at all."

"I know who he works for, and that is more than sufficient. Quinn and Voight are not accepted in polite society."

"Aren't we sanctimonious?" she said cattily. "Everyone in town knows you have political arrangements with them. Doesn't that scandalize the family name?"

"Not in the least," Magruder huffed. "Politics oftentimes requires alliances of an expedient nature. That doesn't mean I would invite them into my home."

"Or into your daughter's bed."

"I'll thank you to keep a civil tongue in your head, young lady."

"You drove Jack off and you expect me to be civil? You don't understand at all, do you?"

"Understand what?"

"You broke my heart, Daddy. You broke it into little pieces, and I'll never forgive you. Not ever."

Libbie crushed her cigarette in an ashtray. She focused all her willpower into a single moment, and brought tears brimming into her eyes. She stood, walking to the door, then turned back. She looked at him with a little-girl-hurt expression.

"I feel all dead inside, Daddy. I only wish you knew."

The front door opened as she moved into the hallway. Sherm stepped into the foyer, closing the door, and walked toward her. He saw the tears glistening on her cheeks.

"Libbie." He stopped, taking her arm. "What's the matter?"

She swiped at her nose. "I'm surprised Francis lets you stay out so late. You're such the devoted husband."

"I was at a beauty pageant meeting. I saw the lights still on and thought I'd stop by."

Sherm was co-chairman of the International Pageant of Pulchritude. Young, shapely contestants came from all over the world to participate in a swimsuit revue, which was held every year in late spring. The pageant drew crowds of fifty thousand or more, pumping revenue into the town's economy, both legal and illicit. Oliver Quinn was the other co-chairman.

"How very timely," Libbie said in a wounded voice. "Did you and Mr. Quinn discuss my scandalous little romance?"

Sherm squinted at her. "What the devil are you talking about?"

"Ask Daddy."

She walked to the stairway. She bowed her head, sniffling loudly, and mounted the stairs as though sapped of energy. A small, hidden smile touched the corners of her mouth.

She thought Jack would have been proud of her.

The moon stood high at midnight. Nolan was alert for a signal as he steered the *Cherokee* south into the Gulf. Whizzer Duncan, armed with a Thompson submachine gun, was beside him in the cockpit. The fleet of lugger boats manned by his rumrunning crew plowed along in his wake. The dim glow of a lantern suddenly appeared off the starboard bow.

Nolan turned the wheel over to his pilot. Some minutes later, the motors throttled down, they swung in under the lee of the *Shark*. The schooner, painted black and almost invisible in the pale moonlight, swayed at anchor against gentle swells. The lugger boats stood off from the *Shark* as Nolan clambered up a rope ladder.

Captain Rob McBride waited amidships. "Jack, my boy!" he called out with a jaunty laugh. "I've missed the sight of you, and there's a truth."

"Goes both ways, Rob." Nolan handed him a manila envelope stuffed with cash. "Sixty thousand and not a penny less. I know you'll count it."

"Why of course I will, laddie. What's a count between friends?"

A short while afterward they stood watching crates of liquor being off-loaded onto the lugger boats. McBride, one eye on a net slowly clearing the hold, glanced at Nolan. He grinned his pirate's grin.

"Tell me, Jacko," he said. "Have you ever given any thought to smugglin'? There's far more money in it, and pleasurable work it is."

Nolan looked at him. "You offering me a job?"

"Aye, indeed I am! I've just bought another schooner and I'm lookin' for a captain with a head on his shoulders. We'd go partners."

"A speedboat and a schooner are just kissing cousins. I'm no sailor, Rob."

"Nothin' to it," McBride assured him. "A couple runs with me and you're ready for the high seas. You'll be lazin' about in Jamaica with rum punch in one hand and a lass in the other. Never a better place to hang your hat."

"Well, it's a twist," Nolan said with a humorous smile. "I never pictured myself as Blackbeard."

"I've been watchin' you, laddie. You're tough and you're smart, and you've got what it takes to make a smuggler. Put on your thinkin' cap."

"I might just do that, Rob. No harm in thinking, is there?"

"None a'tall!"

The lugger boats loaded, Nolan went down the ladder to the *Cherokee*. As they pulled away from the schooner, he looked back and saw McBride in the spill of light from the lantern. The old pirate waved, and Nolan tried to picture himself flying the Jolly Roger. Then, almost unbidden, he took it a step further.

He wondered how Libbie would like Jamaica.

Chapter Twenty-One

Stoner enjoyed watching her dress or undress. Either way, he thought of it as his own personal floor show, naughty but nice. He couldn't imagine that anyone on a burlesque stage had ever done it better.

Janice artfully played to her audience of one. They were in the bedroom of the suite, with Stoner seated in a chair by the windows. She knew there was no serious risk of hanky-panky when she was dressing; he seemed fascinated by what went into the creation. Undressing was an altogether different matter, somehow more provocative. Day or night, she was almost assured they would end up in bed.

The sun dipped below the horizon like a cauldron of smothered coals. Stoner was already attired in his tux, apart from his jacket, which was hanging in the closet. Outside the hotel, Seawall Boulevard was jammed with weekend tourists, a typical Friday night. Later, he and Janice would pretend shock when Captain Purvis and his Rangers raided the Hollywood Club. But that was later, and he saw no reason to let it intrude on the moment. He was watching the floor show.

Janice was naked. She felt his eyes on her as she stepped into her panties, then slipped into a bandeau brassiere designed for gowns cut low in the back. She next adjusted the straps on an elasticized garter belt, carefully rolled on sheer silk hose, and snapped the tops into fasteners. Her slip was crepe de chine, snug around the hips and trimmed in delicate lace. The slip was short, hugging her knees, and displayed the shapely curve of her legs. She moved to the vanity table.

The ritual of a woman dressing seemed to Stoner a work in progress. Her eyebrows were plucked, made fashionable by the French designer Erte, and she penciled a fine, thin arc in black. Kohl was applied around the eyes to give them an almond shape, then highlighted with blue eye shadow, and dark mascara was used to enhance the curl of the eyelashes. Her rouge was worn in the manner currently in vogue, concentric patches which accentuated her cheekbones. Her lipstick, a cherry red, was painted on like a bright rosebud.

The last touch was dabs of Shalimar on her neck, wrists, and behind her knees. A miracle of modern marketing, Shalimar meant "abode of love" and signified the passion of Shah Jahan, who built the Taj Mahal for the woman of his life. The fragrance was warm and sensual, exotically oriental, and widely believed to have a seductive effect on men of all ages. Janice knew it certainly worked on Stoner, and secretly thought of it as catnip for the boudoir. She smiled at him as she posed in a sleek evening gown that emphasized what it concealed.

"There!" she said with a coquettish little wink. "Olive Eberling never looked so good."

Stoner grinned. "You'll make the ladies jealous tonight."

"Flattery will get you *anything*, precious."

"I'll hold you to it after the raid. We'll have reason enough to celebrate."

"Darn," she moped, the sparkle suddenly gone from her eyes. "I hate to think it's going to end so soon. I've gotten to like being rich."

"Don't let down now," Stoner cautioned. "We've come too far to drop the ball. We're almost there."

"Oh, you needn't worry about me, Sherlock. I'm still up for the game."

"I like your spirit, Dr. Watson. Like your cute outfit, too."

"I think you like it better off than on."

"Yeah, maybe so, but you're dressed now. Time to go to work."

"Once more into the breaches, boys and girls. We'll fight the good fight tonight."

"Let's go get 'em, tiger."

The Hollywood Club was packed. Tonight was Sophie Tucker's closing night, and she'd again drawn a full house. Stoner and Janice were by now regular patrons, and the maitre d' greeted them with an obsequious bow. Their usual table was reserved by the dance floor, and waiters descended on them hardly before they were seated. Stoner, whose mood was already celebratory, ordered champagne.

The orchestra wailed away at the *St. Louis Blues*. The music of the Roaring Twenties was conspicuously lacking in nostalgia, the traditional ballad replaced by blues and jazz. Songs were abbreviated, a series of vocal ejaculations evoking a sense of primitive rivalry, or spiritual misery. Jazz in particular was brazenly defiant, music in the nude, rapid and feverish and exciting. A jazz musician's triumph was erratic syncopation, a bizarre and outré rhythm.

Janice, all but jiggling in her seat, thought it was the cat's meow. Blues and jazz had come upriver from New Orleans, spreading across the land so quickly it seemed an overnight sensation. In an era desperate with the need for escape, and cynical of anything conventional, the stuttered wailing of a saxophone became the salvation of white America. The big thing that year was the music of Jelly Roll Morton, and with it, a frenzied new dance. The orchestra segued into the Black Bottom.

Oliver Quinn stopped by the table. "Good evening," he said with the charm reserved for wealthy patrons. "Enjoying the music?"

"I just love it!" Janice cried. "Bob's such a stick-in-the-mud about anything new. I can't get him on the dance floor."

The floor was crowded, men flailing their arms and

women waggling their pert little bottoms with abandon. Stoner was not surprised by Quinn's cordial manner, for he'd lost something over three thousand in six nights at the casino. He saw nothing of Jack Nolan, who usually assisted Quinn in greeting the club's steady clientele, particularly high rollers. He wondered if Nolan was off on another rumrunning operation.

"I wish I could help, Mrs. Eberling," Quinn said, smiling at Janice. "Unfortunately, I'm not too much on these new dances myself. I seem to miss the beat somewhere."

"Know exactly what you mean," Stoner said with a haughty gesture toward the dance floor. "Give me a foxtrot any old day. That's my speed."

Quinn nodded affably. "We try to provide something for everyone here at the Hollywood Club. I'd say the casino is more your speed, Mr. Eberling."

"Well, that's yet to be proved," Stoner said ruefully. "You boys are into my pocket pretty deep. I'm lookin' to make a comeback."

"I'm sure you will, and then some. Your luck's bound to change."

"We're sure enough gonna find out tonight. I aim to hit the craps table like a bulldog on a bone."

"Mr. Quinn," Janice said, dismissing the subject with wifely disdain. "I understand the Ritz Brothers are opening tomorrow night. Are they as good as everyone says?"

"Even better," Quinn assured her. "They're born clowns, the jesters of Broadway. The best comedy act you'll ever see."

"Oh, I just can't wait!" Janice exclaimed. "You be sure to reserve our table, you hear? I adore comedy."

"You always have a table with us, Mrs. Eberling. We appreciate your patronage."

Quinn wandered off to greet other customers. Stoner watched him with an amused look. "Tomorrow night he'll wish he'd never seen us. Talk about a rude awakening."

"Careful, Mr. Eberling," Janice said sweetly. "Don't

count your chickens before they hatch. Isn't that what ranchers always say?"

"You're thinking of chicken farmers, Olive. Ranchers raise cows."

"Six of one and half a dozen of another, Roberto. You know what I mean."

"Honey, we're gonna take this place like Grant took Richmond. You wait and see."

The houselights dimmed as they finished their dinner. Trumpets blared and drums rattled as Sophie Tucker strutted onto the stage, framed in a rosy spotlight. "The Last of the Red Hot Mamas" wore a spangled gown that left little of her zoftig figure to the imagination. She carried a large feathered fan that swished with sexual innuendo.

She opened her closing show with what audiences now thought of as her signature song. The orchestra led her into *There'll Be a Hot Time in the Old Town Tonight.*

"I should be back by ten."

"You need your sleep, Ira. You're not getting any younger."

"Yes, dear."

"You're not listening to a word I say. You never do."

Naomi Aldridge was seated in an overstuffed chair. Her crocheting needle moved with steady precision as she worked on an elaborate lace doily. She was short and plump, and believed that men were overgrown boys who required constant bossing. She darted Aldridge a sharp look.

"No later than ten, you hear me?"

"Yes, dear, I hear you."

Aldridge gave her a peck on the cheek. He went out the front door and walked to his Chevy, which was parked in the driveway. The house, a modest two-story Victorian, was on a quiet, tree-lined street west of the business district. He backed out of the driveway and drove toward the Strand.

The problem, as Aldridge saw it, was that they'd

never had children. Whether Naomi was barren or he was sterile seemed to him a moot point. All her friends had children, and with age, she'd grown increasingly bitter with her empty nest. He felt her frustration, but at times she could be a handful. She treated him more like a mother than a wife.

On the way downtown it occurred to him that he had no room to talk. In private moments, he sometimes wished Earl Durant was the son he'd never had. He liked to think that his son would have been just as intelligent and re-sourceful, though perhaps not so foolhardy. He still couldn't understand Durant's obstinate refusal to leave Galveston. Discretion, given the situation, was absolutely the better part of valor.

Downtown, Aldridge turned north on Fourteenth Street. The Knights of Pythias building was located on the Strand at Fourteenth, and tonight was the night for the weekly board meeting. The Knights of Pythias was a fra-ternal and benevolent organization that devoted its re-sources to a range of charitable causes. He'd been a member for twenty-three years, and was quite honored to serve on the board of directors. His particular interest was the plight of needy children.

Aldridge parked the car around the corner on Four-teenth. He got out, dropping the keys in his suit pocket, and walked toward the Strand. A dark four-door Buick coasted to a halt beside him, and two men jumped out, crossing to the sidewalk. One was lean and wiry, the other was stout as a bull, and in light from the street lamp, he recognized them as hoodlums. Underlings, but nonethe-less men known to virtually everyone in town. Turk McGuire and Whizzer Duncan.

"Don't give us no trouble," Duncan said in a clipped voice. "Come along nice and peaceful."

"What's the meaning of this?" Aldridge searched the street for any sign of help and saw no one about. "Take your hands off me!"

"Get in the Goddamn car."

McGuire grabbed him by the scruff of the neck and bodily lifted him into the backseat of the Buick. Duncan hopped into the passenger seat and McGuire crawled in beside Aldridge, slamming the door. The car pulled away, braking at the corner, then crossed the intersection headed south on Fourteenth. Aldridge, still trying to collect his wits, realized there were four men in the car. He looked at the man seated on his left.

"Evening, Mr. Aldridge," Nolan said with a roguish smile. "Hope the boys weren't too rough. We had to move right along."

"I resent being manhandled," Aldridge said indignantly. "What is it you want with me?"

"Just business, Mr. Aldridge. Nothing personal."

"I demand an explanation."

"Well, you might say you're our hostage. We're holding you for ransom."

"I don't believe you," Aldridge said. "This has to do with Earl Durant and the bank, doesn't it?"

"You'll find out soon enough." Nolan lit a cigarette, exhaled smoke. "Just play along and don't worry about it. We're not going to hurt you."

Aldridge didn't buy it. They had abducted him by force, which under Texas law was punishable by life in prison. Even worse, he could identify them, and they weren't the sort of men to chance a live witness. He thought it very unlikely he would ever see his wife again.

The Buick turned a corner, moving west on Stewart Road. Nolan stared out the window, smoking his cigarette in silence. His crew had tailed Aldridge for the last three days, looking for the right moment to make the snatch. He had decided on Aldridge, rather than the Ludlow girl, for what seemed to him the most practical of reasons. Aldridge, who handled the day-by-day operations of People's Bank & Trust, was the better bargaining chip. Durant could never run the bank by himself.

Nolan was nonetheless troubled. Until he found a way out for himself and Libbie, he had to stall for time with Quinn and Voight. Grabbing Aldridge would make them think he was on the job, and perhaps string them along a few days more. Yet he was under orders to dust Durant by the weekend, and he'd already decided it would never happen. Somehow, between tonight and Sunday, he had to come up with a ploy that worked for him and Libbie, *and* Durant. He didn't have the least idea how he would pull it off.

Some six miles west of the downtown area, the car turned north onto a dirt road. Aldridge saw Sweetwater Lake on their right, a part of the Island that was largely uninhabited except for scattered farms. A short distance down the road, the driver turned onto a dirt track that meandered through a stand of trees and ended at a clearing overlooking the lake. Closer to the water, visible in the pale moonlight, was a ramshackle cabin. The windows were dark.

The men climbed out of the Buick. McGuire took a firm grip on Aldridge's arm, and with Nolan leading the way, they walked to the cabin. Inside, Nolan struck a match, lighting a coal oil lamp, and the sudden flare revealed what looked to be a backwoods camp for fishermen and hunters. There was a main room with a woodburning stove, rickety table and chairs, and a window looking out onto the lake. Through a door was a small bedroom, with two iron-framed single beds and a window at the side of the cabin. The smell of the place was musty, ripe with odors.

"All the comforts of home," Nolan said with a casual wave of his hand. "Think of it as your hideaway, Mr. Aldridge. You get your choice of beds."

Aldridge felt dizzy with fear. "I take it I'm being held prisoner."

"Let's say you're our guest. We stocked the place with groceries and Whizzer's not a bad cook. You could do worse."

"How long do you intend to hold me?"

"I'll let you know when I know."

Duncan and the driver, Lem Brewster, were assigned to stay behind and guard Aldridge. Nolan motioned to Duncan as he went out the door with McGuire. They stopped in the shadow of the cabin.

"No rough stuff," Nolan said pointedly, staring at Duncan. "Anything happens to that old man, I'll have your balls. Got it?"

"Hey, Jack," Duncan said with a wiseacre grin. "No need to throw your weight around. I'll treat him like he was my own father."

"Just make sure there's no slip-ups."

"What if he tries to escape?"

"You better hope you can outrun him. Otherwise you'll have to outrun me."

Duncan frowned. "I don't get you, Jack. What's the old fart to you?"

"We're not playing twenty questions here. Do like you're told, understand?"

"Yeah, sure, whatever you say."

They left Duncan standing in front of the cabin. McGuire got behind the wheel of the Buick, starting the engine, and Nolan took the passenger seat. A short while later they turned on to Stewart Road and headed back to town. McGuire glanced across at Nolan.

"What was that with Duncan? You think he'd croak the old guy?"

"Whizzer's got a mean streak that pops out now and then. Better safe than sorry."

"Why you so worried one way or the other?"

"Without Aldridge we don't have the bait for Durant. You follow me, Turk?"

"You're sayin' we need him alive to set the trap, right?"

"You just won the nickel cigar."

McGuire was Quinn's man, loyal to the last. Nolan knew that everything he'd said tonight would be reported to Quinn, and not long afterward, to Voight. The problem he'd now set in motion was running a con with no end in sight. No clear way out.

He thought he might yet get himself killed.

Traffic was heavy on the causeway. The crush was particularly bad on Friday nights as weekenders rushed to join the revelry. The Island was a carnival in motion.

There were three cars in the Ranger convoy. Captain Hardy Purvis and four men rode in a Buick, the doors emblazoned with the Ranger emblem. Directly behind were two Chevrolets, standard departmental patrol cars, each carrying five men. One man in every car was armed with a Winchester pump shotgun.

The traffic inched off the causeway at a sluggish crawl. Taillights blinked along the esplanade of Broadway, where cars were jammed bumper-to-bumper, barely moving. The towering electric sign at roadside—GALVESTON, THE TREASURE ISLAND OF AMERICA— seemed to mock those stranded in traffic. Their weekend was off to a slow start.

Hardy Purvis checked his watch. The raid on the Hollywood Club was scheduled for nine o'clock and it was now eight-fifty. He cursed, surveying the traffic jam, all too aware his raiding party would never make it across the Island in ten minutes. His anger was compounded by the thought of Stoner waiting in the casino, tonight's plan stymied by their late arrival. He opened the door and stood on the running board, scanning the street ahead. He saw no break in the traffic.

A part of his anger was born of resentment. For three days he had stewed on what he considered an affront to his rank and his years of service. Colonel Garrison had effectively placed him under the command of a sergeant, and there was nothing for it but to swallow his pride. But now, the damnable Friday night traffic was about to make it appear he couldn't execute the simplest part of the plan. Garrison was sure to rate his performance tonight with the

deadliest threat to a Ranger's career, the ominous Four
Ps: Piss Poor Prior Planning.

Purvis made a spur-of-the-moment decision. Far better to announce your arrival, he told himself, than to be
thirty minutes late. He turned, looking at the Ranger cars
directly behind, and rapidly pumped his arm up and down
in the air. Then he stepped off the running board and slid
back in the passenger seat. He motioned to the driver.

"Let's have the siren and the chase lights."

"You sure, Cap'n?" the Ranger said blankly. "They'll
hear us a mile away."

"Goddammit!" Purvis thundered. "Don't argue with
me. Do it!"

The driver hit the switches. The siren blasted a shrill
wail and the bubble-gum lights on top of the Buick began
flashing. The cars to their front were stuck in traffic, nowhere to go and unable to move out of the way. For a
moment, with Purvis glowering like a singed rooster, they
sat locked in place. He abruptly flung an arm off to the
side.

"Take to the curb," he ordered. "Get around 'em,
Goddammit!"

The Buick bounced over the curb. Two wheels on the
street and two wheels on the lawn of a house, they lurched
east along Broadway. The patrol cars followed, sirens
blaring and lights flashing, plowing ruts in one lawn after
another as they bumped down the street. Purvis ordered a
right turn at the corner of Broadway and Fiftieth. They
headed south toward Seawall Boulevard.

Twelve minutes later the cars skidded to a halt in
front of the Hollywood Club. The sirens wound down
with a mournful screech and the bubble-gum lights
winked off as the Rangers piled out and rushed the door.
The doorman, resplendent in top hat and tails, quickly
moved aside. He waved them on with a pearly grin.

"Good evening, Cap'n," he said in a piping voice.
"Mighty fine to see you again."

Purvis slammed through the door. The Rangers,

formed in a tight phalanx, followed him down a hall lined with exotic plants. As they disappeared into the club, the doorman moved to a small button secreted behind one of the plants, mounted on the wall. He pressed it three times.

"Yessir, Cap'n," he said merrily. "Welcome to the Hollywood Club!"

Stoner was standing at the craps table. Another customer was rolling the dice and he was betting the numbers on the felt layout. Out of the corner of his eye, he saw Janice playing the slots along the far wall. He sneaked a peek at his watch.

Seven minutes past nine. He wondered what was keeping Purvis and his Rangers. Early that morning, he'd driven into La Marque, using the phone booth in the pharmacy, and called Houston. Purvis, irked at being questioned, had assured him the raid would come off as planned. Nine o'clock sharp.

So where the hell were they?

Three sharp blasts sounded on a gong. Stoner turned and saw the hammer pounding on a fire alarm at the rear of the room. For a moment, everyone in the casino froze, and then Dutch Voight appeared in the doorway of the office. He raised his arms as the fire alarm went silent.

"Ladies and gentlemen," he called out. "We are about to be raided by the Texas Rangers. Please follow the directions of the housemen and don't worry about a thing. Just stay calm."

The dealers and croupiers instructed the customers to pocket their chips and move back from the tables. Voight waited until everyone was clear of the equipment and then stepped into the office. Through the open door, Stoner saw him walk to his desk, stoop down, and pull a lever mounted in the floor. A low hum of machinery vibrated through the casino.

The slot machines folded like Murphy beds, rolling into the walls. The reverse sides of the slots, now facing outward, were framed posters of popular motion pictures.

The floor separated beside the craps tables and the roulette tables as housemen hurriedly slipped elasticized covers over the equipment. In the next instant, the gaming tables rotated 180°, turning top to bottom as the floors cranked back into place. The bottoms of the tables, when they appeared, were baize-covered billiards tables. The cue sticks and balls were quickly removed from compartments along the edges.

Stoner was no engineer, but he immediately grasped the fundamental concept. Beneath the floor, and in the walls, was a massive hydraulic system, powered by electricity. He suddenly understood why the casino had been built at the end of the T-head pier, suspended over water. Below the casino, probably housed in steel and hidden from view, was a custom-designed marvel of hydraulic engineering. His respect for Quinn and Voight went up a couple of notches.

Even as he watched, the blackjack tables revolved into the floor, replaced by backgammon and bridge tables. Housemen produced cards and chairs, got the guests seated at the tables, and then mingled with the crowd. Gamblers who only moments ago were tossing dice and playing roulette now took up cue sticks and began banging balls around on billiards tables. The swiftness of the transformation was startling, hard to comprehend unless seen firsthand. A casino had been converted into a social club in less than three minutes.

Janice paused at Stoner's side. "Have you ever!" she said in a breathless voice. "Houdini has nothing on these people."

"Maybe he designed it for them," Stoner said with a bemused look. "I wouldn't have believed it if I hadn't seen it for myself."

"Sweetie, we're talking serious magic here."

"Yeah, and all without smoke or mirrors. A nifty operation. Damn nifty."

Voight walked to the front and unlocked the heavy oak doors. Hardy Purvis and his Rangers burst into the room as though storming fortified battlements. From the nightclub, announcing their arrival, came the strains of the orchestra playing *The Eyes of Texas*. Everyone looked up as if sharing a private joke.

"Come right in, Captain Purvis," Voight said with a wry smile. "What can we do for you tonight?"

"None of your wisecracks, Voight." Purvis glowered around at the billiards tables and backgammon players. "We're here to shut you down for good."

"Well, in that case, be my guest."

The Rangers conducted their usually thorough search. As with previous raids, they tapped the walls, stomped on the floor, and inspected the billiards tables. Stoner was impressed, and relieved, that Purvis never once looked in his direction. He thought the Ranger captain was a surprisingly good actor.

The search lasted almost thirty minutes. Finally, with a parting shot at Voight, Purvis led his Rangers back through the nightclub. The orchestra playfully announced their departure, and the audience joined in the spirit of things. Their voices carried through the lounge to the casino.

> *"The eyes of Texas are upon you*
> *All the livelong day!"*

"Well, Sherlock?" Janice whispered, her eyes bright with excitement. "What do you think?"

Stoner grinned. "I think Saturday night's our night. Our last night."

Chapter Twenty-Two

Durant got to the bank about eight-thirty on Saturday morning. The doors opened at eight but he was rarely ever there on time. The bank functioned just as well with or without him.

Nothing about People's Bank & Trust interested Durant. At first, when he'd decided to stay on, he had attempted to assume the duties of president. But he soon realized that the thing holding him in Galveston was his determination to thwart William Magruder. The bank itself was like a yoke around his neck.

There was never a moment he didn't resent how the bank had changed his life. He'd been in Galveston almost four weeks, and not a day passed without some bitter reflection about Hollywood. Though he kept in contact by phone, his friends in motion pictures were beginning to doubt he would ever return. He wasn't all that certain himself.

The phone conversations with Tom Mix and others in the film industry were frustrating. He found it impossible to unburden himself and tell them the truth. How could he explain that the mob had tried to kill him and would try again? How could he explain refusing to run and not come off sounding like some dime-store hero in a low-budget film?

The upshot was that he fudged the truth. He told them that selling a bank was far more difficult than he'd ever envisioned. Yet that explanation wore thin, particularly over a period of weeks. His friends listened, sometimes with sympathy, but they really had no interest in his problems. People in motion pictures were single-minded about their work, and they were quick to point out that Hollywood had a short memory. Your reputation was pegged to what you did today. Everything else was history.

The mere thought of it put Durant in a bleak mood. He wasn't sure he would get out of Galveston alive, much less return to the life he'd known in Hollywood. Entering the bank, he dreaded yet another day of twiddling his thumbs while pretending he understood balance sheets and financial summaries. Catherine intercepted him outside his office.

"Good morning." Her usual cheeriness seemed off a note. "Have you seen Mr. Aldridge?"

"No," Durant said. "He's not here?"

"Not yet. Fortunately, Mr. Jenks knows the combination to the safe. Otherwise we wouldn't be open for business."

Jenks was the head teller, Aldridge's principal assistant. Durant was at a loss. "Have you tried Ira at home?"

"Mrs. Aldridge called here." Catherine looked perplexed. "She said he went out last night and hasn't come home. She's so upset she started crying."

"Did she say where he went last night?"

"Some sort of meeting at the Knights of Pythias."

"Did she try calling any of the other members?"

"Early this morning she talked to two of them. They both said Mr. Aldridge didn't attend the meeting. Don't you think that's awfully strange?"

Durant felt a sudden chill. For four days, since his meeting with Jack Nolan, he'd expected another attack by the mob. He'd taken Catherine out twice in that time, always armed with his Luger, and always on guard against another assault. Yet nothing had happened, and with every passing day, he'd grown increasingly wary. He wondered now if they had decided on a different tack.

"I'm very worried," Catherine said, interrupting his ruminations. "Shouldn't we call the police?"

"Let me talk with Mrs. Aldridge first. Maybe there's something we. . . ."

Jack Nolan walked through the front door. Whatever doubt Durant might have had abruptly turned to certainty. Catherine saw the change in his expression and looked around, watching as Nolan moved toward them. Her mouth ovaled.

"Oh, God," she said on an indrawn breath. "I'm going to call the police."

"No," Durant said crisply. "Let me handle this."

Durant reassured Catherine with a touch on her arm. He entered the office, closing the door, and seated himself behind his desk. Nolan took a chair, tapping a cigarette from a pack of Luckies, and clicked a lighter. He lit up in a haze of smoke.

"We've got Aldridge," he said, pocketing his lighter. "Or maybe you hadn't noticed he's missing."

"I noticed," Durant said without inflection. "What do you want?"

"Same thing we wanted all along. Sell your bank to Magruder and you get Aldridge back in one piece. Otherwise. . . ."

"You'll kill him."

"Your words, not mine."

Durant stared at him. "Do you enjoy hurting old men?"

"Not my style." Nolan exhaled a cloud of smoke. "Look, chum, it's just business. Nobody has to get hurt."

"Why the turnaround? I thought you were after me, not the bank. Magruder refused my last offer."

"So he's in the market again."

Nolan was playing a new angle. Late last night, in an effort to stall for time, he'd talked to Quinn at the club. He suggested that Magruder would be even more in their debt if they convinced Durant to sell the bank before killing him. Quinn, after only a moment's thought, agreed.

Whether it was the late hour, or simply that he was pleased with himself, Quinn was in an expansive mood. He mentioned having met with Magruder on charity matters Friday afternoon, and then bragged about finally discovering the importance of People's Bank & Trust. Magruder, in a rare moment of candor, let slip that the bank controlled property he needed to complete his new resort project. His on-again, off-again ambivalence was now understandable. He might not get the bank, and the property, if Durant were dead.

Quinn then convinced Voight to follow Nolan's suggestion. By arranging for Magruder to acquire the bank, they positioned themselves to take a piece of the action on the resort project. Magruder had always insisted that they stay out of the hotel business; but with the debt so large in their favor, he could be persuaded to accept them as partners. Voight liked the idea so much he agreed to let Durant live a little longer. Still, he insisted that the bank deal be closed by Monday. He wanted Durant dead by Monday night.

Nolan had bought less time than he'd hoped. Yet he knew that running a con required not just craft but flexibility. By Monday he might think of a new angle that would spare him from killing Durant. Somehow, though he couldn't have explained it, he saw a link between sparing Durant and finding a way out for himself and Libbie. He thought perhaps it was Irish superstition, the ancient Gaelic belief that God granted favors for favors done. Whatever the reason, he'd already decided he would never kill Durant.

"Your move, slick," he said now. "The bank or Aldridge?"

"How do I know you'll let him go?"

"Hey, what more do you want? You've got my word."

Durant placed a call to Magruder's office. He went straight to the point when Magruder came on the phone. "Your mob buddies are holding Ira Aldridge hostage. How would you like to buy a bank?"

Magruder hesitated, as though digesting the news. "How much do you want?"

"One hundred thousand, and it's not negotiable. I get my price or your pals can keep Aldridge."

"Quite frankly, I am tired of haggling with you, Mr. Durant. Your terms are acceptable."

"How soon can your lawyer draw up the papers?"

"I'll have him work on it over the weekend."

"Tell him to work fast. I get Aldridge back by Monday or it's no deal."

Durant hung up. He nodded curtly to Nolan. "Satisfied?"

"You're a tough cookie," Nolan said, stubbing his cigarette in an ashtray. "What if he hadn't met your price? Would you've walked away from Aldridge?"

"Like you said before, it's just business."

"Well, whatever the case, looks like we're on hold till Monday. I'll see you around, slick."

Nolan rose with an unreadable smile and went out. When the door closed, Durant told himself it was all hot air and soap bubbles. Even if he sold the bank, they would never run the risk of a live witness who could charge them with felony abduction. Aldridge would be killed.

So all he'd done today, Durant realized, was to buy some time. He had to find another way to bring Aldridge home alive. And the clock was ticking.

He had to get it done before Monday.

The spotlights cast flashing beams a thousand feet into a moonlit sky. Tonight was opening night for the Ritz Brothers, and a line of cars crept forward outside the Hollywood Club. Parking attendants rushed to keep them from blocking the entrance.

Stoner and Janice arrived in their canary-yellow Packard. She wore a gold lamé gown with a matching stole, and he was attired in a tuxedo and cummerbund. Earlier, when they were dressing, he had wedged a Colt .45 automatic into the cummerbund, at the back of his trousers. In his hip pocket, he carried a leather badge holder with the shield of a Texas Ranger. He felt confident that tonight's raid would close the place down.

The nightclub was packed. Quinn, ever the genial host, greeted guests as they came through the doors. He looked the debonair showman in a white dinner jacket, a scarlet boutonniere blazing from his lapel. His manner was lighthearted, almost ebullient, the impresario staging yet another extravaganza. Jack Nolan, in a double-breasted tux, was at his side.

"Mr. Eberling! Mrs. Eberling!" Quinn offered them a warm handshake as they entered the club. "Your table's reserved, just as you requested. The best seats in the house."

"We're much obliged," Stoner said, noting that Nolan was back on duty tonight. "You folks sure know how to treat your customers right. Wasn't I just sayin' that, Olive?"

"Yes, you were, sweetheart." Janice dimpled her cheeks in a bubbly smile. "We just love your club, Mr. Quinn. You're sooo gracious."

Quinn preened. "Nothing's too good for our guests. We even bring in the Texas Rangers for added entertainment. How'd you like our little improvisation last night?"

"Oh, an absolute riot!" Janice squealed. "Honestly, those Ranger boys were fit to be tied. I could hardly keep a straight face."

"Same for me," Stoner added, bobbing his head in admiration. "We were sayin' Houdini must've rigged them topsy-turvy tables. Regular magic show."

"We're proud of it ourselves," Quinn said with a beaming grin. "The Rangers are always good for a few laughs. I get a kick out of it."

"Bet you do," Stoner said, forcing himself to smile. "Speakin' of laughs, we're lookin' forward to the Ritz Brothers. Hope they're as funny as the Rangers."

"Funnier by far," Quinn assured him. "I know you'll like the show. Enjoy yourselves."

The maitre d' led Stoner and Janice to their table.

Nolan watched them as Quinn turned to greet other guests. All through the conversation he'd been reminded of Tuesday morning, at the tobacco shop in La Marque. He still thought it strange that a wealthy high roller would be standing around a phone booth, waiting for calls. But he decided once again to say nothing to Quinn or Voight. He had all the problems he could handle for the moment.

Stoner, after being seated at the table, was having second thoughts himself, He was glad to see Nolan in the club, for the mob's enforcer, more so than dealers or pit bosses, deserved to be arrested. But he filed a mental note to keep an eye on Nolan when he made his move on the casino. No need to get careless and risk getting himself shot. He'd staked everything on pulling it off tonight.

"I'm so proud of you," Janice said, after the waiter had taken their orders. "The way Quinn was talking, I thought for sure you'd belt him in the puss. He has nothing but contempt for . . . well, you know who."

Stoner's mouth curled in a cagey smile. "Before the night's over he'll have nothing but respect for you know who. We'll wipe that grin off his face."

"I still think you're a model of restraint."

"Well now, Olive, you were pretty good yourself. Nobody could've done it any better."

"You're so nice to say so, Robert, honey lamb. I just love working with you . . . among other things."

Stoner laughed. "Don't go practicing your wiles on me."

"Why not?" She gave him a lewd wink. "Don't you like it?"

"What do you think?"

"Oh, I think you do."

"I think you're right, Mrs. Eberling."

"I'm always right, Mr. Eberling."

The houselights dimmed shortly after they finshed their dinner. A buzz of excitement went through the audience, for everyone eagerly anticipated the show. The Ritz Brothers were an antic trio—Al, Jimmy, and Harry—

celebrated for their slapstick humor. The oldest was twenty-five and the youngest nineteen, and they were already stars of vaudeville and the Broadway stage. Their act featured dizzy comedy routines and raunchy songs.

The orchestra brought them skipping onstage in baggy pants and floppy jackets. Their first number was a bawdy tune about a one-eyed nymph and her energetic lover, a peg-legged sailor. The audience followed the lyrics with gasps and giggles from the women and guffaws of laughter from the men. The end of the song prompted the crowd to a wild round of applause.

The orchestra stilled, and without missing a beat, the brothers went into a comedy routine. Al, the oldest, began talking about the dumbest man he'd ever known. "So dumb," he said with a straight face, "that he only took a bath when it rained."

"Hey, that ain't so bad," Jimmy said, rolling his eyes. "I knew a guy one time, when they said brains, he thought they said trains. He got on the wrong one."

"You wanna hear dumb?" Harry jumped in with a goofy smile. "Fella in the neighborhood, you gave him a penny for his thoughts—you got change!"

The crowd responded with a wave of laughter. Quinn, ever constant to his superstition about opening nights, was standing at the back of the room. His girlfriend, Maxine, looked like she'd been poured into a silk dress that revealed every curve. Her hair was piled atop her head in a French twist and her breasts threatened to spill out of her low-cut gown. She hugged his arm.

"Oh, Ollie, I just love opening nights. It's all so swell!"

"There's no business like show business, Maxie. Nothing even comes close."

"And you're the best showman there ever was. I mean, golly, you're an artiste!"

Quinn chuckled. "Don't tell Dutch."

Durant stepped out of a taxicab. The doorman was busy with people waiting for their cars to be brought around, and didn't pay him any attention. He walked into the Hollywood Club.

The layout was generally familiar. From what he'd heard around town, there was a nightclub, and then, at the end of the T-head pier, the casino. He moved through the entry hall, opening a set of glass doors, and heard the sound of an orchestra. He was alert to any sign of Jack Nolan.

All day, Durant had deliberated on a course of action. The police would be of no help, and if he waited until Monday, he knew Aldridge would be killed. Even if he sold the bank, he was convinced the mob would eliminate the only witness. Then, at the first opportunity, they would kill him.

There was nothing for it but to take the fight to them. He wouldn't allow Aldridge to be killed, and the only way to stop it was to force their hand. Whether it was Quinn or Voight, or maybe both, he meant to offer them their lives in exchange for Aldridge. The only place he knew to find them was the Hollywood Club, and he'd waited until they were busy with a Saturday night crowd. Surprise was his one advantage.

The orchestra was playing dance tunes. On the way in, Durant had noticed a billboard advertising the Ritz Brothers, and he assumed the show was over. The nightclub was nonetheless still crowded, and several couples were dipping and swaying on the dance floor. The maitre d' stopped him at the door.

"May I help you, sir?"

"You sure can." Durant had already concocted his story. "I represent Al Jolson and Mr. Quinn asked me to stop by when I was in town. Trouble is, we've never met, except on the phone. Could you point him out?"

"Certainly." The maitre d' nodded to a man talking with several guests at a table. "The gentleman in the white dinner jacket."

"Appreciate your help."

"Not at all."

Durant intercepted Quinn as he turned away from the table. "Hello, Quinn," he said, blocking the club owner's path. "We need to talk."

Quinn smiled amiably. "I don't believe we've met."

"I'm Earl Durant."

"Well—" Quinn seemed momentarily at a loss. "What can I do for you, Mr. Durant?"

"Act like we're old pals." Durant brushed his suit jacket aside, tapping the butt of the Luger in his waistband. "Don't sic anybody on me or I'll kill you. Got it?"

"You'll never get out of here alive."

"How would you know? You'd already be dead."

Quinn thought about it. "What do you want?"

"Ira Aldridge."

"Sorry, never heard the name."

"Yeah, you have," Durant said. "Where's your office?"

"At the back of the casino."

"Let's go."

The two bruisers at the rear of the nightclub opened the door into the lounge. Quinn nodded to them without expression. "This gentleman's with me."

Durant followed him through the lounge. There were people sitting around drinking and talking, and a waiter bustled past with a tray of cocktails. At the heavy oak doors to the casino, Quinn took a ring of keys from his pocket. He unlocked the door and they moved inside.

There were two hundred or more people crowded around the gaming tables. As Durant nudged Quinn forward, the hammering clang of a fire-bell went off with an ear-splitting din. For an instant everything in the casino seemed arrested in motion, then the fire bell stopped. A man suddenly vaulted on top of one of the craps tables.

"Texas Rangers!" Stoner shouted, the Colt automatic in one hand and his badge in the other. "This is a raid and you're all under arrest. Don't anybody move!"

Durant and Nolan saw each other at the same moment. Nolan was on the far side of the room, his hand edging inside his jacket, when he spotted Durant standing behind Quinn. A look of astonishment came over his face, and as Durant slowly wagged his head, he removed his hand from his jacket. A man in a double-breasted tux rushed toward the office.

"Hold it, Voight!" the Ranger commanded. "Take another step and I'll drill you!"

Voight abruptly stopped, then spun around, his face a mask of rage. "Eberling, you're a dead man."

"Sergeant Clint Stoner," Stoner informed him. "Stand right where you are."

"You're still dead," Voight growled. "Nobody makes a monkey out of me."

"Just stay put." Stoner swung the pistol around, the sights trained on Quinn. "Glad you could join us, Quinn. Get that door open—now!"

Quinn hesitated only an instant. The gun at his front was more threatening than the one at his back, and he hardly glanced at Durant as he opened the door. Captain Hardy Purvis and his squad of Rangers were just entering the lounge. They rushed through the door of the casino and spread out, some armed with revolvers and others with shotguns. Purvis snorted a barking laugh when he saw the gaming paraphernalia still intact. He looked at Stoner on top of the craps table.

"Well done, Sergeant," he said in a loud, authoritative voice. "We'll take it from here."

"Cap'n, it's all yours."

Stoner swapped a glance with Janice. She was standing by a slot machine, and she smiled proudly as he hopped off the craps table. The Rangers, with Purvis directing the operation, began separating club patrons from the casino staff. The guests were herded out the door and released, while the housemen were held under guard along the far wall. Durant, who appeared to be with Quinn, allowed himself to be forced in with the staff members. He was thinking fast, searching for an angle.

Hardy Purvis shouted a command. The five Rangers

with shotguns moved about the room and systematically blasted holes in the tops of the gaming tables. Purvis turned with a spiteful grin and looked at Voight and Quinn, who were standing at the front of the loosely bunched housemen. The roar of the shotguns reverberated through the casino like rolling claps of thunder.

Voight and Quinn watched the carnage with hollow stares. Durant seized on the diversion, backing away to stand by Nolan. His voice was muted by the steady barrage of gunfire. "Let's make a trade."

Nolan gave him a sideways glance. "Trade for what?"

"Tell me where you're holding Aldridge. I'll never let the Rangers know you were involved."

"Two of my boys are guarding him. No way you'll get him out by yourself."

"I'll take my chances."

Nolan quickly assessed his situation. The casino would be shut down, and along with the others, he would be arrested. The last thing he needed was a felony charge for abduction, and if he worked it right, tonight's raid might provide an out for himself and Libbie. He thought it was worth a shot.

"Do we have a deal?" Durant goaded him. "Or do I talk to the Rangers?"

"Are you on the square? You won't turn me in?"

"You've got my word. Give me Aldridge and you're in the clear."

Nolan told him about the cabin on Sweetwater Lake. The men around them were distracted as one table after another was blown apart, and his voice was muffled by the drumming roar of the shotguns. He quickly gave Durant directions to the lake and the turnoff to the cabin. He ended with a warning.

"Watch yourself," he said soberly. "The boys I left out there are both shooters. They play dirty."

"I'll keep it in mind. Thanks, Jack."

Durant brushed past the men in front of them. He made a snap decision to say nothing to the Rangers. The story would require too much explanation, and he couldn't risk being slowed down. Once the shooters heard about the raid, they might very well panic and kill Aldridge. He had to move quickly and find the cabin. Tonight.

"Sergeant Stoner," he said to the man who had taken the casino. "I shouldn't be held here. Your Rangers made a mistake."

Stoner looked him over. "Who are you?"

"I'm Earl Durant," Durant said, moving forward. "I own the People's Bank & Trust."

"Durant?" Stoner paused, the name somehow familiar, and suddenly it came to him. "Aren't you the banker working with the reformers?"

"How'd you know about that?"

"Doesn't matter how I know. I saw you come in with Quinn just before the raid. Why were you with him?"

"Quinn and Voight threatened me," Durant said honestly, motioning to the club owners. "I came here to have it out with them."

"All by yourself?"

"I'm all I've got."

Stoner glanced around at Quinn and Voight. The shotguns abruptly stopped firing, and they were now staring at Durant with murderous scowls. Stoner thought their expressions spoke to the truth of Durant's story.

Hardy Purvis, with the look of Caesar triumphant, drifted over. "What's going on here, Sergeant?"

"Just a mix-up, Cap'n," Stoner said. "This man's not part of the casino crew."

"Then get him out of here," Purvis said, jerking a thumb at the housemen. "I want the whole bunch hand-cuffed."

Stoner nodded. "You're free to go, Mr. Durant."

"Thanks for your help, Sergeant."

Durant walked to the door. As he went out, Stoner borrowed handcuffs from a couple Rangers and moved across to Quinn and Voight. He clamped the cuffs around their wrists with a little chuckle.

"I have to tell you it's a real pleasure. Never had so much fun in my life."

"You and me aren't finished," Voight said, his eyes dark with menace. "I'll see you around one of these days."

Stoner smiled. "Not if I see you first."

By midnight, Voight and Quinn and their men had been transported to the county jail. All the nightclub guests, as well as the orchestra, the Ritz Brothers, and the kitchen staff, were ordered off the premises. A stout chain was snapped in place across the front doors with a padlock.

The lights went out at the Hollywood Club.

Chapter Twenty-Three

Durant held the speed to a sedate twenty miles an hour. He was on Stewart Road, west of town, looking for the turnoff to Sweetwater Lake. He knew it was somewhere off to the right, but he was wary of missing the turn. A half-moon, directly overhead, was almost as bright as the headlights.

Earlier, when he'd left the club, he realized he needed a car. The problem stumped him for a few seconds, and then the solution came in a moment of what he considered poetic justice. All the parking attendants were gathered by the front door, talking excitedly about the Rangers' second raid in as many nights. He walked off into the parking lot.

Nolan's cherry-red Stutz Bearcat was three rows down. Durant had driven practically every car ever manufactured in his years as a stuntman. Even more important, he'd worked with mechanics whose knowledge of the internal combustion engine was essential to any stunt involving a car. A minute or so under the hood and he had the Sutuz hot-wired and the engine purring. He drove out of the parking lot headed west.

Durant thought Nolan would appreciate the irony. But as he passed the amusement piers, which were ablaze with lights and crowded with tourists, he experienced a moment of uncertainty. For the job ahead, the odds would have improved greatly if he had enlisted the aid of the Rangers. Still, even in hindsight, he knew it would have taken half the night to persuade them that a man held captive was more important than closing down a casino. And in the process, simply mentioning the cabin on the lake, he would have betrayed Nolan to Quinn and Voight. He felt he'd had no choice but to play a lone hand.

Nolan had told him the turnoff was five or six miles west of town. Off to the right, glistening in the moonlight, he saw the glassy surface of Sweetwater Lake. The highway made a sharp curve and then, less than a mile farther on, he spotted a dirt road angling off to the north. He turned onto the road, working the clutch and shifting down into second gear, cutting his speed to a crawl. He doused the headlights.

The moon cast a spectral glow across a land flat as a dime. Up ahead, perhaps a quarter mile past the turnoff, he saw the dirt track that Nolan had described. There was a slight shoulder on the road, and he coasted to a halt, letting the hot-wired engine die as he released the clutch. After hooking the gearshift into reverse, he stepped out of the car and gently closed the door. A faint breeze drifted down from the northeast.

The dirt track was bumpy and rutted, barely wide enough for a car. Trees bordered either side of the lane, and Durant caught a whiff of wood smoke on the breeze. He pulled the Luger from his waistband, clicked off the safety, and walked forward through dappled moonlight. A hundred yards or so ahead, he came to a clearing, where a small cabin was perched on the shore of the lake. Off to the right, he saw a one-holer privy, which meant the cabin didn't have indoor plumbing. He paused at the edge of the treeline.

The cider glow of a lamp lighted a window at the front of the cabin. Durant heard the muted sound of voices from inside, and he waited a moment, slowly reconnoitering the open terrain for any sign of movement. He stepped from the shadow of the trees, carefully avoiding the shaft of light from the window, and circled around from the south. He eased forward, a step at a time, along the front wall.

The voices were now more distinct. He stopped beside the window, listening a moment, then gradually

moved his head past the casement. There were two men
seated at a table, playing cards, their faces bathed in the
glow of a coal oil lamp. One was wiry and beady-eyed,
and the other was thickset with a thatch of bushy black
hair. A wood stove was positioned against the wall nearest
the lake, and opposite the men was a door that apparently
led to another room. There was no sign of Aldridge.

Durant ducked below the window. On the other side,
he passed by the door and turned the corner on the north
side of the cabin. A window was set into the wall, and
again, gingerly, he eased his head around the casement.
The spill of light from the front room revealed a crude
bedroom, devoid of furniture except for two single beds.
Aldridge was asleep on one of the beds, lying on his back,
his features visible in the dim lampglow. The men kept
an eye on him through the door.

Nolan's warning came back to Durant. The men were
shooters—mob parlance for killers—and unlikely to be
taken without a fight. A moment ago, watching them play
cards, he'd observed they were in shirtsleeves, their coats
off, each of them carrying a revolver in a shoulder holster.
The idea of busting through the door, particularly if it was
locked, would alert them before he ever got inside. The
alternative was to break the front window and shoot them
where they sat, without warning. The notion was fleeting,
quickly discarded as unworkable. He couldn't picture
himself an assassin.

Which left only the door. He went back around the
corner of the cabin and moved along the wall. His one
hope was that the door was unlocked and he could burst
inside before they had time to react. There was a slim
chance that if he got the drop on them, they would surrender without a fight. The odds were long but the situation left him short on options. His throat dry, he dropped
to one knee beside the door, the Luger gripped tightly in
his right hand. He reached with his left hand to test the
doorknob.

"I gotta take a piss."

"Lem, you oughta get your kidneys checked."

"Hey, you gotta go, you gotta go."

The men's voices carried clearly from inside. A chair scraped against the floor and heavy footsteps crossed toward the door. Durant quickly pulled back, rising to his feet, and flattened himself against the wall. The door opened in a sudden flood of light and the thickset man with bushy hair stepped outside. He walked to the treeline, unbuttoned his pants, and pulled out his pud. A stream arced outward and splashed on the ground.

Durant ghosted across the clearing. He jammed the muzzle of the Luger into the man's spine. "Don't say a word."

The man sucked in a breath. He stood stock-still, and his steamy stream abruptly went dry. Durant nudged him with the pistol. "Put it in your pants."

Hastily, the man tucked himself away. Durant spoke into his ear. "I'll be right behind you. Walk back in there like you've finished your business. One peep, one wrong move, and you're dead. Let's go."

Durant marched him to the cabin. As they came through the door, Whizzer Duncan looked up from shuffling the cards. He saw something odd on his friend's face, and then, in the silty lamplight, he saw Durant. The cards fluttered from his hands and he kicked back his chair. He clawed at his revolver.

"Move, Lem!" he shouted. "Goddammit, *move!*"

Brewster struggled to break free. He heaved one way, then the other, but Durant had a tight grip on his shirt collar. As he was jerked back into place, Duncan whipped the revolver from his shoulder holster and fired. The slug hit Brewster in the sternum and he grunted, then slumped forward. He dropped heavily to the floor.

Durant leveled the Luger in a fluid motion. He stitched three red dots on Duncan's shirtfront, the shots not a handspan apart. Duncan stumbled backward in a nerveless dance, tripping over his chair, and fell to the floor. He groaned, splattered with blood, and by some inhuman effort of will raised his gun in a shaky hand. Durant shot him in the head.

The room was pungent with the acrid smell of gun smoke. Durant stood there a moment, staring at the body, then slowly lowered the Luger. He knelt down, pressing a finger to Brewster's neck, and found no pulse. Then, still dazed by the swift brutality of death, he remembered why he was there. He walked to the bedroom door.

Aldridge was cowering behind the bed. He looked at the figure silhouetted by lamplight in the doorway and pushed to his knees. His voice was a strangled rasp: "Earl?"

"It's over," Durant said with quiet resignation. "They're dead."

"How in God's name did you find me?"

"I'll tell you later. It's a long story."

"Yes, of course . . . later."

"Let's go home, Ira."

On Monday morning a crowd began gathering in Superior Court. The newspaper had reported the Rangers' raid on the Hollywood Club, and there was widespread interest in the case. Many thought a conviction would mean the beginning of the end for Galveston.

Captain Hardy Purvis, with Stoner and Janice, was seated directly behind the prosecution table. Stoner was in uniform, the sleeves of his shirt adorned with sergeant's stripes, a holstered pistol at his side. He and Janice were prepared to testify about their undercover assignment and their roundabout infiltration of the casino. Purvis believed they had an airtight case.

Quinn and Voight arrived shortly before nine o'clock. They were accompanied by Nolan and twenty-two housemen who had been arrested during the raid. Early yesterday morning, in a hastily convened court session, all of them had been released on bail. Quinn and Voight joined their attorney, Lester Maddox, at the defense table. The others took seats on benches at the left side of the courtroom.

County Prosecutor Sherwood Butler arrived as the benches filled with spectators. He had spent a good part of Sunday with Purvis and Stoner, reviewing the facts of the case. His manner was that of a man pressed to take on an unsavory task, and he had been less than forthcoming in his discussions with Purvis and Stoner. He nodded to them now, quickly averting his eyes, and seated himself at the prosecution table. He opened his briefcase and removed a single sheet of paper.

A door opened at the rear of the courtroom. The bailiff jumped to his feet. "This court is now in session, the Honorable Thomas Woodruff presiding. All rise!"

Judge Woodruff mounted the steps to the bench. A large man with florid features and graying hair, he wore a voluminous black robe and a benign expression. After lowering himself into a high-backed leather chair, he opened a file folder as the bailiff ordered everyone to be seated. He peered down from the bench.

"This is a preliminary hearing," he said in a deep voice. "The accused are Oliver J. Quinn and Edward S. Voight and twenty-three of their employees, charged with operating an illegal gambling enterprise. We are here to determine whether or not the accused should be bound over for trial."

A murmur of anticipation swept through the spectators. Judge Woodruff waited until they fell silent, then looked from the prosecution table to the defense table. "Mr. Butler, Mr. Maddox," he said in acknowledgment. "Are you ready to proceed?"

"Yes, Your Honor," Butler said.

Maddox half rose from his seat. "The defense is prepared, Your Honor."

"Very well," Woodruff said. "For the record, the accused pleaded not guilty in a bail hearing yesterday morning. Mr. Butler, what say you for the state?"

Butler got to his feet. "Your Honor, I have here a

copy of the state statute governing such matters." He walked forward and placed the single sheet of paper before the judge. "Under the statute, the state feels there is insufficient evidence to warrant a felony indictment. We move that the charge be reduced to a misdemeanor."

"Wait a minute—!"

Hardy Purvis bounced out of his seat and pushed through the balustrade separating the spectators from the court well. His features were wreathed in anger.

"Judge, just hold on," he fumed, striding toward the bench. "You can't allow this travesty to go on. There's been a fix put in here."

"Stop right there," Woodruff commanded. "I will not have disruption in my courtroom."

"Your Honor, I'm a captain in the Texas Rangers!"

"I don't care if you're John the Baptist. You will not upset these proceedings."

"I raided the place," Purvis said hotly, shaking his fist in the general direction of Quinn and Voight. "Saturday night me and my Rangers caught 'em red-handed. I know a felony arrest when I make one."

"You are out of order." Woodruff squinted down at him from the bench. "Mr. Butler represents the state and has every right to put forth any motion he sees fit. Return to your seat."

"Butler's been bought! Don't you see what I'm telling you, Judge? It's been fixed!"

"Bailiff, escort this man from my courtroom."

"You can't throw me out of here. I'm a Texas Ranger!"

"You will be a Texas Ranger in the county jail unless you obey the orders of this court. Bailiff, show him out."

The bailiff was a stout man with rubbery jowls. When he started forward, Purvis turned about and stalked back through the balustrade. Stoner gave him a weary shrug as he went past, as if to say they'd played into a rigged game. Purvis marched out of the courtroom.

"Mr. Butler," Woodruff said in the sudden silence. "Do you have anything to add?"

"No, Your Honor," Butler said in a low voice. "The motion stands."

"So ruled." Woodruff nodded to the defense counsel. "Mr. Maddox, the charge has been reduced to a misdemeanor offense. How do your clients plead?"

"Guilty, Your Honor," Maddox replied, as though reading lines from a script. "My clients beg the court's leniency in view of the fact that they have never before been arrested. This is their first offense."

Judge Thomas Woodruff fined them each one hundred dollars. The crowd broke out in applause, and Woodruff, unable to suppress a slight smile, quickly retired to his chambers. Voight peeled off hundred-dollar bills from a wad of cash and settled the fines with the court clerk. Nolan led the band of grinning housemen up the aisle.

Stoner watched with a bitter expression. His mind played back over the last month, and he thought justice bent like a reed before the wind when county officials were on the pad. He got to his feet, Janice at his side, as Quinn and Voight came through the balustrade. Quinn was in a chipper mood, and he put out a hand, stopping Voight in the aisle. He smiled at Stoner.

"You missed your calling, Sergeant. You should have gone into show business. You're quite an actor."

"I'm strictly an amateur," Stoner said. "You boys wrote and directed your own little drama here today. Shows you what bums with money can do."

"Hey!" Voight pushed forward with a rough look. "You remember what I told you, hotshot. You'll get yours."

Quinn warded him off. "Dutch, let's call it water under the bridge. Sergeant Stoner was just doing his job."

"I still am," Stoner said sharply. "You want threats, I'll give you one. Let's talk about Earl Durant."

Voight bridled. "What about him?"

"I don't know the whole story. All he said Saturday

night was that you're after him. I'm telling you to lay off."

Quinn and Voight exchanged a glance. Two of their men had been killed Saturday night at the cabin on Sweetwater Lake. They were stymied as to how Durant had found the cabin; but they were certain he'd killed the men. Quinn looked back at Stoner. "What's Durant to you?"

"Just another innocent party," Stoner said. "Anything happens to him, you boys won't know what hit you. I'll take it real personal."

Quinn laughed. "Sergeant, I don't think you care one way or another about Durant. I think you're ticked off about the casino."

"If you're saying I hold a grudge, you're absolutely right. I'll get you bozos any way I can."

Later, in the car crossing the causeway, Stoner was still steaming. He thought he'd wasted nearly a month of his life, and all for nothing. His threat about Earl Durant had been made in earnest. He would welcome the opportunity to come after Quinn and Voight.

"I almost hate to leave." Janice was staring out the window as seagulls floated lazily over the harbor. "Even if things went wrong, we still had some good times here. Didn't we, pumpkin?"

Stoner was forced to smile. "You're easy to take on a regular basis. Never thought I'd hear myself say that."

"Oh?" she said, looking at him with surprise. "So, what are you saying?"

"Maybe we ought to play house more often."

"I don't believe it! Are you serious?"

Stoner thought perhaps he was . . . maybe.

Late Friday morning Durant came through the door of the bank. He was carrying a legal portfolio, and he glanced at a calendar on the wall behind the tellers' cages. The date was October 5.

Catherine was typing a letter. She paused, looking up with a humorous smile, as he stopped at her desk. "Almost lunchtime," she said. "Some people would say you're keeping banker's hours."

"Not much longer." Durant grinned and patted the legal portfolio. "I've just come from Walter Kline's office."

"Everything's set, then? You're really going to sell the bank?"

"Lock, stock and barrel. By this afternoon I'll be an ex-banker."

She pouted. "It won't be the same without you."

"You never know," Durant said, his grin wider. "How about dinner tonight?"

"I thought you'd never ask."

"It's a date."

Durant motioned to Aldridge, who followed him into his office. The older man appeared recovered from his ordeal, and they had agreed never to speak of it to anyone. The police hadn't yet uncovered a suspect in the killings at Sweetwater Lake, and Durant intended to keep it that way. He meant to leave Galveston a free man.

In the office, Durant seated himself behind his desk. He opened the portfolio and placed a document in front of Aldridge. "Kline covered everything from A-to-Z. Look it over and see what you think."

"You're sure about this?" Aldridge said, pulling his chair closer to the desk. "Anything could happen in five years."

"Ira, I've never been more sure of anything in my life."

Durant was in a buoyant mood. On Monday morning he had received a call from Clint Stoner, the Texas Ranger. Stoner was on his way back to Austin and had stopped at a phone booth in La Marque. The purpose of his call had little to do with Quinn and Voight getting off on a misdemeanor charge. Everyone in town had already heard about the political shenanigans in the courtroom that morning. And hardly anyone was surprised.

Stoner's call was more of a personal nature. He explained that he had confronted Quinn and Voight in the courtroom and put them on warning. Should anything happen to Durant, he would bring the full force of the Rangers to bear, and at the very least, send them to prison. Durant gathered that the Ranger, though concerned for his welfare, was more interested in keeping the heat on Quinn and Voight. Stoner ended the call by saying he thought Durant's troubles were over. Mobsters, perhaps more than anyone else, understood a threat.

The call restored Durant's resolve that he would escape Galveston alive. Then, early Monday afternoon, he had received a call from Jack Nolan. Dumbfounded, he listened as Nolan explained William Magruder's true interest in People's Bank & Trust. Magruder was in the midst of planning a resort hotel, and the bank owned property essential to the project. The land alone, Nolan went on, was why Magruder had gotten the mob involved. Durant was floored by Nolan's sudden revelation.

"I don't get it," he'd said. "Why are you telling me all this?"

Nolan had laughed. "Let's just say I'm wiping the slate clean."

"What slate?"

"Galveston."

The call ended on that cryptic note. In the space of a few hours, Durant felt he'd been handed a new lease on life. Sergeant Clint Stoner had bought him immunity of sorts from the mob, and Diamond Jack Nolan had revealed the source of all his problems. By late Monday afternoon, working with Aldridge, he had identified the piece of property so vital to Magruder's hotel project. A few minutes later, he'd offered Aldridge a deal no one could refuse. He saw it as his ticket out of Galveston.

Early Tuesday, Durant went to see his late uncle's attorney, Walter Kline. He instructed Kline to draw up two contracts, one for the sale of the bank, and one for the land contiguous to Magruder's property on Seawall Boulevard. The bank contract transferred ownership of

People's Bank & Trust to Aldridge for ten thousand dollars down, paid out of bank funds, and ten thousand a year for five years. The contract for the land was drawn between Durant and William Magruder.

"Looks fine to me," Aldridge said now, placing the contract on the desk. "Those are the most generous terms a man could hope for."

Durant, as president of the bank, had loaned Aldridge the down payment on a personal note. He dismissed his generosity with a casual wave. "Ira, I think Uncle Joe would rest easy knowing the bank's in safe hands. Let's get it done before you change your mind."

Catherine was called into the office. She was a notary public, and after they signed the contract, she witnessed their signatures. Durant, grinning broadly, clasped Aldridge's hand with genuine warmth.

"Congratulations, Ira, you've just bought yourself a bank."

Ten minutes later Durant walked into the waiting room of Magruder & Company. Ellen Morse, Magruder's secretary, remembered his previous visits all too well. She rushed around her desk and blocked the door to the inner office.

"No farther, Mr. Durant," she said acidly. "Leave now or I'll call the police. I mean it!"

"Don't worry, your boss will want to see me. Tell him Santa Claus is here."

"I beg your pardon?"

"Just tell him Christmas came early this year. Mention a piece of land on Seawall Boulevard."

"You wait right where you are."

She disappeared into the office. A moment elapsed, then she opened the door, motioning him inside with a suspicious little frown. Magruder was seated behind his ebony desk, fingers laced over his expansive belly. His eyes were hooded, and alert.

"Well, Mr. Durant," he said without expression. "I

must say you bear scant resemblance to Santa Claus. What's this about a piece of land?"

"Merry Christmas." Durant took the contract from his jacket pocket and dropped it on the desk. "Read it for yourself."

The contract was two pages long, double-spaced. Magruder scanned through it quickly, then turned back and read it line for line. He grunted something unintelligible, his mouth pursed in thought. He finally looked up.

"You're a surprise a minute, bub. How'd you find out about the hotel?"

"What's the difference?" Durant said, taking a chair. "Do you want the land or not?"

"Not for fifty thousand."

"The price isn't negotiable. I'm sure I could find other buyers."

Magruder studied the contract. "I see nothing in here about the bank."

"That's true," Durant said with a tight smile. "You'll be happy to know that I'm leaving Galveston. I've just sold the bank to Ira Aldridge."

"Aldridge won't last six months."

"You're wrong there. He'll last the same way my uncle lasted all those years. Lots of people in town don't like you or your bank."

"Nonetheless, the bank made the deal more attractive. I dislike competition."

"You're wasting my time. You wanted the land and it's right there in front of you. Take it or I'll put it on the open market."

"You always were a hard one, weren't you, bub?"

Durant stood. "Is that a yes or a no?"

"Keep your pants on," Magruder said gruffly. "I'll call my secretary in and have her witness our signatures. How do you want your money?"

"A cashier's check."

"You don't trust my company check?"

"I don't trust you."

Ellen Morse, also a notary public, witnessed the signing of the contract. She was then dispatched to Magruder's bank and returned a short while later with a cashier's check. Magruder waited until she was out of the room.

"Fifty thousand," he said, passing across the check. "I believe that concludes our business."

"One last thing," Durant remarked. "You know Walter Kline, the attorney?"

"Yes, I know him."

"I've left a long, detailed letter in his safe. Guess what it says about you and your mob buddies?"

Magruder scowled. "Have you lowered yourself to blackmail?"

"Let's call it insurance. Anything happens to me—anywhere, anyhow, anytime—Kline will deliver it to the attorney general and every newspaper in Texas. Think about it."

"I'll be glad to see the last of you, Mr. Durant."

"The sentiment's mutual."

Durant walked out of the office. He thought the warning delivered by Sergeant Stoner offered a degree of protection. Yet he felt even more certain about the letter in his lawyer's safe.

William Magruder knew when to call it quits.

Chapter Twenty-Four

The Hollywood Club was back in operation. By Saturday evening, the casino had been restored to its former elegance, with new gaming tables delivered by truck from the manufacturer. The raid of a week ago might never have happened.

Quinn thought of it as a cloud with a silver lining. The raid had brought the club even more notoriety, and reams of free publicity. Newspapers in Houston and other cities carried tongue-in-cheek articles comparing the Texas Rangers to the bumbling Keystone Cops of movie comedies. The Associated Press put the story on the national wire in what amounted to journalistic satire.

The publicity provided promotion as well for the club's latest headliners. Saturday night was opening night for the acclaimed dance team of Fred and Adele Astaire. A brother-and-sister act, the Astaires were two of the most popular figures in show business. Their singing and dancing career began as children in vaudeville, and now, in their twenties, they were the darlings of Broadway. Their most recent stage hit was the musical comedy *Lady, Be Good!*

The house was sold out. Quinn, with Nolan at his side, was stationed by the door to greet arriving guests. Those who were regular club patrons inevitably stopped to chat a moment about the raid, and congratulate Quinn on outwitting the Rangers in court. The cynicism of a generation was never more apparent than in their amusement at law enforcement officers being ridiculed in the press. Quinn treated it with witty nonchalance.

The Magruders arrived shortly before seven o'clock.

The party included Magruder with Opal on one arm and Libbie on the other, followed by Sherm and his wife, Francis. The women wore expensive gowns and diamonds, except for Libbie, whose beaded flapper dress revealed a good bit of leg. Magruder's expression was that of a man who had been shanghaied away from his pipe and slippers. His eyes flashed with anger when he saw Nolan at the door.

"Good evening," Quinn said smoothly, the hand behind his back motioning Nolan to stand aside. "Always a pleasure to have the Magruders as our guests."

"Speak for yourself," Magruder grumped. "My daughter insisted on dragging us down here to see the Astaires. She says they're the most sophisticated thing on Broadway."

"Class with a capital C," Quinn assured him. "Adele and Fred have taken dance to the pinnacle of the art. I'm sure you'll enjoy the show."

"I think I'd need rose-colored glasses. I'm here under protest."

Libbie carried a white plume fan. She raised it in an airy movement, shielding her face from Quinn and her father, and lowered one eyelid in a slow, suggestive wink. Nolan caught the wink and looked off into the club, amused by her audacity but forcing himself to hold a sphinxlike expression. Then the maitre d' stepped forward, cued by Quinn, and led them to a table near the dance floor. The orchestra was playing the *Sugartime Rag*.

Magruder, at Libbie's insistence, ordered champagne. After glasses were poured, and the waiter had taken their dinner orders, he excused himself. He threaded his way back through the tables, stopping here and there to greet friends, and approached the door. Quinn spotted him coming and saw the stinging look of anger he shot at Nolan. Magruder stopped a short distance away.

"What is it, Bill?" Quinn said, moving forward. "Something not right with your table?"

"No, no." Magruder leaned closer, lowering his voice.

"I trust the personal matter we discussed is no longer an issue."

Quinn appeared confused. "I thought Monsignor O'Donnell would have passed along my message. Jack Nolan will never see your daughter again. You have my word on it."

"I wasn't referring to Nolan. Although I do appreciate your discretion in that regard. I'm talking about Earl Durant."

Magruder had called Quinn yesterday afternoon. He'd briefly explained the land deal, and then elaborated on the fact that he was no longer at odds with Durant. He hadn't mentioned the letter in Walter Kline's safe, or that it would cause him irreparable harm if Durant met with foul play. He had simply expressed his concern for Durant's continued good health.

"All taken care of, Bill," Quinn said with a raffish smile. "I talked it over with Dutch and we'll respect your wishes in the matter. Nothing will happen to Durant."

"Splendid," Magruder said, visibly relieved. "I'm once again in your debt, Ollie. Thank you so much."

"Hey, that's what friends are for."

Quinn watched him walk back to his table. Yesterday, after the phone call, Quinn had indeed talked to Voight. The upshot was an argument, with Voight still strongly determined to put Durant on ice. But Quinn had eventually persuaded him that Durant was worth more to them alive than dead. At the right time, they would call in the chit on Magruder—a debt that had gotten three of their men killed—and make themselves silent partners in the resort hotel. Voight, however grudgingly, finally conceded that business was business. He agreed to let Durant skate.

Later that evening, when the show began, Quinn joined Maxine at the back of the room. Fred Astaire, who was widely regarded as the greatest tap dancer of the era, always opened the show with a solo routine. Quinn watched the nimble little man skip around the dance floor, feet tapping with swift grace to the beat of the music. He smiled at the sheer delight of it all.

"Maxie, there's something mystical about it, isn't there?"

"Of course there is, sugar," she purred, molding herself tight against his arm. "I get dizzy sometimes just thinking about you."

"Yes," Quinn said absently, watching Astaire. "That, too."

The sky was clear and black as velvet, bursting with stars. Tiny streaks of lightning, distant on the southern horizon, flickered over the Gulf. High tide brought an indigo surf pounding against the shore.

Durant and Catherine walked along a pathway above the beach. They were beyond the amusement piers, still loud with weekend tourists and incandescent with a swirl of colored lights. A woman shrieked in the distance as a roller coaster plunged into the depths of clattering tracks.

Earlier, over dinner at Delmonte's, Durant had been unusually quiet. Catherine was subdued as well, for she sensed there was something of farewell in the evening. The bank was sold, the land deal was closed, and he'd engineered an armistice, if not peace, with the mob. She knew he was thinking now of Hollywood.

Durant was actually thinking of her. Scarcely a month had passed since they'd met, and oddly, he found himself unable to say good-bye. His life was restored to some degree of normalcy, though he was still watchful, and for the moment, still carried the Luger. Yet he had more money than he'd ever imagined, and he could have easily booked passage on the noon train. There was nothing holding him in Galveston . . . except Catherine.

They stopped where a stretch of opalescent beach glittered beneath starlight. He put his arm around her waist, and they watched a moment as whitecaps rippled landward across the Gulf. She was overcome by the certainty that he was about to say something she didn't want to hear. Something kind and gently endearing, and final. She willed herself not to cry.

"I'm going back to Hollywood," he said, staring off at the distant waters. "Talked to Tom Mix on the phone this morning. Told him I was through with stunt work."

"Oh?" She struggled to control her voice. "What will you do?"

"Well, I asked him to give me a shot at directing one of his pictures. I think it's time I took the leap."

"And will he . . . let you direct?"

"We shook hands on the phone. I'm all set for his next picture. We start filming in two weeks."

"That's wonderful!" she said, forcing herself to sound thrilled. "I just know you'll be a great success. I'm so happy for you."

"Yeah, it's a big break," Durant said thoughtfully. "Tom always said I should be a director, and he's got the clout to choose who's behind the camera. I'm lucky to have him in my corner."

"Why, I'd bet anything it's only the beginning. Douglas Fairbanks and who knows who else will want you on their pictures."

"You're right, it could lead anywhere. I've got money to invest, and in Hollywood, nothing talks louder than hard cash. A good picture with Tom Mix could open all sorts of doors."

"Of course it will," she said vividly. "You'll be a mogul in no time. I just know you will."

"I'll settle for director." Durant hesitated, as though searching for the right words. "The thing is, I need you in my corner, too. I want you to come with me."

She caught her breath. "How do you mean . . . come with you?"

"Well, you know . . ."

"No, tell me."

"I'm trying to say we'll be married in Los Angeles. I want you to be my wife."

Her heart hammered wildly. She suddenly seemed

unable to breathe, and her voice failed her. She leaned into him, her head against his shoulder. He pressed his face to hers.

"What's wrong?" he asked. "Are you worried about your mother?"

"No, not at all." She wrapped herself in his arms. "Mama's life revolves around her friends and everything here on the Island. She'll do just fine."

"So we're off to Hollywood—if you'll marry me."

"Yes," she whispered tenderly. "I'd love to marry you."

Durant kissed her full on the mouth. She hugged him fiercely, and then, unable to restrain herself, she began laughing. He looked down at her with a bemused smile.

"What's so funny?"

"You're the one who should be worried about Mama."

"Me?"

"You know how she is about motion pictures. She'll insist on visiting us."

"And—?"

"She'll want to meet every movie star in Hollywood."

"Well, why not?" Durant said with a chuckle. "Nothing's too good for the grandmother of my children."

"Children?" Catherine said. "What happened to the honeymoon?"

"We'll get an early start."

"How early?"

Durant grinned. "On the train to California."

Libbie came down the staircase one step at a time. A few of the stairs creaked with age and she paused, fearful of awakening her father. She was carrying a small valise, with a change of clothing, her cosmetics, and her jewelry. The lights were off throughout the house.

The grandfather clock in the hallway chimed four times as she tiptoed across the foyer. She unlocked the front door and stepped outside, gingerly closing the door until the latch clicked. As she started away, it occurred to her that she would never return to the house, and she placed her key on the doorstep. She hurried off into the night.

Nolan was parked around the corner, on Twenty-ninth Street. His Stutz Bearcat, stolen from the club parking lot last Saturday night, had been found by the police the following morning outside City Hall. Nothing had been damaged, though he discovered the car had been hot-wired, and he suspected he knew the name of the thief. The gas gauge was down just enough for a round-trip to the cabin on Sweetwater Lake.

Libbie opened the passenger door. She tossed her valise in the back and scooted across the seat into his arms. "Hi there, handsome," she said, kissing him with nervous excitement. "Been waiting long?"

"You're right on time." Nolan felt energized himself, somewhat like the first night he'd led a rumrunning operation. "Any trouble getting out of the house?"

"You'd be surprised the things a girl learns in college. I used to sneak out of the sorority house the same way."

"You're sure about this? It's not some college prank where tomorrow's just like usual. We're burning our bridges."

"Of course I'm sure!" She took his face in her hands and kissed him hard on the mouth. "You'll never, ever get rid of me. I hope you know that."

"I wouldn't have it any other way."

Nolan started the car. The streets were deserted, and five minutes later, they rumbled over the causeway. Libbie glanced out the window at the darkened harbor, and then turned in her seat, looking back at the galaxy of street-lights on the Island. Her family, all of her friends, the people she'd known all her life passed through her mind in fleeting images. She silently said good-bye to Galveston, a small lump in her throat. She knew she would never return.

"Any regrets?" Nolan asked quietly.

"No, just memories," she said, moving closer, her hand tucked into his arm. "I'm leaving nothing behind that really matters. What about you?"

"Not even memories. Quinn and Voight weren't exactly family. I've forgotten them already."

"Yes, but will they forget you?"

"I told them I was taking Sunday off. We'll be long gone before they know the difference."

"You didn't answer the question," she said, poking him in the ribs. "Or maybe I didn't ask it right. Will they *forgive* you for walking out on them?"

"Doesn't matter," Nolan said with a rakish smile. "I've got too much on them and their whole operation. They'll let bygones be bygones."

"You sound awfully sure of yourself."

"Well, that's how the rackets work. You never cause trouble for a guy who's got the goods on you."

Nolan disliked starting out with secrets. Still, given what Quinn and Voight would learn on Monday, the truth might frighten her even more. He reassured her with a light-hearted chuckle. "Don't worry your pretty head about it. Nobody's gonna be looking for me."

"But if they were," she said, unable to shake the thought, "you could always find another job of some sort. You could succeed at anything. Anything at all!"

"Go straight?" Nolan scoffed. "Too late for that in this lifetime. I'm a gangster."

"Yes, I know," she said with a little laugh. "I think that's why I fell for you. I never could resist a rogue."

"Yeah, that's me all right. A rascal through and through."

"So tell me, my darling rogue—where are you taking me?"

Nolan grinned. "I thought our first stop would be Louisiana."

"Really?" she said, her expression puzzled. "Why Louisiana?"

"Couple reasons. One, they don't have a waiting period for a marriage license. So we'll find ourselves a justice of the peace and make it Mr. and Mrs."

"Oh, jeepers, Mrs. Jack Nolan! I love the sound of it."

"Only right that I make an honest woman of you."

"I couldn't agree more," she said happily. "Where will we go on our honeymoon?"

"That's the second reason," Nolan told her. "I thought we'd spend a week in New Orleans. Lots to see in the Old French Quarter. The natives call it the *Vieux Carre*."

"Who cares what they call it? You'll be lucky to get a peek at it, Mr. Nolan."

"Why's that?"

"Because Mrs. Nolan intends to keep you in bed the entire week."

"Do you?" Nolan said with mock irony. "Guess I'm marrying the right woman, after all."

"You certainly are," she purred, nuzzling his shoulder. "And after I've worn you out in New Orleans? What are your plans for the rest of our lives?"

"How do you feel about the tropics?"

"Something like Hawaii, or Tahiti?"

"No, I was thinking more of Jamaica."

"Oh, I adore the Caribbean. Who do you know in Jamaica?"

Nolan told her about Captain Rob McBride. He finished with a wry shake of his head. "The old pirate offered me a ship of my own. You'd be Mrs. Captain Nolan."

"I love it!" she cried gaily. "And smugglers must make tons and tons of money. Don't they?"

"We'd be living in the lap of luxury. I'll get you one of those villas overlooking the sea."

"And you really aren't changing occupations so much, are you? You'll still be my rogue."

"A seafaring rogue," Nolan amended. "I'll fly the Jolly Roger in your honor."

"I can't wait!" She hugged his arm. "When do we leave?"

"A week from Monday. I booked passage on a ship out of New Orleans."

"Oh God, Jack, we'll have a marvelous life, won't we?"

"Yeah, I think the world's gonna be our lollipop."

The lights of Galveston Island faded as they drove off the causeway. Neither of them thought to look back.

Opal Magruder came downstairs about nine Sunday morning. She was refreshed from a good night's sleep, humming a tune she'd heard at the Hollywood Club last night. She moved along the hallway to the dining room.

Magruder was seated at the head of the table. His plate was piled high with waffles, scrambled eggs, and thick slices of ham. He looked up with a nod. "Good morning, my dear."

"Good morning, William."

Opal helped herself from warmer trays on a sideboard. She took her place at the opposite end of the table and unfolded her napkin. The maid came out of the kitchen, filled her cup with coffee, then returned through the swinging door. She picked at her eggs, nibbled on a piece of toast.

"Weren't the Astaires wonderful?" she said, trying to make conversation. "So graceful, like two young swans."

"Yes, I suppose." Magruder pretended no great interest in the arts. "For my money, dinner was the best part of their show."

"We really should go out more often. All you ever think about is business and more business. You should take the time to stop and smell the roses."

"I'll leave the roses to you, my dear."

Jason, the chauffeur and sometimes butler, came through the door. He walked to the head of the table and placed the Sunday *Galveston Daily Chronicle* at Magruder's elbow. He waited for Magruder to look up.

"Something else?"

"Yessir." Jason placed a house key on the table. "I

found this on the doorstep when I went to collect the paper."

"Did you try it?" Magruder asked. "Does it fit our door?"

"Yessir, it does."

Magruder studied the key with a perplexed expression. His gaze shifted to the opposite end of the table. "Where's Libbie?" he said. "Have you seen her this morning?"

"Why, no, I haven't," Opal replied. "Girls do need their beauty rest. She's probably sleeping late."

Magruder grunted. "Go upstairs," he said to Jason. "Tell Miss Libbie I want to see her down here."

"Yessir."

Jason went out the door. Magruder unfolded the newspaper and began pursuing the front page. "Now that's progress," he said, tapping the paper. "Wall Street can now talk by radiophone with the London stock exchange. Quite a boon for world trade."

Opal nodded. "How nice."

"One day we'll have that for the cotton exchange."

"I'm sure you will."

Their conversation lapsed into silence. A few minutes later Jason returned with a lavender-scented envelope and placed it beside Magruder. "Miss Libbie was not in her room," he said. "Her bed appears not to have been slept in. I found this on the dresser. Will there be anything else, sir?"

"No, that's all."

Magruder opened the envelope as the butler walked to the door. There was a single sheet of stationery, with Libbie's initials printed at the top. He scanned the contents and his features flushed with rage. He angrily shook the letter.

"We're ruined," he said, his jowls quivering. "She's eloped with a gangster. Do you hear me, a gangster!"

"Yes, I know," Opal said calmly. "We had a long

talk last night after you went to bed. She told me all about her young man."

"And you didn't say anything to me? You didn't try to stop her?"

"Libbie is a grown woman and she knows her own mind. Why would I stop her?"

"Why?" Magruder exploded. "Because we'll be disgraced, that's why! Have you suddenly gone senile?"

Opal pushed back her chair. "You really are an old fud, William. I often wonder I've stayed with you all these years."

"What in God's name are you talking about?"

"Our daughter's happiness. Or have you forgotten what it was like to be in love?"

"Her happiness," Magruder said with heavy sarcasm. "For your information, her happiness will be our scandal. What does love have to do with it?"

"Everything."

Opal turned with great dignity and walked from the room. Magruder was taken aback, thoroughly baffled by her cool, inimical manner. After a moment, he snatched the letter off the table and hurried along the hall to his study. He placed a call to Sherm's home.

"I have to talk with you," he shouted into the phone. "Get over here right now!"

Some ten minutes later Sherm came through the door of the study. Magruder, who was seated at his desk, silently handed him the letter. Sherm read it once, then twice, and slowly shook his head with disbelief. He dropped the letter on the desk.

"I thought it was over," he said dully. "I thought Monsignor O'Donnell put a stop to it."

"Don't fault him," Magruder grouched. "All the blame goes to our friends Quinn and Voight. Quinn gave me his word on it."

"When was this?"

"Last night, at the club. He said Nolan would never see Libbie again. And this morning, she's gone!"

Sherm lowered himself into a chair. "From the sound of it, Nolan pulled the wool over their eyes. He and Libbie had this planned all along."

"I don't care," Magruder raged. "Quinn gave me his word, *his word!* I'm going to destroy both of them— Quinn and Voight."

"You're forgetting something."

"What's that?"

"They could destroy us," Sherm said. "Anything we use against them, they could turn it around on us. We'd go down in flames with them."

"I—" Magruder's features were ashen. "How did it come to this?"

"In for a penny, in for a pound. We have to think of the business before anything else. We have too much to lose."

Magruder slumped in his chair. "My God, my daughter a gangster's moll. I'll be the laughingstock of Galveston."

"What the hell, Pop," Sherm said with grim humor. "We've been sleeping with the mob for years. Why not Libbie?"

Later, when Sherm was gone, Magruder sat staring at the letter. The lines blurred, and he wondered where she was, how he'd lost her. He damned Quinn and Voight and Nolan.

And most of all, he damned himself.

Chapter Twenty-Five

The dome of the state capitol glittered beneath golden sunlight. The day was bright and crisp, and cumulus clouds drifted high in an azure sky. Congress Avenue was clogged with traffic.

Early Monday morning Stoner parked his car at the side of the capitol. He had been granted a week's furlough, and after leaving Galveston, he'd leisurely toured the coastline with Janice. They had arrived in Austin yesterday evening and he'd dropped her off at her apartment. Their parting had been bittersweet.

For almost five weeks, they had been inseparable. Their undercover assignment had cast them as man and wife, and they had shared not only a brief marriage, but the constant hazard of duping the mob. The experience had brought them closer together, and kindled a sense of mutual trust that few married couples ever achieved. They were, more so than most couples, a team.

Yet something had changed within the last week. As they drove the coast, stopping at Padre Island and Corpus Christi, any further talk of marriage had been put on hold. Their last night on the road, spent at the fabled Menger Hotel in San Antonio, had led to a frank discussion about the future. Janice, no less than Stoner, wanted some time to think. Neither of them felt compelled to rush things.

Their lovemaking that night had been tender, fervid but poignant. Whether they were in love, or simply great together in bed, seemed to them a moot point. They enjoyed one another, there was humor and laughter mixed with their passion, and they would forever be linked by the excitement and danger of what they had shared in

Galveston. Hardly needing words, they knew they wouldn't date anyone else once they returned to Austin. They just wouldn't get married—for now.

Stoner mounted the broad, stone steps to the capitol building. He was still assigned to Ranger Headquarters, and he'd been ordered to report to Colonel Garrison upon returning from furlough. Even though he and Captain Hardy Purvis had submitted written reports, he thought Garrison probably wanted a firsthand account. On the second floor, he tugged his uniform jacket tight and entered the reception room. The secretary, still wearing her hair in a chignon, greeted him with a pleasant smile. She ushered him into the office.

Homer Garrison rose from behind his desk. He extended a firm handshake and motioned Stoner to a chair. "Welcome back, Sergeant," he said. "How was your furlough?"

"Good, thank you, sir." Stoner seated himself, his Stetson hooked over a knee. "Spent some time on the coast not doing much of anything."

"Well, you certainly deserved the time off. How is Miss Overton?"

"She's just fine, sir. She asked me to pass along her regards."

"From your report, I gather she performed admirably in Galveston. Quite brave of her, working undercover."

"Yessir, she's a regular little soldier. And a real good actress, too. She had them all fooled."

"Commendable." Garrison slid an envelope across the desk. "There's a check in there for a thousand dollars. Please ask her to accept it with my compliments."

"That's very generous, Colonel." Stoner slipped the envelope inside his jacket. "I know she'll appreciate it."

"Not at all. She did a crackerjack job. Tell her I said so."

"Yessir, I will."

"And now to you." Garrison tapped a file folder on

his desk. "Captain Purvis gave you high marks in his report. I endorse the commendation."

"Thank you, sir," Stoner said, his features sober. "Captain Purvis did a mighty fine job himself. Too bad it was all for nothing."

"I wouldn't agree, Sergeant. You and Miss Overton accomplished something thought to be impossible. We finally know how that damnable casino disappears."

"Colonel, that turned out to be the easy part. What good's it do if we can't get a conviction?"

"You're talking about the prosecutor and the court being fixed?"

"Yessir, I am," Stoner said shortly. "Crooked judges just let the mob thumb their nose at the law. The almighty dollar calls the tune in Galveston."

"Unfortunately so," Garrison acknowledged. "We nonetheless learned a valuable lesson. Our efforts must be directed at attacking the mob in other ways."

"I don't follow you, Colonel."

"Suppose there was a method that couldn't be overturned in the courts. Would that get your attention?"

Stoner sat straighter. "Yessir, it sure would."

"I suspected as much."

Garrison went on to explain. For the past week, he had been huddled in meetings with the attorney general. Their purpose was to find a legal mechanism that would negate the mob's influence with prosecutors and courts. After several days of reviewing the Texas statutes, a junior staff member came up with a technicality in the laws directed at illegal gaming. The simplicity of it made it virtually foolproof.

The attorney general, under Texas law, had no prosecutorial powers. Yet the lawmakers, with an eye toward unscrupulous business practices, had given the attorney general the power of civil injunction. Once a law officer presented evidence of illegal gambling, the technicality applied as it would in any business enterprise. A court was required by law to issue a restraining order that halted gambling operations for ten days. And a judge was allowed no discretion in the matter. The restraining order must be issued.

There were further complexities on the theme. After ten days, if the evidence warranted, a civil injunction was mandated by the law. In the event the injunction was violated, the gaming club owner was automatically sentenced to three days in jail. By law, the attorney general was permitted to attach several injunctions together, each of which added to the jail sentence. There was no jury trial involved, and the process could be repeated endlessly. A judge who tried to tamper with the civil code faced the very certain risk of impeachment.

"Water on stone," Garrison concluded. "Not as quick as criminal charges, but the end result is the same. The mob will ultimately be worn down and worn out."

Stoner nodded hesitantly. "Colonel, you're talking a long time. Months, maybe even years."

"Exactly right," Garrison agreed. "Which demands that we have the right man for the job. I believe you're our man."

"Well, sir, if you'll pardon the expression, I'd give my left nut for another crack at Quinn and Voight. I consider those two unfinished business."

"I expected nothing less. How would you feel about working under Captain Purvis?"

"I'd like that just fine," Stoner replied. "Captain Purvis and me look at things the same way. We're both sore losers."

"Excellent," Garrison said. "As of today, you are transferred to the Houston office. You will head up a new division, the Rackets Squad. How does that sound?"

"Colonel, I couldn't ask for anything better. Any limits on how hard I push Quinn and Voight?"

"Your sole purpose will be to break the back of the mob in Galveston. You'll have a free hand."

"I'll leave for Houston tomorrow."

"One other thing."

"Yessir."

Garrison removed a leather badge holder from his desk drawer. He opened it, placing it on the desk, points of light reflecting off a gold shield. "Sergeant, I suggest you take those stripes off your sleeve. Effective today, you're Lieutenant Stoner."

Stoner accepted the badge holder. He stared down at the gold shield a moment, then looked up with a wide grin. "Well, sir—" he faltered, groping for words. "You sort of took me by surprise. I don't know what to say."

"Don't say anything," Garrison said with gruff good humor. "Just bring me Quinn and Voight."

"You can count on it, Colonel. One way or another, they're done."

Later, as he was leaving the capitol, Stoner wondered how Janice would feel about moving to Houston. Then, in the next instant, his mind turned to Galveston, and the mob. Quinn and Voight thought they'd seen the last of him, and he laughed, imagining their reaction when they got the news. Life was sweet.

Justice, with a dab of retribution, was sweeter still.

Voight made his usual Monday morning trip to the bank. Sherm Magruder, all the while he was exchanging bearer bonds for cash, expected some remark about Libbie and Nolan. When nothing was said, he decided to follow the advice he'd given his father. He acted as though it was business as normal.

Barney Ward was waiting in the reception area. Like everyone else, he knew a transaction had taken place, even though he wasn't aware of the details. His job was to act as bodyguard, ensuring that Voight and the briefcase made the appointed rounds in safety. He followed Voight out of the bank.

Five minutes later they entered the Turf Club. There was little action on a Monday and the bookmaking parlor was practically empty. As they crossed the room, Joe Reed came out of the manager's office with a bundle of mail. He saw Voight and hurried ahead to hold the elevator door.

"Just in time, boss," he said with a beaming grin. "I was on my way up with the mail."

"I'll take it." Voight stuck the bundle under his arm. "Seems like all the bills show up on Monday. Never fails."

"Same with me." Reed waited for Voight and Ward to step aboard the elevator, then closed the door. " 'Course, I let the little woman handle it. I hate payin' bills."

"Good idea," Voight said as the elevator shuddered upward. "How's Leann doing these days?"

Reed was always impressed by Voight's memory for family. "She's just fine, boss," he said, bobbing his head. "She'll be tickled you asked."

"Give her my best, Joe."

"I surely will, boss. Surely will."

The elevator bumped to a stop at the third floor. Reed opened the door, and Voight and Ward stepped off. There were several men in the athletic club, working out with weights and punching the heavy bag. At the end of the hall, Turk McGuire was posted outside the office. Voight nodded to him.

"I don't see Jack anywhere. Has he been around this morning?"

"Haven't seen him, boss," McGuire said. "Maybe he had a late date."

"His love life's his problem. Call him and tell him to trot it on over here."

"Sure thing, boss."

Voight went through the door to the office. Quinn was seated at his desk, poring over the legalese in an entertainment contract. He looked up as Voight dumped the mail in front of him, then moved to the safe and began working the combination. Quinn set the contract aside and began sorting through the mail.

"Helluva note," Voight said over his shoulder. "Going on noontime and Jack hasn't shown up."

"You're right," Quinn said. "Especially since we gave him yesterday off. Any of the boys know anything?"

"I told Turk to call him and tell him to get a move on. We're running a business here."

Voight placed the bearer bonds in the safe. He closed the door, spun the combination knob, and set the briefcase on the floor beside his desk. After taking a seat, he nipped the end off a cigar and lit up in a cloud of smoke. He glanced across at Quinn.

"Anything important in the mail?"

"Nothing—" Quinn hesitated, staring at a plain white envelope. He opened it, quickly read the note inside, and his jaw dropped. "Jesus Christ!"

"What?"

"Jack won't be answering his telephone. Here, read it for yourself."

Voight took the note. He recognized Nolan's loopy scrawl even before he began reading. The message was short and to the point.

> *Dear Dutch & Ollie,*
> *Sorry I wasn't able to give you more notice. Figured a letter was the best way to let you know I've quit. Libbie Magruder and I will be married and long gone by the time you get this. Your secrets are my secrets unless you send somebody looking for me. Let's just live and let live, and nobody gets hurt.*
>
> *Your pal,*
> *Jack*

"Sonovabitch!" Voight grated, his eyes rimmed with anger. "He quit us and ran off with that little broad. Goddamn him!"

"Postmarked Saturday," Quinn said, holding up the envelope. "That means he had everything planned out and probably took off Saturday night after the club closed. He played us along like we've got strings."

"Nobody quits me and gets away with it. Dirty bastard knows our operation inside out."

"Read the note again," Quinn said. "That part about 'live and let live.' "

"Yeah?" Voight flung the note on his desk. "So what?"

"Jack's telling us to leave well enough alone. He won't turn on us, because if he did, we'd turn on him. We all know who's at the bottom of the Gulf."

"You're saying we just grin and bear it. Pretend like he didn't crap on the guys that treated him like family. That's it?"

"That's it," Quinn said evenly. "There's nothing to be gained in trying to square accounts. We'd just hurt ourselves."

Voight seemed reluctant to let it go. "What about Magruder?" he said. "He'll be plenty pissed that our boy Jack went bye-bye with his daughter. How's that gonna affect business?"

"In a way, Jack did us a favor. I think this gives us some added leverage."

"How so?"

Quinn smiled. "Magruder wouldn't want it known he has a gangster for a son-in-law. I think we can make him jump through hoops—to keep his secret."

"You've got a point," Voight conceded with a grumpy smile. "He wouldn't want us leaking that to his society swells, would he? We've got his fat ass over a barrel."

"Dutch, I believe we've come out of this smelling like a rose."

"Yeah, maybe so, but I'm still burned. Jack was the best damn rumrunner anybody ever saw. Who the hell we gonna get to replace him?"

"We'll find someone," Quinn said without concern.

"After all, that's why we built an organization. No one man is indispensable."

"Ollie, when you're right, you're right." Voight blew a perfect smoke ring and watched it float toward the ceiling. "We practically own this Island, and five'll get you ten we've seen the last of the Rangers. We're sitting pretty, top of the world."

"Never rest on your laurels."

"What's that supposed to mean?"

Quinn signed the entertainment contract with a flourish. He held it up like a trophy. "I've just booked Mae West for a two-week engagement."

Mae West was one of the hottest stars on Broadway. She was infamous for risqué songs and racy comedy, and only recently, she'd been arrested for appearing in a scandalous play titled *Sex*. Her name alone conjured visions of raw sensuality.

"God," Voight moaned. "What's she gonna cost?"

"Sixteen thousand."

"Are you nuts? *Sixteen* thousand!"

"For two weeks," Quinn reminded him. "It's a steal, Dutch."

"I still say you're nuts," Voight grouched. "No broad's worth that much."

"Has Mr. Showbiz ever led you wrong?"

"Ollie, you'll be the death of me yet. Honest to Christ."

Voight furiously puffed his cigar. Quinn chuckled softly, leaning back in his chair, and visualized Mae West strutting about on the stage. Her brassy voice came to him amidst thunderous applause from the crowd.

His chuckle became deeper, and with it, the certainty that Galveston Island was the playground of America. He told himself the Hollywood Club would last forever.

For he was, with no jest whatever intended, Mr. Showbiz.

Alma Ludlow stood on the platform outside the Santa Fe depot. She waved to Catherine as the train chuffed smoke and slowly pulled away from the station house. Her hanky was sodden with tears.

Catherine turned from the window as the train gathered speed. She dabbed at her eyes and smiled sadly at Durant. "Mama doesn't believe we'll really get married. She thinks I'm running off to live in sin."

Durant laughed. "We'll send her a photostat of the marriage license. She'll know it's official, then."

"Yes, of course, that's a marvelous idea! She'll have something to show her friends."

"I don't get it. Why would she give us her blessing if she thought we wouldn't be married? She acted happy enough."

"Oh, she's very happy," Catherine said with conviction. "She couldn't imagine anything grander than living in Hollywood. So that makes it perfect for me."

"She never said a word," Durant remarked in a puzzled voice. "Yesterday, she fussed over me like I was a member of the family. She asked me to call her 'Mom.' "

"She thinks it's a fairy tale come true. Her daughter off to Hollywood with the big movie director. She's dying for an invitation to come visit."

All day Sunday had been spent at the Ludlow house. Catherine was busy preparing for the trip, packing bags to take on the train and boxing odds and ends to be shipped later. Her mother was back and forth, helping her pack in between peppering Durant with endless questions about movie stars. Dinner that evening had been something of a farewell supper, a quiet but happy celebration. Alma Ludlow had cooked all her daughter's favorite dishes.

Durant had booked a private compartment for the trip to California. The compartment was spacious, with double bunk beds that converted into a couch, a sitting area by the window, and a lavatory with a small shower stall. Catherine had been surprised and pleased, and her mother was thrilled that she was traveling in such luxury. But now, as the train trundled north over the causeway, she stared out the window at the sunlit harbor. Her features were pensive.

"Feeling sad?" Durant asked, noting her expression. "Sorry to be leaving your mother?"

"No, not at all," she said with a quick smile. "I'm sure Mama will invite herself to California for Christmas. She hinted at it last night."

"Why the sad look then?"

"Oh, I was just thinking about those gangsters. Quinn and Voight and all the others."

"What about them?"

"Well, in a way, I suppose it is sad." She glanced out the window and caught a last glimpse of the Island beneath a midday sun. "After everything you went through, almost getting yourself killed, and nothing's changed. They still run Galveston like it was their own little kingdom."

"Maybe not for long," Durant said. "You remember the Ranger I told you about? Sergeant Stoner?"

"Yes, the one who helped you that night at the casino."

"I got a call from him this morning, just before I checked out of the hotel. Caught me by surprise."

"Why would he call you?"

"Well, he didn't know I was leaving Galveston, and he thought I'd want to hear the news. He was flying high."

"You make it sound like good news."

"Good as it gets," Durant said with a grin. "Stoner's been promoted and put in charge of a Rackets Squad. His only job will be to nail Quinn and Voight."

"Omigosh!" Her eyes were round as buttons. "Do you think he can do it? Does he really have a chance?"

"I think Quinn and Voight are in for rough times. Stoner's determined to close them down."

Durant was glad to see the last of Galveston. There were no fond memories left behind, and his most fervent wish was that Stoner would rout the mob and drive them off the Island. Yet, odd as it seemed, he hoped Jack Nolan would somehow escape the law. Another time, another place, and they might have been friends.

All things considered, though, he felt himself the luckiest of men. He'd fought the mob and Magruder to a stalemate and he had cashier's checks for sixty thousand in his wallet. Even more, he would soon direct his first motion picture, and something deep inside, visceral in its certainty, told him it was only the beginning. And best of all, he was returning to Hollywood with Catherine.

"Let's forget Galveston," he said, taking her in his arms. "From here on, it's just you and me. Nothing but good times ahead."

"Ummm, I like the sound of that." She snuggled closer, her head against his shoulder. "Tell me stories about making movies, something outlandish. Anything at all."

"Anything at all covers a lot of ground. What would you like to hear?"

"Tell me how you first met Douglas Fairbanks."

"The first time was when we were shooting *The Mark of Zorro*. I did most of the stunts."

"And Mary Pickford?"

"Oh." Durant smiled, laughter in his voice. "Mary's another story entirely."

"Are you saying—" Catherine suddenly gasped, her eyes luminous with wonder. "You don't mean it . . . do you?"

"Well, you have to understand, that was before she met Doug. She'd just come to Hollywood."

"Yes?" Her curiosity overcame her. "And?"

"You really want to hear this?"

"I'm dying to hear it."

"You're sure?"

"I'm sure!"

Durant told her everything. Almost.

Epilogue

Galveston Island remained the mecca of gambling and vice for more than three decades. Civil injunctions filed by the attorney general were a nuisance, but the Hollywood Club always reopened and stayed open. The mob came to look on it as just another cost of doing business.

Oliver Quinn and Dutch Voight ultimately wearied of the battle. Age, and a fortune stashed away in bearer bonds, influenced them to sell their interests to a new generation of mobsters. These new overlords of crime were smart and sophisticated, but they were caught in the tidal undertow of a changing morality. The Texas Rangers finally turned out the lights on Galveston in 1957.

Diamond Jack Nolan became a smuggler, operating out of Jamaica. In 1928, during a run of bootleg liquor to Miami, his schooner was caught in a storm off the Florida Keys. The *Libbie*, named in honor of his wife, went down with all hands aboard. Elizabeth Magruder Nolan, the mother of two strapping boys, lived out her life in Jamaica, in her villa by the sea. She never remarried, and she never returned to Galveston.

Clint Stoner rose to the rank of captain in the Texas Rangers. For twenty years he stormed Galveston, raiding casinos and gambling dives, plastering the town with civil injunctions. His obsession with the mob left little time for a private life, and he and Janice Overton gradually drifted apart. He retired in 1946 and watched his successors close down Galveston eleven years later. Yet he remained a legend to all of Texas, the Ranger who never quit.

Earl Durant and Catherine Ludlow were married in October 1926. His first film, a Tom Mix western, revealed a remarkable talent as a director. He was in the vanguard of those who made the transition from silent movies to sound, and he worked with stars of the era in comedies as well as drama. He went on to make thirty-four films, and he won the Oscar for *Northern Lights* in 1932. He and Catherine had three children, and were among the first to build a mansion in Beverly Hills.

Cuddles the parrot lived to be sixteen. In 1927, when Oliver Quinn married Maxine Baxter, Cuddles was moved from the club to the penthouse suite in the Buccaneer. Quinn, whose many business affairs occupied his time, felt a talking parrot would be the perfect companion for Maxine. The first time Cuddles saw her in a negligee, he let loose a loud wolf whistle and squawked: "Ohboy! Ohboy! Lookathetits! Lookathetits!" Maxine, always receptive to a compliment, thought he was adorable.

America's Authentic Voice of the Western Frontier

Matt Braun
Bestselling author of *Bloody Hand*

HICKOK & CODY

In the wind-swept campsite of the Fifth Cavalry Regiment, along Red Willow Creek, Russia's Grand Duke Alexis has arrived to experience the thrill of the buffalo hunt. His guides are: Wild Bill Hickok and Buffalo Bill Cody—two heroic dead-shots with a natural flair for showmanship, a hunger for adventure, and the fervent desire to keep the myths of the Old West alive. But what approached from the East was a journey that crossed the line into dangerous territory. It would offer Alexis a front row seat to history, and would set Hickok and Cody on a path to glory.

"Braun tackles the big men, the complex personalities of those brave few who were pivotal figures in the settling of an untamed frontier."
—Jory Sherman, author of *Grass Kingdom*

"Matt Braun has a genius for taking real characters out of the Old West and giving them flesh-and-blood immediacy."
—Dee Brown, author of
Bury My Heart at Wounded Knee

AVAILABLE WHEREVER BOOKS ARE SOLD
FROM ST. MARTIN'S PAPERBACKS

HC 8/02

**Before the legend,
there was the man . . .**

And a powerful destiny to fulfill.

On October 26, 1881, three outlaws lay dead in
a dusty vacant lot in Tombstone, Arizona.
Standing over them—Colts smoking—were
Wyatt Earp, his two brothers Morgan and
Virgil, and a gun-slinging gambler named
Doc Holliday. The shootout at the O.K. Corral
was over—but for Earp, the fight had just
begun . . .

WYATT EARP

MATT BRAUN

IN 1889, Bill Tilghman joined the historic land rush that transformed a raw frontier into Oklahoma Territory. A lawman by trade, he set aside his badge to make his fortune in the boom-towns. Yet Tilghman was called into service once more, on a bold, relentless journey that would make his name a legend for all time—in an epic confrontation with outlaw Bill Doolin.

OUTLAW KINGDOM

MATT BRAUN

AVAILABLE WHEREVER BOOKS ARE SOLD
FROM ST. MARTIN'S PAPERBACKS

OK 5/96